SWEET BLACKMAIL

"But Kate," he said softly, "I thought I'd made it clear. There's only one way you can convince me you deserve to be free."

"I thought you were joking," she whispered, her breath gone.

"Did you?" He took in the parted lips and pinkening cheeks, the dread reflected in her clear, azure eyes. He let his gaze fall to her breasts, the soft, swelling curves uncovered now by her low-necked dress.

"Do you mean it?" she asked in a strangled voice.

"I always mean what I say," he told her smoothly.

"I would rather rot in prison for the rest of my life than give you the satisfaction!"

"Would you, Kate? Even if I said I'd take great pains to assure you that you were satisfied, too?"

"Ha!" she snorted. "I very much doubt that."

"Don't be too sure, my love. . . ."

Sweet Treason

Patricia Gaffney

LEISURE BOOKS  NEW YORK CITY

A LEISURE BOOK®

April 2000

Published by
Dorchester Publishing Co., Inc.
276 Fifth Avenue
New York, NY 10001

ISBN 0-8439-4802-7

The name "Leisure Books" and the stylized "L" with design are
trademarks of Dorchester Publishing Co., Inc.

Printed in the United States of America.

*This book is for my parents,
for Jeff, for Susan,
and always for Jon.*

PART I

CHAPTER 1
Inverness
Summer 1741

The stillness over the valley was almost absolute; the only sound was the high, pesky hum of bumblebees in the heather. Overhead, an eagle soared in lazy circles. Lured by the fragrant hush, a family of deer was about to venture out to taste the new grass along the stream bank—when a low rumble sounded in the distance. The stag lifted his head, ears twitching. In no time the rumble grew to a roar, like a gang of wild children let loose in church. Every creature in the meadow scurried for cover as three riders broke from a copse at the foot of the valley.

In the lead was a girl, with flushed face and flying red hair, howling and whooping like a madwoman as she urged on her enormous black stallion. Close behind on a smaller horse came a lad with the same red hair and a comical look of manly determination on callow, boyish features. Nearly upon him, a big, handsome fellow on a bay charger cursed cheerfully as his hat blew off in the wind.

"Whoa, Rory, give way!" the big man shouted.

"Never! You'll have to catch me!" the boy hurled back.

"Right you are!" He dug his heels in harder while he maneuvered his mount to the boy Rory's right flank, and quickly the bay gained on the little mare. "There, you're caught, then," he flung over his shoulder as he broke away, grinning when the boy's sweat-stained face registered surprise and then consternation. "And now for you, Kate McGregor!"

Ahead of him, shoeless, capless, and with bare legs flashing whitely under rose-colored silk skirts and innumerable petticoats, rode Katherine Rose Lennox Brodie McGregor, only daughter of the Laird of Braemoray. And she was damned if she was going to let Michael Armstrong beat her in a horse race.

"In a pig's eye!" she called back inelegantly, a determined set to her delicate jaw. "To the Knob!"

"What?" bellowed Michael.

"The top of Royce Knob! The loser's a muttonhead!"

The sound of her joyous, uninhibited laugh sent a tremor through Michael Armstrong. He realized he was paying more heed to the heady sight of Katherine, his beautiful Kate, bent low over the stallion's neck and moving as gracefully as some goddess on a swan, than to the managing of his own horse.

As for Katherine McGregor, she was oblivious to everything except pure, glorious enjoyment of the moment. Even the appealing prospect of besting her betrothed was forgotten in the sensual delight of the flower-scented wind in her hair and on her pinkened cheeks, and the sensation of complete oneness with the powerful animal beneath her. It seemed to her a perfect moment in time, an instant when all the ingredients for happiness, even ecstasy, were abundantly present. Later, when so much was lost, she would look back and remember, and think: that was riding, that was being courted; that was the essence of my youth.

At the far end of the valley rose a stubby, ungainly protuberance with a thatch of trees like hair on top: Royce Knob. Casting a quick backward glance, Katherine started up the stony face, praying the stallion wouldn't stumble. She'd easily outdistance Michael on the straightaway because her horse was swifter, but his was stronger. She could hear the bay clattering over rocks and bits of scree behind her and knew with a thrill of excitement that he was closing the gap. "Up, Prince! Up, boy," she urged in the rich, intimate tone that up to now she'd not used on any but her beloved horse, and so was unaware of its devastating potential. The huge stallion responded with a last great bound of his hindquarters and triumphantly achieved the summit. Michael gained the peak moments later, his horse blowing and stamping as though in hurt pride.

Doubt momentarily clouded the girl's lovely features. "You didn't let me win, did you, Michael?" she asked suspiciously.

"Ach! No. Though 'tis a handy excuse I wish I'd thought of," he said as he wiped sweat from his face with a big linen handkerchief.

"Ha! I knew it!" She bent over the stallion's neck and embraced him exuberantly. "Ah, my beautiful Prince! What a lovely boy, what a bonnie fellow you are."

"I wish you loved me half as much as you love that animal, Kate," Michael sighed in a mock-aggrieved tone.

Katherine smiled and might have responded, but at that moment her brother and his horse, a mare called Bungle who had an uncanny knack for living up to her name, struggled over the crest of the knob. Boy and mare looked equally winded, and Rory was mad as well.

"Frigging horse would chase a goddamn bloody rabbit, and just as I was about to overtake you both!"

At the age of thirteen, Rory had discovered the joys of cursing. Whenever out of earshot of his parents or his teachers, he never missed an opportunity to punctuate every sentence, every utterance, with as many oaths as the syntax could bear without losing all meaning. Katherine

had learned that reacting to his blasphemies only egged
him on to new heights of foulness, and now she simply
ignored him.

"Next year when Papa gives you a *real* horse, you'll beat
us both, I've no doubt," she placated him, and Rory
brightened. "But in the meantime, the loser must walk
the horses."

"Balls! You never said that!"

"I did. Did I not, Michael?"

"Oh, aye. Loser walks the horses. 'Twas quite clear."
Michael nodded solemnly.

"Crap, turds, horse manure." Rory jumped down from
his mount and seized Katherine's bridle. "I think you're
both lying. You just want to be rid of me so you can be
alone and say idiotic things to each other. But it won't
work; I'll simply walk them about in a circle, with you in
the middle. Now, off, get off and let me begin."

They dismounted, Michael looking a bit crestfallen.
Katherine found a clump of heather beside a fir tree and
threw herself down upon it. "Oh, Michael, look at the
sky. Have you ever seen anything so perfect?"

"Never," he returned feelingly, not looking up. He was
hypnotized by the enticing sight of his fiancée, sprawled at
his feet in the freest of postures, presenting an irresistible
combination of seductiveness and innocence. Her gown
was of dusty rose silk with lace at the sleeves and neckline.
The tight bodice, accentuating the narrowness of her waist
and exuberant upthrust of womanly breasts, was em-
broidered with light green flowers against the same pink as
the dress. She was taller than average, slender but strong,
and she moved with an easy grace that was delightful to
watch, entirely natural and wholly feminine. The apricot
complexion was flawless except for a thin peppering of
freckles across the bridge of her small, finely formed nose.
To say her eyes were blue was as lame and inadequate as
saying the sea is blue; her surroundings and her moods

dictated their color—turquoise in daylight, violet indoors or when she was angry, and a seemingly infinite variety of hues and intensities in between. She had a sunny disposition, and often exasperated less light-hearted souls with her cheerfulness. She was gentle, generous, and affectionate, and loyal to a fault. And, miracle of miracles, she was without a particle of vanity.

"Oh, what a lucky sod I am!" Michael marveled aloud. *His* Katherine. Betrothed since childhood, he'd always been fond of her. Yet never in his rashest dreams had he imagined the skinny, coltish tomboy with the wild red hair would grow into this beautiful half-girl, half-woman, whose perfect face monopolized his daydreams and whose soft, budding body haunted his sleep.

Coloring a little under the warmth of his regard, Katherine sat up and patted the ground beside her. "Come and sit, Michael. If you must say idiotic things, at least say them only to me."

"Oh, I heard him," Rory called disgustedly. "Makes a fellow want to puke."

"Move farther away, then," Michael suggested mildly, dropping down beside Katherine. "Mayhap to Aberdeen," he added in an undertone, making her giggle.

"I saw the road soldiers again today," Rory went on, oblivious. "They were down by the Tooey, watering their horses. I told them they'd better get their ugly fat arses off our land, so they left."

"Ach! Rory. Such a liar you are. You never did anything of the sort," his sister clucked.

"I did! Well, I would have, but by the time I reached 'em they were gone."

"Papa says they're dangerous, Rory. Don't go near them again."

"Your father's right," Michael confirmed.

"I don't care," Rory muttered stubbornly. "Bloody,

filthy English bastards. They think their wretched roads can tame us, but the Highlands will always be free!''

Katherine smiled, amused at how much he sounded like their mother, whose politics where the English were concerned made the Cameron clan seem conservative. ''I wonder what they were doing so far north,'' she mused. ''Do you think they mean to extend the road from Iverness?''

The thought was disquieting. For the past thirty years, Englishmen under General Wade had been building roads in the Highlands, much to the fury of loyalist Scots who viewed the roads as an invasion into their sovereign territory and a threat to one of their major strengths—their inaccessibility.

''Oh, 'tis not likely,'' Michael reassured her.

''No, 'tis more like they simply lost their way. Being Englishmen, what can you expect?'' Rory snorted. He abandoned the horses to crop on the meager grass and sat down beside them. Katherine reached over and pushed the hair out of his eyes, hair the same reddish-gold color as hers, glowing a fiery orange now in the bright sunshine. He pulled away impatiently, at the age when a feminine touch only causes irritation. ''Michael, tell us again about Bonnie Prince Charlie,'' he urged, shaking the older man by the boot and fixing him with earnest eyes. ''He rides and shoots every day, doesn't he? And he goes on forced marches to keep himself fit. And he's a big, handsome man, and he's just waiting to come out of exile and take back the Stuart crown. Tell us, Michael.''

Katherine laughed. ''What's left to tell?''

Michael smiled tolerantly. ''Oh, aye, Rory, he's a fine figure of a man. As soon as enough of the clans come out for him, I've no doubt he'll invade England and drive King George all the way back to Hanover.''

''I wish Father would come out for him,'' Rory said, sounding wistful.

Katherine shook her head. "Father's not a fighting man. He's determined to stay neutral when the war comes."

"*I* shall not be neutral," Rory declared. "Perhaps by then you'll have a regiment, Michael, and I shall be in it. But when do you think the clans will be ready? What if it happens before I'm old enough to fight?"

"Not likely, lad. The Scottish Jacobites won't come out for the prince until France declares her support, and the French won't support him until the Jacobites pledge theirs. 'Tis a vicious circle. The time is now to rally the clans, but the leaders are lazy. Lovat does nothing with the McKenzies, Sir James Campbell is half-hearted with the MacLeans, MacLachlans and MacDonalds. . . ."

Katherine had heard this sort of talk for years, and until recently it had always held her spellbound. She was as fervent a supporter of Charles Stuart, the Bonnie Prince, as young Rory, if a trifle more sophisticated politically—though *only* a trifle, in truth—and she enjoyed spinning romantic fantasies about the prince and a Stuart restoration as much as her brother did. Lately, though, her mind was on other things. She'd turned sixteen in May, and it seemed to her whatever springtime force made the buds on the dogwoods burst into white-leaved splendor or the crowberry and lupin spring up overnight like whiskers on the meadow had also awakened something new within herself this year, causing her to see the whole world in an intriguing new light. Today, for example, as Michael spoke and Rory interrupted with excited non sequiturs, she found herself listening more to the sound of her fiancé's voice than to the sense of the words. Smiling dreamily, her mind half-engaged, she lost herself in trancelike contemplation of his skin, the way his straight, silver-blond hair grew, the shape of his shoulders, the strength of his hands. They were to marry in a year's time; this certainty had been a pleasant if not particularly thrilling prospect to

Katherine all her life. But now the subject had taken on a wholly new sort of interest. She had a clinically correct but emotionally vague notion of what men and women did with each other when they were married. The knowledge that soon the mystery would be solved in the most direct and personal way she could imagine—or rather, *not* imagine—filled her with delicious, trembling dread.

But first there was one more year of school to be gotten through, she remembered sourly, wrinkling her nose and turning down the corners of her wide, exquisitely formed mouth. Why couldn't her father let Rory and her be educated at home like all their neighbors and friends? Why did he persist every year in sending them away to Paris or Florence or Holland, where they must always struggle with unfamiliar languages and unknown classmates? This year it was to be Paris again, and she cringed at the thought. School was so stuffy and tame and boring. There was nothing to do except read books and change clothes and speak French, a dandified language if there ever was one. She would much rather speak Gaelic, wear Rory's old breeches, and ride horses on the moor.

But on this subject her father was adamant. When she was twelve, the night before he'd sent her off to Milan to study, she'd cried bitterly and begged him to let her stay home for just this one year; why, she'd even have a tutor, she'd offered eagerly, if he wouldn't allow her to attend the village school with the other children. But he'd shaken his head and put his hands on her shoulders in his heavy, melancholy way. "Poor Kate," he told her, "you're only a child, you cannot see the handwriting on the wall. 'Tis better that you and Rory be educated as Europeans, for there's no future for a young person here in Scotland."

"But why? *Why?*" She had not understood at all and was appalled that her own father could voice such a treacherous sentiment. But he would not explain, and the next day he'd sent her away.

Since then she'd come to know he feared a terrible calamity if Scotsmen rose up and tried to install the exiled Charles Stuart or his father as king of England. He and Michael argued endlessly about it, though neither man ever budged an inch. Katherine hated to disagree with her mild, scholarly father, but in this instance she sided wholeheartedly with her fiancé and yearned with all the passion of youth for a Stuart restoration.

"Look at the sun setting on the *house*, Kate," Rory was saying, as though he'd said it at least once before, and Katherine realized with a start that she'd been too intent on the fine golden hairs growing on the back of Michael's big hand to follow the conversation.

"Beautiful," she murmured automatically. "Oh, *beautiful*," she said again, really looking. Darragh was on a cliff overlooking a tributary of the Findhorn, with the wilds of Dava Moor behind it. The center of the house was a centuries-old war tower, with more modern additions on either side. It was gaunt and fortresslike, and Katherine knew that most people thought it bleak, even ugly. Oh, but how she loved its lonely, windswept look and the color of the stone when the afternoon sun struck it and seemed to set it on fire.

"You love it, don't you, Kate?" Michael asked, smiling at her in that new way he had which made her feel slightly dizzy.

"Aye, I do," she admitted. After a moment she said briskly, "Right, then, we'd best be getting along home. And we must ride slowly; Innes will scold us if the horses are winded." Nominally, Innes was her father's caretaker; in fact, he ran the entire estate, a happy circumstance that allowed Angus to spend virtually all his time in his library.

"Yo, Prince!" Katherine called, scrambling to her feet. Michael and Rory groaned reluctantly but rose with her. The stallion trotted over and shook his big head in anticipation.

"Oh, bloody hell. Dirty, stinking beast, diseased whore, syphilitic daughter of a—''

"Rory!'' Katherine cried, exasperated. "What on earth is the matter?''

"Bungle! The splay-legged bitch has strayed again. Oh, bloody hell. And it's not bleeding funny! She's down by the Tooey getting a drink, I've no doubt. Now I'll have to walk her home, the bloated old hag. Damn her filthy—''

"Oh, for the lord's sake, Rory, go and get her. We'll be right behind you.''

Rory departed, scrambling down the slippery hillside and muttering obscenely.

Katherine sent Michael an amused look, then glanced down at her bare foot in confusion. She looked back to see if she'd mistaken his expression. She had not.

"Why do you stare at me like that, Michael?'' Her voice was soft and lilting; she had no idea how beguiling she was.

"Don't you know, Kate?'' It occurred to him she really might not, that she was still too much of a child to understand the effect of those guileless eyes, orchid-colored in the fading afternoon light, or the mobile, expressive mouth, exquisitely sensitive, made to be kissed.

Katherine fingered the silver buckle on Prince's bridle and pretended a deep interest in his mane. Michael was only half right. She was sheltered, but she was sixteen years old and she'd had opportunities by now to observe the effect on men of her blossoming womanhood.

"Perhaps I do,'' she admitted. But then her courage fled. "No—no, I do not.'' The impossibly long, coal-black lashes fluttered a moment before her gaze swept away.

Michael was undone. "Then I must tell you,'' he murmured, striding toward her, unable to keep his hands from seizing her shoulders and pulling her to him. "All the long day I've been hoping young Rory would take himself off for a wee minute, so I could do this.'' He kissed her, long and fervently. It was not their first kiss, but to Katherine's mind it was their best yet. She put her arms around his neck and pressed her body against him, allowing herself to enjoy the strong, hard feel of him, safe in the knowledge that he wouldn't hurt her and that he would stop, as he always had, before things went too far.

''I love you, Michael,'' she said simply when the kiss was over and he'd pulled back to look at her.

''Oh lord, Kate, I do love you!'' he responded exuberantly, hugging her and spinning her around. ''How can I wait another year to have you?''

This was the part in their recent conversations that intrigued Katherine. What exactly did he mean, to ''have'' her? To have marital relations with her, of course, to have ''intercourse,'' as the priest called it. But surely not in the way of animals she'd witnessed at times on her father's estate, not that brief, urgent coupling of sheep or cattle. No, when Michael said he wanted to ''have'' her, it sounded like so much more, it sounded like heaven on earth. It meant some mysterious union of bodies, minds, and hearts that promised a joy she could not even dream of.

''I don't want to wait, either,'' she told him truthfully. ''But I suppose we must. It's what everyone does. And yet it doesn't feel right to wait, does it?''

''It feels bloody awful,'' he agreed heartily. They stood holding each other until Katherine slid her arms from around his waist with a reluctant sigh.

''We must go.''

''Aye, I suppose we must. Your father will skin me if I don't have you home before dark.''

''Innes might,'' she corrected, laughing; ''Father would not even notice.''

They led their horses down the stony hill carefully and started across a meadow that ended in a wooded copse along the banks of the Tooey, a quiet tributary that was really more a stream than a river.

"Will you take supper with us tonight?" Katherine asked, smiling up at him winsomely.

"I wish I could, but I cannot."

"Oh, pooh. Why not?"

"I've promised to meet my cousin."

"Ewan MacNab?"

"Aye."

She sighed inwardly. She had a low opinion of his cousin Ewan, a reckless, unprincipled ruffian who played at revolution as though it were a game. Her father detested him and deplored Michael's association with him. She didn't know what the two of them talked about when they were together, but she speculated. She longed to ask Michael directly what his ties were to the Jacobites and what role he played or hoped to play in gathering the clans. But he always dismissed her curiosity with a joke or a clever change of subject, making her feel like a child. It was frustrating, and all she could do was pray he wasn't involved in anything dangerous.

They reached the end of the meadow and entered the wood on a path so narrow they had to go in single file. "Master Rory!" Michael called out in his vibrant baritone. The sun had set moments ago. There was still light in the clearing, but here in the forest near the river it was all murky shadows. The river was just ahead; Katherine could hear its muted gurgle beyond the next turn in the path. There would be a small clearing, a sandy patch of ground under a stand of willow trees, and it was there she expected to find Rory.

"Well? What ails you and your nag? Move along, slow-bellies." Michael was standing with his hands on his hips, wondering why they'd stopped.

"Michael." Something in her voice made him frown. He dropped his horse's reins and in three steps he was beside her.

The clearing was not empty, though Rory was nowhere to be seen. Instead three men were there, and something about them, something beyond the fact that they stared back stupidly but malevolently in a kind of drunken, loutish tableau, made Katherine catch her breath with a sudden chill. When Michael came up beside her, her relief was palpable. "Road soldiers" Rory had called them: common laborers not fit for the regular English army. Two lay on the ground and one leaned against a tree, holding a near-empty gin bottle. That one's the leader, Katherine found herself thinking, though the term seemed scarcely appropriate. He looked the youngest, and his slate-gray eyes had a reckless, flamboyant glitter that outshone the drunkenness.

"Look what we got here, Billy," he said softly to a dark, oily-skinned man with a mean slit for a mouth and dead black eyes. Billy rose to one elbow and continued a silent, blank-faced watching that struck Katherine as more reptilian than human. The third was stretched out full-length in the dirt, a huge, flabby fellow with pale blue eyes and red lips. His egg-shaped head was turned toward her and he was smiling vacantly. All of them were watching her with such unwholesome avidity, she thought of starving dogs chained just out of reach of a meal.

She stole a glance at Michael. He held himself stiffly and a muscle twitched in his jaw. The look in his eyes sent her a warning. Normally the mildest of men, his temper was ferocious when provoked. And if Katherine was sure of anything, it was that now was not the time for a confrontation. She put a hand lightly on his sleeve and cleared her throat.

"I beg your pardon, but you are on private property," she trilled, as though speaking to the deaf.

No response, just that unsettling staring. After a long moment the dark one slithered to his feet; the fat one sent

her another imbecilic smile. The third, the leader, took a
final swallow from the bottle, then held it up to the light
to confirm its emptiness. He looked at the bottle; he
looked at Katherine. His smile, the look in his cold gray
eyes—she knew what he was going to do the instant before
he did it. His arm flashed back and then forward with
blinding swiftness, and with a crash the bottle shattered
against a tree three feet from her head.

Prince reared in fright. Michael grabbed his bridle and
brought him down, rubbing his head until he was still.
Katherine wrapped her arms around herself to still her
trembling. She heard the men's ugly laughter, saw
Michael take a menacing step toward them. Then she
noticed that the one who had thrown the bottle wore a
rope around his waist for a belt, and in it was a pistol.

"Michael! Stop!"

"Michael, stop!" the fat one mimicked, laughing
stupidly and lumbering to his feet like a great cow.

"What do you want here?" Michael asked quietly.
Apparently he'd seen the pistol; Katherine offered up a
prayer of thanks.

"Why, we're just passin' the time o' day, mate. No law
against it, is there?" The leader, handsome in a heartless,
disturbing way, smiled as if he knew a secret joke. "How
come you ain't wearin' a skirt? I thought all you Scottish
blokes went around bare-assed." He laughed again,
joined in a moment by the fat one. Billy remained blank-
faced; he'd never stopped staring at Katherine.

The fat one waddled closer, mesmerized. She tensed,
but he stopped when he was four feet away. With a start,
she realized he was holding a short, thick stick in his
pawlike hand. "Gor, but she's pretty," he breathed
through thick lips. "Can we have her, Wells?" he asked in
a childish whine. "Can we?"

Wells smiled his slow, crooked-toothed grin at the
expression on Katherine's face. "Now, Thomas, what

makes you so unaccountable anxious? Though I admit you've a rare good notion for once.''

Michael backed up swiftly to stand in front of Katherine. She touched him, just for the feel of something solid. "I'm warning you, if you even touch her, any of you—''

"You'll what?'' Wells slowly pulled the pistol from his belt and pointed it at Michael's head. "Fact is, me and my friends ain't had us a sample of anything female in a tedious long time, and we've grown amazing hungry.'' His tone was mockingly apologetic. "Now, I can see this fair wench has a tender place in 'er heart for you, and mayhap you return them same fine sentiments. But a man's got to share and share alike in this world if he wants to get along. Am I right, Billy?'' Billy shifted his dead black eyes to Wells briefly, then resumed his silent, serpentlike study of Katherine. Wells sighed. "A man o' few words, is our Bill,'' he smiled tolerantly. "Now, where was I? Oh, yeah.'' As if in a dream, Katherine heard the gun cock, saw the flash of Wells's grin, heard him speak in a friendly, casual drawl. "I'm givin' you a choice, cove, and a passin' generous offer it is. I can shoot you now or you can take a turn on her with us. And I'm even gonna give you ten seconds to decide.''

Katherine reached out to grip Michael's arm and moved from behind him. Dry-mouthed, she watched the three men step closer, forming a semicircle around them. With the horses at their backs, they were effectively surrounded. She tried to draw a deep breath.

"You're mad,'' Michael was saying. "Listen to me, I can give you money.''

Wells held out a hand, palm up.

"I haven't any with me, damn you, but I can get it!'' The desperation in his voice frightened her more than anything.

Wells seemed to weigh the proposition for a moment

before shaking his head. He looked at Katherine and
licked his lips vulgarly. "No, I think not. I misdoubt it
would be enough."

"But—"

"No, I said! Now make up yer mind, we're tedious tired
o' waitin'."

"I know what I'd do," said Billy, a sudden humorless
smile breaking over the expressionless face.

"I know what I'd do," Thomas echoed foolishly.

Michael turned his tortured face toward Katherine once,
then looked away. She heard him speak, heard his
anguished tone, but the meaning of his words was lost
until all at once it exploded in her brain. "I'll join you.
Just don't kill me. For God's sake, don't kill me."

Katherine gasped and her hands flew to her face in
horror. Not—not happening, her brain sputtered. She felt
an arctic coldness rush through her chest. A black, liquid
pit of terror was opening before her. She stepped away
from Michael wordlessly, unmindful of the soft, cynical
"Ahh" from Wells. In that moment, that second when their
attention was fastened on her so intently, Michael sprang.
In one great leap he was across the clearing, and in another
instant his huge hands closed around Wells's neck. The
gun fired; Katherine screamed.

"Run!" Michael grunted as he bore a red-faced Wells to
the ground. Wells struck out blindly with the empty pistol
but the blow glanced harmlessly off Michael's shoulder.
"Run!" he called again, but Katherine was paralyzed.
Billy hopped from one foot to the other, as indecisive as
she. Then, slowly, like a great beast of burden, Thomas
began to move toward the struggling pair, the club held
high in his hands. Katherine felt a cry of panic rise in her
throat as he lumbered closer. Michael heard and looked
up, but it was too late. With a horrible, crunching thud
the club struck his right temple and he sprawled forward in
a heavy, lifeless heap.

Wells lurched to his feet, holding his throat and cursing

foully. Half-blinded by tears, Katherine tried to dart past
him to Michael, but his hand flashed out and grabbed her
by the hair. He jerked her to him viciously. Her back was
against his chest, his other arm encircled her waist.

"No, you don't! Rest easy and you'll end up enjoyin'
yerself. Hold, I said. Ow! Why, you bitch—" Releasing
her hair, he twisted her around and slapped her hard in
the face. The shock of the blow set her brain on fire. Fear
evaporated and she felt full of a white light of pure,
blinding fury. Spitting like a wild animal, she leapt on
Wells and attacked him with fists, nails, elbows, knees,
feet, until he fell back with a disbelieving oath. "Get 'er
off me!" he screamed, shielding his face with his arms. His
nose was bleeding and there were deep scratches on his
neck. The other two were watching wide-eyed from a
distance, Thomas still clutching his wooden club.

Snarling, Katherine gathered herself for another frantic
assault, but suddenly she froze and the fire died out of
her. Following her appalled gaze, Wells turned around
and saw a boy at the edge of the clearing, his face twisted
with a look of terror and indecision. He took one tentative
step toward them.

"Run, Rory! Run!" Katherine screamed, pulling at her
hair frantically.

"Get 'im," Wells told Billy shortly.

For a split second Katherine thought Rory meant to
stand and fight. But when Billy whirled and sprang at him
with the agility of a monkey, Rory cast one agonized look
back at her and scampered into the trees. Billy was after
him in an instant. The thrashing sound of trampled
undergrowth diminished quickly, and then there was
silence.

He's fast, Katherine told herself, fighting down panic;
he'll get away.

Wells was grinning at her knowingly. "Billy'll get 'im,
whoever he is. Billy's the fastest." He took a step toward
her. "Me, now, I ain't fast a'tall. I like to take my time."

Katherine backed away. She heard Thomas giggling behind her and then felt his enormous hands on her arms. Without thought, she bent her head and bit down as hard as she could until she tasted blood. He yelped and jumped away, holding one hand between his knees and crying like a child.

"Idiot!" Wells spat, furious. He considered Katherine through narrowed lids for a few seconds before his face cleared. "A woman like you needs holdin' down," he told her, smiling. "I like a lively roll-about, but you take it a deal too far." While he spoke he was untying the rope he wore around his waist. He coiled it in his hands teasingly, enjoying the look of abject horror on her face. Then all at once he sprang. She fought with all her strength, but this time he was ready. Before she could land a blow, he forced her backward until she fell over the leg he cocked behind her knees to trip her. She landed hard on her back, her breath gone. Turning her over roughly, he pushed her face into the dirt while he dragged her arms behind her back. He was tying her and she had no strength left to resist. She cursed him from an unknown reservoir of vileness until she choked on dust and her own tears. When he pulled her back to face him, her rage sputtered out and turned to primitive, unspeakable fear. He straddled her and struck her in the face with the back of his hand. "That's for my nose," he said matter-of-factly. Then he looked up. "Ah, here's Billy." He turned toward the dark little man who stood over them, breathing hard. "Well?"

"I did for him. He was just a kid."

Katherine closed her eyes, and something in her let go. She heard their filthy talk, felt their cruel hands as they tore at her clothing, but it was all through a purplish haze of unreality. It didn't matter anymore what they did to her or that they would kill her when they were through. Nothing matters, nothing matters, she sang to herself, blocking out the touch of hands on her body. If only she could remain detached, if she could stay up here in the purple cloud, away from the horror—

But now Wells was clutching the sides of her face and shouting at her. "Look at me! Look!" She opened her eyes and it was as if she were staring into Satan's face. "Say my name." She shook her head in denial and disbelief. "Say it!" He hit her again.

"Wells!" she choked, seeing him now only vaguely through a haze of tears.

"Wells," he repeated, satisfied.

Bile rose in her throat at his painful, intimate touch. He leaned closer and told her in a hoarse whisper what he was going to do to her. She felt herself about to fly into madness, and in desperation her mind seized on the feel of the rope. It hurt her, it was so tight. She twisted her swollen wrists to feel the burn more acutely of the rope on her wrists. Her senses shut down and she focused obsessively on the feel of the rope on her wrists, burning, stinging, tightening, constricting. She saw through a curtain of bright red light, and the hateful sound of Wells's voice was lost in a deafening roar that filled her ears.

Suddenly the sound of a shot demolished the delicate barrier around her consciousness, and when she opened her eyes Thomas was falling slowly and soundlessly to the ground beside her like a felled tree. The earth shook when he landed, and she saw a gaping black hole beginning to fill with blood in the side of his neck. Billy's screech was like that of some exotic bird as Innes, her father's caretaker, aimed his other pistol and shot him in the heart.

Wells rose slowly to his feet. There was no fear in his eyes; incredibly, he still wore a ghost of his cocky grin. Katherine had a sudden understanding that he was mad.

Innes, unarmed now, watched from his horse at the edge of the clearing while Wells drew a knife from his boot. The caretaker kicked his horse into a walk and

approached the crouching, smiling figure warily.
Katherine tried to sit up, to warn him that this was not a
man but the devil himself, but she couldn't move and all
that came from her throat was a low, desolate howl. Innes
circled closer. When he was six feet away, Wells sprang
and plunged the knife deep into the horse's neck. An
ungodly gurgling sound came from the animal's chest as it
slumped to its knees and fell sideways, lifeless.

Innes' leg was pinned beneath the horse's flank; he was
struggling desperately to free himself while Wells backed
slowly toward Katherine's stallion. Just as he gained his
feet, Wells leapt effortlessly to the horse's back and
laughed out loud. Innes stopped in mid-stride toward
him, arrested by the unmistakable note of lunacy in the
sound.

"You won't forget me, will you? Wells is my name!"
He jerked the rearing stallion around and galloped into
the woods.

"They tied me, Innes. They tied me."
"Shh, lass, I know." He was covering her with his coat
and trying to help her sit up. He held her for a moment
and then began to untie the savage knots that bound her
wrists. "Ach! Ye're all bloody from the ropes."
"They tied me."
"Hush, now, it's all right."
"They killed Rory."
"Nay! Oh God!" Tears sprang to his eyes and ran down
his leathery cheeks. They cried together, holding each
other, not speaking.

"Is Michael dead?" Katherine asked after a long time.
But she already knew the answer.
"Aye, lass, he's gone."

The moon climbed higher and shone with a chillier
brightness, silvering the trees in icy light. Somewhere an
owl hooted in the black woods. The sound of rushing

water against the stream bank was peaceful. Katherine wept because she wasn't dead. If she turned her head she could see the white of Michael's shirt where he lay on the ground a few feet away. Somewhere in the woods Rory lay battered and broken, her beloved brother, her childhood's best friend.

And slowly, as the moon rose higher and dappled the woods with gently moving shadows, despair gave way to fury, grief to vengefulness. In that hour her innocence died. Where a flower had bloomed there was a thorny stalk, and its veins ran black with the bile of hatred. When her father came she had no tears, and the hate-filled words tumbled from her lips like sharp stones: "Papa, we must kill them!"

CHAPTER 2
The Scottish Lowlands
November 1745

"Oh, balls—sir. Prince Charles is finding plenty of supporters now because the people are sick of kings who can't even speak English. But he'll never succeed because he's underestimated how indifferent the English Jacobites are to a Stuart restoration. Though they've little more enthusiasm for the House of Hanover, after watching it squander their wealth on one useless foreign war after another."

Colonel Roger Denholm folded his arms and leaned back in his chair to consider this remark. Coming from a major in the Royal Dragoons, the head of a regiment of His Majesty's cavalry, a lord and viscount of the realm, and the future Earl of Rothbury, it was at the very least injudicious. But considering it came from James Burke, it was exactly the kind of thing the colonel had learned to expect.

Why, blast the man, he wasn't even in uniform, he was in evening clothes, and it was half past ten in the morning. Irritated, he surveyed the indolent figure who lounged against his desk as though it were his instead of Denholm's. The lean build and graceful carriage gave no clue to the rock-hard physique under the perfectly tailored evening costume, and the fine-boned hands didn't look like those of a battle-tried cavalry officer. He wore his sleek black hair tied back with a ribbon. The aristocratic face was dominated by an aquiline nose that ended in a point, and the slightly flared nostrils gave him a not wholly undeserved expression of arrogance. His eyes, a stunning silver-blue, could glow with vital intensity; but they also had a habit of registering total bored disdain that had been known to devastate and enrage.

And, Denholm knew, his glib tongue and unorthodox, if not to say inflammatory, views on the current monarchy were becoming a source of irritation to his superiors. But what really bothered the colonel was that James Burke was a soldier in command of a regiment, and lately he was growing reckless. Recklessness was not a quality in an officer the colonel was prepared to tolerate.

"And so, Major Burke, you would say Charles is on a suicide mission?" he asked mildly.

"I would, sir. I think his cause is doomed to spectacular failure."

"I wish I could believe that. The man has an uncanny ability to arouse emotions. He's young, he's handsome; he's fighting ostensibly for his father, not himself. He cuts a romantic figure in his tartan plaids. He appeals to the women—why, look at his reception in Edinburgh."

"Puh," scoffed Burke. "Women don't fight wars."

"No?" Colonel Denholm's expression was enigmatic. He sat up and his tone grew businesslike. "I've mixed reports of you from the Duke of Cumberland. He calls your exploits at Fontenoy 'brilliant but erratic.' What do you say to that?"

"I was wondering when we would get to the point, sir," Burke murmured, permitting himself a small smile. "My opinions on the Young Pretender's chances of becoming king may be interesting, but I couldn't quite see you summoning me from Dumfries just to hear them."

"Quite. Let me be frank, James. The truth is, I'm not pleased with your recent performance, not pleased at all. You have the makings of a splendid officer, but lately something's gone awry."

"I cannot agree." Major Burke uncrossed his long, elegantly booted legs and rose from the edge of the desk to his full height. He peered down his nose at his superior in a manner that managed to stop just short of insolence; at the same time, there was something in his eyes, a fleeting look of indifferent acknowledgement, that suggested he was not really much affected by the colonel's assessment. At Fontenoy his best friend had been killed. He felt grateful to Cumberland for only calling his behavior "erratic"; in truth, he'd been a wild man.

"Your agreement is inconsequential." Denholm glared at him speculatively through his eyeglass. "You've achieved a certain notoriety as a daredevil and a risk-taker, a man without fear for his own life and limb. Methinks it's boredom, though, not patriotism that spurs you. 'Tis a pity you haven't the stomach to conduct yourself like a proper lord; you might even go home and help manage your father's estates."

"My stepmother is doing that very nicely," Burke noted dryly.

"The point is, you endanger others' lives when you risk your own. That's something I can't allow." He took note of the major's stiffening jaw and cold blue stare, and continued levelly. "I have a new assignment for you, James. You won't be leading troops, not for a while. Instead I want you to insure the safe transport of a prisoner to the garrison at Lancaster, from where the prisoner will later be escorted by a platoon to London."

"A prisoner? You want me to escort a *prisoner*?"

"Indeed, a very dangerous criminal. I wouldn't entrust this formidable duty to just anyone." Burke did not much like Denholm's tone, nor the decided twinkle in his eye.

"Do you know a lieutenant-colonel named Maule, James? Yorkshire fellow, under Grenfell's command."

"Fat bastard with red hair?"

The colonel winced. "I believe that's the one."

"I've met him once or twice. Bit of a pig, I thought."

"Yes, well, be that as it may, Lieutenant-Colonel Maule may have been the victim of a clever little plot. Then again, he may not." In spite of himself, Burke felt a faint stir of interest. "Until a week ago, Maule and a small company were trailing, at a safe distance, Prince Charles's troops as they marched from Edinburgh to Carlisle. Their object was to gauge the strength of Charles's army and advise General Wade on whether or not he should engage the prince at Carlisle. Maule claims the documents in which he confided this vital intelligence were stolen from him two days before Carlisle fell to Charles without a fight."

"You say he 'claims' it."

"Lieutenant-Colonel Maule is not a reliable officer. I would go so far as to say he's not a man of good character —I speak in confidence now, of course." Burke nodded solemnly. "Perhaps he lost them, perhaps they never existed, perhaps he sold them. On the other hand, perhaps his story is true."

"And what is his story?"

"It's a rather old one, not very imaginative. He says the young lady he won in a card game, and whom he very generously set up as his mistress that very night, was in fact not what he thought her to be."

"You mean a prostitute."

"A camp follower. A poor Scottish girl of easy virtue who slept with English soldiers for money. There are many such in these unsettled times, as I'm sure I've no need to tell you."

"Mm. And what does he think she really was?"

"A spy."

"Could she not be both?"

"Yes, I suppose."

"Have you met her?"

"Indeed, I have."

"What do you think?" He stood up suddenly, interrupting the colonel's answer. "Wait a bit—*This* is the dangerous criminal you want me to escort to Lancaster? This—*girl*?"

"*Sit down*, Major Burke. I'll tolerate no more outbursts. Do I make myself clear?"

"Perfectly."

"Good." Denholm leaned back. He fished a handkerchief out of his waistcoat pocket and began to polish his eyeglass. "Let's be frank, James; we've known each other a long time. You need a change. You've become more of a liability than a boon to the king's cause. I'm doing you a timely service, whether you believe it or not."

"Forgive me if I can't summon up much gratitude," he returned sourly. A *prisoner*, for God's sake. How had it come to this? Not long ago he'd been in Flanders, leading a cavalry regiment; now he was about to escort a Scottish prostitute to Lancaster.

"Nevertheless, I'm relying on you to put your mind to this affair and try to discover whether we're dealing with a spy or just a whore who's had the misfortune to be in the wrong place at the wrong time. If the latter turns out to be the case, then we must turn our attention to Maule. I must tell you, I don't trust the man."

"And how do you propose I find this out? Sir."

"Oh, James, I leave that entirely up to you."

"Thank you very much. What's the girl's name?"

"Her name is Katie Lennox."

"You say he won her in a card game?" Distaste colored the major's pale, aristocratic features.

"From her current 'protector,' another Scotsman. Ewan Ramsey, by name."

"And what became of Ewan Ramsey?"

"Not much is known about him. Apparently he left the district before the disappearance of Maule's documents. He was a gambler who also sold gin to the soldiers; and she was a hanger-on, not too discriminating in her personal attachments. They were known as a fun-loving, loose-living pair."

"Known by whom?"

"The soldiers. Maule's company."

"Then the acquaintance was—"

"Short, yes. We're speaking of a matter of days, a week at most."

"And how long was she Maule's mistress?"

"Two days."

Burke pulled at his top lip thoughtfully.

"Maule says she came along with him quite readily, that she had an eye on the main chance and thought she could do better with an English officer than a Scottish gambler."

Burke grunted. "She sounds like a rare treasure."

"James—" The colonel stopped. His uncharacteristic hesitation drew Burke's attention. "I'm sure I can count on you to be objective about this woman. What I mean is, she being Scottish, and in view of what happened, ah—"

"That was a long time ago, sir." He kept his face impassive, his tone colorless. "I can assure you it will have no effect on my ability to assess fairly this girl's credibility."

"Of course, of course." The colonel seemed relieved the topic was closed. "Now, when you arrive in Lancaster, I want you to make a report to the military authorities there. Nothing formal, just a summary of your impressions. It won't be binding one way or the other, of course, but it'll be helpful."

"Shouldn't there be another woman along, someone to act as a—a—"

"A chaperone?"

"Well, yes, something of the sort."

"Ah, James, your blue blood is showing. Whatever this girl is, her *reputation* is not at stake. And naturally I would trust you to behave at all times in a gentlemanly way."

"You may rest easily on that score, sir," Burke replied haughtily. "Scottish whores are not precisely my cup of tea."

"No," Colonel Denholm said dryly, "I imagine not."

It wasn't really a cell; there were no barred windows, no straw-covered floor or steel grate in a studded door. It was a room, the bedroom, in fact, of one Silas Ormsby, before His Majesty's Twenty-First Royal North British Fusiliers had requisitioned his little cottage as a temporary gaol while they provisioned themselves with grain and cattle from the neighborhood. It was reasonably clean, furnished with a small, bug-free cot, a wooden chair, and an empty chest of drawers. Still, its dimensions were six feet by eight, its door was unfailingly locked, and its one small window was boarded up with planks. A cell by any other name is still a cell.

After three days and four nights, Katherine Rose Lennox Brodie McGregor, the Lady Braemoray, was well aware of, one might say intimately acquainted with, every spare inch of her accommodations. She knew that three normal strides or five mincing steps took her from the door to the far wall. She'd reckoned to the minute how long a three-inch piece of candle could illuminate her quarters, however dimly, and she was on easy terms with a family of brown mice living in the thatched ceiling overhead. She had discovered early on the slender crack between two boards nailed over the window, and was by now fully conversant with the view it provided of Mr. Ormsby's turnip patch, and beyond it the broad expanse of wheat field, currently dotted with the dun-colored tents of Colonel Denholm's cavalrymen. Most of all, she was agonizingly aware of the chain of events that had brought about her captivity in this no-name village west of Dumfries in the southernmost lowlands of Scotland.

It was her own fault, that much was certain, though it was a singularly uncomforting thought. She had simply stolen the documents one night too soon, one night before they had planned it. And when she'd fled to Ewan's room at the inn afterward, he had not been there because he hadn't been expecting her. How galling it was to think if she could have brought herself to stay with Lieutenant-Colonel Maule only one more day, the papers would have been in Owen Cathcart's hands by now and she herself safely home in Edinburgh. She would be savoring the rebel army's easy defeat of Carlisle, not waiting in a cell for the king's soldiers to decide whether she should live or die. Oh, *damn* her timidity, her weakness, her—she didn't know what to call it. And it was terrible to consider that had she to do it over, the chances were good her courage would be found wanting again. In her life she had been given one opportunity to strike a blow against the English, to fight back with one small reversal after all the crimes committed against her and her family. And she had failed.

And yet—and yet—he was such an *animal*, such a filthy, horrid *brute* of a man, the living essence of Englishness to Katherine. She sat up on the cot and hugged herself, chilled by a sudden memory of Maule, of the way he'd touched her that first night. Cathcart's and Ewan MacNab's objective had been to establish her in a close relationship with Maule so she would have access to his private papers. They'd succeeded beyond their wildest imaginings when he had taken a fancy to her and "won" her with a hand of piquet on the very first night they'd met. He'd immediately brought her to a "guest house," which was really little more than a brothel, and very soon Katherine realized she'd started something she might not be able to finish. What she had earlier imagined would be an unsavory but necessary bit of business—sleeping with an English soldier to obtain military secrets—swiftly became unthinkable. Before things had gone too far that first night, there had been a knock at the door—a staff sergeant calling Maule away on urgent business—and she'd almost fainted with relief. That was the moment when she should have known she was not going to be able to go through with it. The door wasn't locked; she could have walked out. And during the long night and the long day following, while she waited for him to return, a dozen times she had almost done just that.

But hate is a strong motivation, revenge even stronger, and Katherine had nurtured both in her breast for four long years. She might have gone on for four more that way, or forty, if the English had not committed one more atrocity against the McGregors. Three months ago, in August of 1745, they had murdered her father.

And so she had not walked out. She had stared out the window all day at a dirty courtyard littered with dog and horse offal, thinking how appropriate such surroundings were for the coming assignation. And when he'd finally come, she'd suffered his pawlike touch until she knew she was either going to faint or scream, and then she'd distracted him by calling the maid and ordering a meal and a bath. After that he'd begun to drink steadily, and she'd entertained a wild hope that alcohol and fatigue would render him too tired to want her, giving her a second reprieve. But a bright, indefatigable gleam in his porcine eyes told her that was not to be. He'd made her sit beside him on the bed while he stroked her arm, sloshing whiskey around in his glass.

"By God, you're a beauty. I mean for a Scotswoman," he amended automatically. "Ugly race in general. Have you English blood in you somewhere? You must have."

"No' as I know of, milord." *You repulsive swine.* One hand unknowingly made a fist.

"Never mind. Tell me your name again."

"Katie Lennox, sar. I cum from Edinburgh, which is where I met me friend Ewan Ramsey, him as who you slickered last night in the—"

"I asked you your name, not your bleeding history!" he cut her off irritably. Just then he reached up and grabbed her chin, making her face him. "Let's get something clear, girl. I paid thirty guineas for you, more than I've ever paid for a woman, and I mean to get my gold's worth. Pay close heed to me, now. There are certain things I like and certain things I don't like, see?" He squeezed her face painfully and proceeded to tell her what he liked and didn't like. Katherine made herself go numb. She stopped listening and watched how his lips moved over his yellow teeth, how his snoutlike nose quivered over certain vowel sounds. When the sense of what he was saying threatened to intrude, she concentrated on how much her jaw was hurting. She felt tears sting behind her eyes and swallowed back a sob. It doesn't matter, she told herself, it'll only be for a few hours. I *will* bear it.

There was a rap at the door and two serving girls entered with the bath.

When they were gone and he started to undress, she fled to the table in the corner and poured more whiskey into his glass. She glanced up once at the mirror on the wall in front of her and saw him take a leather pouch out of the inside pocket of his uniform coat and place it on top of the high bureau. Her mouth went dry. She knew for certain he had not left the room last night with that leather pouch. It must be the information they were waiting for! It *had* to be. Now was the time for Maule's scouting party to send the intelligence they'd been gathering to General Wade; otherwise it would be too late to advise him before Charles's army got to Carlisle.

A thousand thoughts raced through her brain. She ought to stay, that was the plan, they'd said three nights.

But if she could get the pouch now, there would be no *reason* to stay. Surely the crucial thing was the information, not the time. It wasn't cowardice, it was—*expediency*, it was—

"Come wash my back, girl!" Maule bellowed from the tub, breaking in on her fevered reasoning. She stood still for a long moment, and then her hand went deliberately to the empty whiskey bottle on the table. She took it by the neck and held it behind her skirts. Maule had his broad white back to her and she went toward him slowly. "Did you hear me?" he barked impatiently.

"Aye, sar. I'm just here." She saw there were long red hairs growing out of the tops of his shoulders. He was nearly bald without his wig. She decided to hit him right on top of his head, in the middle; it was the widest part and afforded the largest target. She brought the bottle up high, feeling quite powerful and cold-blooded, when her hand began to shake uncontrollably. She gripped the bottle more tightly in desperation, but it was no use: she couldn't do it! Then Maule turned his head and she saw his face, even uglier now because of his anger, and before his expression could change she brought the bottle down on him with all her strength. It caught him on the top of his forehead. He slumped forward and his face hit the water as glass fragments fell into the tub all around him. She heard a bubbling sound, and with a gasp of horror she realized he was drowning. His head was slippery with blood, and it was hard to pull the heavy weight of him back out of the water. She leaned him against the back of the tub, and immediately he began to slide down on his spine. She grabbed him under the arms from behind and hauled him up again, groaning with effort. He stayed still, but she thought it wouldn't be for long. She ran to the washstand by the bed and took up the big pitcher and basin. She filled both with dirty bath water, and the level in the tub sank down so he was sitting in only a few inches of water. She thought he would probably not drown now.

She went to retrieve the leather pouch he'd put on the bureau. A hasty search confirmed that in it were the very documents she'd been sent to secure, and relief made her feel light-headed. She wrapped it securely in her shawl and took a last look around the room. She wanted to shout out loud for joy! Her eye fell on Maule's clothes, draped over the bed, and an impish smile lifted the corners of her mouth. She picked up his breeches, went to the dying fire, and coaxed it into life. The flames bit readily at the dry material, and before long there was nothing left but a handful of brass buttons and a bad smell in the air.

With a sigh of satisfaction, she opened the door and slipped from the room.

But I was a day too soon, she sighed, leaning against the boarded-up window and listening to the rumble of her stomach. It must be nearly time for dinner, she reckoned. Black bread, a bit of cheese, and a mug of beer: she knew the menu by heart. It was coarse and meager, but it usually didn't have any bugs in it.

But why couldn't Ewan have been at the inn when she'd gone there that night? And what had possessed her to sit and wait over an hour for him, until Maule's men had simply walked in and arrested her? She'd gone straight to the only place they knew to look for her, and she'd let herself be captured like a rabbit in a snare. What a fool, what an idiot, what a—Ah, but that did no good. She'd called herself every name she could think of and she was still locked in this cell, and she was still probably going to hang.

One thing she would *not* be punished for was assaulting an officer of the king. For his own reasons, Maule had not reported the fact that she'd knocked him unconscious with a whiskey bottle while he sat in his bath. His version was that she'd crept out with the documents while he was asleep. She wondered how he'd explained the goose-egg on his forehead. Perhaps it was high enough that his wig covered it.

There was a rattle at the lock, and the door to her cell swung open. Katherine blinked in the sudden brightness, shielding her eyes with her hand.

"Well, and how are we farin' this fine day, Mistress Lennox?"

"Why, Master Blaine, we're in fine whack, as usual, wi' naught t' complain aboot bu' a pressing wish to be awa'! And how's yerself?" Katherine stood up straight and put on her friendliest smile, at the same time folding her arms across her chest and endeavoring to keep as much distance as possible between herself and Corporal Freddie Blaine. Her gaoler was a rather likable fellow, for an Englishman, but he had swallowed whole the confection that his prisoner was a wanton, fun-loving strumpet, and he was fond of giving her arm a pinch or her rump a pat at unexpected moments, endearments Katherine was not truly alarmed by but heartily wished would go no further.

"Oh, I'm tip-top, Katie, but wantin' to be away as much as you. Well, almost as much." Corporal Blaine laughed boyishly. "They say Wade will march to try to recover Carlisle, and Charles is already heading south and getting away. And here I am, playing nursemaid to a bleedin' female, no offense, when I could be pottin' Highland rogues with my musket. It ain't fair, I'm bound."

"Ach, but 'tis a desperate fugitive I am, so ye'd best keep up yer guard, Corp'ral." Suddenly she frowned, hands on hips. "Well, and where's me dinner? Here I am fair starvin' t' death, countin' the minutes before ye bring me mouth-waterin', ever-changin' repast, and there ye stand, bare-handed. Has the royal army run out o' spoiled meat, then?"

The corporal laughed again and ran a hand through his

straw-colored hair. "I'm afraid your dinner will have to wait, Katie. Colonel Denholm wants to see you again." He spread his hands apologetically at her stricken look. "It won't be so bad, I'm sure, for he's a decent fellow."

His decency wasn't what cowed Katherine, it was his shrewdness. He was not a fool, and she dreaded another of his close interrogations. Well, she hadn't given herself away yet and could only pray her luck would hold. But the strain of walking a tightrope was beginning to tell, and she was not sure how much longer she could play her part.

"He's got a swell with him this time," Corporal Blaine continued. "Looks like a duke or an earl at least, though I heard someone call him Major. He ain't in uniform, though." Katherine stored this bit of information away. "And someone else is said to be comin', too." He paused for dramatic effect.

"Who?" she asked at last, out of patience.

"Someone you know."

She froze. Oh God, she thought, have they caught Ewan MacNab? It's all up, then, for they must know everything.

"Someone you're not overly fond of, I hear." Her face remained a blank. Corporal Blaine gave his last hint. "Someone who's wearin' his breeches today, for which we're all mightily grateful."

Katherine burst into laughter, relief making her feel giddy. Corporal Blaine watched her in awe, struck by how pretty she was even now in her tattered, filthy dress, and with hair that looked like mice could be living in it. They'll not hang *her*, he thought with certainty; they couldn't, even if she was a spy, which of course she wasn't. He'd put his money on Maule as the heavy in this affair, and he bet any court in the land would do the same after one look at her.

He recalled the time and turned businesslike, addressing her briskly. "Right, then, we'd best be goin'.

I've got to bind you this time, worse luck.'' He ducked outside the door for a second and returned with a short length of rope. When he saw her face, he frowned. "Hullo—what is it?"

She was pressed against the far wall, white-lipped, watching his hands as though they held a deadly viper. "You—ye'll not really tie me, will you, Freddie?" she faltered, the light gone from her eyes and replaced by a fearful pleading.

The corporal was astounded by the change in his fiesty, tough-talking charge. "But I must," he declared helplessly. "New regs from headquarters, just this week. Cumberland says we've been too soft on prisoners and wants a crackdown."

"But—'tis just a few steps! I shan't try to escape, Freddie, I promise you." She tried to laugh.

"I'm sorry, Katie, I must. 'Twould be my hide if I didn't. Here, now, turn around, there's a good girl."

"Oh God, no, don't—" The corporal took her firmly by the shoulder and pulled her away from the wall. "At least not in back, for the love of God!" she managed to say, though her lips trembled so she could scarcely speak.

Bewildered, the young corporal shrugged and began to tie her wrists together in front, making sure the knots were secure but not uncomfortably tight. When he was finished, he studied her face, and he had an eerie feeling she was no longer aware of him, or of anything else. He had an urge to touch her, to put both hands on the tops of those lovely white breasts her shabby, low-cut gown exposed. She'd tantalized him for days with her bawdy tongue and ladylike ways, a strange combination that made her more attractive to him than any whore he'd ever known, and he'd known a goodly number. Something prevented him, perhaps her fear or maybe his own better nature, and instead he chastely tightened the two

ends of her shawl around her shoulders and led her outside.

It was not a long walk down the dusty lane to Colonel
Denholm's headquarters, only past another cottage or two
and an occasional knot of cavalrymen engaged in desultory
military exercises. But to Katherine it seemed as though
she'd been sucked into a whirling tunnel, black but for
brief flashes of garish light at the edges and no end in
sight. Soldiers looked up from their tasks and saw her, and
expressed their stunned appreciation in the way soldiers
do, with whistles and shouts and vulgar proposals. If she
heard them she gave no sign, only held herself tightly as if
to prevent pieces from flying away. Flashes of an ancient
memory, blood-soaked and violent, threatened to overwhelm her; she knew if she let it happen, if she lifted the
veil and beheld the naked horror, she would start
screaming. Through the sheer force of her will she held it
at bay, never weakening her grip on the curtain that kept
the horrific vision shrouded from her mind's eye.

Wind blew her bright, tangled hair about like a red
flag, but she did not notice it; the day was blustery and
cold, but she didn't feel it. Once she stumbled and was
grateful for a firm hand on her elbow. Then she was
vaguely aware that Freddie was gone and she was in
Colonel Denholm's office. He'd stood up and was
speaking to her, not unkindly, and now he was introducing someone else, someone who did not stand up. She
barely glanced at the second person and had only a fleeting
impression of someone very large, dressed all in black. She
tried to attend to Denholm's words, but it was impossible.
She twisted her wrists painfully against the bonds to try to
clear her head. Denholm had asked her a question, but she
didn't know what it was. There wasn't enough air in the
room, she could hardly breathe. Her knees were about to
to give way, the roaring in her ears was louder now, the
room began to dip crazily—

Suddenly a mammoth, dark-clad figure descended on her like a great bird of prey. Before she could scream, her wrists were seized; she saw a flash of silver, and all at once the rope fell to the floor and her hands were free!

CHAPTER 3

She took a deep breath, and the blood returned to her cheeks in a rush. She felt the ground beneath her feet, solid and trustworthy. The fog that had blurred her vision receded, and she became aware that a man in a black coat was holding her firmly by the elbows and looking down at her through eyes of the most extraordinary ice-blue. Her gaze dropped involuntarily to his unbuttoned waistcoat and casually tied, snow-white cravat, upward to his rather harsh, unyielding jaw, and then to the most beautiful mouth she'd ever seen. It was wide and generous, and simultaneously reckless and sensitive, with a small white scar just above the top lip that exotically skewed its sensual symmetry. He had an eagle's beak of a nose, and above it those steely eyes were staring at her with such riveting intensity that it was a long moment before she realized her own hands were gripping his upper arms in a paralyzed sort of way. She heard Colonel Denholm clear his throat as if for the second or third time, and she blushed deeply, pulling her hands away. The man before her smiled a slow, provocative smile and moved negligently aside. She saw him put a short, narrow-handled knife into the inside pocket of his coat before he leaned back against the wall beside Denholm's desk. He folded his arms and stared at her in a way she could only call arrogant, and somehow insulting as well. Obviously this was the "swell" Corporal

Blaine had told her about. She felt a sudden dislike for him, and an infinite wariness.

Major Burke was feeling wary as well, for this girl was not what he had expected. He'd been prepared for one of those hard-eyed, gutter-smart camp followers who dispensed their inexpensive favors, along with the pox, in every country where soldiers fought or marched or encamped. If she were one of them, he could only rue what he'd been missing, because he usually made it a practice not to consort with prostitutes. It wasn't necessary. His wealth, position, and looks routinely commanded entree into the highest circles of society, where literally scores of titled women seemed dedicated to allowing him to seduce them. Sometimes it struck him that the women he bedded were scarcely better educated and usually no more entertaining than common whores, but at least sleeping with them was healthier.

But this girl confounded him. For one thing, he had no ready category in which to put her. She was certainly dressed for the part in her tattered blue gown, cheaply made and cut so low in the bosom it seemed to him one deep breath might send those luscious white breasts tumbling out. He amused himself imagining it. Would she be embarrassed and blush again, as she had just now when he'd caught her staring at him? What a lovely color she'd turned, underneath all the dirt. And what did you call hair that color, he wondered, imagining what it might look like combed.

But it was her face that gave her away. Whores simply didn't look like that, at least none he'd ever seen. They didn't have guileless, intelligent eyes or silky, apricot complexions, straight little noses and long, dusky eyelashes, mouths so vulnerable and perfect you wanted to—He frowned and put his hands in his pockets, annoyed with his thoughts and unconsciously assuming that insolent look for which he was famous. Of course she was a

whore; what else could she be? She might look like a lady
but she could not be one. This girl had been Maule's
mistress, after all. That made her a very cheap piece
indeed.

"Are you all right now, Miss Lennox?" Colonel Denholm was saying, seated again at his desk. They were in the
large, low-ceilinged front room of what had been until
recently the village tavern, and the sweet smell of stale
beer still hung lightly but unmistakably in the air. The
colonel's desk was to the left of a large fireplace, and
Katherine had to curb an impulse to move nearer to its
crackling warmth and thaw the three-day chill in her
bones. Instead she stood stiffly in the center of the room,
unconsciously rubbing her wrists and thinking at least it
wasn't necessary for her to pretend to feel nervous, for she
was nervous.

"Oh, aye, sar, 'twasn't nothing, only a wee bit of a
gray-out, as ye might say. I'm righ' as rain now, thanks
ever sae kindly." She spoke in her fastest, thickest brogue,
and was gratified to see Major Burke lean forward slightly
as if struggling to understand her.

"Good, excellent. I trust you're being treated well
enough in the lockup, are you? Plenty of food and all
that?"

"Oh, aye, sar," she answered sincerely, blinking her
eyes in appreciation. "It beats me mum's cookin' all t'
hell. And truth t' tell, I've slept in plenty worse places in
my day. Plenty worse." She gave the last word her longest
treatment, "werrrse," and nodded wisely in the manner
of a very old woman who has slept in hundreds and
hundreds of places. Briefly she wondered if she was over-
doing it.

"Ah, very good. Well, as I was saying, this is Major
James Burke, who will be taking over the investigation of
the charges against you for a while."

This was not good news, Katherine instantly perceived.

She looked at Burke with welling suspicion. He bowed to
her deeply, too deeply, with a smile full of easy insolence.
A wave of annoyance washed over her. He was making fun
of her! With an effort she forced herself to curtsey to him
in the humble peasant style she'd taken pains to learn.

"What I'd like you to do, Miss Lennox," the colonel
was going on, "is to take a seat here," indicating a
straight-backed chair in front of his desk, "and tell Major
Burke exactly what happened between you and
Lieutenant-Colonel Maule."

"Between me and the colonel, sar?" she asked in a voice
full of dismay. She looked down modestly as if to hide a
blush. "Oh, I could no' do that, sar. 'Twouldn't be
seemly a'tall!"

Burke snorted.

"No, no," Denholm coughed. "What I meant was, tell
us how you *met* Maule and, ah, so forth and so on."

"Oh, that! You want me t' tell all tha' again, then?"

"If you would be so kind. And if you'd endeavor to
speak quite slowly and distinctly, we would both
appreciate it so much."

"Very good, sar." She sat down demurely and folded
her hands in her lap. Clearing her throat with self-
conscious formality and fixing both men with a look of
wide-eyed candor, she began her tale. "Weel, 'twas this
way. Me and Ewan was in Lockerbie, see, and one night
Ewan gets into this card game, and—"

"What were you doing in Lockerbie?" Burke interrupted peremptorily. He could see she had her little story
all prepared and ready to recite; he wanted to see if he
could rattle her.

"Why, I was wi' Ewan."

"How did you come to be in Lockerbie with him?"

"We were travelin', and we—we were just there!"

"Where had you traveled from?"

"Oh, from all over. We'd been in Abington and
Moffat—"

"Where did you start out from with Ramsey?"

Katherine could see what kind of inquisitor Major Burke was going to be: relentless. She decided to inject some truth into her story. "From Edinburgh, sar."

"Do you come from Edinburgh?"

"I—I've passed part o' me life there. Me mother bides there." This much was true.

"Her name?"

The man spat his questions at her as rapidly as rifle fire. She was momentarily addled. Was it dangerous to tell him her mother's first name? No, of course not, she remembered; she'd already given them a false last name herself, that of her father's mother. "My mother's name is Rose Lennox."

"And your father?" Burke continued remorselessly. Colonel Denholm had sat back in his chair and was observing the interview with interest.

"He's—dead." Her voice was colorless.

"His name, girl."

"I—I—"

"Yes?"

"I dinna ken his name."

"And how is that?"

"My—me mother doesna ken it, sar."

"Ah. I see." Burke leaned back, satisfied her confusion and embarrassment were real.

Katherine squeezed her hands together in her lap and gritted her teeth. She marveled at the cold rage that welled up in her. How easy it had been to tell Colonel Denholm these monstrous lies about her beloved mother and father, and how wrenchingly difficult it was to say the same words to this abominable English major.

"How did you meet Ramsey?" Burke went on after a moment.

Denholm, she recalled, hadn't asked her this particular question. Something perverse in her wanted to shock the major out of his insufferable superiority. She looked at him intently but innocently. "I met him in the alley behind McTavish's Tavern on Black Horse Lane. He was pissin' against the wall and I was pukin' up a quart o' McTavish's sorry rum punch into a trash heap." She thought his aristocratic paleness grew distinctly paler and she settled back in her chair, pleased. She even crossed her legs, revealing an audacious glimpse of shapely ankle beneath the torn skirt. She went on with relish. "We seemed t' hit it off righ' from tha' moment, me and Ewan. He was devilish handsome and he had a real way aboot him. Quite swept me off me feet, he did."

"I haven't a doubt of it," Burke said coolly. He was beginning to conceive a dislike for the woman.

"So we became a couple, like, and we had some high good times together. He was a grea' one fer gamblin'. Why, he'd bet on anything, anything a'tall. He'd wake up in the mornin' and look out the window and say t' me, 'Wha' d'ye bet it'll rain today, Katie, me love?' And if I'd say, 'Nothing, love, fer there's no' a cloud in the whole bloody sky,' why, he'd say, 'Very well, then, wha'll ye bet it'll *no'* rain?' Oh, aye, he'd take any side of a wager, just fer the thrill of it, like, and sometimes—"

"Yes, yes," Burke cut in impatiently, "young Ewan was a gambling man. Now tell me how the foolish fellow came to squander away such a fine treasure as yourself, Miss Lennox."

The sarcasm in his tone galled her. "Oh, Major Burrke, tha' was a sorry night, tha' was." She wiped away an imaginary tear and snuffled pitifully into her filthy handkerchief, ignoring his skeptically cocked eyebrow. "Ewan's luck went sour in Lockerbie. He couldna win a bet on wha' time o' the day it was, and that's the truth. He was doon t' naught but a few farthings one night in a pub called the Green Goose in High Street. Do ye know it?"

"I fear not."

"Lots of sojers from the local regiment go there. Ewan took me wi' him, as usual; said I was his good luck piece."

"I'm sure of it." He smiled, positive her pun was unintended.

"There was this lootenant-colonel there who was just lookin' at farst, no' playin', I mean. He was sorta watchin' me, too, ye might say, out o' his piggy little eyes, and fair givin' me the jitters. I dinna ken, something aboot him, the way he stared—I plain didna like him!" She was speaking truthfully now. She let her mind go back to that night, the one she and Owen Cathcart and Ewan MacNab had planned for weeks in advance. "The colonel could see, as anyone wi' half an eye could see, tha' Ewan was almost flat. He'd said no' a ward all the long night, just watched the play and stared at me in his spooky way, when all of a sudden he says t' Ewan, 'You've about lost it all, you barelegged, frozen-assed Scot, but I see you've got one last stake to put up. That is, if you're half the gamesman you take yourself for.' " She saw Major Burke suppress a smile at her deep-voiced, deliberately clumsy attempt at an English accent, and she felt a small thrill of triumph. " 'And wha' migh' tha' be, Yer Excellency?' asks Ewan, in tha' comical way he had wi' English sojers. Say wha' ye will aboot my Ewan, he wasna afraid o' anyone, no' even a bloody lootenant-colonel in the bloody English army! Beggin' yer pardon, I'm sure."

"Quite wonderful. Do go on."

" 'And wha' migh' tha' be, Yer Excellency?' says Ewan," she repeated, savoring these embellishments. " 'Why,' says the colonel, 'that fetching bit of baggage behind you, sir.' Ewan gasps in horror. 'You mean my wife, sar?' 'Your *wife!*' says the colonel, and laughs out loud. In truth, sar, everybody laughed at that," she admitted mournfully, hanging her head. "So I drew meself up, I did, and told the English bloody colonel as how my Ewan would never think o' puttin' up *me* in a wager, and anyone who thought otherwise was a bone-headed thickwit and a pure fool t' boot!'' Her voice grew pitiful. ''Then I looked doon at Ewan t' back me up, like, and tha' was when I spied the gleam in his eye. Damn him t' bloody hell!'' She resorted to her handkerchief again, boo-hooing into it most pathetically.

The two men glanced at each other. ''There, there,'' said Denholm tentatively.

Burke was not so kind. ''Stop that damned cater-wauling, woman, and get on with it.''

''I'm sorry, sar, but it fair breaks me heart t' think aboot it.''

''Then don't think about it! So Maule won you in the damned card game. What happened to Ramsey?''

She shook her head miserably. ''I dinna ken, sar, for I never saw him again.'' That much at least was true. Damn him, why couldn't he have been waiting in his room? It was bitter to think her life might be forfeit because Ewan MacNab had lingered over his supper.

''Very well, we'll leave that for now.'' Burke pushed himself off from the wall and came toward her. He sat on the edge of Colonel Denholm's desk, not three feet from her knees. She felt threatened, endangered by his nearness, and somewhat spellbound by the directness of his silver-blue gaze. It was clear to her which of these two Englishmen meant her no good. ''Who is Owen Cathcart?'' he asked suddenly.

Taken off guard, Katherine felt her heart miss a beat. ''Owen Cathcart?'' she repeated stupidly, buying time. One hand fluttered to her hair; she patted some wild strands down nervously. ''Why, he's—just someone I know. Why d'you ask?''

''Because he's reputed to be a spy and you've been seen with him in this neighborhood.''

''Owen?'' she cried incredulously. ''Owen Cathcart a spy? Why, he's naught but an auld mon who's been nice

t' me. He likes his bit o' fun, and he's rare generous wi'
his purse to a lass. Weel, if he *is* a spy, I know naught of
it!'' She sat up suddenly with a worried frown. ''Hullo—If
you find Ewan, you wouldna tell him aboot me and Owen,
would you? Wha' I mean is, there's a nasty jealous patch
in Ewan, and there's no sayin' wha' he'd do if he found
out. No' but wha' he doesna have a bit of his ane on the
side whenever he likes it, mind, but lord help me if I
should throw that up in his face! Whoo, wouldn't he be
half mad? But wha' I say is, wha' a mon doesna ken canna
bite him, and besides, sometimes a gel has t' hae a bit o'
somethin' extra t' tide her over till her real mon gets flush
again. So where's the harm done?'' She shrugged broadly
and sent Burke an ingenuous smile, inviting him to
challenge this unassailable piece of logic. He was looking
at her with cold distaste. She could tell from the curl of his
lip what he was thinking: that if she was not a spy, she was
a worse trollop than he's first suspected. It was exactly
what she wanted him to think, but it gave her surprisingly
little pleasure.

''So you became Maule's mistress,'' he said after a
pause, his voice tinged with acid as he considered the
distasteful alliance.

''Aye.'' She met his uncanny blue eyes and held them,
determined not to look away first. He would *not* make her
feel ashamed.

''Where did he keep you?''

Swallowing, she willed herself not to react to his callousness. For heaven's sake, she wanted him to believe her,
didn't she? ''At a guest house. Mrs. Talbot's, in—''

''Water Street. I know it. Guest house, you call it? He
wasn't exactly going into hock on your behalf, was he?''

She said nothing, hiding her dislike in a blank stare.

''Never mind, let's get to the point. Colonel Denholm
says you were apprehended four nights ago with a packet
of documents containing vital military intelligence and

you've had nothing of consequence to say for yourself ever since. The penalty for treason is hanging, as I'm sure I've no need to remind you. You've had ample time to ponder your plight; now is your opportunity to explain anything you'd like. Come, girl, what have you to say?" He spoke sternly, as if to a child, in his oh-so-refined accent, and Katherine was filled with irritation at the high tone he took with her.

"I will tell ye the truth, Major Burrke—and Colonel Denholm. I had no' spoken earlier for I was too ashamed. And because, as ye say, the penalty fer treason is hangin', but fer thievery 'tis only imprisonment."

"Thievery, is it?" Burke's face was alight with cynical interest.

"Aye, sar, and hard it is fer me to admit it. And I can promise you, 'twould never have cum to all this if he hadna been sae cruel, the black-hearted bastard!" She looked at Denholm apologetically. "Beggin' yer pardon, sar." The colonel waved his hand. She took a deep breath. "There were things he wanted me to do, things he—wanted to do to me." She was suddenly loath to go on with this story and she could not look at either man. She felt a hot flush crawling up her neck as she remembered the things Maule had said to her before she'd willed herself to stop listening to him, forcing herself not to make the mental connection between him and that other thing, that awful other thing she refused to think about ever, ever—except today when Corporal Blaine had tied her hands and she'd remembered—

She stood up abruptly, shuddering, her arms wrapped around herself. Burke stood, too. She expected him to sneer at her, but his lips were set in a grim line and she had the impression that if she took a step toward him he would touch her. She turned away, confused. After a few moments of silence she heard him say quietly, "Go on, please."

She turned around. She had herself under control again. She decided it was time to enlarge a bit on Maule's baseness. Gripping the back of the chair, she addressed a spot on Colonel Denholm's desk. "When I would no' do wha' he wanted, he beat me. With his hands, usually, but once wi' his belt. And if ye dinna believe me, I can show ye the bruises, for they're still there." Well, she reasoned, the only reason he had *not* beaten her was because she'd escaped from him too soon, so it was hardly a lie at all. Not that she cared.

She went on resolutely. "On the second night, I saw him take money from the pocket of his coat and put it in a pooch. I—"

"A pouch?" Denholm interjected.

"Aye, a pooch. I looked awa' lest he see me watchin', but I *sensed*, do ye ken, that he put it on the high bureau next t' the bed. After—after—you know—I waited until he was asleep. Then I crept out o' bed and put on me clothes. I was shakin' like a leaf fer I knew wha' he'd do if he should wake. It was dark, o' course, and I couldna see what all was on the bureau, but I—" she hung her head in apparent shame—"I made a grab fer what I thought was the money—and I ran!"

It sounded plausible to Katherine's ears. She kept her head down awhile longer, feigning embarrassment. When she finally looked up, Burke and Colonel Denholm were regarding her with identical expressions of suspended judgment. She saw she hadn't completely convinced them, yet neither were they inclined to hang her immediately from the nearest gibbet. She felt a sudden burst of hope.

"He must've had *two* pooches, d'ye see? And unlucky gel that I am, I chose the wrong one. Anyway, wha' would I be wantin' wi' documents? I canna even read! If he hadna been sae beastly t' me, I'd never've stolen from him, either. 'Tis no' my way, though I wouldna expect ye

t' believe it. Beggin' yer pardons, I expect yer like most
men—if a gel is forced t' take up wi' men in an easy way t'
make her living, then she must be the kind who'll steal
and lie and cheat and every other evil thing under the sun.
But 'tis no' always sae simple.'' She sat down again and
folded her hands in her lap, the picture of wounded
dignity.

Burke swept her a low bow and placed his hand over his
heart. ''Madam, I'm moved. And I'm obliged to you for
this timely lesson in masculine magnanimity.''

''Ye're welcome, Major,'' she returned sweetly. She
stared down demurely at the floor, thinking she had done
the best she could and there was nothing to do now but
wait. She was admiring the high polish on Major Burke's
Hessian riding boots, which he wore somewhat incon-
gruously with his evening clothes, when he got up suddenly and began to pace about the room in a restless,
distracted way. She watched him covertly from under the
long fringe of her lashes. His clothes were of the very finest
quality, she noted, and they fit him in a way that spoke of
the fashionable world's most expensive tailoring. And yet
he was decidedly no fop. He disdained a wig or even
powder for his hair; and although his suit was elegant, it
was simple in the extreme. He had a proud bearing and his
high cheekbones and fine black brows gave him a haughty
expression, but she suspected his undeniable refinement
was deceptive. She recalled perfectly how his arms had felt
under her fingers, and she observed with tempered appreciation the hard muscles in his thighs, the flatness of his
belly, the breadth of his shoulders as he prowled back and
forth beside her.

''So Maule beat you, did he?'' She started in surprise
when Colonel Denholm spoke suddenly. She had forgotten all about him.

''Oh, aye, sar, and in a most cruel and heartless way.
And the werrst of it was, I'd done naught t' desarve it. Oh,

Ewan's gi'en me a cuff or a kick, lord help us, and so has one or two o' me other sparkers, truth t' tell, but Colonel Maule whacked me aboot fer the pure pleasure of it, or so it seemed t' me, sar. I vow, I believe the man is deranged a bit in his attic, if ye ken what I mean.''

"That's a bloody lie! This woman is a vicious trickster, a flaming Jacobite, and a traitor to the crown!"

At the sound of that hated voice, like the bark of a half-mad dog, Katherine shot up out of her chair and backed against the desk, small fists clenching unconsciously.

"Ah, Lieutenant-Colonel Maule," intoned Colonel Denholm, rising from his chair and speaking with exaggerated calm, "the very man we were talking of. Do you know Major Burke?"

"Lieutenant-Colonel Maule," Burke drawled, in a tone of voice edging perilously close to disrespect. He made no bow or move to shake hands, and the inclination of his head was infinitesimal. He had always disliked Maule. Now he despised him.

"Burke," acknowledged the other man, reddening with anger and swatting sharply at his boot with a riding crop. He turned back to Denholm. "I didn't mean to barge in, but I couldn't stand by and let this whore defame me. What she says is a lie, I never touched her. She's a thief and a spy, and she ought to hang!"

"Ah, well, we shall have to see about that, I expect," the colonel returned mildly. "Why don't we all sit down and talk it over calmly." Katherine sat back down stiffly; Burke and Maule remained standing. "Ah, well. Very glad you happened by, Maule, for there's something I was wanting to ask you. Miss Lennox has had the goodness to explain how it came about that she stole your leather pouch."

"Oh, she has, has she?" he snarled, watching her with loathing out of his small, piglike eyes.

"Indeed. Seems she thought she was robbing you, as

she'd seen you put gold in your purse before, ah, retiring for the night."

"Put gold—! Bah, it's a stupid lie, I never put money in that pouch. Keep my money in my belt, always have. Take a look if you don't believe me." He began to unbuckle the black waist belt he wore around his uniform breeches.

"Oh God, save me! 'Twas tha' self-same belt he beat me with! Don't let him touch me again!" Katherine shrank back against her chair with a remarkably fine show of terror.

"Why, you falsifying bitch—" Maule took two steps toward her, his riding crop raised high in the air. She put up her hands instinctively and shut her eyes. When she opened them an instant later, Burke was standing between her and Maule, a hopeful expression in his eyes and a ready look in the set of his shoulders and the flexing of his hands. Maule lowered the crop, his face livid with suppressed fury, and stepped back. Burke's alert posture relaxed slightly but he remained where he was, with one hand resting casually on the back of Katherine's chair. Maule turned to the colonel and spoke through clenched teeth.

"If you would allow me five minutes alone with this slut, sir, I warrant we'd soon have the truth out of her." This injudicious suggestion caused Denholm to purse his lips and stare at Maule calculatingly.

"Weel, if *tha'* doesna prove the truth o' wha' I've been sayin', I dinna ken wha' does," Katherine declared triumphantly.

Seeing his error at the exact moment she spoke, Maule's temper flared anew. He began to curse her in the most abusive way, accusing her of every vileness his infertile imagination could muster. She was shocked into open-mouthed staring when he raged that, for thirty guineas, she hadn't even been any good in bed. "Lay there like a bag full of turnips, and too damned skinny by half!" Had he lost his mind? Had the blow to his head addled his brain? No; more likely he simply couldn't admit to these men he'd not consummated their revolting alliance. It added unhoped-for corroboration to her story, and she knew she should feel glad. But when she saw the look on Major Burke's face—disgust, disdain, and something else she couldn't define—she blushed to the roots of her hair.

"I tell you, Colonel," Maule continued to rail, showing no sign of winding down, "the woman's a liar, a thief, a Jezebel, a turncoat, and a traitor."

"What about a Judas Iscariot? You left that out." Burke's voice seemed to rise with an effort from untold depths of boredom. The whole unsavory story was beginning to annoy him. Maule and this girl, together, naked in a bed—He had a sudden vision of it and it set his teeth on edge.

Maule slashed viciously at his boot with his riding crop. "You may scoff, Major, but it's because of her Carlisle fell to the Pretender's brat, without even a fight!"

"Carlisle fell because Wade is a senile old windsucker and he didn't put up a defense," Burke drawled, adjusting the lace at his sleeve so it fell in more graceful folds.

"Good God!" roared Maule, shocked to the core. "Are you mad, sir? I tell you she's a traitor, and she should die like a traitor!" He whirled on Katherine. "I saw them kill a spy once," he told her in a voice heavy with hatred. "Up around Loch Ness near the Carriearrack Pass it was, not three months ago. Old man, name of McGregor. Quite a hero among some of the Scottish swine now, but he wasn't no hero when the Black Watch caught him recruiting the clans and hanged him on the spot for a traitor." He grinned at how pale she had suddenly gone; at last he was getting to the she-devil! "And do you know what they did then? They cut off his head and stuck it on a pike, and they left it in front of Fort Augustus till it rotted. Aye, and then they cut out his heart, and they—Oof!'' He wasn't prepared for the hissing dervish of fury that came at him with the force of a small battering ram. He fell back with an oath and tried to shield his face with his arms, but already there was a bloody scratch down the side of his fleshy jaw and the mark of small, even teeth on his thumb. The onslaught was over as suddenly as it began when Burke grabbed Katherine around the waist and jerked her away. She was so angry she literally saw red. That pig, that bastard, that *animal!* That such a one as he should have the gall even to speak her father's name, much less describe to her how they'd murdered him! Never had she wanted to kill anyone so much as she wanted to kill Maule. A brief struggle told her there was no escaping Burke's iron grip. But he could not stop her tongue, and for the next minute the air was shaken by a raging, spitting harangue that left all three men startled and speechless.

For Burke's part, he had never heard such epithets from a woman, nor indeed from very many men. He began to feel hugely entertained, quite enjoying the feel of Katie Lennox in his arms as she twisted and sputtered in fury, when it dawned on him all at once that she had entirely lost her brogue. In fact, if one could separate the matter of her speech from the manner, one would have to say she spoke in perfectly refined accents, with only the lightest touch of a Highland lilt in her r's and o's. A glance at the other two told him the colonel had made the same observation but that Maule was oblivious, still caught up in his own anger and busy nursing his hurt thumb.

Burke gave Katherine's diaphragm a quick squeeze, cutting her off in mid-expletive. ''Enough, woman,'' he ordered shortly, and set her down without unnecessary gentleness in her chair.

''You see what a shrewish bitch she is?'' Maule began, seeming about to launch into a counter-invective.

''Oh, have done, sir,'' Colonel Denholm told him

wearily but firmly. "There is nothing to be gained from all this bitterness, and I'm tired of hearing it. It's not for you to decide what she is, Maule, nor for me, either. Major Burke is leaving in the morning with this lady for Lancaster, from where she'll be taken in due course to London and there judged by a military court. We have your statement, we know your side of the story—"

"My *side*! I should certainly trust the authorities to take 'my side,' as you call it, over that of a common whore."

"Well, which is it, sir, a common whore or a dangerous spy?" Burke asked softly.

"Damn your impertinence, Major—"

Colonel Denholm stood up. "All right, Maule, thank you for your trouble. You'll doubtless be hearing more from me on this in due time. You're excused now."

Maule looked as if he would like to murder Burke and do something unspeakably worse to Katherine, but he wisely bit back whatever last words he might've been harboring, saluted the colonel smartly, and walked out.

There was a moment of relieved silence. When Katherine looked up, she was unsettled to see the major and the colonel regarding her with considering expressions, Burke's more dubious than thoughtful. She felt called upon to say something.

"Weel, I canna say I'm sorry *he's* gone. Wha' a rum party, eh? But after a' that, it's t' be you and me, Major Burrke, off t' Lancaster together. Only fancy! I've never been south o' Ecclefechan, meself, and that only fer a day or two once wi' Ewan. Bit of a holiday we had, I recollect, wi' a picnic and—"

"Peace! Hold your tongue, woman, or you'll find yourself with a gag over your mouth all the way to London." Exasperated, Burke dropped into a chair by the fire and glowered at her, long legs stretched out before him.

"Miss Lennox," Colonel Denholm said quietly. Instantly she was on guard. "Would you be good enough

to explain how it is that your Highland manner of speech
has a certain on-again, off-again quality?''

"My—what, sar?" She was appalled, but truly puzzled;
she thought she had been amazingly consistent.

"Your brogue, girl," said Burke roughly. "When you
were chewing the hide off poor Maule, it disappeared."

She opened her mouth but no words came out. She felt
herself flushing. She laughed nervously and twisted her
hands in her lap. She knew she was making a botch of it,
but no explanation leapt to her rescue; her mind was a
perfect blank.

"I canna think wha' you mean! Are you sure?" They
stared at her in silence. "Weel, I mean, mayhap when I'm
tha' angry it just goes awa', or something o' tha' sort. I
recollect now the same sor' o' thing happens t' me cousin
Jenny, only the other which-way. Why, when she gets her
quills up and really flies into the trees, you never heard
such hair-raisin' curses in yer life, and her most times the
mealy-mouthedest goody-goody you could know. It fair
makes yer blood turn blue t' hear her, I vow—"

"By the way," Burke cut her short, "why *were* you so
angry?" She looked blank. "Was it because he was
describing a hanging?" She said nothing. "No, I think
not," he speculated, watching her. "You went white as a
sheet as soon as he mentioned the fellow's name.
McGregor, was it? One might almost think you knew
him." Katherine could only shake her head mutely.

Colonel Denholm finally broke the silence. "You've
been out of the country, Major. The man's name is
commonplace now in the Highlands. He's become a
regular martyr to the cause among the supporters of the
prince. Doubtless she heard it that way."

Katherine found her voice. "Aye, that's the way of it,"
she managed softly. "I'd heard he was a brave mon, and
although I dinna hold wi' politics myself, I could no' but
admire his courage." She looked down, unable to meet
their eyes.

No one spoke for a few minutes. A gust of wind sent a sudden puff of smoke into the room and a log fell out of the hearth on the floor. Burke got up and kicked it back into the fire with his boot. The colonel rang a bell on his desk and stood up.

"That's all for now, Miss Lennox. For your sake I hope you've been candid, for otherwise it will go hard with you."

"Oh, indeed, sar, I've told you naught bu' the truth."

"The major will want to be leaving quite early in the morning, so make sure you're ready. Have you anything else to wear besides that, ah, dress?"

"Nay, naught but wha' I'm standin' up in, as they say," she replied cheerfully. She spread her skirts coquettishly, seeming oblivious to how stained and disreputable they were. "I suppose it could use a bit of a press, eh?" The expression on Major Burke's face almost made her laugh.

"Do you ride?" he asked without much hope.

"Aye, I do! Ewan taught me last spring on the loveliest donkey you ever saw. Raspberry was her name, and if we didna half go canterin' aboot the country like crazy, I dinna ken—"

"Oh God!" Burke stared up at the ceiling beseechingly. "Just tell me, sir, what I did to bring about this punishment. I have to know."

"That'll do, Major," Denholm admonished with a quivering lip. "And you, miss, will do well to mind everything the major tells you on the journey. He's not without influence among the authorities and his report will weigh heavily with them."

"Oh, aye, sar, I'll be as good as gold," she assured him, missing Burke's look of surprise at the colonel's words. "He'll have naught t' complain aboot from me, for I'll be as quiet as a wee mouse."

"Good, very good. Ah, here's Corporal Blaine to take you back. I wish you luck, Miss Lennox."

Katherine was standing motionless beside her chair, struck dumb by the sight of the corporal advancing on her with a short piece of rope in his hands. Her lips felt too stiff to form the question in her mind. Then Burke was beside her, his hands in his pockets, and he was drawling in his supercilious way, "I say, is there really any need to bind this dangerous criminal again, Colonel?" and rocking leisurely back and forth on his heels.

"No, no, certainly not," Denholm acknowledged readily. "Just take her along, Blaine, that's fine."

The room steadied and Katherine was able to move beside the corporal to the door. She turned back with a look of gratitude for Burke, but he had already walked away and was stirring the dying fire with a poker.

CHAPTER 4

"Katie, I've got to say I've seen you lookin' better," pronounced Corporal Freddie Blaine, a grin splitting his homely face. "Truth to tell, there's not much more'n a hair's difference between you and a sack o' flour." He laughed uproariously at his joke, heedless that the object of his mirth found no humor in it at all. Katherine was scowling down at the heavy, dun-colored bag of a garment that fell to the floor around her feet with all the grace of a wrinkled bedsheet, and wondering if this was Major Burke's conception of a joke.

"Freddie, he canna really mean fer me t' wear this. Tell me again what he said," she demanded, sparks of anger beginning to ignite in the sea-blue eyes.

"Only that you should put it on quick, and that I should bring you straightaway to the stableyard where he's waitin'. Oh, and he said to tell you to throw yer other gown away. 'That unspeakable rag,' he called it. Said if he was me he'd burn it."

Katherine shook her voluminous skirts in frustration. "I'll no' even be able t' walk in this. You could fit three o' me inside! He's tryin' t' bait me, that's what. 'Unspeakable rag,' is it? Why, the bleedin' twit. Here, gi' me me gown, Freddie, I'll no' throw it awa'. I'll keep it fer a rainy day. Cum, then, we mustn't keep his highness waitin'. Where's me shawl? I ought t' tie it aboot me waist just t' keep me skirts off the ground!'' So saying, she marched out of her cell, her gaoler stepping smartly to keep up.

Outside, the sky was leaden and a cold rain fell lightly but steadily. Sidestepping a puddle, Corporal Blaine remarked that it was a wonder the major would set out on a day like today, what with the rain and all. ''At least you're ridin' and not drivin'; a coach would take three times longer, the roads bein' what they are.''

''I expect the major canna wait t' be rid o' me, and would ride out in a blizzard if need be,'' Katherine replied grimly. Already her shoes were soaked and the hem of her dress was covered with mud. By the time they reached the stableyard her temper was badly frayed, and it didn't help that Major Burke's first words were somewhat less than cordial.

''Where the hell have you been? I meant to be off half an hour ago.''

He was in regimental uniform, though without his sword, and despite her annoyance a part of Katherine's mind had to admit he did look splendid. But there was something about a uniform that made any man look strong and handsome, she reasoned, conveniently forgetting Corporal Blaine.

Blaine was saluting Burke and explaining that there had been ''some difficulty with the dress'', when Katherine interrupted irritably. ''Major Burrke, wi' all due respect, I'm no' in Newgate yet and I dinna see why I should dress like an inmate. Or did Freddie get it wrong and ye really intended this thing fer the horse?''

Burke's scowl disappeared and he smiled in amusement. ''No, it's for you, Kate. And although it has a tragic way of hiding your charms, I thought that preferable to halting all the manly traffic between here and Lancashire while the lads made fools of themselves over you. It's ugly and you don't deserve it, but it covers you up.'' His eyes dropped regretfully to her bosom and lingered there until she felt her cheeks redden. She was utterly disconcerted. He had called her "Kate," not "Katie" and not "Miss Lennox"; and he'd spoken warmly, not sarcastically, just as though he didn't despise her. The smile that softened the harsh planes of his face brought her up short and dispelled her anger as if it had never been. "And besides," he went on more practically, "I'd lose my commission if I delivered you to the authorities with the ague." He turned to the corporal. "Well, Blaine, that's all; you can go."

"Yes, sir." Corporal Blaine saluted again, but something prevented him from leaving. He looked at the ground, glanced up at Katherine, then back to the ground. "Well, Katie," he said indecisively.

Katherine reached for his hand impulsively and shook it. "Goodbye, Freddie! Thank ye fer bein' sae kind t' me; I won't ferget ye."

"Nor I won't forget you either! God bless you, love; I hope it turns out well for you." He saluted Burke a third time, looking sheepish, and hurried away. Katherine watched him go a bit wistfully; he had been kind to her in his way, and he'd even managed to cheer her up a little during the dark days of her confinement.

"Do you always seduce your gaolers, Miss Lennox?" Katherine stiffened and turned slowly to face Burke. Disdain was back on his face and his tone was sneering.

Her chin went up and a scathing retort almost tumbled from her lips, but she bit it back in time. "Only when it suits me purposes, Major Burrke," she purred matter-of-factly, but with eyes still blazing. "The comforts o' home are sadly lackin' in prison, as ye might imagine, and sometimes 'tis worth a gel's while t' make friends wi' her keeper." It was hard not to look away from his expression of contempt, but she managed it, with a thudding heart and cheeks suffused with a blush born of anger and mortification. "Do I take it ye dinna approve?" she challenged him after a long moment.

"Approve!" He smiled thinly. "Oh, no, I approve heartily of it; what's more, it's exactly what I would expect." He turned away and strode across the yard to a tying-post where three horses were tethered, two with saddles and one bearing supplies.

Katherine took two deep breaths and succeeded in subduing most of her anger. It would be the height of folly to give in to emotion at this point in the charade, and she vowed not to let Major Burke provoke her again. She had to begin to think like the profligate strumpet he took her for; then his insults would have no sting. Hard though it might be, she had to cease being Katherine McGregor and throw herself wholeheartedly into the role of Katie Lennox.

She composed her features into what she hoped was an idiotic simper and tripped after him, holding her sodden skirts high enough to give him a provocative view of her ankles.

"Ooh, wha' a pretty horse. What's his name?" she asked, knowing full well she was a mare. "Can I pet him?" She reached up and touched the mare's nose gingerly, then snatched her hand back as if afraid of being bitten. "He's so tall, how shall I ever get up on him? Can he go really fast?" Burke's look of pained forbearance was very satisfying. "Is this a side-saddle, Major? Only fancy, I'll be ridin' him just like a lady. Wi' Raspberry I rode astride, I recollect, sorta like ridin' a log. Whew! if my arse wasna half sore. I told Ewan, I said—"

"Cease, woman! I'm a mild and pacific man, but much more of that and you'll provoke me to unwonted violence."

"Oh, la, such grea' werrds you do use. Freddie told me ye were a lord o' some sort, and now I can credit it."

Ignoring her, Burke wrestled a bundle of heavy cloth out of one of the boxes on the packhorse. When he shook it out she saw it was an enormous cloak made of fine gray wool, with a hood lined in black velvet. "Here," he said shortly, settling it around her shoulders and buttoning the frog fastener at her breast with impersonal fingers. "The good mother who provided your fetching frock had no coat to offer, so you'll have to make do with this for now."

Katherine ran her hands down the front of the cloak, marveling at the softness of the material. "Ach, no," she began reluctantly, " 'tis a wondrous thing, but I collect 'tis yers, and if ye gi' it t' me, then ye'll have naught fer yerself. Here, ye must take it back—Oh!"

With a grunt of impatience, he seized her around the waist and hoisted her up on the saddle. He adjusted the stirrup length and thrust her foot into it, his hand around her ankle in a most familiar and peremptory way. "Hold the reins like this," he ordered, putting them in her hands and pressing her fingers down as if she were a child. She had to hide a smile.

"Like this?"

"No, damn it, like *this*."

"Like this? Aye, I see; I think I've got it now. Weel, I must say, Ewan was a much *nicer* teacher than you, Major Burrke, no' half so testy."

Muttering something unintelligible, he left her and mounted his own horse, a gray stallion with massive hind-quarters and a small, intelligent head. But her horse was likely-looking too, she thought, with a powerful chest and well-muscled legs. It crossed her mind that if it came to a race, her mare might give Major Burke's stallion a run for his money.

They set out on the muddy, rutted road eastward toward Dumfries, a distance of some ten or twelve miles. From there they would turn southeast, skirting the Solway Firth. If the rain didn't worsen, Burke hoped to reach Gretna Green by nightfall. On the morrow they would drop down into England and head south, bypassing Carlisle, and with luck be deep into Cumberland by the end of the day. It all

depended on the weather, though, and he didn't much
like the look of the clouds which seemed to start a few feet
from their heads. At least the girl sat her horse well and
didn't bounce up and down, as he'd feared she would. In
fact, she had light, even hands on the reins and a surprisingly graceful carriage. Some people were natural
riders, he supposed; he was glad to see she was one of
them.

They rode in silence for a while through the gentle
Lowland countryside. There were few villages in the pre-
dominantly sheep-rearing landscape, although the wide,
lonely valleys enclosed rich farmlands. Katherine was
thinking they were all very well, those soft, rounded hills
and quiet glens, but there was no *drama* here. The
Highlands were less hospitable and much poorer but, to
her mind, infinitely more beautiful.

All at once it struck her, more forcefully than at any
other time in the last three months, that she might never
again see Darragh, and most certainly she would never live
there. After her father's execution, all his lands and
property had been forfeited, and she and her mother had
been forced to move from Inverness to Edinburgh. They
were not poor, because Katherine's grandfather's un-
entailed fortune had passed directly to her on her
twentieth birthday. But her spirit had withered in Edinburgh, and her existence there was empty and meaningless.

She stared blindly ahead, helplessly overtaken by
sorrow. Pain stabbed at her like a knife with the
knowledge that not only could she never be at Darragh,
but neither would she ever see her gentle father again, nor
Rory, nor Michael. Nor would she ever have her mother
again as she had, for grief had driven Rose McGregor mad.

But the most agonizing thing she must live with, the
thing that had not gone away even for a minute in the last
three months, was the awful truth that she was the indirect

cause of her father's death. If she—along with her mother—had not nagged, scolded, and cajoled him every day for the past four years to take up his responsibilities as head of the Invernesshire McGregors and gather them in support of Charles Stuart, the kindly, aging scholar would never have left his beloved library and set out on a mission for which he was disastrously unprepared and unsuited. It was her fault, all her fault, but she'd known of no other way to thwart the English and aid the rebels. She was a woman; she couldn't fight. And so she'd urged her father to ride to his death, with proud words and empty patriotic phrases, and she would live with the burden of her guilt for the rest of her life.

It was rare that she gave in to the despair that constantly lurked beyond the edges of her mind, and she had to wonder at how badly timed its arrival was now. Burke was looking back at her and she turned her head to avoid his eyes. But he slowed his horse and waited for her to come up beside him.

"Are you ill?" he asked, frowning.

"No." She had difficulty swallowing the lump in her throat; her heart felt swollen with sadness. "No, I am not ill." She smiled tremulously; her eyes were their truest blue through a blur of unshed tears. Burke watched her but said nothing. "I reckon I'm gettin' the hang o' this horse-ridin'," she managed after a minute, leaning forward and patting her mount between the ears.

"I reckon you are," he agreed quietly. They rode on a ways. After a quarter of a mile he saw she was herself again. "You said, 'No, I am not ill,' " he announced suddenly. Katherine looked at him quizzically. "You didn't say, 'Nay, I'm no' ill.' " His Scottish accent was distressingly accurate. She felt her face redden. "I've never *known* such a woman for blushing," he exclaimed, distracted. "But come, admit it, this rough brogue you affect is a sham. There's no use in going on with it, you'll only tire yourself out. We've a long way to go, remember; only think how much easier it'll be for you if you let yourself speak naturally." He was looking at her expectantly, one brow arched in that infuriating way he had.

"I—I think ye must have naught but cobwebs in yer attic," she said, looking away. "I dinna even ken what ye're blabbin' about."

"Oh, Kate, Kate," he said sternly, shaking his head like a disappointed schoolmaster, before spurring his horse into a trot and resuming his place in front.

From there to Dumfries, Katherine pondered her dilemma. On one hand, if he was not bluffing, the game was up and there was no need to continue playing this cumbersome part. And he was right, it was a tiring performance. She'd made a mistake in the beginning by doing it so broadly; it made it difficult to be consistent and too easy to lapse into parody. On the other hand, what if he wasn't as certain as he pretended and was really only trying to trick her into dropping a major part of her disguise? Then, too, she had a vague notion that somehow her brogue provided a way to keep them at a distance from each other; it was an obstacle, a social buffer that kept him away from her, literally and figuratively. She had a suspicion their relationship would be very different without it.

By the time they entered Dumfries, she had arrived at a decision.

She'd thought they would be stopping for a meal, so she was surprised when Burke led the horses over to the side of a small store. In the window was an engraved shop bill announcing "Mrs. Cheatham's Frock Shop: Best and Most Fashionable Ready Made Frocks; Suits and Waistcoats of Fustian, Ticken, and Holland; Also Footwear, and Undergarments." Burke sprang off his stallion and tethered the three horses, then went around to help her dismount. He stretched his arms up to her, but she spoke before he could lift her down.

"Major Burke, I've been thinking over what you said,"
she told him in her natural voice, a soft, lilting accent with
only a hint of a burr around the r's. " 'Tis true I was
exaggerating a wee bit, but I had good reason for doing so
and I beg you will let me explain."

He had been resting his hand on her hip with unconscious familiarity. At her words, his eyes widened and
he snatched it away. Katherine was dismayed: his reaction
was exactly what she had hoped it would not be. He
thought her a lady!

She spoke quickly to repair the damage. "Everything
I've told you about myself is true! 'Twas only the *way* I
told you that wasn't altogether sincere. And I've an
explanation for that."

His ice-blue eyes measured her under lids grown heavy
with skepticism. Rain ran off his tricornered hat in steady
rivulets. She thought he looked very big and very
dangerous. She was afraid she had made a serious mistake.

He put up his hands again and grasped her around the
waist. "I look forward to hearing it, Kate," he said
quietly, an ominous set to his lips. He set her down slowly
and deliberately, and he did not immediately let her go.
She had to tilt her head back to meet his eyes and the hood
fell away from her hair; the rain misted her lashes, making
her blink. "You might say I'm eager to hear it. I think at
dinner you'll tell me all about it." His hand moved to her
elbow in a painless but unbreakable grip, and he led her
around the corner and into the shop.

Katherine went along blindly, her mind preoccupied
with the question of what in the name of God had
possessed her to give away so much of her disguise, freely
and without duress? He'd *tricked* her, that's what, with
his persuasive talk of how much *easier* it would be for her.
Oh, she'd been a fool! Her thoughts raced along,
searching out details for the new story she would tell him,
so that inside Mrs. Cheatham's store she didn't take
immediate note of her surroundings until the good woman

spoke.

"Good afternoon, madam; good afternoon, officer,"
she greeted them cheerfully. "And what an afternoon it is;
more fit for ducks than humans, I'll vow." She stopped
when she got close enough to see the seriousness of
Katherine's disarray. She looked flabbergasted. "Well!
Well, now, I say, you've—you're—" Words failed her.

"We need a dress," Burke intoned calmly, at his most
lordlike as he stared down his nose at Mrs. Cheatham.

"A dress! Yes, just the thing."

"Something simple and serviceable. Warm, not
fancy—"

"And pink!" chirped Katherine.

"Decidedly not pink," Burke corrected coldly. "Something in brown or gray, I think. And a warm riding coat as
well, if you have one. Do you sell shoes?"

"Yes. I mean, no. That is, boots; I sell boots." Mrs.
Cheatham was flustered.

"Even better. This is likely-looking." He held up a
rather sober gown of dark gray worsted, trimmed with
maroon ribbons.

Katherine wrinkled her nose in disgust. "Likely-looking
for a funeral, mayhap," she declared contemptuously. Her
face lit up at the sight of a satin dress in canary yellow,
suitable for a formal evening party. "Ooh, look! Yellow's
my color, and look at all these cunning little bows down
the front. May I have this one?"

"Assuredly not. We'll have the gray."

"I won't!" she cried peevishly. "You can't make me
wear that ugly thing." She stamped her foot in a vulgar
way. "Besides, it wouldn't fit, it's miles too big."

"You'll wear exactly what I tell you, and I'll brook no
argument."

"You'll brook no—Why, you—" Her cheeks reddened
with frustration. All the words she wanted to say were
either too educated-sounding, like "You unconscionable

prig! You arrogant, overbearing boor!'' or else they were
vulgar, and she had no wish to shock poor Mrs. Cheatham.
The shopkeeper was looking from one to the other in
distress, fearful of a full-scale brawl breaking out in her
store.

"I believe the gray would fit," she offered timidly,
"though 'tis hard to tell with your, ah, *cape* on, madam.
But perhaps I have something else that might answer. I
have in mind a dress over here." She searched among an
assortment of gowns in a cupboard. "Yes, here it is." She
held up a forest green velvet dress with an underskirt of
lighter green, trimmed at the sleeves with cream-colored
lace, and with a bodice of very delicate green and black
brocade. It was simple but stunning. Katherine held her
breath; she didn't know whether to praise it or jeer at it.

"You don't look quite so mulish, Kate. Does that mean
you like it?" Burke said idly, fingering the material. "It
might serve," he continued, not waiting for a reply. "Are
your boots of good leather, madam?"

"It's not nearly so nice as the yellow," Katherine noted
firmly, "but I suppose it will do. Yes, I'll wear it."

"Your opinion wasn't solicited," he pointed out,
turning again to Mrs. Cheatham. "We'll have the green.
Now, where are your boots?"

In the end, Burke purchased not one but two dresses, a
riding coat, boots of soft morocco leather, two shifts, and
two pairs of silk stockings, all of the highest quality Mrs.
Cheatham offered and all in the very best of taste.
Katherine learned that it made no difference whether she
professed to like something or to hate it; Burke paid no
attention and bought exactly what he wanted—which
fortunately was exactly what she would have chosen herself. She made a point, therefore, of always exclaiming
over the loudest or the gaudiest thing, the one that came
closest to vulgarity, or at least to excess, for Mrs. Cheatham
sold nothing that was truly vulgar. His largesse surprised

her until he explained coldly that they would be together for some time, perhaps as much as a week, and to see her in the same gown every day would offend his senses.

"Mayn't I wear the green one now?" she asked when he instructed Mrs. Cheatham to put everything but the riding coat and boots into boxes.

"No."

"Why not?"

"Because I have said so."

"But why? Or would explaining it to me be 'brooking argument'?"

He frowned at her sarcastic tone, then sighed testily. "You may not put on the new gown now for two reasons. One: We don't have time. Two: It would be folly to change into clean clothes before you've bathed, there being such an inordinate amount of filth on your person. It would be like putting a new blanket on a horse that had just stumbled into a mire." He smiled, pleased with the analogy and the look of indignation on her face. "By the way, didn't they give you water to bathe in when you were in gaol?"

"Water to bathe in!" She laughed derisively at such a naive idea. The major had obviously never spent time in a military prison. "Oh, to be sure, in a great copper tub, with fine-scented soap and fancy perfumes, and a towel so soft you could lose yourself in it for days. But I told the guard to take it all away, it was just too fine for the likes of me!"

She thought Burke's pale cheeks reddened the tiniest bit, but "Hmpf" was all he said. "Are you finished, madam?" he asked Mrs. Cheatham, whose fingers had gone lifeless over the string on the last box.

"Y-yes, I'm just done. Now, let me see, that comes to twenty-six pounds, four shillings, for the lot."

"I must say," Katherine observed while Burke paid, "the king's army is a lot more generous than I'd've expected."

Burke's brows shot up. "The king's *army*," he repeated, sounding surprised. "Never mind. Here, give me my cloak and put on the coat. Change into the boots as well."

Katherine stood stock-still while the truth dawned on her. "You mean—You're saying *you*—"

"For heaven's sake, Kate, close your mouth." To her amazement, he went down on one knee, lifted her foot from the floor and removed her shoe. She had to put a hand on his shoulder to keep her balance. He slipped her new boot on, then did the same with her other foot. He stood up, slapping his palms together. "My cloak," he said, one hand outstretched. Dazedly, she unbuttoned it, shrugged it off and handed it to him. He threw it over his shoulders with a flourish. It looked better on him than her.

"I—I really did think they would pay somehow, pay you back later or have some sort of fund. Otherwise, I would not—" She stopped, confused. She was mixing up her roles, she perceived, for Katie Lennox wouldn't give a hoot who paid for her fancy new clothes.

"Otherwise, what?" Burke prompted, helping her on with her riding coat, a fashionable affair of dark blue wool, with fur-trimmed collar and cuffs. "Otherwise you would not have accepted them?" He smiled cynically and without humor. "Forgive me, my dear, but I find that difficult to believe."

Good, she thought, but she was blazingly angry. "Otherwise," she blurted out without thinking, "I would have asked what conditions went along with the accepting of them!"

"Would you indeed?" he asked, unperturbed. "Perhaps we'll speak of that later. Come along."

"Oh, no, we'll never speak of it, I can assure you of that!" She knew she was taking the wrong tone, but she couldn't help herself; she was furious.

Mrs. Cheatham was standing by the door, wringing her

hands. "Good afternoon to you," she trilled hopefully.

"No?" Burke looked at Katherine with interest. "Really? Sometime you must remind me to ask you why. I had thought you lacked that particular kind of scrupulousness." He started out the door, one arm full of boxes. "You've been more than kind, madam," he told Mrs. Cheatham, handing her something Katherine couldn't see; but the woman's suddenly mollified face gave her a clue. "Come, Kate."

Outside, while Burke packed the new purchases onto the back of the supply horse, Katherine had a chance to subdue her temper. She'd done it again, she scolded herself, given way to wholly inappropriate indignation. If she weren't more careful, she'd find herself at the wrong end of a noose with nothing to comfort her but the knowledge that through it all she had behaved like a real lady.

Burke seemed to know his way around the town. He led her unhesitatingly along a cindered sidewalk past several more shops to an alehouse called the George and Dragon. Inside, the air was hazy with chimney and pipe smoke, and the bar area was filled with the usual taproom wags and characters. They looked Katherine and Burke over carefully, but not with as much amazement as Mrs. Cheatham had, before returning to their pipes and pints and conversation. Burke held a chair for Katherine at a table beside the great fireplace. He took off his wet cloak and hung it on a hook before the fire, where it immediately began to steam.

The waiter appeared, saying today there were veal cutlets, pigeons, asparagus, lamb, salad, apple pie, and tarts.

"Are you hungry?" Burke inquired neutrally.

Katherine made an indifferent face. "I could eat a little something," she said offhandedly. She'd lost weight in the last five days and her stomach had shrunk to concavity; it was rumbling now in indignant alarm. But she'd be damned if she'd let Lord High and Mighty Burke know.

Burke smiled slightly and told the waiter to bring some of everything, and a pitcher of his best ale. At Katherine's look he shrugged. "The army does pay for meals, you know, so you needn't be concerned about any—what was it?—*conditions*. Same for lodgings, by the way."

She could not think of a suitable reply.

The waiter brought ale and poured it into two mugs. Katherine realized she was sipping hers too daintily, took a sizable swig, and went into a coughing fit. When she recovered, Burke was looking at her appraisingly.

"How does it compare with McTavish's sorry rum punch?" he asked blandly.

"Favorably; it merely went down the wrong pipe," she replied tightly, wiping her eyes with her napkin. "Honestly, Major, everything I've told you about myself is true. You can't blame me for wanting to sound a bit crude, can you? Be frank: Now that you know I can speak proper English, aren't you more inclined to think me a spy?" He was silent. "Of course you are. 'Tis only natural. And since I knew you and Colonel Denholm would feel that way, I only exaggerated a wee bit, made myself out to be quite common in my speech. And then I began to have such a good time of it, I guess I got a bit carried away. I wanted to see how far I could go."

Burke looked thoughtful. "I apprehend you haven't lost your brogue entirely, so I take it at least you are Scottish?"

"Oh, aye, through and through. That is, at least on my mother's side. As I mentioned, m-my mother—"

"Wasn't sure who your father was. Yes, you mentioned that."

The meal arrived. Katherine immediately forgot her resolve not to let Major Burke have the satisfaction of seeing how hungry she was. It didn't matter to her that he spent most of the time watching her instead of attending to his own meal; she was too intent on satisfying her appetite.

"Are you finished?" he asked once, noticing she'd laid down her knife and fork.

"Actually, I was only kind of . . . resting."

"Ah."

"Were you going to eat that little piece of meat?"

"This? No, would you like it?"

"Only so it doesn't go to waste."

"Of course."

"Do you know, in some places they just throw it away?"

"Not here, though, I expect."

"You can never be sure."

"Too true. Will it bother you if I smoke?"

"Oh, no. My fa—my *friend*, a gentleman I used to know, smoked all the time. I rather like it."

"Have you had that many gentlemen friends, then, Kate?" He drew out a clay pipe from his coat and began to fill the bowl with tobacco. "Hmm?" he prodded when she hesitated.

"I have, you know," she admitted with charming reluctance. She lowered her voice confidentially. "It may sound shocking, but the fact is, I *like* men. And then, of course, a girl who's unschooled and unskilled has to make her way somehow in the world."

"Indeed she does. Usually she gets married, however."

"We-el," she said consideringly, "it's not that I haven't had offers."

"I would be astonished if you had not."

"And it's not that I'm against marriage, not in itself. It's just that I haven't happened upon the right man yet."

"A rich one, of course."

"There, I knew you would understand."

"What about Ewan Ramsey?" He blew a short puff of smoke at the ceiling, unaccountably irritated.

"Oh, Ewan's all right, though he'll never amount to

anything.''

"Setting your sights on higher game, eh?''

"Well, a girl's got to look out for herself.''

"Is your mother living?''

"Aye, in Edinburgh.'' She pushed the last plate away and dabbed at her lips with her napkin. "My mother was very beautiful when she was young. Ach, she's beautiful now to me, though broken down and sick. When she was a young girl she went into service in a gentleman's house in Edinburgh. She was got in the family way soon enough and was let go. As I said, she was pretty, and she was young and without much sense, so it was impossible to say exactly who the father might be. Well, she had me, and I don't know how we lived for the first nine years of my life, though I expect I can guess.''

She took a sip of ale. It wasn't as difficult as she'd anticipated to spin this yarn. She thought of it as just a story, a fairy tale about imaginary characters such as she might have told Rory when they were children. Rory had always said she was the world's best teller of tales.

"Anyway, when I was nine, my mother took a post as housemaid in the home of a great lord. His wife had lately passed away with the smallpox, and before long it pleased him to make Mama his mistress. He took a great liking to me as well, for some unaccountable reason; I wasn't much to look at, that's for certain.''

"You astound me.''

"He said I was like the daughter he'd never had. He talked to me all the time, just as though I was grown up. And he educated me in a small way, taught me to speak proper English and took me to the theater sometimes, and once to the opera. I've often wished since then that he'd taught me to read; then I might have become a governess and been respectable. But there's no use crying over spilt milk, I always say. He was a kindly man, and lonely after his wife died. I truly believe he might have thrown everything away, married Mama and adopted me as his very own child, but it wasn't to be. He was killed in a coach accident when I was thirteen, and Mama and I were thrown out into the world again on our own.'' She made a brief show of weeping into her napkin.

Burke turned his head to hide the amusement in his eyes, not persuaded for a minute by this display of sentiment. Her story was plausible, but something told him she was making it up out of whole cloth. It scarcely mattered to him, though, so absorbed was he in the melodious sound of her voice and the subtle play of expressions across her lovely face. At that moment he could have listened to her recite the tax rolls and been content.

''We went north after that to try our luck around Inverness,'' she continued, snuffling a little. ''When I was sixteen I went into service in a so-called gentleman's house. Under-housemaid I was, and a more miserable time I never spent. After a year I was sacked. The mistress said I put on too many airs, but really she was afraid for her son. And well she might have been, for he'd already seduced me, had his fun with me, and given me up! 'Twas my first taste of men's fickleness, and it taught me a valuable lesson: Don't be a fool and give yourself to a man who can't return the favor with anything more substantial than hugs and kisses.''

''Clever girl,'' Burke murmured, watching her through lazy, narrowed lids.

''Well, things went downhill from there for a while. Mama said I took up with bad companions, but I was young and I was learning my way. One thing I found out is that it's easier to live off a man's money in return for being friendly than it is to work yourself to the bone in some swell's house for miserable wages and no chance in sight to pull yourself out. I watched what happened to my Mama, and I'd rather die than let it happen to me!'' She felt quite worked up; she even brought her fist down on the table with a little crash.

Burke signaled the waiter for the bill, unimpressed. "And Ewan? Was he a way out?"

"Nay, but he was fun for a while. We had some gay times," she recalled fondly. "But it was time to move on, for he was beginning to tire of me."

Burke stood up. "Now, *that*, Kate, has to be the biggest lie you've told all day."

"I'm not lying!" She stood up, too, shocked and wounded. "How can you think it, after I've told you things I've never told another living soul?"

"I'll admit it's a good story; parts of it may even be true. But you'll never get me to believe any man could tire of you, Kate. You're too *entertaining*."

The rain had subsided to a misty trickle but the wind was picking up; Katherine was grateful for the warmth of her new coat. While she was mounted on her horse and waiting for Burke to finish untying the other two and join her, she heard a commotion behind her in the street. She turned and caught a hasty glimpse of a man with a broom chasing a barking dog, who was chasing a hissing cat. Before she could react, the cat zipped between her horse's legs, the dog in full fly behind it. The mare screamed with fright and reared. Coming down, she ran sideways two steps, lunged forward and reared again, pawing the air with her forelegs. Keeping her seat, Katherine leaned far forward over the horse's neck, pulling firmly on the reins with steady, even hands. The mare thudded back to earth and backed up angrily. Katherine kept a short rein and murmured soothing sounds, still bent low over the mane. The horse trotted around in a circle for a few seconds, shaking her head and snorting with indignation, and then quieted. "Good girl, goood girl," Katherine crooned, patting her neck.

The man with the broom, a fishmonger, came toward her with his broom hand outstretched and his other hand over his heart. He was sorry, he was wretched with contrition, but the cat had stolen the mackerel and he'd taught the dog to chase off marauders; it wasn't his fault, it was the cat's fault, and if he ever saw it again he would make it pay; he only thanked God she wasn't hurt, such a beautiful lady, and such a magnificent horsewoman as she was, too.

Katherine laughed and was about to reassure him when her eye chanced to fall upon Burke, and the words died on her tongue. He was coming toward her slowly; in his face admiration and anger were struggling for dominance. Anger won. He reached for her horse's bridle too suddenly and the mare almost reared again. He brought her down forcefully and held her steady with his long-fingered, sensitive, and somehow dangerous-looking hands. Katherine stared down at them for a long moment before she could bring herself to meet his eyes. There was a menacing glint in their cold blue depths. His mouth was grim and the little scar over the top lip had gone whiter with anger. She felt a tiny thrill of fear and decided to brazen it out.

"Jesus, Mary, and Joseph, did you see that? I vow I thought my time was up! I just held on for dear life, and the Lord must have been smiling down on me. If my heart isn't half racing!" She put her hand over her chest solicitously. "Does that happen very often? Why, it's a wonder the streets aren't littered with corpses! What a dangerous pastime this horse-riding is!" She faltered, unwilling to keep rattling on in the face of that icy stare, now tinged with scorn.

"Are you finished?"

She took a deep breath and nodded once.

"Good."

He led her horse over to where his was still tied. He

mounted the stallion and took up the long lead to the packhorse. Katherine fell into step behind them as they moved sedately down the street and out of the town. Once she looked back at the fishmonger, standing in the street and watching them go, and she waved at him forlornly. She wished she were staying behind, huddled in the warm chimney corner of the George and Dragon and drinking a cup of chocolate, instead of setting out on a cold November afternoon for England behind this hostile, unpredictable major, whose power over her fate and fortunes was growing more unendurable every minute.

They rode through a rough and rumpled landscape of grassland, heather, and gorse before the road turned toward a river and followed its slow, serpentine path between tree-draped banks. They saw hardy sheep on the upland grazings, and once they passed a group of delicate roe deer nibbling at the bracken on the far bank. Red squirrels scampered in the bare boughs overhead, readying their nests for winter.

The road widened as it turned eastward, leaving the river behind. Burke slowed his horse and waited for Katherine to come up. The peacefulness of the landscape had somewhat lulled her apprehensions, and she was able to face him with a degree of equanimity.

"I want to know what else you've lied about," he announced abruptly, and her calm was shattered. "You're digging a grave for yourself, Kate, or whatever your name is. The more lies you tell, the greater your chance of being hanged for a traitor. Do you understand that?" Underneath the sternness there was a kind of entreaty that was new. She was taken aback by it before she considered it was undoubtedly another one of his tricks. "Do you, Kate?" he went on insistently. "You're not what you profess to be, and I'm bound to say that to the military men in Lancaster. The more you lie, the worse it will be for you. Tell me the truth about yourself. Now."

In a pig's eye, she thought grimly. What did he take her for, an imbecile? "Very well, Major Burke," she imagined herself saying, "I can see there's no use trying to fool you! I'm a rich, titled lady from Inverness with a grudge against England and all the English because they defiled me and slaughtered my family. I support Charles Stuart against the king and I tried to aid him by stealing enemy secrets. There, I've told you everything. Now what will you say to the military men in Lancaster?" Pah! What sort of a fool did he think she was? He was the fool, because it seemed that for some reason he still thought she was *not* a spy, in spite of all the inconsistencies in her story. He thought she was something, but he didn't know what. Well, let him stew in it, the arrogant English bastard.

No. Sober reason told her her best chance still lay in convincing him she was a whore. She couldn't abandon her story about Ewan and the card game and Maule winning her, and how else to explain that sordid business except to stick to her identity as a prostitute? Why couldn't he believe that, anyway? She thought she'd done a brilliant job portraying a loose woman. Could it be she was too naive? Could he tell that all her knowledge of sexual immorality came from schoolgirl gossip and romance novels? It was a sobering thought.

"I haven't lied about anything else," she murmured with downcast eyes, "though I don't blame you for doubting me. I didn't tell you I could ride for the same reason I exaggerated my speech: I knew it would make a false impression. It's true, I do seem to be getting into more trouble every minute, but honestly, Major Burke, I'm being straight with you now. I've got no more secrets, so there will be no more surprises. I beg you to believe me!" She looked up at him with a troubled brow, her eyes limpid with sincerity. She saw she hadn't persuaded him.

She had an inspiration.

"There really was a Raspberry, you know," she giggled.

"Ewan was so excited when he gave her to me. He'd won her at cards, of course. He wanted to call her 'Pair of Aces,' but I wouldn't let him. Well, you have to know Ewan, he's a very proud man in his way and he took offense at what he called my 'highfalutin ways.' I think it made him feel beneath me when I talked proper English, so I would put on a bit o' a brrogue wi' him, too—though no' half such a one as I used wi' you!" She laughed merrily at the memory, studiously avoiding his eyes. "Anyway, when he brought me the little donkey, I pretended I couldn't ride because I knew it would set him off if he knew I could. It was the lord I was telling you about, my mother's lover, who taught me to ride. And so when *you* asked me, why, I just naturally said I couldn't, as I had with Ewan, feeling it would make my story more believable. I wish now I hadn't done it, because I can see you're thinking if I lied about that, what else have I lied about? Well, aren't you?"

Burke grunted. His expression had become noncommittal, which Katherine considered a giant step forward.

"But the rest is all true. Lieutenant-Colonel Maule really did win me in the card game, as he himself admits, and perhaps I might have become his mistress if he hadn't been such a ready hand with his belt. But I've got my own principles, and I don't hold with a man bashing a woman for no reason. So I stole his money, or so I thought, and ran back to Ewan's room, thinking I'd stay with him until we were out of the dreadful Lowlands and back in Edinburgh or another big city where I could start over. I told myself I wasn't really stealing, because the colonel owed me something. Well, it wasn't my fault he'd already given Ewan thirty guineas for me. Somebody owed *me* something for *myself*." She was frowning with earnestness; she'd forgotten it was a story. She saw herself as a wronged woman, struggling to survive in an unfair world controlled by men.

"Well, Kate," Burke said after a moment, breaking the

silence. She was encouraged when his lips curved in a smile, but there was something in his eyes she couldn't decipher. He was looking at her in a way that suggested he was assessing more than her credibility. "What you say may well be true, but I confess my mind still teems with doubt. I would be loath to convey the wrong impression of you to the men at Lancaster. It occurs to me there might be something you could do to help convince me."

CHAPTER 5

He'd spoken so reasonably, so matter-of-factly, it was several seconds before his meaning dawned on her. She searched his cool blue eyes to make sure she hadn't mistaken him, and was thankful when a tiny flicker of amusement, quickly hidden, marred his solemnity.

"You're teasing me," she chided, lowering her gaze so he couldn't read her expression. She laughed shakily and drew a deep breath, realizing she had stopped breathing after he'd spoken. Her heart was racing and her palms were perspiring; it was as though she'd narrowly avoided a terrible accident.

"Perhaps a little," he admitted, enjoying himself. "But if you consider, it's not such a wild notion, is it? You tell interesting stories, Kate, but it's impossible to say whether they're true. Now, I'm an astute sort of fellow, but I'm not a wizard. I think I'll have to resort to less conventional means than is usual with a prisoner to test your credibility."

Her face was a study in consternation. He couldn't help laughing, and once more relief flooded through her like a dam bursting. "You *are* a caution, Major Burke," she gushed. She cast about in her mind for a way to change this unsavory topic. "Do you think we'll make Gretna Green by nightfall? 'Tis such a dark day, I can't tell whether it's late or not. How many days do you think we'll be to Lancaster? I suppose it depends—"

"After all, what would one more man matter, Kate?"
he interrupted, continuing his train of thought. "You've
had so many, as you told me yourself. And it would give
me something—how shall I put it?—*substantial* to tell
them in Lancaster."

She felt a flash of temper. "I *have* had many men, but I
choose them for myself! I won't have one *forced* on me.
Now, have done with your mockery, Major. If you can ride
any faster, I think it would behoove us to make haste
before it grows too dark to see the ruts!"

He cocked one eyebrow at her and she realized she was
speaking too naturally, sounding too highborn. But she
didn't care, she was too riled. What a lewd, scheming,
blackmailing wretch he was! Just like all of them, every
rotten, bloody Englishman she'd ever met. She hated the
lot of them and wished them all eternal damnation. She
felt furious with herself as well for not having foreseen this
unwelcome turn of events. She knew Burke was leering at
her in his beastly way, but she would not give him the
satisfaction of a glance. At last he tired of baiting her and
spurred his horse into a trot.

They didn't reach Gretna Green before dusk, but had to
put up at a mean little inn some distance west. The Swan
was literally in the middle of nowhere, with nothing for
miles on any side except lonely valleys and steep-sided
glens. The landlord was a Scotsman named McKie, a
white-haired, corpulent overindulger with a bottomless
appetite for gin and wenches. His establishment was dirty,
loud, and overpriced, largely because he preferred
drinking bouts and long dalliances with whores to
maintaining it.

Burke didn't like the look of the filthy stableyard. He
told Katherine to go in while he had a word with the
ostler. She was grateful, for she was stiff with cold and the
novel experience of riding all day. Once inside, though,

she thought she might have done better to wait for him after all.

The first floor was one large room. To the left was a small dining area; to the right, a huge fireplace with a scattering of chairs and benches around it where the serious drinking was done. Half a dozen imbibers turned as one at her entrance, and all conversation halted. Somewhat daunted, she started to raise her chin and give them back a dignified stare when she recalled herself. She smiled tentatively, wondering what Katie Lennox would do at this moment. She was saved from a wrong guess by the hearty greeting of McKie himself, who came out from behind the long bar at the back, wiping his hands on a soiled apron.

"Weel, now, look wha' the fog's blown us, lads! Welcome t' the Swan, miss, ye're a mighty fine sight on a sorry night. Travelin' alone, are ye? Ye look froze straigh' through. Cum over t' the big fire and warm yer lovely self. A glass o' somethin' t' take the chill out, am I right? Don't move a hair, I'll be back before ye can whistle!" He had taken her by the elbow and steered her across the room to the fireplace, where she was left standing with her back to the flames and a dozen eyes trained intently on her slender figure.

"Hello," she said softly, mostly to break the silence, and a chorus of halloos went up all around her. She smiled shyly and the men smiled back, enchanted. " 'Tis a bit nasty out," she observed.

"Aye, it is!" they all agreed.

"The fire feels lovely."

"Aye, it does!" They nodded vehemently.

There was a breathless silence while they waited for her next penetrating observation. Just then McKie returned with a steaming mug. "Here, miss, 'twill warm yer insides. Ye dinna need a thing done t' yer outsides," he smirked; "they're perfect as they are."

This drew an appreciative laugh from the drinkers,

although one coughed uncomfortably and spoke up.

"Where do ye come from, miss? If ye don't mind me askin', that is." He was much younger than the rest, with reddish hair and a handful of freckles across his nose. With a stab, Katherine thought of Rory; he would have been about this boy's age now. He wore a green and black tartan across his shoulder, which further endeared him to her.

"From Edinburgh." She took a sip of the hot rum and had to stifle a cough. "Delicious," she told McKie, with watering eyes.

"Aye," he chuckled, "I make it myself. 'Twould warm a bear's arse on a bad night." He was about to beg her pardon when she surprised him by smiling. "By God, ye're a bonnie lass!" he cried impulsively, echoing the precise sentiments of every man in the room.

"Where're ye bound for?" pursued the red-haired youth. He hadn't taken his eyes from her for a second.

"For Lancaster."

"Lancaster!" One of the other men, a skinny, scraggly-haired fellow in a dirty jerkin, spat on the floor in disgust. "Why would anyone be wantin' t' go there?" he inquired of the room at large, and there was a murmur of unanimous perplexity.

"I don't go because I want to," Katherine said with a melancholy smile. There was a pause.

"Are ye runnin' away?" ventured the boy.

"Nay," she told him. "I wish I were!" She took another sip of her drink, hoping they would not ask her any more questions. She thought she had probably said too much already.

The sound of the door opening broke the sad little spell she'd unwittingly cast, and all eyes turned from her to Burke.

He took in the scene with a glance. "Well, Mistress Lennox, you've wasted no time getting to know the locals, I see." His voice sounded gruff in the quiet room. It was not a remark calculated to win him friends, nor was the sight of his English cavalry uniform after he'd swept off his cloak and hung it on a peg. "Who's the innkeeper here?" he inquired somewhat irritably.

"That's meself, Jonah McKie at yer sarvice. Ye look all done in, officer. Will ye be needin' a nice room and a meal?" The landlord was at his most obsequious, relying on years of experience to tell him which of these two it would pay him to flatter.

"Two rooms, with keys. One for me and one for my prisoner. Come, Kate."

Katherine gasped. There had been no *need* for him to say that; he'd done it just to embarrass her! She set her cup on the mantelpiece and turned back with a proud set to her jaw. She'd taken a step toward him when the red-haired youth stood up and barred her way.

"Hold on! How do we know she's yer prisoner? What's she done? How do we know ye're not *kidnappin'* her?"

Burke was very wet and very tired, and something about the intimacy of the scene he'd walked in on nettled him. He hadn't left the woman alone more than five minutes, and already she had a roomful of drunken protectors, including this plaid-wearing puppy who looked as if he'd be more at home in a schoolroom than a public house.

"What's your name, son?" he asked tersely, reining in his temper.

"Tom Cleland, and I ain't your son," the boy retorted hotly. "What's she done? Are ye goin' t' tell us or not?"

Out of patience, Burke snapped, "What she's done is none of your business. Now, step out of the way, boy, or I'll have to teach you a lesson in manners."

He couldn't have said anything more inflammatory to young Tom Cleland. He blushed to the roots of his red hair and drew himself up to his full height, still blocking Katherine's way. His fists clenched aggressively and his narrow chest expanded. Katherine's heart went out to him because he was so young and so intent on proving he was not. "Then ye'd best begin now," he stuttered wrathfully, "because she ain't goin' until you say what she's done!"

Katherine thought Burke looked more irritated than angry, but the boy was clearly spoiling for a fight. She reached out and touched him lightly on the shoulder. "I'm grateful for your concern, sir, but I would not have you risk your liberty for my sake. I'm Major Burke's legitimate prisoner. He escorts me to Lancaster, where I'll doubtless be tried as a spy!"

"A spy!" exclaimed Tom, and the word was repeated around the room wonderingly. "For the Bonnie Prince?" he guessed, trying to disguise his eagerness.

"Aye, for the Bonnie Prince," she confirmed. "Though, of course, 'tis not true, not a word of it."

"Of course not!" "Nay, it ain't true!" "Not a word!" Not one of them cared whether she was a spy or not, but each seemed ready to defend her to the death. Perceiving that things were getting out of hand, Burke started to speak, but Katherine forestalled him by bestowing a beautific smile on them all, especially Tom Cleland, and making her graceful way through them to stand by Burke's side. The look he gave her was not pleasant.

"Supper's in twenty minutes," McKie announced a bit nervously. "Mayhap ye'd like t' go up and see yer rooms farst, General? Scrape the mud off your boots and what have ye?" Burke favored him with a slight nod. "Then if ye'd be good enough t' cum wi' me, I'll show ye the way."

A trained soldier, Burke couldn't refrain from looking behind him as he followed McKie and Katherine up the stairs to the second floor; but now that the primary diversion was gone, the men in the taproom were already returning to their cups with only a few disgruntled mutterings. All except for Tom Cleland, who glowered furiously until the turn in the stairway blocked him from sight.

The rooms McKie showed them were at the end of a long hall, next to each other and separated by a thin wall; they were depressingly small, and meagerly furnished with only the bare essentials in tasteless, castoff furniture. The landlord handed two keys to Burke and gave him an exaggerated wink. Katherine was standing in the hall, looking dispiritedly in at the room assigned to her, but she plainly heard what McKie, a few feet away, said to Burke in an undertone. "Beats me why ye're wastin' yer brass on two rooms, General. If it was me, I'd be givin' it to her every chance I could between here and Lancaster. Weel, I mean, who'd care? Who'd even know? If she's a spy, it'd only be what she desarved, am I right?"

Burke glanced over McKie's shoulder at Katherine. She was staring back at him rigidly, cheeks aflame, with a look of combined loathing and apprehension clouding the clear blue-green of her eyes.

"You're a pig, McKie. Get out of my sight."

"Eh?" The innkeeper was genuinely surprised.

"You're not fit to lick her boot. Take yourself off or I'll throw you down the stairs." This was delivered in a frighteningly quiet tone that had the cutting edge of a razor.

"Oh, now, guv'nor, ye've taken me wrong! I was only havin' a bit of a joke, is all. Why, I—" Burke took a menacing step toward him. "Ow! I'm goin', I'm goin'. Sober down, guv!"

"And send someone up with our baggage," Burke called after the hastily retreating figure. "Now!"

A sound came from the bottom of the stairs, something midway between acquiescence and a curse.

"Miserable pig," Burke muttered, turning back to Katherine. She still stood in the doorway, frozen in an attitude of astonishment. "Well, what did you expect?" he asked, exasperated by her look. "Did you think I'd agree with him?"

"I—I—" She didn't know what she'd thought, but she

hadn't expected him to be so—*protective*. "Well," she found her tongue, "after this afternoon, I wasn't certain what your intentions were."

He leaned against the door frame beside her; she found his nearness disturbing. "Ah, *my* intentions. That's a different matter, isn't it?" He smiled at her obvious discomfort. "I'd like to think my intentions and the jovial McKie's wishful thinking are two different things."

"I would like to think so, too," she retorted quickly, "but I fear the truth is they come miraculously close to each other!"

Burke gave an appreciative laugh, which only deepened her frown. She turned on her heel and walked into the room. She would have closed the door, but he was right behind her.

He glanced around quickly. He went to the casement window, opened it, and peered down. There was a sheer drop of twenty feet to a dirty courtyard below. He closed the window and drew the curtain over it. "I wouldn't try jumping," he observed dryly. He took another quick look about him, but there was nothing to see. "Make them give you a longer candle." He moved past her to the door. "I'll knock in fifteen minutes; be ready. And, Kate—see if you can do something about your hair."

Katherine lay back in the wooden tub and watched the warm, soapy water ebb and flow lazily across her nipples. She sighed with contentment, relaxing completely for the first time in many days. What a grand and glorious thing was a bath, she reflected, especially after one had been denied the experience for nearly a week. Burke had suggested this one right after supper. No, not suggested; ordered. She'd wrinkled her nose in pretended disgust at the idea. "A bath? Who needs a bath?" she'd exclaimed in feigned shock. But inside, her heart had pounded with anticipation.

She stuck a foot in the air and washed between her toes, feeling the ache in her back and thighs from the long ride begin to melt away. She sighed again and closed her eyes. She could almost fall asleep, she thought, right here in the tub. McKie's supper had been poorly prepared but plentiful, and she'd devoured quite a lot of it as well as two glasses of wine. The fire in the grate was small but burning brightly, and for the first time in days she felt truly warm. She must have dozed a few minutes, because she noticed with a start that the water was cooling fast and she hadn't yet washed her hair.

Rubbing soap into the long, heavy locks, she thought back over the evening. Before supper, after Burke had left her alone, she'd debated whether to change into her new green velvet gown or continue to wear the shapeless gray tent he'd given her that morning. But then on an impulse she'd rejected them both and unpacked the dirty, tattered dress she'd worn for so many days in gaol. Her whore's gown, she called it. It had been bright blue when new, but now it was dull with soil and wrinkles and stains. It was cheaply made out of inexpensive material, and although she'd worn it for many days, she still could not quite get over how low it was cut in the bosom. Her mother would surely have labeled it ''common,'' or worse. She'd spent a long time picking it out because she'd wanted it to be perfect, and she thought she'd succeeded very well: it looked exactly like the sort of gown a penniless, wayward girl of easy virtue would buy whose primary object was to attract men.

That was how Katherine wanted to look tonight. She knew she'd lost a lot of ground today by revealing she could speak English and ride a horse as well as Burke, and she was afraid there were other, subtler things she'd given away, too. She had a vague notion that putting on the blue dress would be akin to getting back into character, whereas donning the new velvet would come too close to displaying her true self.

When she'd opened the door to him, Burke's eyes had widened in surprise for a split second before narrowing in cynical amusement. "You just can't keep yourself covered up, can you, Kate?" he'd drawled, an unpleasant smirk twisting his lips. His gaze had dipped to her breasts, which strained against the cheap material, the nipples barely covered, until a hot flush had crept up her neck and into her cheeks. "The boys below will be sorely grateful, I'm sure. What a *generous* lass you are." It had taken every ounce of willpower not to snatch up her shawl and put it across her bosom like a shield, and even more not to slap his impudent face. Instead she'd sent him a simpering smile and flounced out the door in front of him, pretending she'd taken his words as a compliment.

Meals were taken communally at the Swan. Burke held a chair for her at the head of a long, rectangular table, and the others, most of the men she'd met in the taproom and a few strangers, took seats around them. Again she wished desperately she'd brought her shawl; the frankly lustful stares that met her were demoralizing, and pretending to enjoy and encourage them was exhausting.

One look at Tom Cleland told her he'd spent the last half hour drinking, and he patently did not hold his liquor well. His face was flushed and he couldn't seem to stop talking. Most of his remarks were directed to Katherine. He wanted to know everything about her; he seemed to have fallen in love with her. She found it easy to deflect his questions and was not in the least offended by his manners, for although he was thoroughly smitten, he was never anything but respectful. She thought again of how much he reminded her of Rory.

His attitude toward Burke was another matter, and she could see trouble brewing early on as his thinly veiled insults intensified. By the end of the meal he was completely drunk. He almost fell over when he suddenly pushed his chair back and clutched at the tablecloth to haul himself to his feet. He stood swaying, his mug extended over the center of the table where a pitcher of water had been placed. There was a reckless gleam in his eye. "I pr'pose a toast!"

Katherine was afraid she knew what was coming; she glanced at Burke apprehensively, wondering if he would understand. Jacobite supporters declared themselves clandestinely by toasting the king with their glasses held over a bowl or pitcher of water; it meant, "To the king over the water," or James, Bonnie Prince Charlie's father, for years an exile in Italy.

"To the king!" cried Tom.

"To the king!" echoed the others, holding up their mugs and glasses.

"I seem to be out of wine." Burke leaned across the table and picked up the pitcher. He poured water into his glass, then set the pitcher down beside his plate. "To the king."

He raised his glass slightly and his eyes locked with Cleland's. The youth flushed bright red and his face became a contorted mask of indecision. After many seconds, discretion lost the battle; with a furious oath he hurled his untouched mug across the room. It broke against the wall with a shattering crash. He lurched around the corner of the table, seeming intent on throttling Burke, and without thinking, Katherine jumped up to block his path. He careened into her and sent her flying backward across her chair and onto the floor, where she landed with a painless but loud crash. Struck dumb with horror, Tom stared down at the beautiful lady he'd given his heart to, who was struggling to rise while tugging feverishly at the top of her gown to re-cover her suddenly naked bosom. He never saw the iron fist streaking toward his chin; he was out cold before he hit the floor.

Katherine leaned over the grate in the small fireplace

and rubbed her hair vigorously with a thick towel. Lord, but it was lovely to be clean again. She had no nightgown, so she'd put on one of the new shifts Burke had bought her. It was of fine soft linen, cream-colored, with white silk ribbons threaded through the sleeves and neckline. She liked it enormously; she had to admit it compared favorably with the ones she had at home. But that was hardly surprising; she imagined the major had a wide and minutely detailed experience of ladies' underwear.

She thought fondly of the tongue-lashing she'd given him tonight after he'd leveled poor Tom Cleland. "Bully," "vicious savage," and "barbaric monster" were among the milder things she'd called him. Unfairly, she now thought, though without much remorse, because if ever a man needed silencing Tom Cleland had. But she'd felt so sorry for him. She remembered how he'd looked, stretched out flat on the dusty floor beside her, so young and helpless. And so outclassed by the man who stood, hands on hips, gazing down in obvious disgust at both of them. She'd been conscious of looking extremely ridiculous, huddled next to an unconscious drunk on the floor of an alehouse, half naked and surrounded by ogling onlookers. At the same time, she knew this scene was exactly the kind of sordid illustration she needed if she were ever to convince Burke or anyone else that she was a tramp, not a spy. So, in a horrible kind of way, the evening had been a success.

She picked up a pearl-inlaid silver brush on the mantel. It was beautiful, she thought idly, but then everything Major Burke owned seemed to be of the finest quality. He'd thrust it into her hands tonight, telling her to "Use it, for God's sake!" before closing and carefully locking the door and going to his own room, unknowingly leaving her with the two things she wanted most in the world—a hot bath and a hairbrush. She began to brush her long, silky hair, enjoying the feel of it in her hands, tangle-free at last. She was suddenly so tired, and it always took such a long time to dry her hair because it was so thick, and so blasted *long*. But her father had loved her hair and had asked her not to cut it, so . . . . She felt the familiar jolt of pain and had to squeeze back tears for the second time that day. Now was not the time for mourning, she scolded herself. She'd done enough of that before and would undoubtedly do more once she was out of this predicament, one way or the other. She had to keep her wits about her no matter how tired she was, for her life might depend on it. The lives of Owen Carthcart and Ewan MacNab might depend on her as well, because if she were found out, they would inevitably fall with her. She had no love for Ewan MacNab, her dead fiancé's reckless cousin, but she wished him no harm. And Owen Cathcart was a decent man, a dedicated Jacobite; of the three of them, his loss would be the most serious blow to the cause of the Stuart succession.

She couldn't keep her eyes open another minute. She threw down the brush and blew out the candle on her tiny night table, then went to the window and pushed back the curtains to let in the moonlight. There was a full moon tonight; in its silver glow her room was almost as bright as day. She tiptoed across the cold floorboards and crawled between the sheets of her narrow bed. It was lumpy and the linen was not perfectly clean, but it felt wonderful all the same. For a moment she watched the shadows from the dying fire play across the ceiling. Was Burke's bed just on the other side of the wall? she wondered sleepily. The thought gave her a shivery feeling. She fell asleep imagining how he looked when he slept.

Burke was not asleep. He lay in bed, sipping from a glass of brandy and trying to read Voltaire in French by the feeble light of one candle. But fragments of images kept intruding between him and the page, until finally he closed his eyes, closed the book, and gave himself up to the visual memories.

They were all of Kate. Kate in the oversized gown he'd given her, sparks flying from her turquoise eyes, and her scolding him vigorously in her exaggerated brogue. Kate at dinner this afternoon, trying so hard to disguise her ravenous appetite, and him without the heart to tease her. Kate's horse rearing and her hanging on like a leech, not frightened at all. Kate in the taproom surrounded by admirers, looking like a disheveled angel. And Kate sprawled on the floor beside her unconscious champion, red-faced with mortification, then cursing a blue streak when he'd offered his hand to help her up.

He had argued with Colonel Denholm over this assignment because he'd thought it would be dull. Dull! He didn't know when he'd had a more interesting day. The girl intrigued him, he had to admit it. She had more twists and turns than a maze. And she was such an enchanting little minx with her saucy tongue, her wild red hair. Teasing her was an irresistible pleasure; she blushed so charmingly and so easily, he felt compelled to say anything that might bring on that lovely rose color.

But most of all he was captivated by the mystery of her. If she was a whore, she was the oddest one he'd ever met. And if she was not, then what was she? Respectable? Educated? But why would a lady throw everything away to spy for the Jacobites? Patriotism? Loyalty to the Stuarts? It was impossible to credit. Political fanaticism was usually a man's sport, for one thing, and for another . . . He sighed and rubbed his eyes tiredly; he was too weary to think.

He put down his book and tossed off the last swallow of brandy. If the weather was fine, he had two, maybe three more days to discover what she was, as much as a week if it rained. He remembered how she'd looked when he'd suggested a quick way to find out if she was as indiscriminate with her bed partners as she claimed. She had seemed well and truly shocked, which was interesting in itself. But the more he thought of it, the more the idea appealed to him. "Scottish whores are not precisely my cup of tea," he recalled telling Denholm. No, but then he thought of how her mouth looked, how the top lip turned up ever so slightly in the most exquisitely seductive way. He thought about what it would be like to kiss her, to touch her face, to hear her begin to moan with pleasure. . . .

There was a sudden loud thud against the wall beside him. He sat up, listening intently. Was she trying to escape? He distinctly remembered locking her in. He heard muffled sounds, impossible to say of what, and then all at once there was a short scream, cut off quickly and followed by the sound of a slap.

Burke leaped to his feet and grabbed the key to the other room from the mantel. Stark naked, he charged out the door and down the short hall to Katherine's room. Her door was still locked. He unlocked it and threw it open. It struck the wall with a resounding crash and he strode through. What he saw in the moonlight chilled his blood for an instant, then made it run hot with fury.

Jonah McKie had his nightshirt on over a pair of breeches. His florid, white-whiskered cheeks were doubly livid from drink; his eyes seemed about to pop from his head. Huffing and puffing from the strain, he was holding a pillow over Katherine's face while the fingers of his other hand fumbled at her breast. He was dodging her kicking legs and clawing hands while trying to cover her body with his, but he was too fat and too drunk to subdue her. Katherine's shift had come up over her knees as she flailed about on the bed; Burke could hear her gasping raggedly under the pillow.

Growling like a wild animal, he grabbed McKie by the scruff of his neck and the waistband of his breeches, picked him up as if he were no heavier than a saddle, and hurled him across the room. He hit the wall head first and collapsed in a loose heap.

Burke turned back to the bed. Katherine was sitting up, holding the pillow against her chest. He saw that she was panting and wild-eyed, but apparently not injured. He turned his attention back to the landlord.

McKie was groaning and holding his head, and stinking like a gin mill. Burke hauled him to his feet and dragged him savagely out of the room. He hustled him down the hall to the top of the stairway, where he seriously contemplated throwing him down the steps. It would probably kill him. With profound reluctance he settled for punching him with all his strength in his flabby belly, then snapping his head back with a stunning blow to the jaw. There was a satisfying crunching sound, and McKie slid slowly down the wall to the floor, unconscious.

Doors opened along the hall and curious heads poked out to find out what was causing the din. Burke's nakedness and the bloodthirsty look on his face had a marvelously dampening effect; all the doors closed as swiftly as they had opened.

He went to his room long enough to pull on his breeches, then hurried back to Katherine. She was sitting on the edge of the bed, still clutching the pillow. She looked heartbreakingly young, and he could see she was in deep distress. He took a step toward her the same moment she came off the bed. They met in the middle of the room; his arms went around her in the most natural embrace. At first she was stiff and silent, but as he held her she began to tremble violently. Her teeth chattered and he knew she was struggling hard not to cry.

He picked her up and carried her back to the bed. Keeping her in his arms, he sat down at the head, resting his back against the wall. She drew herself up into a tight knot on his lap and buried her face against his chest. Her hands were clenched into fists; she pressed them against her lips to still her rattling teeth. He pulled the blanket up over her shoulders and held her tightly. Her feet were freezing. He began to massage her feet and calves with soothing, impersonal fingers, and very gradually he felt her body begin to relax.

She took a long, shivery breath. "He had a key," she said shakily. Burke felt her soft breath stir the hairs on his chest. He smoothed the fragrant, softly curling hair back from her brow and gazed down at her. Her skin shone with a white radiance in the moonlight. One hand lay trustingly against his chest, palm open, and the other was holding closed the two halves of her torn shift. The need to kiss her rose in him like a strong thirst.

Her voice came again, light and tremulous. "What did you do with him?"

"I dimmed his lights," he growled into her hair.

"You didn't—"

"No. But I wanted to."

She heaved a gusty, childlike sigh. "I think he was drunk."

He smiled. "I believe you're right."

He lay for a long time breathing in the clean scent of her warm body, marveling at the pleasure it gave him to hold her, until it gradually dawned on him that she was asleep. Her long, inky lashes lay like an eagle's wings across the milk-white cheeks. He wanted to hold her all night, but his right leg was asleep. With infinite care he sat up, cradling her like a sleeping infant in his arms. He put his legs over the side of the bed and stood up.

"Burke?" Her eyes were a soft, bottomless violet in the moonlight.

"Shh." He laid her down gently and pulled the covers around her shoulders. "Go to sleep, love. Close your eyes. You're safe."

She sighed and was instantly asleep again. Burke stood for a long moment watching shadows move across her face and across the fan of bright hair against the pillow. Finally, regretfully, he left the bedside and padded across the room. He closed the door quietly behind him and locked it.

CHAPTER 6

By midmorning of the next day they'd skirted Carlisle without meeting soldiers from either faction in the rebellion and were moving at a steady pace southward into Cumberland. Katherine had traveled to London numerous times in her life but always by a more eastern route, either by boat from Inverness along the coast or overland via Edinburgh and Newcastle. She'd never been farther west in England than Bath, and she was astonished by the breathtaking beauty of this land of tarns and fells—or lakes and hills. It wasn't easy, but after a half day's ride she was forced to admit—to herself, never to Burke—that this lake country was as gorgeous as her beloved Highlands. In a quieter way, of course; not so wild or so gloriously inhospitable. But there was a sublime gloominess in the bleak tarns and the menacing cliffs above them, the remote, boulder-strewn valleys and windswept heaths, that appealed to a part of her that had always loved wild, foreboding landscapes. It was unfortunate that this magnificently lovely one had to be an *English* landscape.

Thoughts of the night before intruded on her consciousness from time to time as they rode along, but the astonishing thing to her was how little affected she was by what had happened. Last night's events ought to have brought back a flood of unbearable memories; but strangely, they had not. Her strongest recollection was not of waking up with a hand over her mouth and a man whispering urgently, "Oh, me lovely, me beauty, Jonah won't hart ye—" No, her vividest memory was of lying in the warm enclosure of Major Burke's arms afterwards, feeling his breath on her hair, his hands soothing her, his heart thudding strongly under her hand. She had never in her life felt so safe.

Safe! How utterly ridiculous. She thrust the thought away; what a silly goose of a girl she was becoming. But the image that replaced it was even more unsettling. It too was of Burke, of the way he'd looked last night in the moonlight. Like some avenging god out of a Greek myth, fierce and invincible. His body had seemed to glow in an unearthly silver light, with bluish shadows modeling all the interesting planes and hollows. Her heart had taken wings when she'd seen him. The sleekness and power of his finely muscled back, his long thighs, his hard, sculpted buttocks—

She shivered, and didn't know why. She was honest enough to admit that her reaction to Burke's nude body had not been revulsion. This in itself was bewildering, because her only other experience of male sexuality had been a vicious, degrading experience. She'd thought it would always be that way, and now she had to allow for the possibility that it would not. Her feelings were hopelessly confused. Part of her felt the timid stirrings of gladness, part of her was appalled. That an Englishman—worse, *this* Englishman—could evoke anything in her except disgust was almost too much to bear. She resolved to think no more of it.

She'd decided to put on the second of her new dresses that morning, and a glance in the wavy old mirror in her room had been at once gratifying and worrying. She looked quite nice, she thought, flower-fresh and neat as a pebble. Her gown had a rust-red linen skirt with a glazed linen bodice of the same color, ornamented in a white and blue floral pattern, and the low neckline was trimmed generously with white lace. She looked the way she would want to look if she were safely at home, setting out on a pleasure trip or accompanying her mother on a ride. But that wasn't how she wanted to look now! And yet what could she do? She couldn't keep wearing her "whore's gown"; Burke wouldn't allow it. He'd probably burn it if he ever saw it again. From the way he'd gawked at her this morning, she supposed he approved of her looks. He'd even said something nice about her hair. She forgot exactly what; his thunderstruck gaze had unnerved her. She'd taken the ribbon out of the neckline of her ruined shift and tied her long tresses back in a sort of loose bun at the nape of her neck. She wished she had some pins to hold it more firmly, but this would have to do. But it wasn't his approval she was seeking, she reminded herself; if anything, it was his disapproval. Well, if she couldn't *look* like a slut, she would have to *act* more like one. At that, her mind shut down.

She glanced over her shoulder. Burke had abandoned his former position in front and taken to riding about four steps behind and to her left. The better to stare at her, she reckoned irritably. He'd been doing that all morning and it was beginning to annoy her. At first she'd ignored him, then she'd tried to stare back and embarrass him. Ha! The man was incapable of embarrassment. He would smile his slow, lazy smile until she looked away, usually blushing because of something in his eyes she could not quite name. Oh, she probably could if she tried, but she had no wish to think any more about Major James Burke at all.

But he did look exceptionally handsome this morning, she mused a moment later. He'd abandoned his uniform—"It inflames 'em too much, Kate," he'd told her; "all they want to do is rescue you"—and put on a tan buckskin hunting coat over a white cambric shirt and black breeches. She'd thought it impossible for him to look more masculine than he did in his uniform, but she'd been wrong. Well, she reflected, it was lucky she was not at all susceptible to such frivolous things as good looks, at least not in Englishmen; otherwise Major Burke might have turned her head.

They had been traversing a lane that ran along a ledge high above a valley crisscrossed with stone walls. Halfway down the stony fell was a circular hollow filled with inky black water, and a sheep trail led to it from the lane. Unexpectedly, Burke turned the horses into the little trail to the corrie. Katherine could not think why they were stopping until he took a bundle from the packhorse and spread its contents out on a flat rock.

"Hungry?" He put his hands up to help her, but she deliberately jumped down unaided before he could touch her.

"Starved!" she exclaimed, going over to the food and examining it with interest. "Meat pies! Where did you find them? And cheese, and fruit—Burke, how marvelous!"

"So," he said, folding his arms, "at last I discover a way to make you smile."

She ignored this, beginning to divide the food into two portions. "Will you have the fruit now or later? Oh, and a tart; how delicious it looks. I'll save mine for later. Why don't you sit down?" When he remained where he was, she put her hands on her hips and faced him, clucking her tongue in exasperation. "I was not aware you were trying to make me smile, Major Burke," she snapped, out of patience with his staring. "If you were, you have a most peculiar way of going about it, and 'tis no wonder a meat pie has better luck!" No, no, no, that was the wrong tone, not at all what Katie Lennox would say. But Burke burst into such an infectious laugh, it wasn't long before she gave up trying to look stern and began to laugh with him. What she'd said suddenly seemed very funny. When they regained their composure and settled down to the meal, they felt more at peace with each other than they had all morning.

Replete, Burke leaned back against a rock and crunched down on an apple. "So you're from Edinburgh," he said with difficulty.

"What?"

He swallowed and repeated himself.

"Aye," she responded, perfectly at ease. A crisp breeze had sprung up and was blowing the morning clouds away; patches of blue were reflected in the black water of the corrie when the wind rippled its surface.

"Were you there, then, when Charles invaded?"

"Invaded? Ha!" she scoffed. "There was not even a fight."

"No? I'd heard there was looting."

"Nay!" she denied hotly. "Why, the Highland soldiers were so brave and orderly, they would not even accept drink when it was offered them by the townspeople."

"You don't say."

"Indeed I do. And at Prestonpans, Charles ordered the king's wounded to be treated as humanely as his own." She stopped, recalling herself. "I—I've no head for politics, as I told you before," she acknowledged somewhat belatedly, "but I don't think anyone could say the rebel army hasn't fought valiantly. At least, this is what I have *heard*; I've no way of knowing, and probably you would know much better than I."

Burke smiled slightly. "Why does he always go on foot, I wonder. The man's a trained pedestrian." Katherine frowned with pique but kept silent. "And I can't say I've much admiration for his intelligence, Kate. He should have realized by now his cause is without a solid political basis. The lairds who've joined him so far have done so out of honor, or a desire for adventure, or—"

"*Honor*, of course, is something most Englishmen

wouldn't understand,'' she interrupted, stung.

"Unless they were forced to join him,'' he continued, unperturbed, "as they were in Atholl by having their houses burnt over their heads.''

"That's a lie!'' she cried, shocked and outraged.

"No, Kate, it's not a lie,'' he said quietly. The blue of the sky was reflected in his eyes, revealing a bitterness she'd never seen. "There are never completely good or completely bad sides in a war, love. Only groups of men killing each other, usually on foreign soil, for reasons that become murkier the longer they fight.''

She was startled by his tone. "But *you* fight. And kill, presumably.''

A look flashed across his face and was gone before she could decipher it. "It's true, I have killed. I've seen hundreds of men die. Once it was exciting to risk my life against another man's, but not any more. It sounds trite, but I'm sick of fighting.''

It didn't sound trite to Katherine at all. She'd seen killing, too, and had no wish to see any more, ever. She waited for Burke to say more, but his unexpected candor was at an end. "But how can anyone be loyal to a king who cannot even speak English?'' she asked finally.

"Ah, you're mixing him up with his father,'' he smiled. "This George is learning English, I'm told.''

"But—he's *German*.'' The word seemed to her to sum up everything that was wrong with him. "He's not English.''

"But, Kate,'' he countered, "neither are the Stuarts. They're half French and half Scottish. And wholly un-English.''

She grinned. "Trrue, but 'tis tha' half bit o' Scot tha' makes 'em sae bonnie!'' She decided then it was useless to pretend complete disinterest in the Stuart succession; she would never carry it off. Instead she would make herself out to be a typical Scot, with all of a Scot's prejudices and prickly pride, and still not give herself away as a Jacobite.

Burke watched her for a few moments in silence, then shook his head and stood up, stretching. "Stir your stumps, woman, or we'll never make Windermere before dark."

They walked their mounts back up the narrow trail to the road, where Katherine allowed Burke to give her a leg up on her horse. His hand on her ankle was not as impersonal as it had been the first time he'd put her up, she noticed, and the look he gave her was anything but indifferent. He seemed to be seeing her in a new light, and for the life of her she didn't know why. But she was quite sure it was not the kind of light she wanted to be seen in.

"Tell me more about yourself, Kate," he suggested after a period of silence. They were riding past a stone ruin, overgrown with brambles and wild rose vines. The sun had come out, turning the sodden grass slopes from dun-colored to bright emerald. Meadow birds on flickering wings darted from one patch of cover to another.

"Nay, Major, why don't you tell me something about yourself? You've heard enough about me, surely. 'Tis a dull time I've had, anyway, compared to the life of a soldier. You must've been to so many strange and exciting places, won't you tell me about them?"

"You're such a transparent little piece, Kate. You don't fool me for a minute."

"I haven't the slightest idea what you're talking about. Just tell me this: are you really a duke?"

He laughed. "No, only a mere viscount."

"A viscount! Only think. Is that higher than an earl?" She screwed up her face in pretended perplexity.

"No, though I suppose I will be an earl when my father dies."

"Then *he's* an earl?" Burke nodded. "How grand. How do you address an earl?"

"Well, in my father's case, he's the Earl of Rothbury."

"So you're the Viscount of Rothbury?"

"No, I'm the Viscount Holystone."

She shook her head in pretty confusion. "So what should I call you? Sir, or my lord, or—"

" 'Your Royal Highness' will do."

"You're teasing. Is it wonderful to be rich and have a title?" She made her voice sound wistful.

"It has its advantages."

"But why did you join the army? Why not just be a gentleman of leisure?"

"For adventure. For a change. So I wouldn't have to go into politics as my father wished. And I didn't fancy lolling about in drawing rooms while hopeful mamas hauled out their daughters for my inspection."

"No? Why not? I should think that would be quite diverting."

"No, no, too boring. Besides, what if I'd met one I liked? Then I should have had to marry her." He raised his aristocratic brows in an expression of supreme distaste.

Katherine laughed. "Would that be so terrible?"

"Horrible. The end of everything. You know, Kate, they end books with 'And they lived happily ever after' because the authors can't think of anything interesting that could possibly happen to the happy couple after they tie the knot."

"I cannot agree with you," she said after a moment's thought. "I can't think of anything more interesting than trying to make a good, happy life with someone you love."

"Why, Miss Lennox, you surprise me. I thought your sole criterion for a happy life was wealth."

"Not my sole one, Major; my principal one. I expect I shall marry for money and then take a lover."

"Only one?"

"Oh, no, not necessarily. But one at a time," she said, pursing her lips scrupulously. "Where does your family live?'' She thought it best to change the subject.

"In Northumberland. Not twenty miles from the Cheviot Hills.''

"Nay! Really? Why, you—you're almost—''

"Almost in Scotland? Aye, t'be sure! That's why you like me so much, Kate.''

"I don't like you at all.''

"What? You wound me to the quick. Why don't you like me?''

Because you're English, she almost said. "Because you're taking me where I don't want to go.''

"Ah.'' He smiled sadly.

"And did you go to fancy schools when you were a boy?'' She felt safer when he was doing the talking.

"Yes, yes.''

"Are you a snob?''

"A snob?'' he repeated, surprised. "Why do you ask?''

"Oh, no reason.'' She hid a smile at the way he stared down his long nose at her, with no idea how imperious he looked.

"I've never really thought about it,'' he said truthfully. "But never mind that, Kate; I have much more important things to ask you.''

"Very well,'' she sighed resignedly. "Fire away if you must, Major Burke.''

They were riding abreast because the lane had widened as it dipped down the boulder-strewn, bracken-covered fell and leveled off on the valley floor. She looked across at him expectantly, marshaling her wits and preparing to wax eloquent on the subject of her deprived childhood, her wayward adolescence and misspent youth.

"First of all,'' Burke began, sounding businesslike, "do you charge money when you sleep with men, Kate? Hmm? Or do you have 'protectors,' as it were, who pay you for your services in a more indirect way?''

She opened her mouth but no sound came out. For once

she was too shocked to blush. She studied his face intently
for some tiny sign that he was joking, but there was none.
She looked straight ahead at the stony path and blurted
out the first thing that came into her head. "Both! I have
both. Both kinds of men."

"I see. When you have one of the former kind, the
more casual, short-term lover, if you will, what exactly do
you charge? What are your rates?"

She laughed a short, nervous laugh. "Oh, it depends."

He kept looking at her. "On?" he prodded finally.

"On, um, the circumstances. I mean, I have to take
everything into account. You've no idea."

"No. Exactly. Hence the question."

"Yes. Well, I mean, it depends on the person, doesn't
it? And—my *mood*. And where we *are* at the time. So
forth and so on," she muttered almost incoherently.

"Just a general figure, Kate. To give me an idea."

She cast about in her mind wildly. A figure! Good lord,
she had no idea, not the least notion of what a prostitute
charged. "Major Burke, it's so difficult to say," she
stalled, trying for a sophisticated tone.

"Of course. A range, then."

"A range. Mmm . . ." Her mind went blank. "Anywhere between ten and twenty pounds."

"Ten and twenty pounds?"

"I mean guineas. Ten and twenty guineas." She didn't
have the nerve to look and see how he had taken this. "As
I say, it all depends."

"Yes, of course." There was a pause while he seemed to
think this over. "I know my questions seem a bit personal,
but I hope you can understand why. I'm trying to get to
the bottom of our dilemma, you see." His tone was a little
too reasonable, a little too solicitous to be quite genuine;
but there was enough doubt in her mind to prevent her
from challenging him. "How many men have you had, do
you reckon? You're not very old, of course, so—"

"Dozens! Hundreds!" She thought for a second. "Dozens," she concluded positively.

"Really?" This time there was definitely a gleam of something in his eye, and she caught it just before he bent low over his horse's neck to brush a clod of mud from his chest.

"Why are you asking me these questions?" she demanded suspiciously.

He turned an innocent face to her. "Why, Kate! I'm testing your story, of course. Surely you don't think my interest is merely prurient."

She blushed, but she had the wit to retort, "I haven't the vaguest idea what 'prurient' means."

"Ah, no, of course. Well, Kate, one last question. How many positions do you know?"

She looked blank. Positions? What was he—Suddenly she understood, though by instinct and nothing else. She felt her face growing hot again and looked away. She took a deep breath and turned back to face him. "Major Burke," she said levelly, "I know more positions than you have ever dreamed of in your life." She held his eyes for so long that for once he looked away first. But she'd seen his nostrils flare and the color in his cheeks deepen ever so slightly, and she knew she had scored. Emboldened, she pursued the conversation that a moment ago had seemed excruciating. "You thought me shy and awkward just now, didn't you? When I couldn't answer your questions right away, you thought me inexperienced. Yes? Well, I'd like you to know, Major Burke, there are many men who will pay twice, even three times the usual rate for that kind of naivete. In my business, you see, innocence pays."

Oh, how gratifying to see consternation on *his* face for a change, rather than feel it on her own. And anger, too, she saw now, and wondered what had provoked that. When he spurred his horse without another word and went ahead of her, her victory was complete. She didn't ask herself why this particular victory did not taste sweet.

They made good progress as the afternoon wore on, but with each passing mile Katherine's spirits sank a little lower. It was all very well, winning a verbal battle with Burke; but the dismal fact remained that if the weather held, they would reach Lancaster after one more long day's ride. Then he would go away, and there would be new men to convince. She felt the urgent need to do something now. Cathcart and Ewan MacNab were not going to rescue her, she now knew; whatever was going to happen would be up to her. Colonel Denholm had said Burke had influence with the Lancaster authorities. She'd done all she could do, all she *would* do, to persuade him to make a favorable report. But if she could get him to let her go *now*, then a favorable report wouldn't be necessary. If he would let her go *now*—but what would induce him to do such a thing?

They were at the foot of a long valley, cross-hatched with steep-sided becks and winding sheep trails, culminating in a narrow passage between two distant fells. The valley was grassy and fairly flat, and it reminded her of the wide meadow at Darragh where she and Rory and Michael used to race their horses. She had an idea.

"Major Burke!" she called, causing him to slow his horse and wait for her to come up. They hadn't spoken for over an hour; the major's face was completely expressionless. "I have a proposition for you." She colored when his lips quirked and a cynical light appeared in his hard blue eyes. Bastard! she fumed. Who did he think he was to judge her? "A proposal, I mean," she corrected testily. "A wager."

"A wager, Kate?" His tone held mild interest.

"You're a cavalryman; I imagine you think you've quite a lot of skill with a horse. And I will say you handle your mount with a middling degree of competence."

"I'm much obliged to you for that."

ਨਂਂਂਂ

"You'd not be risking much by betting you and your horse can beat me and mine to the other end of the valley, just where the two hills run together there at the mouth, would you?"

He surveyed the prospect, then glanced briefly at Katherine and her mare. "No," he agreed with a small, disparaging smile, "I don't expect I'd be risking much. But what's the wager, Kate? What do you win if I lose?"

"My freedom!" She couldn't keep the note of passion out of her voice. "If I win, you let me go!"

"But Kate," he said softly, "I thought I'd already made it clear. There's only one way you can convince me you deserve to be free."

"I thought you were joking," she whispered, her breath gone.

"Did you?" He took in the parted lips and pinkening cheeks, the dread reflected in her clear, azure eyes. He let his gaze fall to her breast, the soft, swelling curves uncovered now by her open coat and low-necked dress. Her right knee was hooked around the pommel of her saddle; her skirts hid the outline of her legs from his view, but he remembered perfectly from last night how long, sleek, and supple they were.

"Do you mean it?" she asked in a strangled voice, recalling his attention with difficulty.

"I always mean what I say," he told her smoothly. He could guess what she was thinking. Her lovely face was clouded with tumultuous indecision. It was a pleasure to watch her; her thoughts always paraded across the mobile, expressive features with such transparent clarity.

She reached a decision. "I would rather rot in prison for the rest of my life than give you the satisfaction!" she declared feelingly.

"Would you, Kate?" he responded, unruffled. "Even if I said I'd take great pains to assure that you were satisfied, too?"

"Ha!" she snorted. "I very much doubt that."

"Don't be too sure, my love." His eyes gleamed maddeningly.

"I think you're afraid to race," she accused, trying a different tack. "You couldn't bear to be bested by a woman, so you refuse to take a chance. How cowardly!"

He laughed gleefully at that. "Kate, these barbs at my masculinity pierce me to the core. But tell me, what makes this race worth my while? You gain your freedom, but what do I receive?"

She hadn't thought of that. What could she give him? Nothing came to mind.

"It must be something quite valuable, don't you think? Something of comparable worth against your liberty. Hmm." He stroked his chin thoughtfully. "Well, let's have our race first. If I win, I'll name my prize then. Are you game?"

There was something seriously flawed about this arrangement, but Katherine had begun to see the race as her only chance, and she had enough confidence in her skill as a horsewoman to overlook the consequences of losing.

"Aye, I'm game," she said fiercely. She peered across the valley. Half a mile away the hills converged, forming a natural mouth or alleyway. "Do you see where that line of trees begins on the left? Just there, at the first tree, the race will end. Agreed?" She was stripping off her coat as she spoke; she threw it down on a dry boulder.

"Agreed." Burke dismounted and hobbled the packhorse. He shed his own coat and tossed it over hers, then remounted his stallion. His movements were relaxed and easy; there was a slight smile of anticipation on his lips. His manner contrasted sharply with Katherine's. She was like a coiled spring, her eyes bright with excitement, her jaw set determinedly. She lined her horse up carefully, making sure Burke's stallion's forelegs weren't an inch closer to the finish line than her mare's. Burke was having trouble keeping a straight face. He grinned outright when she threw her right leg over the mare's neck and sat her like a man, providing him with a brief but engrossing glimpse of white calf amid a profusion of lace and petticoats.

"I'll give you a head start since you've only one stirrup," he offered generously, blue eyes twinkling.

She wanted to refuse, but discretion won out over pride. "Very well, but only to that black rock yonder," she agreed, pointing. "Are you ready?" She glanced over at him. He'd rolled up his sleeves and thrown off his cravat. She was momentarily daunted by the rippling muscles in his forearms and the way his powerful black-clad thighs gripped the sides of his horse. But the cocky, self-assured expression on his arrogant face annoyed her so much, her will to win tripled. She looked ahead grimly, and her long, strong fingers tightened convulsively on the reins.

"Anytime, Kate," he drawled.

She inhaled deeply. Then she kicked her booted heels into the mare's sides, simultaneously giving her a sharp whack on the rump, and they were off.

She reached the black rock in about ten strides, and couldn't resist a backward glance to make sure Burke hadn't cheated on her head start. He had not, but the first massive lunge of the big stallion's forequarters seemed to fill up half the distance between them in no time. With a thrill of panic she turned her attention to her horse, lying low over her neck and calling out urgent inducements. The mare responded eagerly with a new burst of speed, and they sailed over the banks of a fast-moving brook as easily as if they were flying. The ground passing under them was a blur. Oh, what a lovely mare, Katherine exulted. More than halfway to the goal, she cast another look behind. When she saw how far back Burke was, her heart soared. The wind snatched the ribbon from her hair and the bright

locks fell down her back in a shower of red and gold. She
could have laughed out loud from sheer happiness. Only a
little farther and she would be free. Free! Should she just
keep riding, or stop and bid farewell to the major? She
guessed she would stop, if only to see the look on his face
when . . . Something on the periphery of her vision made
her turn her head. Oh God, Burke was less than twelve
feet behind! With a howl of fury she tried to kick her horse
into a stronger gallop, but the mare was already running
faster than she ever had and there was nothing left in
reserve. Slowly, relentlessly, her lead dwindled to nothing.
Burke, his shirt flying whitely behind him like a sail,
passed her just before she reached the stand of copper
beeches on the left, the goal line.

Disappointment engulfed her like a huge wave, leaving
her limp. Tears threatened behind her eyelids but she
blinked them back angrily. So close! To think that a few
feet of English soil stood between freedom and captivity—
God, it was bitter. When Burke turned his horse and
trotted back toward her, she had to choke back a searing
curse; she would rather die than let him know how
devastating this loss was.

They sat their horses six feet apart on the mossy ground,
breathing hard and eyeing each other warily. "I win,"
Burke announced unnecessarily.

All of a sudden Katherine remembered the other half of
the wager. Bitterness and disappointment faded to insig-
nificance in the face of this new threat. She stared back at
him, suddenly feeling like a rabbit in a snare.

"Get down off your horse."

It was not a request. She yearned to refuse, but to do so
would reveal that she was afraid of him. She couldn't even
admit that to herself.

She sprang from her horse agilely, and Burke jumped
off the stallion at the same time. He was beside her in
three strides. She'd forgotten how big he was; on horse-

back they were nearly the same height.

"Well, Kate." His forehead was beaded with perspiration; his hair gleamed sleekly in the setting sun. His shirt was half unbuttoned, and she could see the black hairs that curled damply on his chest.

"Well, Major?" She thought her voice sounded amazingly steady.

"I'm ready to collect my prize." His smile set her teeth on edge. "But what shall it be? Something of great value, I think; after all, if you'd won, I'd have given you your freedom, that most precious of gifts. But what have you to give me?"

"Nothing!"

"Nothing?" he repeated, with exaggerated surprise. "Oh, Kate, think again."

"I—cannot."

"Then I shall have to choose for you. I choose—" he narrowed his eyes in mock concentration—"I choose . . . let me see, what shall it be? A kiss."

Relief struggled with alarm. She had thought he would want more, but this was bad enough. He closed the distance between them in a step and her panic rose. No one had touched her since . . . She put her hand against his chest to hold him away. "Burke, I don't want to!" she said simply.

"But you must," he whispered. He took her hand and brought it to his mouth; she felt the heat of his lips on her palm, the inside of her wrist. He pulled her closer, putting her arm around his neck and bending over her, his other arm circling her waist. There was a fraction of a second when he paused, when she really could have pushed him away, but it was gone before she recognized it. His wide, reckless mouth met hers, and after that she thought she would wait a little while before pushing him away. She kept her eyes open; it gave her a sense of control. Gradually she felt herself becoming absorbed in the taste and texture of his mouth and the feel of his breath on her skin. After a minute or two and the kiss didn't end when some subconscious timekeeper told her a kiss ought to end, her eyelids fluttered closed and her body softened against him. He felt so solid and real, so . . . But now she felt the tip of his tongue between her lips, and it shocked her to her toes. With a little startled cry, she pushed him away and stepped back, more out of breath than she'd been after the race.

"Ah, Kate," Burke murmured, shaking his head, "just when it was getting good." His eyes were cloudy. For once he wasn't smiling.

She drew a shuddering breath. "A kiss is a kiss," she told him shakily. "You've been paid, Burke; now it's finished." Her face was flushed and her lips were tingling.

"You look like you've been kissed, lovely Kate, but not nearly enough." He moved toward her, one hand outstretched.

"No!" A thrill of apprehension went through her. "Enough, Burke, it's done."

He stopped. "Very well," he sighed. He was his old self again, smiling his mocking smile. "But to say a kiss is a kiss demonstrates a sad lack of appreciation for the finer points, my love. I begin to see why you're not more successful in your chosen profession."

Katherine drew in her breath, offended. "I meant," she flared, "that kissing *you* is just a kiss. An artist needs inspiration to do his best work, and in your case I was denied that."

He looked unaffected by this insult. "Are you an artist, then?"

"That, Major Burke, is something you will never know."

He walked over to her horse and caught the bridle. He brought the mare back and clasped his hands to give her a leg up; she accepted his help stiffly. Once she was in the saddle, he stood looking up at her, amusement still lighting his eyes. He grasped her knee familiarly and gave it a squeeze.

"You know, Kate, with a history like yours for losing wagers, I wouldn't bet on that. I wouldn't bet on it at all."

CHAPTER 7

They didn't reach Windermere that evening. Near Helvellyn they came upon such an inviting little inn that Burke decided to stop for the night, even though there was still another hour of daylight. The Rose and Crown was a two-story, ivy-covered brick structure, well-proportioned in the new "Georgian" style, with trim, white-sashed bay windows in front and innumerable smoking chimneys poking up from its slate roof. It looked cozy and attractive, and Katherine was pleased they were stopping.

A private chaise had arrived moments before and was unloading its passengers as they rode up. While a groom took her horse, Katherine watched a woman of about forty, richly garbed in a fur-lined cloak and beaver hat with a crimson plume, descend from the chaise with the aid of a liveried footman. After her came a girl of fifteen or sixteen, and then a nondescript, middle-aged woman Katherine took to be a servant. With a slight start, she realized Burke was eyeing the older woman with obvious appreciation, and now he was actually bowing to her. The woman gazed across at him briefly before favoring him with a slight nod; she turned away soon to lead her small party inside the hostelry, but not before she allowed an inviting twinkle to gleam in her eye and the merest hint of a smile to curl the corners of her mouth. For Katherine she had not even spared a glance. They're *flirting*, she thought, piqued. She instantly conceived a dislike for the woman with the red feather which was groundless but profound.

A few moments later she found herself entering the Rose and Crown with her arm tucked in Burke's while he smiled down at her in a proprietary way. The entrance hall was clean and cheerful, with whitewashed walls and sanded floors. There was a public parlor to the right where an assortment of respectable-looking travelers had gathered to sip tea or sherry before supper. A small, balding gentleman in shirtsleeves and waistcoat came bustling toward them, introducing himself a bit shyly as Thomas Beenling, the owner, and welcoming them to his humble establishment. He regretted his wife was presently too occupied with the evening meal to greet them but he was certain she would be anxious to do so later. Burke acknowledged this courteously, then shocked Katherine to her foundations by announcing that he was Mr. James Burke from up around Berwick and she was his wife, and they would be wanting a room! She started to pull away in protest, but his grip on her arm only tightened and his smile widened devilishly.

"Oh, my sweet, there's no need for such maidenly shyness," he admonished solicitously; "I'm sure Mr. Beenling has seen dozens of new brides and grooms in his career, and is the very soul of tact and discretion."

She ground her teeth in renewed fury.

"Newlyweds!" exclaimed the innkeeper, rubbing his hands together happily. "You'll be wanting the Paragon Room, then," he assured him. "It's a suite, with a little dressing room attached, like. Just the thing, says my wife, for the shy bride." He blushed, suddenly comprehending that this speech might not embody the soul of tact and discretion. He signaled for a porter to carry their bags, then led the way upstairs himself.

The Paragon Room was large and comfortably appointed with good plain furniture. An oak four-poster bed stood in the center. As soon as she saw it, Katherine forcibly extricated Burke's fingers from her wrist and went to stand by the window, deaf to Mr. Beenling's description of the comforts to be found in the dressing room and the splendid supper in store for them downstairs at seven o'clock.

At last he was gone, and with the shutting of the door behind him she whirled on Burke furiously, demanding an explanation.

"Why, Kate, I thought you'd be glad," he said innocently, beginning to unpack his portmanteau.

"Glad!"

"I did it for you, sweetheart, truly."

"Don't call me sweetheart!" She longed for something to throw at him.

"Shh!" he hissed, stifling a laugh. "What will the other guests think?"

"I don't give a damn what they think!"

"Tsk, tsk, such language, and from my lovely new wife. I won't stand for that, dearest."

She opened her mouth but no words came out; she was speechless with rage.

"No, but really, Kate," he began again, attempting a serious mien, "you're evidently a woman in chronic need of protection. My knuckles are raw from dealing with your admirers. I need some peace and quiet, at least for one night." He took a heavy military pistol out of his bag and placed it in the drawer of the bedside table, along with a small assortment of books and pamphlets. Then he unfolded a fresh white linen shirt and began to unfasten his cravat. "Don't you think you'd better freshen up a bit before dinner, my sweet? I think we should dress, don't you? Put on your new green gown; I adore what it does for your eyes."

Katherine stamped her foot in impotent fury. "You're a high-handed, double-dealing, foul-minded maggot!"

He had begun to unbutton his shirt. She edged closer to her own small clothes bag. "If I were a man I would deal with you, James Burke!" she threatened feelingly. He was pulling his shirt out of his breeches and preparing to slide it over his massive shoulders. "If you were half the gentleman you pretend to be, you'd—Oh, you are odious!" His shirt was off and he was fumbling at the buttons of his breeches, grinning insufferably. She snatched up her bag and flounced away to the dressing room.

"Don't dawdle, sweeting; we mustn't be late," he called after her, just before the door slammed with a deafening crash.

Katherine stood against the door, breathing deeply. That worm, that despicable insect. He was without a conscience and utterly beneath contempt. And if he thought for a moment his childish ploys would do him any good, he was in for a grave disappointment.

She sat down on the chair before the mirrored dressing table, and was momentarily stunned by her reflection in the glass. Her color was high, her eyes still burning bright with residual anger. She had done nothing to her hair since the horse race; it hung about her shoulders in mad disarray. There was warm water and sweet-smelling soap on the mahogany washstand, and—miracle of miracles!—someone had left half a dozen hairpins in the dressing-table drawer. She took the green dress out and shook it free of wrinkles. She would wear the damned thing, not because he'd told her to but because she had nothing else. Besides, she thought, smoothing the soft velvet skirt with her hands, it really was a beautiful gown.

In fifteen minutes she was bathed and dressed and ready to go, except for her hair. It was galling to have to ask Burke for anything, but the fact remained, he had the hairbrush. Resignedly, she tapped on the door.

"Yes, my love?"

Her eyes closed briefly in disgust. She opened the door a

crack. He was lying on the bed in his black evening clothes, the ones he'd worn the day she met him, reading a book. He glanced over at her interestedly. "May I borrow your hairbrush again, Major Burke?" she asked, stiff-lipped.

"But of course! Forgive me, dear, I should have given it to you to keep." He sprang from the bed and went to the bureau, got the brush and brought it to her.

"Certainly not; it's yours, not mine." She took the brush and started to close the door in his face, but his foot prevented it. She stepped back, disdaining a vulgar physical battle, and he walked in cheerfully.

"I thought I might watch," he smiled, folding his arms and leaning against the door frame. She sat down before the mirror and began to brush her hair, determined to ignore him. "How beautiful, Kate," he said after a moment, with apparent earnestness. "How often do you brush it?" She said nothing. "How many strokes a night, hmm?" She remained silent. She frowned with concentration while she drew the heavy mass of curls and waves back from her face, secured it with the pins, and let it hang down freely at the back. It was a cunning style she'd learned at school in Paris years ago—severe in front, sensual and free at the back and sides. Still frowning, she coaxed a curl to hang down artlessly in front of one ear. "Very clever," Burke noted appreciatively. "That guileless look, eh? You do it so well, my darling."

She slammed the brush down and stood up abruptly. "Are you ready?" she snapped, her eyes sparkling with suppressed ire.

"My God, you're lovely, Kate," Burke breathed, getting the benefit of the full effect for the first time. The dress was a perfect fit, and it became her wonderfully well. He congratulated himself on selecting the very color to accent the green in her blue-green eyes and the coppery-gold highlights in her magnificent red hair. Next to the rich, dark velvet, her skin shone like alabaster, perfectly white except for the delicate apricot in her cheeks and the natural pink of her delectable lips. Her neck seemed almost too frail to bear the heavy head of lustrous hair; he thought of a beautiful flower on a slender stalk. And her breasts, pale and smooth, swelling so enticingly above the tight bodice of the dress, making him want to reach out with both hands—

"Are you ready?" she repeated breathlessly, undone by his scorching stare.

"Oh, Kate," he murmured, shaking his head slowly, "if you only knew."

In the center of the dining parlor was an immense round table, around which were four or five smaller tables for guests who desired privacy. Mrs. Beenling, as large and imposing as her husband was small and self-effacing, led Katherine and Burke to one of these latter, not unnaturally assuming the newlyweds would prefer to dine tête-à-tête. She brought them a special bottle of wine, reserved, she said, for only the weightiest occasions, and heartily wished them well for the rest of their days. Katherine bore these courtesies with the barest civility, while Burke responded with exaggerated goodwill. He toasted her effusively when the proprietress had gone, raising his glass to a long and happy life together, to his great good fortune in finding and winning the woman of his dreams, to their many, many offspring who he prayed would look exactly like her—

"*Will* you stop?" she demanded, irritated beyond measure. "You are behaving like a perfect fool."

"Ah, but it's your own fault, lovely Kate. You bring out the fool in me. I'll warrant no man could sit this close to you for long, bathed in the radiance of your beauty, and not start spouting nonsense. We lose our heads, is what it is . . ." He was staring off into the distance, distracted by something; he seemed to have forgotten what he was saying. Katherine turned her head curiously, following his gaze. Across the way, at another table for two, sat the lady with the feather—though she was without it at the moment—and her daughter or companion or whatever she was, the girl of fifteen or sixteen. The older woman nodded decorously in their direction, though with the same playful gleam in her eye. The girl, who was blonde and blue-eyed and might one day be attractive, looked down at her plate shyly and blushed.

"Do you *know* them?" Katherine asked, more sharply than she'd intended.

"No, of course not." He sounded surprised. "Why should you think that?" When she said nothing, he went on casually, "She's a handsome woman, don't you think?"

"I suppose so," she admitted, though in lukewarm tones. "But older, of course," she could not help adding.

"Mmm," he murmured, watching the lady across the top of his wine glass. "And wiser, I expect."

Katherine was inordinately glad when the food arrived.

"Are you tired?" Burke asked when they had finished.

"Not in the least." She was lying, but she didn't want to go upstairs yet. She had no intention of sleeping with him in that wide four-poster bed, and she simply didn't have the will to fight with him about it right now. So instead they went into the private parlor, a smaller, paneled room with a cozy fire burning in the hearth, where some of the guests were sitting about, reading and playing cards. Burke led her to a Windsor chair by the fire, then took a seat for himself a little distance away. A maid came and asked if they would like anything to drink; Burke ordered brandy and Katherine requested a small glass of port.

A round-faced, bewhiskered gentleman drinking whiskey nodded at Katherine and then demanded of

Burke in a loud, jovial voice, "What do you make of this prince feller, sir? Should we be priming our pistols and locking up our womenfolk or turning over and going back to sleep? Eh? They say he's still at Carlisle, figuring his next move. If he decides to march south and stir 'em up around Lancashire, we'll be right in his path. Think there's any danger in that?"

No, I don't," Burke answered promptly, "though I expect he will come south. I think Charles has four choices. He can remain where he is and wait for a general rising of the English Jacobites. He can march to Newcastle and engage Wade. He can return to Scotland and wage a defensive war until his army is strong enough to take the offensive. Or he can come south, where he may find a goodly number of supporters in Lancashire. I believe he'll choose the latter because his ultimate objective is London, and the closer he gets, the better he feels. But you and yours, sir, will be in no danger. The Highland troops have conducted themselves admirably thus far. I think they'll continue to do so unless their fortunes change considerably. Which they will in the end, but I don't expect it this soon."

Katherine thought this over in silence, wondering how accurate his assessment was. She was gratified by his admission that the Highlanders had behaved gallantly, but disturbed by his opinion that their cause was doomed. It could not be! She knew the rebellion was a bold gamble and that many would suffer terribly if it failed. But the spirit and courage of the rebels were so strong, their ideals so worthy and right, they had to prevail, they simply had to. Otherwise, what had all this been for, this dangerous charade that might well lead to her own execution?

And yet she had known what the risks were and had accepted them willingly, because it had seemed to her after her father's death that she had nothing left to lose. What had changed since then? Nothing. She was only being a coward, losing heart as she neared the time when so-called English ''justice'' would catch up with her. She needed to pull herself together and remember there were many others in the rebellion who had paid and would continue to pay as high a price as she.

Her drink came and she sipped it quietly, only half listening to what Burke and the other man were saying. The fire was warm, the wine potent, and at last she began to relax. Watching Burke light his pipe, she found herself lost in abstract contemplation of his hands, his strong fingers, his big thumb tamping tobacco into the bowl. Her limbs began to feel heavy, weighted. She studied the muscles in his thighs, the light stubble along the line of his jaw, the way his gleaming hair swept back from his high, white forehead. Unwillingly she remembered his kiss, the way he'd touched her. Her response to him had been so strong and unexpected, she didn't know what to think, or how to feel about it.

She closed her eyes to block out the sight of him. She would think about Michael instead. Handsome, strong, blond-haired. Honest brown eyes, a laughing mouth. But these were only words, she realized with a guilty start; for the life of her she couldn't picture his face. She felt ashamed.

She opened her eyes to find Burke staring at her. She colored and looked away, pretending a deep interest in a hunting print on the wall beside her. How appalling to have to admit, as she must if she was to be honest with herself at all, that she was attracted to him. For the last four years she'd been nothing but a hard shell, reconciled to a life of childless solitude, untouched by any strong emotion except a craving for vengeance. She prayed these new stirrings meant she was changing, that other men could make her feel this way, too—that, God forbid, it wasn't just him! Her mind was wracked with questions, and the coward in her hoped she would never learn the answers.

After all, no matter what happened, after tomorrow she would never see him again. And that was fine with her, that was perfectly all right, that was *exactly* what she wanted. And yet—and yet—

Burke was ordering another brandy and asking her if she would like more wine. She seized the opportunity to make her escape.

"No, thank you," she told him, covering a feigned yawn with her hand. "I think I'll go up now. But you have yours, darling, and I'll see you in the morning." She rose and came toward him. "Good night, lambkin," she cooed, touching his cheek with the side of her hand. His eyes were laughing in appreciation. She jumped when he took her wrist and got to his feet in one smooth motion.

"Let me escort you to the door, my angel," he said solicitously.

"It's not necessary, buttercup."

"Nonsense, I insist. You know I can hardly bear to let you out of my sight."

He led her to the doorway, where they stood in full view of the guests in both the public and private parlors. Some were smiling at them fondly, the news of their recently married status having spread until there wasn't a guest at the inn who didn't know of it. Burke was holding her much too intimately for Katherine's comfort, but she felt perfectly safe; after all, what could he do in front of all these people?

"Are you sure you wouldn't like me to come up with you, sweetkin, and help you undress? All those buttons, and you with no maid." His hand was playing with the top of her dress as he spoke and she felt herself growing warm.

She declined softly. "I would rather eat a plateful of worms, my precious heart." She smiled up into his face lovingly.

"Ah, my dove, you pierce me cruelly. Do I take it

you've not reconsidered my earlier offer?''

"What earlier offer was that, rose petal?"

"Why, my generous offer to you to prove yourself, sugarplum. Your last remaining chance at freedom."

"But, darling," she purred, "I thought I'd made it plain: I would much rather hang!"

"Very well, then, have it your way, my dearest pet. Good night."

"Burke, I'm warning you," she hissed when she realized his intention. Too late—the hand that had been holding her waist went all the way around and pulled her close, while with his other hand he took her chin and tilted her mouth up so he could kiss her. Rather than cause a scene, she suffered his touch, albeit she stood as stiff as a statue, eyes wide open. His lips were gentle, almost playful, but then he drew her even closer and moved his hand from her jaw to the back of her neck, tangling his fingers through her hair and kissing her with such ardor that something in her exploded. This time when his tongue invaded her mouth she didn't stop it; she was too caught up in the heady, heart-stopping sensations his mouth was making her feel. Her arms, which had been pressing stiffly against him, relaxed; her palms opened against his chest. A sound came from deep in her throat and her knees began to tremble. Burke chose that moment to end the kiss, knowing much better than she where their passion would lead. But for Katherine it was a cruel, heartless abandonment. She stood swaying slightly, breathing hard, as slowly the room swam back into focus. She heard the laughter and applause of their audience, saw some lift their glasses in friendly salutes, and went white with embarrassment. She threw Burke a swift, anguished look and fled across the parlor and up the stairs, skirts lifted high.

He watched her leave, fighting an all but overwhelming impulse to go after her. Someone clamped a heavy hand

on his shoulder and dragged him back to the fire, where
brandy and hearty congratulations were forced on him by
more than one envious male onlooker. He bore their good
wishes graciously, but his mind was a million miles away.
When the talk became more general, he moved slightly
away from his companions. He relit his pipe and stared
broodingly into the fire. Before long he was struck by the
resemblance between the darting, multicolored flames and
Kate's hair in the full sun. He asked himself why he didn't
go after her. He knew as surely as he knew anything in the
world that if he went to her now she would submit to him.
She reviled him at every opportunity and professed to
despise him, but she could not hide her body's response.
He exulted in the certain knowledge that she wanted him,
very nearly as much as he wanted her. What was holding
him back? In all probability she was exactly what she
claimed to be—at best, an unchaste, loose-principled
wench; at worst, a whore. After all, this was the woman
who had bedded the despicable Maule, had been ready to
become his mistress because he was richer than her
gambler lover. So what were these scruples and whom did
they serve? He could not answer the question. He only
knew that something in him wanted her to ask for it first;
whore or not, he was loath to take advantage of her in a
weak moment. He knew he was being a fool, and it was an
uncharacteristic feeling. And the worst of it was, tonight
was probably their last chance to be together.

   This was such a horrible thought, he decided to drown it
with more brandy. He took his drink closer to the hearth.
As he stared into the flames he gradually became aware of
an intermittent hissing sound coming from the fire itself.
He put his glass down on the mantelpiece and went to one
of the leaded windows. He threw open the casement and
thrust his head out. Drops of water struck him in the face,
borne by a cold, sobering wind. When he drew his head
back in, he was grinning like a small boy on Christmas

morning.

"It's raining like the devil!" he called out to the room at large. "The roads won't be fit for ducks. We'll have to bide another day!"

CHAPTER 8

Katherine closed her eyes tightly and tried to bring back the dream. If she let her mind drift, she could almost recapture it. Rory was there. "Oh, balls, Kate, it's raining, our ride . . ." He was fussing and fuming, she could no longer remember the words. Then somehow they were on Royce Knob, she on the ground with her back against a tree, he with his head on her lap. He was talking excitedly about something, his small hands gesturing. Her fingers played in his bright red hair, the same color as hers. But then the rain came, big, heavy drops that fell on Rory's face and into his wide, staring eyes—

She shuddered and came fully awake, and the dream evaporated. Where was she? The rain was real, she could hear it thrumming against the windowpane. A sound caught her attention and she turned her head sideways on the pillow. Burke. Jesus, Mary, and Joseph, he was lying next to her, fast asleep! She had a moment of blind panic when she couldn't remember what had happened last night. Oh God, oh God, what if—but no, now she remembered. She'd fallen asleep in the chair, with her coat over her for a blanket. He must've put her in bed, that was all. She peeped under the coverlet to make sure she was still wearing her shift. She was. Well, then, no harm done; her pulse returned to normal.

She stole another glance at Burke. She was fascinated by

the way his nostrils flared at the end of his long, regal nose, even in sleep. Perhaps it was the *construction* of his face that made him seem arrogant, she mused. Then she mentally shook herself. What nonsense. He *was* arrogant, and she was being an idiot.

And yet he intrigued her. Last night before falling asleep she'd stolen a glance at the books he'd put beside the bed. It came as a surprise to learn that he was reading *The Divine Comedy* in Italian, as well as a book on Roman military history, a pamphlet containing a debate between two prominent parliamentarians, and a mysterious little volume written in Greek whose very title was too difficult for her to decipher. Surely this was odd bedtime reading matter for a soldier. What sort of a man was James Burke, anyway?

At that moment his eyes opened and he looked straight at her. The sudden flash of blue was dazzling and she blinked in its radiance. She slid backward in a spontaneous retreat, but his hand shot out and took her wrist. "Don't go," he said softly. "Don't spoil the dream." He gazed up at her sleepily; his smile was uncommonly gentle.

"Don't—don't you think we ought to be getting ready to go?" she stammered. She clutched the edge of the sheet and carried it to her bosom, intensely aware of where his eyes had gone.

He listened for a second, then his smile widened. "Can't you hear the rain, Kate? We'll not be setting out today, I'm afraid."

There was a knock at the door and she jumped almost guiltily. Burke cocked a quizzical brow at her, then called "Come in!" A pretty, fresh-faced chambermaid entered, bearing a tray with two steaming cups of chocolate and some buttered bread.

"Good morning," she said shyly, putting the tray down beside the bed and curtseying.

"Morning," Burke returned cheerily, sitting up with his

back against the pillow, unself-consciously revealing that he wore no nightshirt. "What's it like out, then?"

"Oh, sir, it's tedious dismal; you wouldn't care t' be ridin' out today a'tall. Shall I open the curtain so you can see out?" She looked away with a becoming blush from the riveting expanse of chest and shoulders he took no pains to hide.

"That would be very kind," he told her with effortless charm.

She went to the window and pulled back the curtains, revealing a gloomy skyscape of dark gray clouds barely visible through the downpour.

"Dismal indeed!" Burke agreed genially. "No, we won't be traveling today, I can see that." His rueful look was patently insincere.

"Oh, I was almost forgetting," the maid chirped. "The lady just give me this, said I was t' giv it t' you, ma'am." Katherine took the white card she held out across the bed. "She said if you was not going today because o' the rain, she would be pleased t' make your acquaintance—and yours too, Mr. Burke—after breakfast in the private parlor. Said as how she was most anxious for you t' meet her niece as well. She'd be that yellow-haired young lady with her, I expect," she added for their information.

"Mm, no doubt." Burke was peering down at the card in Katherine's hand. " 'Mrs. Celeste Parkington,' " he read aloud, " 'The Hermitage, Sudbury, Staffordshire.' " For an instant his eyes met Katherine's with a look of limpid innocence. "Thank you—What did you say your name was?"

"Trudy, sir," she answered, blushing again, "though I didn't say it before."

"Didn't you? You ought to have, Trudy, with as pretty a name as that."

"Thank you, sir," she curtsied, looking at the floor in confusion.

"Would you tell Mrs. Parkington my mother and I will be honored to make her acquaintance, say around ten o'clock?"

"Your—Oh, sir," she giggled prettily, "you're teasing." She curtsied her way out the door, covering her mouth with her hand.

Katherine's face was a mixture of amusement and irritation when he turned to hand her a cup of chocolate. "Do you flirt with *all* women, Major?"

"Only if they're very attractive or very unattractive," he said airily, biting into a piece of bread.

"And in which category would you put Mrs. Parkington?"

"Definitely the former," he said with his mouth full.

"Well, Kate, should we notice her?"

" 'Notice her'?" she repeated with distaste. How she hated that expression. "Heavens, you *are* a snob."

"I suppose I am," he acknowledged carelessly.

"Don't you think we're all equal in the eyes of God?"

"Doubtless, but not in the eyes of men. And as long as I'm living on earth and not in heaven, I'm obliged to see through a man's eyes."

His breezy attitude irritated her. "You think you're a better person than I because my station is beneath yours, don't you?"

"Not better, precisely; but unquestionably more fortunate."

"No, *better*. Would you marry beneath you?"

"Not unless I wished to be disinherited."

"So you would not? Even if you were in love?"

"But you see, I wouldn't be. I enjoy my life as it is and see no reason to finish it as a pauper." His tone was light, but she could see he was perfectly serious. "Would you?"

She laughed brittlely. "Major Burke, there *is* no one beneath me."

After that she sipped her chocolate cautiously,

endeavoring to keep as much distance between them as possible without falling off the bed. The intimacy of the situation disturbed her, though she could see no immediate way out. She had a suspicion Burke was naked under the bedclothes. They ate in silence for a few minutes before she put down her cup with a show of resolution and turned to face him.

"Burke, I think you should let me go."

"Yes, I know," he agreed mildly. Inwardly he was wondering at exactly what point she'd conceived the notion that he had the authority to do any such thing.

"I mean it. By now you must realize I'm not a spy."

"I realize nothing of the sort." When he turned toward her the sheet slid lower around his hips; she didn't know where to look.

"I think you're teasing me, Major. Surely you can understand why I'm not able to find much humor in your jests."

"Jests?"

"I'm asking you to be serious and see the situation from my standpoint."

He reached over and picked up a lock of hair that lay across her breast. "Very well," he murmured, "I'll try." He was looking at her hair in his hand as if it were a precious metal.

She swallowed, momentarily losing her train of thought. "The fact of the matter is, I could lose my life because of your stubbornness, your refusal to see things as they are. And I cannot believe you would really want to have that on your conscience."

"You have a way of twisting things around, love. You're in an untenable position by your own actions, not mine. I've already suggested a way to help you out of it, but you don't seem to want to take advantage of my offer. I'm forced to conclude from that that whoring is very far from your nature. From there it's a short jump to the next conclusion, that you're a traitor and a spy.''

With an enraged cry, she snatched her hair out of his hand and leapt from the bed, not caring that she wore nothing but her shift. ''Blackmail!'' she hurled at him wrathfully. ''You're despicable, I despise you!''

''That's redundant.''

''Worm! Insect! Disgusting garbage—''

''I warn you, Kate, I won't have my wife insulting me.''

''You're a slimy, miserable excuse for a gentleman! Horsewhipping is too good for you.''

''You know, Kate, what you need is a good spanking.''

''Coward! Pervert! Just try it, you insufferable English twit, and I'll—''

''What?'' He threw back the covers and put his feet on the floor. Katherine shrieked and bolted for the dressing room. She jerked the door open in a panic and slammed it shut behind her, leaning all her weight against it. There was a breathless pause before she heard him chuckling, all the way across the room. He hadn't even gotten off the bed to chase her. She looked down at her shaking hands. She felt like a fool.

''Oh, but surely—why, I thought *everyone* played backgammon!'' Mrs. Parkington's well-bred accents betrayed her astonishment at such a curious departure from the norm.

Katherine shrugged helplessly. ''I—just never learned,'' she lied, beginning to feel more than a little ill-used. She had been sitting in the private parlor for nearly two hours, compelled to listen in abject silence while Burke and Mrs. Parkington traded views on a wide variety of topics, on most of which she was forced to pretend total ignorance. She was tired to death of smiling vacuously while she listened to their personal judgments regarding Handel's latest opera, Walpole's politics, Hogarth's satirical genius. She had opinions on everything, and she considered they were at least as insightful as Mrs. Parkington's. But she could hardly express them and remain true to Katie Lennox, so she was obliged to engage in this mortifying pretense of stupidity.

She found equally unpleasant the necessity to sit idly by while Mrs. Parkington flirted outrageously with the man who, for all she knew, was Katherine's brand new husband. And Burke did nothing to discourage her. Quite the contrary, he seemed completely absorbed in every word the woman uttered. Honesty compelled Katherine to admit Mrs. Parkington was beautiful, intelligent, and sophisticated. But when her every witty remark, every penetrating observation or clever *bon mot* made Katherine seem, by contrast, even more tongue-tied and doltish—well, then, truly it would have taken a saint to like her, and Katherine was not a saint.

She glanced over at Miss Parkington—Jessica—who was reading a book by the window, and felt another jealous pang. How she would love to curl up somewhere with a book on this dreary day and forget all about war and royal successions and Major James Burke. Especially Major James Burke. Suddenly unable to remain where she was another minute while Burke and Mrs. Parkington cultivated an ever-deepening appreciation of each other, she excused herself to go sit beside Jessica.

"What are you reading?" she asked curiously after a bit of small talk.

"Poems," the girl murmured softly, as though slightly ashamed. "Shakespeare."

Katherine was about to ask to see the book when she remembered, just in time, that she was not supposed to be able to read. Instead she questioned Jessica a little on her likes and dislikes. She seemed to be a sweet, quiet child, happy to be concluding this overly long visit with her widowed aunt and going home to her family.

"Jessica!" her aunt called suddenly. The girl stopped

speaking, looking almost guilty. "Whatever can you be telling poor Mrs. Burke? I'm sure she is very kind and obliging to listen to all your chatter." She laughed indulgently, and Jessica blushed; Katherine felt embarrassed for her. "Come over here, child, and sit by me. Read us one of your little poems." Jessica got up obediently and went to sit by her aunt. Burke sat casually, smoking his pipe, but his eyes seemed to miss nothing. Katherine wondered if he'd seen her reach for Jessica's book. "Read us the one about love, Jessie," Mrs. Parkington smiled humorously. "You know the one I mean, the one that goes on and *on* about love." Jessica blushed again and leafed through the pages. Her aunt sent Burke a look of mock forebearance and folded her hands to listen.

"'Take all my loves, my love, yea take them all; What hast thou then more than thou hadst before?'" Jessica began in a soft, schoolgirlish voice.

Katherine recited the words with her to herself, remembering her own school days and how she had loved those sonnets. Life had been so simple. She'd had no cares but which dress to choose for tomorrow or how to achieve the latest French hairstyle. She felt a pang of envy for Jessica's innocence. Hold on to it for as long as you can, she advised her inwardly; you can never know when you will lose it!

"That was very nice, dear. Perhaps Mrs. Burke would be kind enough to read us one of *her* favorites," Mrs. Parkington said graciously when Jessica had finished, as though conferring an honor. Katherine murmured something vaguely negative. "Oh, please do, we should all like it so much."

"I would prefer not to," she said with a little more force.

But it seemed the more strongly she declined, the more strongly Mrs. Parkington importuned her. "No, but really, you must! It's only fair. And then I shall read one, and perhaps Mr. Burke will favor us with one of his.'' She was flirting again, batting her eyelids at Burke with coy proficiency.

Katherine could feel herself beginning to flush. She could not think what to say next. To refuse would seem so churlish, so obstinate; but to say to this handsome, accomplished woman that she could not read would be too humiliating!

''Oh, yes, please do,'' implored Jessica, adding to her discomfiture.

She stole a quick glance at Burke; he was watching her with a bemused, expectant expression. Jessica went so far as to put the book on her lap. She touched it as if it were some foreign object whose purpose she did not understand. She looked up, her face mirroring her distress, and opened her mouth to speak.

''Oh, Katherine, your spectacles!'' said Burke all of a sudden, as though just remembering. ''No wonder, my sweet.'' He turned to Mrs. Parkington. ''You must forgive my wife, she's a bit vain and refuses to wear her spectacles unless I beg her. She can't see a thing without them.''

Katherine looked down to hide her deepening color, ridiculously overwhelmed with relief. Her heart filled with gratefulness. It was an emotion she had never expected to feel where James Burke was concerned.

The afternoon wore on interminably. The Parkington ladies finally went away after dinner, leaving Katherine alone with Burke. The monotonous drumming of the rain began to get on her nerves, stretching them tighter and tighter as the hours dragged by. She snapped at everything he said, feeling trapped by his constant presence and beleaguered by the choice that his very existence reminded her was still hers to make. When he asked without much hope if she played chess, she said yes. She knew it was unwise; Katie Lennox did not strike her as a chess player. But she was tired of pretending to be stupid. And she needed a diversion, something to take her mind off the fact that time was slipping by, and in twenty-four hours she would very likely be locked in a prison cell.

They took chairs opposite one another at a small table before the fireplace. They were alone in the private parlor; all the others seemed to have disappeared to their own rooms for a nap or some privacy before supper. They began with safe, conventional moves, measuring each other's skill. After a time Katherine reverted to her customary style of play, which was bold, often brilliant, frequently disastrous. Burke's way was more patient and methodical, and very deadly. He took the first game and was on the verge of winning the second when an unexpected gambit on Katherine's part caused him to lose his queen and, soon after, the game. He stared at the board for a long time, studying the maneuver that had defeated him, then looked up with admiration in his eyes.

"I congratulate you, Kate; that was a strong, sharp-witted attack. I shall not put myself in such a vulnerable position again, I promise you. Will you play a third?"

"Of course." But it was growing harder for her to concentrate on the game. Just as she had last night, she began to feel a heavy languor stealing over her as she became almost fixated on Burke's hands. When his thumb rubbed absently across the surface of one of his pawns, she felt a dizzying lurch in her stomach. She caught herself imagining what it would be like if he were to touch her again. Shocked by the thought, she made a foolish move and he took one of her knights.

"Pay attention, Kate," he admonished softly. She flushed and tried harder to apply herself. He left the room for a moment while she contemplated her next move, returning with two glasses of sherry. As he gave her the glass, his fingers brushed hers lightly, and a thrill passed through her with the intensity of an electric shock. She put the glass down before he could see how her fingers trembled.

The candle beside them guttered; Burke rose to replace it with one nearby on the mantel. Instead of sitting down again, he went and stood behind her chair while she struggled to concentrate. The board kept going out of focus; she went blind to everything but the fact of his nearness. Her breath came shallowly, quietly, as if she were waiting for something. Her skin felt thin, as though her body fluids were in danger of escaping and flowing into this charged atmosphere of hushed expectancy. Was she ill? What was this feeling, and why did it only come over her when she was with Burke? The treacherous thought intruded, and would not be banished, that even with Michael it had never been like this.

She moved her bishop finally, almost at random. "It's your move, Major," she said after several minutes had passed and Burke had still not resumed his seat.

He picked up a strand of her hair and slowly wound it around his finger. She shivered and kept her gaze downward. "No, Kate; it's yours." This time she did look up, and his eyes captured hers in a look so full of the promise of passion that she felt on the verge of swooning. "Come upstairs with me," he murmured, his voice low but compelling. Time stopped while they both waited to hear what she would say. Her breath hung suspended; her parted lips were an unconscious invitation he was on the verge of accepting when the door opened and Mrs. Parkington swept in.

"Oh, lovely! I thought I was the only one about. Jessie's having a nap, and it seems everyone else is, too. Thank goodness you're here; I shall go mad without any company until supper."

Katherine felt Burke's hand move softly down her arm to clasp her elbow and lift her gently to her feet. With his arm around her waist, he turned toward the older woman.

"And how we should love to keep you company, madam, but my wife is dropping with exhaustion and can think of nothing but her bed. You must forgive us. Perhaps we'll see you at supper."

With that he guided her out of the room, not waiting for a reply, and Mrs. Parkington was left standing in the middle of the parlor, an expression of worldly resignation swiftly disguising the effects of wounded vanity.

Katherine's thoughts were in turmoil all the way to their second-floor room. Burke's hand never left her—her arm, her elbow, her waist; by the time they reached their room, she felt as if his touch were a burning brand. As soon as the door closed she stepped away from him, determined to confront this thing between them once and for all.

"Stop—please! Don't touch me." She put her arm out stiffly, although he hadn't moved toward her. In fact, he turned his back and went to sit on the edge of the desk, one foot propped on a chair and his other leg stuck straight out in front of him. Something about his negligent attitude in the midst of her agitation annoyed her. "We have to *talk*," she insisted, twisting her hands. "Tell me why you won't let me go, Burke! You know what I am, you couldn't possibly not know! I'm a—" She couldn't say it. He raised his eyebrows, waiting. "A whore!" The word almost caught in her throat; she could feel hot tears stinging behind her eyes. "I take lovers for money. I especially like soldiers, and I don't care which side they're on as long as they have enough gold! I would never risk my life for some stupid, idealistic cause I don't even understand. There wouldn't be anything in it for *me*. Don't you see?"

Burke leaned back on his hands, regarding her with a speculative gleam in his flinty blue eyes. "Over and over you tell me what a whore you are, Kate. To hear you talk, you've bedded half the English army and most of the navy as well. You're a rare generous lass, spreading your favors from Dumfries to Aberdeen. You must not have been at Prestonpans or we wouldn't have lost so badly. Had you been there, you'd have raised the troops' morale.'' He grinned. ''Not to mention their cocks,'' he couldn't help adding. Katherine looked away to hide a blush at his crudity, but she was too late. ''What's this?'' he cried. ''Do you redden when I say the word 'cock,' Kate? How can this be? Every whore I ever knew had a veritable arsenal of blunt expressions to describe the body and its functions. They seem to think saying them out loud gets a man more excited, and who am I to say otherwise? And never have I seen one blush at such a tame word as that.''

She turned back to him, her composure restored. ''You mistake me. Of course I've heard language as bad as that, and much worse, I assure you. I am all you say I am, but you're mistaken if you think I'm proud of it. It was circumstances, not choice, that led me into the life I lead.'' She folded her hands and looked down at them gravely.

''Come, now, Kate, that won't do.'' He had an idea. ''Tell me a ribald joke.''

''A—what?''

''All whores have a storehouse of filthy stories. Tell me one.''

She looked at him blankly. She tried to remember anything that might do. Rory had had a limerick; what was it? '' 'There was a young lady from Dornoch,' '' she began falteringly, then froze. She laughed shakily. ''I forget the rest. 'Twasn't a very funny joke anyway.''

Burke shook his head pityingly. ''Oh, Kate, Kate. Do you still insist on telling me you're a prostitute?''

''Yes! I am, Burke. You have to believe me.''

He smiled. She stiffened, knowing what was coming. ''But I don't believe you. And so you have to persuade me.''

She took a half step backward. ''No.''

"Tomorrow we'll reach Lancaster. After a few days a patrol will escort you to London. There you'll be given a fair trial, and men with the proper authority will decide whether you're—"

"Pah!" she spat contemptuously. "You speak of 'fair' and 'proper' as if Englishmen have any notion of what the words mean!"

He waved away the interruption with a patient smile. His voice lowered a note and seemed to fill the room with a new and unwelcome intimacy. "Nevertheless, time is running out for you. You've exactly one more night to prove you're not a Jacobite spy. And I know of only one way that would convince me."

Fear prickled along her spine and made the palms of her hands damp. The walls of the room seemed to be closing in on her. She tried one last volley.

"Are you really so vain you can't conceive of the possibility that I don't want you to touch me?" she sneered. "Even though, as you so gallantly put it, I may have bedded half the English army, cannot your colossal conceit entertain the idea that I might find *you* repulsive?"

"Repulsive?" He stroked his chin and seemed to consider the notion seriously. "I suppose anything is possible. They say there's a first time for everything." His eyes twinkled at her snort of disgust. "I must say I haven't *noticed* any evidence of repulsion on the too few occasions it's been my great pleasure to touch you. Besides, Kate, even if it were true, a real professional would swallow her distaste; indeed, such reservations would be considered a useless luxury if she were in dire circumstances. And if I may say so, my dear, your circumstances are very dire indeed." He smiled in mock sympathy.

She watched him for a second, unwillingly aware of his undeniable and all but overpowering masculinity. His expression was benign but the blue eyes mocked her, dared her to take up his challenge. And how she longed to hurl it in his face. What pleasure it would give her to tell him, and mean it, that gaol, even hanging, was infinitely preferable to submitting to him! For she had no doubt whatever he meant to carry out his threat and deliver her to the English authorities tomorrow unless she gave herself to him tonight. With a muffled cry of despair she spun away from him and went to stare out the window.

Gripping the sill and staring sightlessly down into the dripping courtyard, Katherine tried to face squarely the question of why it was so difficult for her to consent to sleep with this Englishman. Less than a week ago, she had come within a hair's breadth of bedding one of the most *truly* repulsive men she had ever met. It would have been horrid and grotesque, but she would have done it. What had sustained her in those hours was the memory of what Maule's countrymen had done to her father, and before that to Michael and Rory, and the determination to do something to avenge their deaths. Had that determination deserted her? Why now, even to save her own life, was it so hard to make the same choice?

In a rush, the answer came to her clearly. Taking Maule to bed would have been a cold, calculating shot fired in the course of her personal battle against the English, an act not of love but of war. She could have rationalized it out of existence, so that it was no longer a base thing but rather an act of patriotic duty. But James Burke was another story. Oh, not because she felt anything for him—ach! no, she despised him—but because, God help her, something about him moved her in a way she had thought never to experience again. The sound of his voice made her shiver; his nearness did something to the very hairs on her skin. Bastard! She remembered his insolent kiss last night in front of all those people and her knees began to tremble. It was an outrage! A bloody *Englishman*. What she had almost done with Lieutenant-Colonel Maule brought *honor* to her family's name, she reasoned; but to feel this way about James Burke only brought them shame.

She cursed Burke and her traitorous flesh and strove to calm herself. Then she cursed her own cowardice because she could not face the consequences of defying him. She had made her decision.

CHAPTER 9

Burke rested an elbow on his propped-up knee and watched Katherine with seeming negligence. Her pose was artlessly graceful as she leaned lightly against the window-sill, one long-fingered hand tracing a slow pattern against the glass. What a natural elegance, he marveled; whatever she was, he wouldn't scruple to take her anywhere, even to court, where he did not doubt every dandy in London would fall over himself to meet her. But what would be her fate before a military court? Spy or not, if he were among the tribunal, they'd have to hang *him* before he'd allow her to spend one day in prison. The very idea was repugnant; his mind veered away from thoughts of what would likely happen to her in the next few days. But in all probability she was exactly what she seemed—a beautiful opportunist who was accustomed to using her most valuable possession in order to survive. He supposed the next few minutes would help solve the mystery one way or the other, and he rather wondered at his own emotions. Of course it would be best for her if he were convinced, and thus could help to convince the authorities, that she was no spy, no threat whatever to the peaceful reign of King George. And yet, as much as he wanted her, there was something in him that hoped, irrationally and against all probability, that she was no whore.

With a start he realized she was facing him, looking at

him with a sleepy-eyed half-smile he'd never seen. He
cocked an eyebrow inquisitively. For answer she began to
move toward him, so slowly he could hear the sound of her
petticoat against her legs. When she was within an arm's
length of him she stopped—like a good tease, he thought.
The side of his mouth turned up in a slight sneer. So this is
the way it's to be, lovely Kate. He felt a peculiar mixture
of disappointment and rising excitement.

Katherine had stopped, not to whet his appetite but to
regather the courage that had fled during her mile-long
walk across the room. She blanched at the look of disdain
on his proud face and in that moment came very near to
striking him. But no, this was a game to be played subtly.
If she could succeed in seducing him, so there was no
question in his mind that she was exactly what she claimed
to be, then by tomorrow morning she would be free. The
thought gave her courage, and with something approaching confidence she stepped into the V his legs made.

She rested her hands on his shoulders lightly, her fingertips just grazing his neck. Then she dropped her eyes
hastily, before he could see the desire that had welled up
in her so unexpectedly at this simple touch. Dear God, she
thought, what's happening to me? With a huge effort she
kept her hands where they were and raised her eyes to his,
striving for a seductive look. At least he was not smiling
that insufferable smile, she observed thankfully. Holding
her breath, she leaned into him and slowly, softly, placed a
chaste kiss on his lips. She had meant to draw back after a
moment and tease him with another smoldering glance, but
instead her eyes closed will-lessly and she stood for
incalculable seconds, reveling in the cool, firm touch of his
mouth and the soft feel of his breath on her cheek. And
then it seemed no more than natural to put out her tongue
and run it lightly between his still-closed lips, while
tracing the pattern of his ear with a delicate fingernail.
Very soon she wanted more, and she found herself drawing

in with her mouth until his tongue was between her teeth and it was impossible to say who was kissing whom. Her arms encircled him passionately and she pressed her bosom against his chest, losing herself in a tide of desire that grew almost unbearable—then receded suddenly and sickeningly as the thought intruded that as yet he had made no move to touch *her*. If she'd looked down at that moment and seen Burke's white-knuckled grip on the edge of the desk, this blow to her pride would have been averted. As it was, she could only conclude that so far her approach had been too subtle and it was time to employ blunter measures.

Pulling back slightly, she searched his face for a sign that she'd moved him. His eyes had a cloudy, indistinct look that was new, and a muscle in his jaw was twitching. But Burke was only the second man Katherine had ever touched, and in her naivete she was unable to conclude anything definite from these signs. Desperation gave her courage. She reached for his hand and carried it hesitatingly to her breast. She thought his nostrils flared but she couldn't be sure. Then her own eyes closed in exquisite pleasure as his fingers moved softly, exploringly over her bodice. She felt her nipples grow hard under his hand. When his thumb rasped against one teasingly, she moaned low and swayed against him.

Burke stood upright, all pretense of disinterest gone, and gripped her shoulders hard. When he turned her around so her back was to him, she had a moment of panic that he was pushing her away, rejecting her. But soon it was clear he only wanted a better position from which to slide his hands into the bodice of her gown, to hold her breasts as if they were precious jewels and caress her in a way that made her drop her head back against his shoulder and gasp. His mouth came down and took her with a kind of suppressed violence that caused a prickle of fear, dimming for her the aura of white-hot light that had seemed to surround them. The sudden, shocking thrust of his maleness against her buttocks chilled her even more. Her body was poised between passion and panic as the brief, bloody flag of a memory waved across her mind's eye. But Burke was licking her lips with tiny, catlike movements now, and plucking her nipple between his clever fingers like the strings of a well-loved lute, while his other hand rubbed small, widening circles against her belly and pelvis, leaving a wake of heat everywhere he touched. Fear collapsed under the thoroughness of his assault, and suddenly nothing was left but sweet, uncomplicated wanting. Her whole body shook, and sounds were coming from her mouth she'd never heard before. His teeth closed over her top lip as he caressed the soft, captive flesh with his tongue. She groaned, shivering with pleasure, and then he began a slow, intimate exploration of her mouth. She stopped breathing, drunk with desire. Surely her knees were going to give way if he didn't stop. When she was certain she could not bear it another second, he released her and turned her around again to face him.

"Let me see you." His voice was strangely harsh.

It was a moment before she understood what he meant. Then a slow flush crept up her neck and suffused her cheeks, but without hesitation she began to undo the buttons of her gown, not caring if he noticed how her hands trembled. She pulled her arms out of the sleeves, slid the dress down over her hips, and let it fall in a heap at her feet, dimly wondering if this was the way prostitutes stripped for men. It seemed the easiest way, but she was past caring now. She bent to take off her stockings, then loosened the strings of her petticoat, stepping out of it daintily as it joined her dress on the floor.

She stood before him in her shift, the blush resuming its place on her cheeks. She held her arms awkwardly to her sides, resisting a longing to clasp them in front and hide her nakedness. It was a long moment before she could muster the courage to lift her eyes to his face. Her embarrassment was acute. Would he help her now? A glance at his eyes, smoldering blue ice, assured her he would not. His gaze devoured her but his posture was that of a man in no hurry to speed events along. At last, with fingers that wouldn't stop shaking, she pulled at the ribbons threaded through the thin white material. Too soon it was done. With a resigned shrug of her shoulders, she added the shift to the heap of clothing at her feet and stood before him, completely naked.

Burke didn't move. He was under a spell, mesmerized by her astounding beauty. The firelight flickered over her skin, casting beguiling shadows over the soft contours and bathing her in a pale amber glow. Her lovely breasts were ripe and firm; his hands burned with the memory of their heaviness in his palms. He could see the subtle outline of her ribs down her midriff. She had thighs as white as milk, and he was about to discover if they could possibly be as soft as they looked, like desert sand or a baby's cheek. She was so beautiful, he ached. He stared at her, memorized her, until his hungry eyes locked on the auburn triangle between her leg and her cheeks flamed.

Despite the fire's warmth Katherine shivered, chilled by his stillness. Summoning all the dignity that remained to her, she raised her chin and said softly, "Do you not want me after all, Major Burke?"

Then Burke came to his senses. In one long stride he was before her, his fingers threading her hair. "Do I not, Kate? Do I not?" he whispered fiercely before he kissed her hard, hurting and thrilling her. His hands moved down the length of her back, molding the delicate vertebrae and slender shoulder blades, pressing her into his body until she was no longer sure of her own physical boundaries. He kneaded her buttocks in a shockingly intimate way and pulled her hips against his in the age-old rhythm, and then suddenly he pushed her away. Her mouth opened in disbelief, but he'd only stopped to shed his own clothes. He tore hurriedly at the buttons of his shirt and breeches, kicked impatiently at his boots, and then he was naked. His manhood thrust at her, rock-hard and yearning.

Katherine was not afraid, and she knew he was beautiful. Her eyes found his, and at once for her the game was over: her face was a shining mirror of her certainty that what was happening was a miracle.

Confused by her look, Burke ignored it and obeyed his overloaded senses. He put a hand behind her knees and picked her up, loving the solid feel of her full weight in his arms. "Oh lord, Kate, look at you." She wound her arms around his neck and kissed him. Their lips were locked and his eyes were tightly closed, but somehow he found the bed. He laid her down and sank beside her, his mind reeling at her loveliness. He covered her breasts with reverent hands. "Oh God, Kate. Good Lord."

"I wish you would stop praying," she whispered seriously.

He muffled a laugh against her mouth. "I can't help it, you're such a miracle."

Her arms came around him and he kissed her again, touching her everywhere. She went stiff when she felt his hand between her thighs, but only for a moment. Under his tenderly artful stroking her body relaxed and opened, even when he probed to the very core of her, and soon she was twisting against him and murmuring passion-words she would not have believed she could say to anyone. Burke felt her hot wetness and rejoiced. In a moment he was on her, pushing her legs apart with his knees. When he came into her she said his name, and then her head went back against the pillow.

The world slipped away, and she knew nothing but the way her body felt, bones, blood, and flesh, the feel of this man in her arms and between her legs. She gripped his buttocks and stroked the muscles of his sweat-slippery back, and the faint-hearted thought wafted by that she ought to try to reassert some control, bring her rational self back to life. But it was far too late for that, it was out of her hands; her mind was shredding apart at the edges and she was glad. She yielded to her body's higher wisdom and met Burke's slow, shuddering strokes in perfect rhythm. The part of her that had never been touched before, whose invasion she had thought would be painful and degrading, responded to him with joy and a deep delight. She was tight and slippery and hot, and something was about to happen that before now she had only imagined. Burke slowed, then stopped his steady plunging to savor the deep, intoxicating feel of her. But Katherine knew nothing of lovers' timing and his stillness goaded her. ''Don't—Burke, don't—'' She didn't know how to say it. She kissed him and pushed herself against him, making him stroke her again and again and again. He obliged gladly until, with a high, light cry, she burst free and was flying far above everything in a lovely black void lit by the explosion of a million stars. She heard Burke's helpless groan and pulled him more tightly into her until all awareness of separateness was gone. Whose sweat, whose thudding heart and rasping breath she couldn't tell and didn't care. Blinded, panting, she sailed gently around in the void for incalculable moments, dropping impercept- ibly lower with each lazy revolution until at last she felt the ground beneath her again, soft and welcoming and indes- cribably sweet.

She traced the line of his brow with her thumbs and kissed him in a peaceful frenzy of gratitude, her mind only half-engaged. How lovely, how lovely. She'd heard there was pain the first time, but for her there had only been this deep, transporting pleasure. She shifted her position carefully so as not to dislodge him, unwilling to lose him even now. He smiled down at her, his eyes unknowingly reflecting the same awed wonder that was in hers.

"Katherine Lennox." He said the words respectfully. "Kate Lennox. The beautiful Katie Lennox." Katherine colored foolishly. "You take my breath away, Miss Lennox. You've made me your slave."

"Ah, grand, I've always wanted a slave," she murmured, brushing her lips across his lashes.

"Your wish is my command, beautiful Kate. What would you have me do?" She blushed again, this time at the thought that flashed through her mind. Burke, watching her closely, barked with laughter, then groaned in unison with Katherine as he felt himself slipping out of her. That made them both laugh, and before long they were side by side, giggling like children into each other's faces, sharing the pillow.

"Who do you look like, your father or your mother?" Burke asked softly after a few moments, resting his hand in the hollow of her waist.

"My—" father, she almost said, but caught herself in time. "My mother tells me I might look like my father. But I never knew him."

"Ah, I'd forgotten that. What a hard life you've had, Katie Lennox." She shrugged, and he kissed her shoulder impulsively. "Is your mother alive, then?"

"Aye. She lives in Edinburgh."

"That's right, you told me. Is she well? How does she live?"

"I send her money," she lied. "And she is not well."

"I'm sorry. Is she very ill?"

"No, it's—her mind. She grows vague. I think it's her way to escape from the pain of living." She paused, remembering her mother as she'd last seen her. Losing her husband had pried away the last finger of her grip on reality. She could not accept it, and so she had repeopled her world with all the loved ones she'd lost. Katherine had rationalized leaving by telling herself her mother would hardly even know she was gone, her fantasy life was so complete.

Burke watched her stricken face quietly. "Sometimes, Kate, you look like your heart is breaking."

She shrugged again in an attempt to shake off her sadness. When she spoke there was anger buried in her tone. "It's not a good time to be old and vulnerable in Scotland, Major, in case you had not noticed."

Ah, thought Burke, that was better; he could deal with her when she was only angry.

"And you," she said after a time, "how has your family fared during the uprising, living so close to the border? Have you lost anyone you love to a savage Highlander's sword?"

He smiled slightly and shook his head. "They all have such weak arms and poor aim, their swords never meet their mark." Katherine lifted her lip derisively but did not rise to the bait. "Besides, I'm the only son in the family."

"Have you any sisters?"

"I have one sister." He smiled unconsciously and his tone grew warm. "Her name is Diana and she's sixteen years old. One day she'll be very beautiful. And I have a stepsister," he continued more briskly, "the daughter of the woman my father married after my mother died. Her name is Olivia. She's already beautiful."

Katherine's eyes narrowed in thought. "Is she married, this stepsister?" she asked offhandedly.

"No, though not for want of offers. I rather think she's waiting for me."

"How conceited you are," she scoffed, unaccountably piqued.

"Do you think so? Perhaps I have reason to be."

"What on earth for?"

"Why, Kate, not an hour ago you told me I was repulsive. Now here you are, naked in my bed, pining for me to kiss you again and make love to you."

"Ach! Arrogant beast!" She raised up on her elbow and made as if to box his ear, but he caught her wrist and bore her back down to the pillow, laughing and stopping her protest with his mouth. After a time she quieted, and Burke began a slow, dreamy exploration of her body with his hands.

"Did you know I've been wondering since the day we met if your skin could possibly be as soft as it looks?"

"And what have you decided?" she asked, feigning disinterest.

"Mmm. I've decided it tastes even better than it feels."

Her eyes closed as his tongue traced a warm trail along her shoulder, tickled her armpit, then moved to the base of her neck. There he kissed her with a loud smacking sound, causing her to squeal and push him away indignantly.

Burke laughed delightedly. "I'd like to kiss you everywhere, Kate," he told her in a low, husky voice, sending little shivers along the skin of her arms. For a few more seconds he continued to tell her what he'd like to do with her until Katherine, shaken and dizzy, sat up abruptly and put a hand over his lips.

"I fear such manly exertion as that would leave you weak and fatigued unless you were fortified first with a hearty meal. Are you not hungry, Major Burke? I'm starving!" With that she jumped out of bed, clutching the sheet to cover her nakedness, and set about retrieving her clothes from the pile on the floor.

Burke groaned. "Hungry! How can you be hungry now?" He lay back with his arms behind his head, forgetting everything but the pleasure it gave him to watch her.

With her back to him, Katherine suddenly noticed his avid interest reflected in the mirror over the bureau in front of her. "Supper is at seven, Major," she reminded him pointedly, unaware of the interesting spectacle her shapely white derriere presented to his rapt gaze. "Should you not be up?"

"Ah, Miss Lennox, I've been up since I met you, and am particularly so at this moment," he grinned lewdly.

Katherine could think of no suitable response. She kept her head down, seeming intent on rolling her stocking up over her knee.

"I think I like watching you dress almost but not quite as much as I like watching you undress," he went on matter-of-factly, enjoying her discomfort. "You do them both so prettily."

"I should like to see *you* dressed soon, sir," she retorted, straightening up and shaking the wrinkles out of her gown. She thrust her arms into the sleeves and threw it over her head. Burke chose that moment to leap from the bed with a warlike shout and seize her around the middle from behind. Trapped inside the dress with her arms still over her head, she yelped in surprise and irritation, vainly fighting to wriggle free from the constricting material and from Burke's hands which were suddenly everywhere. "Stop it!" she shrieked when he began tickling her, kicking her legs at him blindly and ineffectually, striving to break out of his grasp that brought her half pleasure, half torture. Whoosh! There was the sound of buttons flying as the gown was whisked back over her head and thrown aside. Burke began kissing her, holding her immobile in an iron-hard grasp until she stopped struggling. "Oh Christ, Kate, I want you again. Please," he coaxed hoarsely against her mouth, "let me, let me." He had her against the bed and she felt her knees give way as he pushed her backwards. At once she felt as if she were on fire. She pulled him down fiercely, clutching his shoulders and crying, "Yes! Yes, oh Burke, yes," unashamedly, forgetting everything in the scorching wave of lust that engulfed her. He lifted her shift up over her hips and opened her legs with urgent hands. Holding her waist, he

pushed steadily into her with an oath that was more like a
prayer, then leaned over and pulled her nipple into his
mouth. She cried out almost instantly, her hips jerking uncontrollably while tears splashed down her cheeks. Immediately afterward he poured himself into her, grinding
his teeth and groaning like a man undergoing torture.

They collapsed against each other, spent and shaken and
strangely subdued by the quick intensity of their passion.
Burke drew a ragged breath as he traced the salty line of a
tear down her cheek with his finger, then kissed her with
infinite tenderness. "I didn't hurt you, did I, Kate?" She
shook her head and looked away. "You're so lovely. I
wonder if I'll ever have enough of you," he said seriously,
almost to himself. Then he gently disengaged himself and
stood up, breaking the spell. "But now I *am* hungry.
Enough of this lolling about naked, woman, have you no
shame? Up with you now and into your clothes. Up, I
say!"

Katherine sat up and, with shaking hands, straightened
her shift and retied the bodice. The muscles in her thighs
felt like jelly. Keeping her mind a careful blank, she tried
to attend to what Burke was saying as he pulled on his
clothes. But her thoughts kept returning to a vision of the
scene just played out on this bed, and each time the blood
rushed to her cheeks and she longed for the floorboards to
swallow her up where she sat. Wanton! Shameless! How
could she have behaved so coarsely? She was bewildered
now by the ferociousness of her response. "Yes, oh Burke,
yes!" she heard herself saying, and mentally cringed in
anguish. Well, she thought, pulling herself up, I meant to
play the whore, didn't I? If he wasn't convinced before, by
God, I'll warrant he is now! I was merely throwing myself
into the role to insure that he would believe me. And in
the process I've learned an interesting thing about myself,
that I could play my part with such—*enthusiasm*. Perhaps
I should have made a profession of the stage!

Perceiving dimly that her reasoning was specious and not caring to dwell on the subject any longer, she began to look about for her dress. She spied it in the corner where Burke had hurled it and was about to retrieve it when he swept it up himself and brought it to her. "I promise not to capture you in it this time," he told her with a laugh, while she lowered the dress over her head with new wariness. "Here, let me do that," he said when her fingers fumbled at the buttons.

"I can do it myself," she said irritably, trying to push him away. But he merely continued to fasten up the front of her dress, unruffled.

"I say, you seem to have lost a couple of buttons at the top here. You really ought to be more careful in the future, my dear."

"Oh, you—" She clamped her lips shut and decided not to give him the satisfaction of seeing her lose her temper. When he was finished, his hands lingered on her breasts, as if reluctant to break contact. Unbelievingly, Katherine was stirred anew, and she stepped back from him abruptly as if she'd been burned. Burke raised a puzzled brow. "My pins," she muttered, turning away to search a bit blindly among the rumpled sheets for her scattered hairpins. Then she went into the smaller room and sat down in front of the mirror over the dressing table. She began to brush her hair fiercely, almost enjoying the invigorating pain she was causing.

"My God, woman, you'll pull it out by the roots. I can't stand to watch you. Let me—"

"Damn and blast!" Katherine yelled, slamming the brush down on the table with a crash. "I am twenty years old! I don't tell you how to clean your pistol or shoe your horse, Major High and Mighty James Burke, and I'll thank you not to tell me how to perform my own goddam toilette!" She flounced back around to face the mirror, seized the brush, and proceeded to pull quite a lot of her hair out by the roots.

Burke stood open-mouthed. After a few seconds he erupted in laughter, throwing his head back and bellowing with glee. Katherine watched him venomously out of the corner of one eye while she coiled her hair into a knot and stabbed pins into it at random. Burke sat down on the bed heavily and wiped at his eyes, still hooting softly. When she was ready, she stood up and stalked to the door.

"If you're through making an ass of yourself, do you think we might go down to supper?"

He locked his fingers around his boot and rested his chin on his knee, suddenly in no hurry to go. "Ah, Kate, Kate, you fill with delight and wonder. Women have always been mysterious creatures to me, but you are a complete and total enigma."

"I'm gratified to hear it. May we go now?"

" 'I'm gratified to hear it,' " he repeated, frowning. "Who really taught you to speak like that? It's hardly the idiom of a poor Scottish camp follower, is it?"

She bit her lip. "I told you how I came by my education. Anyway, after—this afternoon, can you possibly doubt that I am exactly what I've said I am? Can you?" she pressed when he didn't answer, merely stared back at her with an intensity that matched hers. She felt a rising panic. "I've kept my part of the bargain, Burke! I've proved I'm not a spy." Still he stared at her without speaking. When she thought she would snap from the tension, he stood up and came toward her, his face unreadable.

"Ah, the bargain. Yes, Kate, you've kept your part of the bargain. Now let's go have our supper, shall we?"

She took a step backward. A feeling of icy dread began to form in the pit of her stomach.

"Wait, Burke. Are you—We—" She searched his face but it was blank; she could read nothing from his features. She took a deep breath. "We have to come to terms. You said you'd let me go if I—proved to you I'm a—whore. I've done what you wanted. Now you must let me go. And I—I want to go now. *Tonight*."

"Kate," he said after a moment's hesitation, "sit down for a minute."

She felt another thrill of panic. "No! Why?" When Burke sighed and ran a hand through his hair with uncharacteristic irresolution, her agitation grew. Finally, when he still said nothing, she confronted him, fear turning her voice to a whisper. "You're not going to let me go, are you?"

"Listen to me, love."

"You bastard!" she hissed. "You're a lying—"

"Stop. I'm not in the mood for one of your tirades. Sit down and listen to me."

"How could you?" Her sea-blue eyes were flashing silver sparks. "After I—after you *made* me—"

"Ha! That won't wash, you know. No one made you do anything." He leaned against the door resignedly and folded his arms. "I'm afraid you're laboring under a misapprehension, Kate, no doubt caused by a great deal of wishful thinking. But if you're honest with yourself, you'll admit I never did say I would let you go. No matter what amorous incentives you offered me," he added with a faint smile.

"*What?*" Her voice was a shriek of disbelief. "That's a *lie*," she sputtered, "you know it is! You said—"

"I said I wasn't convinced you were what you claimed you were, and I was unwilling to convey the wrong impression to the men at Lancaster. It was you who leapt to the conclusion that I would let you go once I *was* convinced."

"Liar!" Her anger was so potent she could scarcely speak.

He shook his head, controlling his temper with difficulty. "Even if I did let you go, how would you make your way? Where would you go?''

"I would go to Edinburgh!" she cried. "If you're worried about the horse, take her back by all means, I can walk! And you can have your damned dress, too, and your coat, your stupid boots—"

"Don't be an idiot. Do you really believe you could walk a hundred miles in the middle of November, in a whore's gown and a worn-out pair of shoes?"

"Yes!" she declared passionately. "To get away from you, I would crawl if I had to!"

His eyes turned to blue ice. "Some would say you already have."

She drew in her breath, stunned. "Judas! Filthy, slimy serpent! Son of a—"

"You're boring me," he drawled, turning away.

"Villain! Even if you never said you'd let me go, you knew I *believed* you would, and you said nothing to disabuse me! You're a wicked, vile, depraved, evil-minded denegerate who doesn't deserve—"

"Oh, for the love of God—"

"*Englishman*!" This was the foulest curse of all; she loaded the word with all the hatred she felt for him at that moment.

Burke stared at her for a long second, then expelled his breath in a short, hopeless sigh. He held out a hand. "Come, Kate. It's getting late."

"*Never*." She shrank away, backing toward the small table beside the bed. Before he could guess her intention, she opened the drawer and seized the heavy pistol he'd put there the night before. In one fluid movement, she whirled around and leveled the gun at his midsection.

Burke stopped dead. If any other woman had brandished a pistol at him, he'd have laughed and taken it away from her. But Katherine had murder in her eyes and the small hand holding the gun was perfectly steady.

"Kate," he said quietly, "don't be a fool."

"I've already been a fool," she responded in the same

even tone, ''and I shan't be again. Now, walk slowly into
the dressing room, Major Burke.'' She inclined her head
toward the little room to her right, keeping the gun
trained on him.

He tried again. ''If you run away, you'll be caught, and
then they'll hang you for a certainty. Can't you see that?
You're sealing your own fate by doing this, love. Come
with me to Lancaster, where I'll tell them you're the
foulest whore this side of Babylon. And then they'll let
you go.''

She smiled unpleasantly. ''You really have a low regard
for my intelligence, don't you, Major? But I am not
debating this with you. Go into that room now, or I will
shoot you.''

He believed her. He circled around her warily and then
backed toward the dressing room. Katherine followed,
keeping her distance. When he halted on the threshold
and seemed about to speak again, she shook her head and
gestured with the gun for him to keep going.

The key was on the inside. With Burke backed up
against the chair in front of the dressing table, there were
only three feet between him and the door. Katherine
pulled the door almost closed and reached around warily
with her left hand to retrieve the key, all the while keeping
the gun pointed at him. It was while she was withdrawing
the key and inserting it into the lock at the front that
Burke suddenly kicked the door closed on her right wrist
and the gun exploded. She heard a grunt of pain and
threw the door open wide in time to see him crashing
backward against the mirrored wall, blood gushing from
his forehead.

She screamed.

Within seconds, a maid—the one who had served them
breakfast that morning—ran into the room. ''Oh, ma'am,
what's happened? I heard—'' She stopped short, suddenly
seeing Burke, and then the smoking gun in Katherine's
hand. Her eyes widened in terror and she began to shriek,

high, piercing screams in rapid succession. In a panic, Katherine dropped the gun and ran past her out of the bedroom and into the hall. A man in a dressing gown watched her go by in amazement. She flew down the stairs, skirts flying, and was pulled up short by the sight of every guest in the dining parlor watching her open-mouthed, some rising from their chairs and coming toward her.

"An accident! Cleaning his gun—my husband—Is there a doctor? Oh, help me, he's bleeding!"

"I'm a doctor," announced a portly, older gentleman with stooped shoulders and a capable air. "What room?" He pushed back his chair and dabbed his lips with a napkin.

"Second floor, the—last room on the right!" She looked up to see the little maid, Trudy, standing at the top of the stairs, hiccuping hysterically and pointing her arm straight at Katherine. "I'll get—bandages!" she cried quickly. "With our horses!" With that she dashed out the front door and around the side of the inn to the stables.

She found the mare quickly, found a bridle for her after another minute.

" 'Ere now, wot's this?" demanded the rough-looking ostler who had been eating his supper by lamplight in the tack room.

"Emergency! My husband's shot, I must fetch a doctor. Take care, she's *my* horse!" She stepped in front of the mare when the groom made a move as if to stop her. There was no time for a saddle. She led the horse outside to the block and mounted her bareback.

"Stop that woman! Stop her!" A man had come around the side of the building and was blocking the exit from the stableyard.

Katherine kicked her horse's sides fiercely and the mare lunged forward. The man fell back in fright as horse and rider flew past. The mare's hooves sent sparks flying off the cobblestones. They passed the inn's entrance at a gallop, and from the corner of her eye Katherine saw a knot of people standing in the door and gaping at her. She bent low over the mare's neck, encouraging her in low, urgent tones, and very soon the sound of shouting receded as she retraced the route she and Burke had traveled so recently.

The rain had stopped and the night air was cool and damp. Wisps of cloud obscured the moon; she had to slow down in order to see to keep the horse on the road. After a ten-minute canter she came to a Y in the road she remembered from yesterday. The road to the left led to Keswick, Burke had told her. She paused irresolutely. Every instinct told her to go to the right, northeast toward home. But reason insisted that was what they would expect her to do. Better to head northwest for a while, skirting the Solway Firth or perhaps even finding a boat to take her across it, before turning east toward Edinburgh.

With a heavy sigh, she turned the mare to the left. Her pace quickened when the moon broke free from the misty cloud cover, slowed when it disappeared again. Predatory owls and their hapless victims were her only companions throughout the long night. At dawn she guided the mare into a small wood to rest. And there, huddled against a tree in the chill morning fog, her head resting on her drawn-up knees, she finally allowed herself to confront the vision she'd been keeping at bay. She relived the horrifying scene over and over, shivering uncontrollably in reaction. Tears streamed down her face as sobs overwhelmed her. The thought struck that she ought to have let them capture and hang her. For although she had not wanted to pull the trigger, had not meant to, and in fact would not have been able to do it, the truth remained, ugly and implacable: she had murdered James Burke.

PART II

CHAPTER 10

A thin wind blew damply across the sodden landscape as, low overhead, gunmetal clouds lumbered toward the watery light in the western sky. Moss-covered boulders lay like sleeping cattle in the fields. A brook overran its steep-sided banks, and the smell of wet earth was dark and pungent in the late afternoon air.

The wind blew a sudden sharp gust, and Katherine hunched lower over her horse's mane, clenching her teeth to stop their chattering. She stared numbly ahead, blind to the slowly passing countryside, intent on nothing but forward movement. The dampness that seemed to have penetrated to her very bones made her hair stand out like a billowy halo. Occasionally a low moan escaped her bluish lips and was snatched away on the chill breeze. She was so hungry she felt light-headed. Fatigue sat on her shoulders like a sack full of stones, and there wasn't a particle of her body that didn't ache with every plodding step of her weary horse.

She was almost to Keswick; only another hour or so, she reckoned. Strange, then, that a sense of aimlessness was growing stronger with every mile, making it hard for her to care what happened next. Listlessly she asked herself what all this haste and stealth were for; what did it really matter whether they caught her or not? She shuddered and tried to push the unwholesome idea from her mind, but it would not be banished. She heard a forlorn but insistent voice inside demanding to know what, after all, she was trying so hard to get back to. A house that could never be her home, a mother who hardly recognized her? A life of numbing loneliness, whose bleak reality was what had propelled her into this bizarre enterprise in the first place? And with that came a new thought, irrational but powerful, that death was following her, overtaking everyone who touched her life, first her family and loved ones and now the only man who—

Her thoughts broke off; that mind path was still too painful to traverse. Since that last wrenching, corrosive outpouring of grief and remorse two nights ago, she'd deliberately made herself numb, conscious of nothing but the horse's next heavy step, the feel of dampness and cold, relentless hunger and bone-deep fatigue. If she allowed herself to confront the reality of what she had done at Helvellyn, she thought she might go mad. At the very least she wouldn't be able to keep running, and they would capture her. And avoiding capture was the one thing, the lone goal she still possessed, that gave her existence any meaning.

A patch of unfamiliar color a ways off to the right nudged her to weary attention. Through a copse of scraggly trees she could make out what looked like a tumbled-down building, perhaps an abandoned cottage. She set up straighter and squinted. She could see part of a thatched roof through the tree limbs and, looking down, the remains of what might have been a path leading from the lane she was traveling. She turned the horse onto the path and walked her cautiously through the copse, straining her ears for a sound. When she was out of the trees and within twenty feet of the cottage, she stopped. All was silent except for a low sighing of wind in the woods behind her. She stared at the half-ruined dwelling intently, noting its one shuttered window and the sagging board that served as a door, now standing ajar. And then she saw the thin trickle of smoke rising from the broken stone chimney at the back, and hopelessness closed over her once more like a cloak. The cottage was inhabited, and Katherine could not allow herself to be seen.

Tears of frustration blinded her. She must turn the horse and go back to that damp, lonely valley. She felt a surge of anger mingled with recklessness rise in her chest. What difference did it make, after all? She'd been riding for two long, cold days from the inn at Helvellyn, and in all that time she'd seen no one. Surely if she were being pursued this way there would have been some sign of it by now. She was on the verge of exhaustion; to spend another shivering, sleepless night without shelter in nothing but this damp linen dress would be suicide. She needed food, and so did her horse. She stared hard at the cottage, then at the woods through which she had come. When she looked back at the cottage, a figure had materialized in the doorway.

She blinked and drew in her breath. Through the gathering gloom she could see it was a woman, a very old woman, dressed in rags and holding a stick in her hand. She took two steps toward Katherine and uttered something in a harsh, unintelligible accent, half challenge, half question.

"Have you a bit of bread, Mother?" Katherine called out hopefully. "I've not eaten in two days."

The old woman scuttled closer at that and held out her hand, blackened palm upward. A gleam of interest briefly lit her coarse, unkind face.

"I'm afraid I've nothing to give you," Katherine said regretfully, holding up her own empty palms.

The woman bared her teeth in a snarl and raised the cudgel menacingly. She pointed it at the mare and said something in her guttural rasp that Katherine took to be an offer of food in return for the horse.

Again she shook her head. "Nay, I cannot give you my horse, Mother, but I would gladly work for you. Mayhap you'll be needing wood for your fire, your clothes washed or mended—" She broke off when the old crone commenced to abuse her with a string of inarticulate epithets. Sensing that further conversation was useless and biting back a few choice curses of her own, Katherine turned the mare around. With surprising agility in one so ancient, the woman charged, brandishing her cudgel high over her head. Katherine kicked the mare hard, but the horse was too tired to move quickly. She saw the stick whizzing toward her, felt a sharp, stunning *crack!* on her kneecap, and yelped with pain and fury. Startled, the mare leapt forward and cantered jaggedly down the path to the lane, with Katherine clutching at her neck to stay aboard. They rode for nearly a quarter of a mile before fatigue finally overwhelmed the horse's fright and she trotted dispiritedly to a halt.

Katherine slid off her back and leaned against the massive shoulder, burying her face in the rough mane. A sob burst from her lips and tears flowed down her cheeks in rivulets. It was too much. She was so tired, she was fainting with hunger, Burke was dead . . . She stepped back and gazed up at the sky. Leaden, dead, it gave back no hope. She felt an urge to lie down on the ground with her arms outstretched and stare up at the flat, gray clouds, to feel the tears on her face and just lie there until darkness came and there was nothing left to see. Then she would close her eyes, and she would hear and see nothing, and it would not matter whether she slept or died.

She shook herself. This was madness. No, not madness, only the borderline of exhaustion. She scanned the western horizon dully. Another hour of daylight at best. Could she reach Keswick? Probably. But what would she do when she got there, penniless and on the verge of collapse? Despair threatened again, but she pushed it away and squared her shoulders. She would do something; she just didn't yet know what.

An accomplished horsewoman, still she had never ridden bareback for more than an hour at a time in her life, and every muscle ached from the unwonted jolting. The thought of remounting was too painful to be borne; she would walk awhile.

Pulling on the unwilling mare's bridle, she set off into the silent valley, empty but for a scattering of sheep and wild goats. A murky sunset was coasting close to the horizon between two distant fells. At least she felt safe here, for she was so patently alone. She scanned the far-off hills, confirming their emptiness of threat or salvation alike, then turned around to peer at the darkening skyline behind her. A blacker dot against the dusky hill she'd just descended caught her eye and made her frown. With a thrill of alarm, she watched while the dot grew larger and transformed itself into a horse and rider. Lacking the strength to mount the mare unaided, she looked about for something to stand on. She spied a boulder on the side of the road ten feet ahead and led the horse over to it hurriedly. Astride, she kicked the mare into a bone-rattling canter and set off down the lane.

A hundred paces later she looked back. The horse and rider had gained on her to a frightening extent. Something about the man riding . . . Unknowingly she let the mare slow to a stop. She was twisted around, peering into the dusk, intent on the fast-approaching rider. Paralyzed, empty-headed, she watched as he drew nearer, until all at once his identity burst on her consciousness like an exploding star. *Burke!* The easy way he sat his horse, his shoulders, the way he held his head—Burke! He wasn't dead, she hadn't killed him! The emptiness she'd been carrying inside was suddenly filled to overflowing and she felt breathless, euphoric. She put both hands on top of her head as if to keep it on. Then a jolt of alarm rocketed through her, as the shattering thought struck home that she was still running for her life!

With a savage slap she galvanized the horse into a gallop. The exhausted mare ran as fast as she could go, but a single backward glance told Katherine this race would be over quickly. There was no place to go but straight ahead; twin gulches lined the rough road at this point and the mare hadn't enough strength to jump across. Even if she had, the stallion would overtake her on the flat before she went fifty paces. Frantically, Katherine looked back again. Now Burke was so close she could see his face. His eyes glowed with a nearly rabid intensity and his teeth were bared in a feral grin. She slashed the reins across the flagging mare's shoulder, but it was no use. The pursuing horse's hooves sounded as loud as the mare's—and now he was beside her!

"No!" she howled in desolate fury as Burke's arm snaked out and seized her around the middle. With no saddle to cling to, she clutched wildly at her horse's mane, but his grip only tightened. She felt herself being pulled off the mare while the two horses cantered blindly down the stony path. She turned her head to the side and bit down on his forearm with all the strength she had left, and was rewarded by a furious cry of pain. His hold loosened fractionally and she felt herself falling. The mare was still running beside her; for a horrifying second she thought she would be trampled under the thudding hooves. But she hit the ground hard and fell forward in time to see both horses trotting harmlessly away from her, before her forehead struck a sharp rock and she lay still, face down in the road.

Burke wheeled his horse around so violently the stallion reared before charging headlong back up the road. He leapt from the saddle while the horse was still running, six feet shy of the prostrate, unmoving form on the ground. He ran to her, knelt, and touched the bright head.

"Kate," he whispered; "Kate!" He turned her over so she lay on her back. A cut above her eyebrow was bleeding profusely. His hands moved over her delicately, searching for broken bones. When he found none, he pulled her to a semi-sitting posture against the inside of his bent knee and held his handkerchief to the wound on her forehead. She made a soft sound in her throat and tried to sit up straighter. His arms went around her, and her head fell against his chest. He felt her hands touching him; he closed his eyes and inhaled the autumn scent of her hair.

With a suddenness that left him dazzled, she jerked out of his embrace and scuttled backwards. Then he saw the knife he kept in his pocket gleaming in her hand. They rose to their feet simultaneously.

She'd already tried to murder him once; he was perfectly sure she wanted to kill him now. That certainty brought back all the fury he'd been riding with for two days, only now it was doubled because she'd made a fool of him a second time. She was backing away toward his own horse, her arm extended so the tip of the knife was pointed at his throat. His anger settled into a cold, menacing resolve. But, God, what a sight she was! Her wild hair was standing on end, her face streaked with blood, her extraordinary eyes flashing their fanatic determination. Oh no, beautiful Kate, he thought with a quieter, more dangerous determination of his own, not this time.

He took a step toward her, then another. She held her ground but he saw a telltale glint of panic in her eyes. With stunning swiftness, his hand flashed out and grabbed her right wrist in a painful grip. Ignoring her startled cry, he bore her arm backward, at the same time pulling her body intimately into his.

"Drop it," he said softly, conversationally, his mouth only inches from hers.

"Go to hell!"

He smiled. He caught her other wrist easily and twisted it behind her back as well, so she was pressed against him and helpless.

"Drop it," he said again, shoving the hand that held the knife higher. Katherine's head went back and her nostrils flared, but her fingers never slackened their grip. She was clenching her teeth to bite back a scream. He pushed higher, a frown replacing the ruthless smile. "Drop the knife, damn it." Something perverse in him wanted to see her beaten. Her eyes fluttered closed; her face was pinched with agony. Still she clutched the knife, as though it were welded to her hand. "For God's sake, I'll break your arm!" he burst out in wonder and consternation. Incapable of speaking, she shook her head. And staring down into that lovely, stubborn face, white-lipped and intent with an obstinacy he could not understand, Burke knew he'd lost. He whispered a fearful oath, then let go of her left wrist and reached around with his free hand for the knife. With difficulty he pried it out of her stiff fingers and tossed it on the ground behind her.

He knew if he released her arm suddenly, he would only cause her more pain. So by infinitely slow degrees he lowered the tortured limb, watching as color of the palest pink returned to her cold cheeks. For the first time he noticed the bluish hollows under her eyes, the weary droop of her shoulders. He no longer wanted to hurt her. Reaching behind her, he gently massaged her upper arm, all the while searching her face for—ah, he didn't know what. She kept her eyes downcast, her silky lashes black against the whiteness of her skin. When her lips began to tremble he was undone, and suddenly he was kissing her. In a rush it all came back, how it felt to hold her, how her lips tasted, the texture of her mouth, her tongue. He felt her soften against him and rejoiced. He was feverishly conscious of every inch of her, molded to the length of his lean, hard body. He wanted her on the ground, under him, arching against him and calling his name as she had before. His hand found her breast and caressed it until the soft peak hardened under his fingers and she gasped into his mouth. He held her tighter and deepened the kiss, drunk with longing, and it seemed their bodies were melting into each other. It was hard to stand upright any longer. With unbearable excitement he realized he could take her here in the wet road, their clothes on. His fingers slipped, trembling, into the front of her gown and gently touched the warm, sweet flesh of her bosom.

Abruptly, as though she'd been bitten by a viper, Katherine pushed him away. Her eyes, dilated with desire seconds ago, shot arrows of fire. "How *dare* you?" she hissed, in a voice full of shock and loathing. She was breathing hard, her face mirroring the battle she waged inside. She wiped her mouth with the back of her hand in a gesture of pure disgust, and then she actually spat on the ground.

For perilous seconds he was afraid he was going to kill her. His hands clenched and unclenched; the effort he made to keep them from encircling that slender white throat was enormous. When he finally spoke his tone was very quiet, but as loaded with hatred as hers. "I want to be there," he said with perfect truthfulness, "when they hang you." For the barest instant he thought he saw a shattered look in her eyes, but then her chin came up defiantly and the look, if it had been there at all, was gone.

"You're an animal," she enunciated, eyes flashing with nothing now but bitterness and revulsion.

He turned his back on her and strode to where her horse was grazing. His heart was hammering in his chest from fury and frustration. He led the mare back and moved toward Katherine to put her up. She stepped away reflexively, her mouth curling with distaste at the thought of his touch. He cursed her viciously, seized her around the waist, and roughly swung her to the mare's back. Then he mounted the stallion and set off at a fast trot without looking back.

Briefly Katherine considered turning around and riding the other way. Instead she squared her shoulders painfully and kicked the mare into a matching trot. She kept a dozen paces behind him, her eyes boring into his back, directly between his shoulder blades. She wished she had a gun.

"A bath first, or supper, my love?" Burke glanced over at Katherine who sat huddled, barefoot, before the just-kindled fire, then turned back to the chambermaid without waiting for an answer. "A bath, I think, with plenty of hot water. And bring a bottle of wine as well. Then supper, here in the room." The maid curtsied and closed the door.

Katherine held her frozen fingers closer to the flames and tried to stop shivering. The brief, jolting ride in the deepening dusk had all but finished her. While dragging herself up the short flight of stairs to their room in this plain but respectable alehouse, she'd experienced a wave of dizziness and had had to grip the bannister to keep herself upright. Burke had spoken sharply from the landing, impatient with her slowness, and she'd looked down to hide her white, perspiring face. Fainting in front of him would be the final humiliation. She glanced up at him now as he leaned against the door, arms folded, regarding her coldly through narrowed lids. They stared at each other in wordless enmity until he shook his head in disgust and went to unpack his bags.

Ten minutes later there was a knock at the door and several servants entered bearing a tub, buckets of steaming water, soap and towels, and a bottle of wine with two glasses. When they'd filled the tub and gone away, Burke sat down on the edge of the bed and lit his pipe.

"Well?" he said innocently, raising one haughty eyebrow and gesturing at the tub with a full glass of wine.

With a shiver she realized he meant to sit there and watch her bathe. Then angry color suffused her cheeks, but she bit back the scathing words on her tongue. What difference did it make, anyway? Let the bastard think he was embarrassing her if it pleased him. The fact was, she was *beyond* embarrassment where he was concerned, beyond feeling anything whatever except loathing and a burning determination to escape from him again, once and for all. For one second the treacherous thought intruded that barely an hour ago she'd let him kiss her, had in fact come bewilderingly close to letting him make love to her in the middle of the road, but she shoved it aside peremptorily; it had no place in the edifice of feelings she was erecting to sustain her through this ordeal, and so she would not consider it.

She raised her eyes and they stared at each other for incalculable seconds in silent, deadly combat. He was daring her. Knowing he thought her too cowardly to accept his challenge gave her the courage she needed.

She stood up. Without looking away, she began to un-button her gown. It was the cold that caused her fingers to tremble so, she assured herself. She stepped out of the heavy, wet dress, hesitated only a second, and pulled her damp shift over her head. She considered fleetingly that she must look terribly thin, then thrust that silly thought from her head as well. What did she care what he thought of her? She stood straight, head erect, hands at her sides, and looked back at him with as clear and untroubled a gaze as she could manage. His expression was not con-temptuous now. It was fierce, frightening in its intensity, and revealed such a concentrated scrutiny of her nakedness that at last she was indeed forced to look away. The tub seemed miles away, the walk to it endless. When she reached it she thought briefly of facing him during her bath; *that* would show him how much his childish game

affected her. But her courage took her this far and no
farther, and she turned her back on him hastily. She
stepped into the bath and sank into the blessedly hot water
with an audible sigh of relief.

Burke sipped his wine moodily, his eyes never leaving
that delicate white back, the slender arms that splashed so
prettily in the steaming water. After a few minutes he laid
his pipe on the table beside the bed and poured another
glass of wine. He crossed the room and stood in front of
the tub, staring down at her with a small, insolent smile.
Unwillingly, she covered her breasts with her hands,
keeping her gaze on a spot on the wall in front of her. His
lip twitched derisively. He wanted to tell her not to
bother, her breasts weren't that remarkable; but this
would have been such a patent falsehood, he couldn't
bring himself to say it.

"Here. Drink it." He handed her the glass. After a
moment she took it. She drew her knees up protectively
and took a small sip, then another.

"Thank you," she said stiffly.

She thought he would go away then, but he didn't.
Instead he went down on one knee beside her, resting his
arm casually on the side of the tub. He dipped his index
finger in the water and traced a pattern on her shin with
apparent idleness. His hand moved slowly up her knee and
caressed it insinuatingly while Katherine held her breath.
When his fingers moved to the inside of her thigh and
exerted enough pressure to press her legs slightly apart, she
gasped and swatted at his hand, sending a small wave of
water over the side and wetting his shirt. He laughed
shortly, his eyes alight with unhealthy amusement, and sat
back on his heels.

"How did you get the bruise?" he asked, glancing un-
sympathetically at her knee.

Her lips tightened. "English hospitality."

He raised one eyebrow in question; but when she would

not elaborate, he disdained to pursue the subject. "Well, Kate, aren't you curious to know why I'm not dead?"

"*Curious* is not the word I would choose," she snapped, eyeing him warily.

He laughed again, enjoying himself. He touched a small red wound at the side of his head, just below the hairline. "If your aim were a little better, I would be, you know. As it was, you only caused me to bleed like a stuck pig."

She forebore to mention that if he had not kicked the door on her wrist, the gun wouldn't have gone off. This was better: she *wanted* him to think she'd pulled the trigger.

"I have many things to regret about my life," she said deliberately. "One of the hardest is that I didn't take the time to become a better shot."

His eyes hardened; his smile turned sour. He reached out and took the soapy sponge from her hand, ignoring her sudden intake of breath. Holding the back of her neck firmly, he began to wash the encrusted blood from the cut over her eyebrow. She winced, and his movements became gentler. "This is not deep," he murmured impersonally. When he was through, he stood up and tossed the sponge into the water. "Hurry and finish before it gets cold. I'm next." He went to the table and refilled his glass. Then he stretched out on the bed, opened a book, and began to read.

Assuring herself first that he was truly preoccupied, Katherine set about washing her hair. She finished quickly and stood up, looking about for a towel. Too late, she realized the maid had put them all on the foot of the bed. Burke turned a page. With a resigned sigh, she stepped from the tub and padded, dripping, to the bed. As she reached the foot, he uncrossed his legs and put one boot on top of the pile of towels. Smiling slightly, he lay the book face-down on his chest and looked up. His eyes took her in with studied insolence, missing nothing. She felt her blood pulsing and jerked at the top towel furiously. It wouldn't budge. His smile widened.

"I never get tired of seeing you in the nude," he said when she turned her outraged eyes to him.

"You can go—to—hell!" she cried hoarsely, tugging once, twice, three times before the towel came free. She wrapped it around herself and stalked rigidly to the fireplace, where she gripped the mantel and stared blindly into the flames, almost weeping with fury. His low chuckle sounded demonic.

After a few minutes her heartbeat returned to normal. She added a handful of sticks to the fire and stirred it with the poker, breathing deeply. Surely he was through playing his stupid, tiresome games now, she thought, bending over and shaking her thick hair before the quickening flames. Then she heard the creak of a floorboard and a second later she sensed his presence beside her. She straightened slowly and looked up at him. He was resting one arm against the mantel and loosening his cravat with his other hand, all the while staring at her like a cat in front of a mouse hole. What now? she wondered tiredly. When he began unbuttoning his shirt, she knew. He meant to undress while she watched. Another witless attempt to embarrass her. For a moment she toyed with the idea of trying to beat him at his own game—watching him with the same rude interest with which he had stared at her, until *he* turned away with embarrassment. But when he reached down and undid the top button of his breeches, the brilliance of this scheme faded and she hastily turned her back on him. He chuckled again. She heard him step closer and felt him begin to comb her damp, curling hair with his fingers. She stood stiffly, determined not to turn around or give him the satisfaction of reacting. But then he was pushing her hair behind her ear and brushing his lips along the side of her neck very softly, his warm, tickling breath causing an uncanny tremor to shiver through her. She tried to step sideways, but his arm around her waist held her still. He pressed against her intimately, and with a kind of horrified wonderment Katherine realized she was aroused. She took a shuddering breath, and as his hand left her waist to cup her breast she broke away. Burke took a step toward her and stopped. They faced each other across a distance of three feet, both breathing heavily. When Katherine thought her voice wouldn't betray her, she spoke. "I cannot bear it when you touch me, Major Burke. Thank God I don't have to pretend to enjoy it anymore."

He *knew* she was lying, but the insult infuriated him all the same. "I should have taken McKie's advice instead of knocking the poor bastard's head off," he snarled. "Remember what he suggested I do to you? And more fool me, I called him a pig."

"He *was* a pig, and so are you—a worse one!"

"But that's what you do to whores, Kate! You of all people should know that!" They were shouting at each other.

"No, *you* should know that—Whores are probably the only women you can get!"

Ridiculously stung by this truthless stab, he hammered his fist against the wall, so unexpectedly she jumped. The towel around her slipped; she clutched at it frantically and took a step back.

"What have *you* got to be so angry about?" she shouted. "I'm the one who was betrayed!"

"Betrayed! Ha!"

"Yes, betrayed! You're a faithless, lying coward, and a conniver, a—a *manipulator* of women—"

"You almost killed me!"

"You deserved it!"

There was a timid knock at the door.

"Come in!" Burke bellowed. Katherine gasped and bent down to pick up her damp shift from the floor.

The chambermaid poked her head in the door, looking terrified. "S—supper, sar?"

"Yes! Bring it!"

"Aye, sar." She pushed the door all the way open and came in, bearing a heavily laden tray on her shoulder. Smells so savory came from the covered dishes that Katherine felt light-headed; for her, the argument was over.

The maid put the tray on the bed and curtsied, eyeing this strange couple warily. The gent had on naught but his breeches and the lady seemed to be hiding behind a towel and her underwear. "Will ye be wantin' another bath, then? This one's all cauld, I expect."

"It's fine," Burke muttered irritably, "leave it. Go away. Wait! Take that dress and clean it." He pointed to Katherine's gown on the floor. "And the shoes, too." The maid gathered up the dirty, damp dress and the soaked shoes, curtsied again, and scurried out.

Burke looked at Katherine, who was looking at the tray on the bed. "Oh, don't wait for me," he grated sarcastically. "I love a nice cold bath before supper."

"It's your own fault," she snapped. She stood uncertainly, wondering what to put on, the wet towel or the wet shift.

Burke sighed and went to the table where he'd left his bag. He rummaged in it briefly and pulled out a clean silk shirt.

"Put this on," he ordered, handing it to her.

She took it, then stood waiting for him to turn around. He did not. She felt her temper rising like a balloon in her chest. "God damn it, stop *staring* at me, you—*satyr!*" Her cheeks were stained with violent color and her eyes flashed dangerously. She even stamped her foot. It was this last which caused Burke to laugh.

He held up his hand placatingly. "Very well, Kate, I'll not stare at you, though I don't think you really know what you're asking. There, I've turned around. You may dance a jig in the altogether, I'll not look at you. And you can believe me, for I'm a man of my word."

"Ha! That you most certainly are not." Nevertheless, she dropped the towel and thrust her arms through the huge sleeves of his shirt, which hung down almost to her knees and could have gone around her twice. She padded across the floor to the bed and crawled between the sheets, drawing the coverlet over her bare legs. She pulled the tray closer and began to uncover the dishes, her face a study in rapt concentration. Burke watched her over his shoulder for a few seconds with a faint, unwilling smile, then pulled off his breeches and stepped into the tepid bath.

What an infuriating woman! He could hear the light scraping of silver on crockery behind him, and occasionally a small sighing sound of appreciation. He supposed she hadn't eaten much lately. He wondered again how she'd come by the enormous bruise on her knee, or for that matter the countless smaller scratches and abrasions he'd noticed on her body. He didn't believe she'd fallen off that docile mare; she was much too skilled a horsewoman. Well, it wasn't for him to worry about what misfortunes had befallen her during the last two days. She'd tried to murder him twice, hadn't she? A woman like that deserved no pity.

He leaned back in the tub and closed his eyes. Immediately a vision formed in his brain, so clear and distinct it might have been real. But it wasn't, it was a memory. Of Kate, standing before him, naked and yearning. A little over forty-eight hours ago, that had been, not long before she'd shot him. Time had a way of changing things. For a few moments he permitted himself to savor the memory of what had happened between them during the long afternoon in the inn, but the images that flooded his brain were simply too erotic to bear. He sat up and began to scrub his face vigorously in the cold water. It did no good to let himself become aroused by thoughts of Katie

Lennox; he vowed he would not touch her again except to torment her for the rest of their time together—which, God willing, would only be two or three days more.

He rose, stepped out of the bath, and walked over to the bed for a towel. She'd already fallen asleep, he saw, still holding a half-full glass of wine. That was doubtless a blessing; if they spoke to each other at all they would only end up quarreling. He watched her while he dried his big body. He'd never known anyone with hair that color; he didn't even know what color to call it. "Red" came closest, but it was a tame, inadequate description; there was too much gold, too much of that indescribable tawny color, and then sometimes it could look as dark as mahogany. He stared at her until he remembered he was cold and hungry, and went to rekindle the fire.

He put on a clean shirt and sat down on the bed. He took the glass from her hand gently. She didn't stir. He lifted the cover from the first plate. Empty. Just a little brownish gravy beginning to congeal. He uncovered the second plate. Empty! So was the third, and the fourth. The fifth plate, dessert, had a half bite of apple tart left on it. He shook his head in disbelief. Damn the woman—she'd eaten his dinner!

CHAPTER 11

"Kate, help! Help us, Kate!"

The ring of terror in the voices made her weep bitterly, but she could not help. Her hands were bound behind her back and the man named Thomas was driving a stake into her belly with his fists. She was choking on her tears, immobile, unable even to scream. Michael and Rory were begging her to save them but she couldn't move, she was lashed to the ground, she could only toss her head from side to side in hopeless anguish. The cries grew fainter as a roaring in her ears increased until it seemed her brain would burst. She felt cruel fingers squeezing her shoulders like talons, and the dream ended as it always did—with the face of Wells filling her vision and exhorting her in tones of unmitigated evil, "Look at me! Look!"

She sat up, panting. Her face and neck were wet with tears, but when she looked at Burke beside her she saw he was still asleep—so she hadn't called out this time. She sank back on the pillow with relief.

After a few minutes the tension began to leave her body as the vividest scenes of the nightmare slowly faded from memory. She felt cold, quiet bitterness settle over her and welcomed it with a tight smile. Years ago, when the dream was coming almost every night, she would stay awake as long as she could; but exhaustion always overtook her and the nightmare would inevitably recur. As time passed it came less and less often; she hadn't had it in months. Now she felt a steely, cheerless satisfaction that it had returned, for it revived the fierce hatred she'd harbored in her heart for so long and renewed her flagging hunger for revenge. She saw she'd been getting soft, allowing James Burke to distract her from her higher purpose. Why this was so she wasn't sure, except that he possessed some base physical charm she had unaccountably responded to in a few moments of feminine weakness. But no more.

She sat up and put her feet on the cold floor. Burke was breathing heavily; he was deeply asleep. Through the window she saw the sky beginning to lighten. She stood up. Her bruised knee felt stiff and her shoulder ached from Burke's nearly pulling her arm out of its socket. Every muscle implored her to lie down and go back to sleep, but the discomfort only sharpened her resolve.

She padded across the floor to the table where he'd left his bags. What would she wear? The maid, she remembered, had taken away her dress and shoes. She rummaged in the first bag quietly until she felt something soft and velvety and recognized it as her green dress. And there were her boots, too. She was glad, relieved—but irked as well, because it meant he'd been sure of finding her. Well, she vowed grimly, he would not find her this time.

She crept over to the chair on which he'd thrown his jacket and slipped her hand into the inside pocket. She had no intention of running away as ill-prepared as the last time. With scarcely a prickle of conscience, she extracted two gold coins from his bulging purse and replaced the purse in his pocket. After a second's thought she decided not to steal his knife. She gathered everything up and slipped soundlessly from the room as dawn was breaking.

In the chilly hallway, she stripped off Burke's white shirt and put on her dress and boots. No shift, no stockings. She tiptoed down the hall to the steps and paused to listen. All was quiet. Gathering her skirts in one hand, she went down the stairs as silently as possible and ran through the empty taproom to the front door. It was locked, but the bolt slipped back easily and in a matter of seconds she was standing outside in the yard, breathing the cold morning air. Pressing close to the side wall of the alehouse and bending low when she came to windows, she made her way to the rear courtyard. There she stopped and glanced around quickly—no time for careful reconnaissance—and made a dash for the stables. She slipped through the heavy barn door without making a sound and stood against it, holding her breath and listening intently. Silence. Relief washed over her; her heart seemed to start pumping again after a long recess.

Now to find Burke's horse, for this time she meant to leave him the tired mare and take his stallion. After all, she reasoned, if she were caught, they would hang her as readily for a horse thief as a spy.

She stepped carefully down the short row of stalls, peering through the dimness for a glimpse of the gray stallion. She saw him in the last stall. He shook his head as if glad to see her. "Hello, beauty," she said softly, reaching up to stroke his nose.

"Why, Kate, what a lovely sentiment."

Katherine pressed her hand to her mouth to smother a scream and leaned weakly against the wall behind her. Burke rose from a crouch beside the stallion like a great black bird. He stepped swiftly around the side of the stall and came toward her, radiating menace. Instinctively she raised both arms for protection, knowing a moment of primitive fear. He stopped, two feet away. When she realized he wasn't going to hit her, she lowered her arms, but slowly and with profound wariness. She couldn't see his face but his anger was a palpable thing. She steadied herself. "I couldn't sleep, I—went for a walk and—"

"Shut up." His voice was like grating metal.

She raised her head defiantly. "I don't care what you think!"

"You'll care when I tie you to your horse by day and to the bed at night."

All the blood drained from her face. She opened her mouth but no words came out; her mind went blank with panic. She felt his hand on her arm, steering her down the row of stalls to the door, holding her steady when she stumbled. Outside, the full light of morning struck her in the face harshly and brought her back to her senses.

"Wait!" She tried to pull out of his grip. He held on but stopped walking and faced her. They were alone in the middle of the earthen stableyard. "Wait," she repeated, stalling. "Really, you—needn't tie me, Major. I promise I won't try to escape again."

"Oh, you *promise*." His smile was a sneer. "Your promises are worthless."

"Please!" she burst out unguardedly. "Burke, for God's sake, don't tie me!"

"Why?" he snapped, watching her.

"Because—I cannot bear it!" She looked away. Already she regretted revealing even this much to him; she was certain he would use it against her. "Burke, listen." She forced herself to speak calmly. "Tying me will only slow you down, and I'm certain you'd like to be rid of me as soon as possible." She placed her hand over her heart and looked into his eyes with a clear gaze. "I give you my solemn oath I will not run away again. I swear it. And I'm a Scotswoman—my word is my bond!"

He looked at her a long time, unable to decide whether her earnest pose was real or only that—a pose. The sun rising behind her set her hair on fire and gave her slim silhouette the grave dignity of a martyr about to face some horrible death. But he was determined not to be fooled again, seduced out of his senses and deprived of his judgment simply because she was beautiful. On the other hand, she was right, tying her would slow them down; and right again—he couldn't wait to be rid of her. They were already overdue in Lancaster, and he had more important things to do than chase a traitorous whore all over the lake country. But the question remained, could he believe her?

At last he broke the silence, speaking as if from a deep well of suspicion and reluctance. "You'll give your word, then?"

"Aye, my word!" Her eyes lit up hopefully.

He closed the space between them in one step and took hold of her shoulders. "Then so be it, Kate, but I warn you. If you're lying, you'll regret it more than you can possibly imagine."

"I am not lying," she said almost inaudibly. Her throat felt dry and a momentary shiver passed through her.

"Good." He watched her for another minute, then walked away.

Katherine sagged with relief. She followed behind him meekly as he strode toward the alehouse. What a near thing that had been, she thought shakily. She expected he would be watching her closely all morning. In that case, she would have to postpone her escape until the afternoon.

The chance came an hour after lunch.

They were on a narrow, steep-sided trail that wound in tight curves around the clifflike sides of a fell when Katherine spotted what looked for all the world like a pumpkin in the middle of the road, not twenty feet ahead. She rode closer and stopped in front of the pumpkin—for indeed, that was what it was—and turned a bemused look toward Burke, who had come up beside her. Together they contemplated the incongruous object until their attention was caught by a hoarse cry just beyond the turn in the road ahead of them. Burke frowned a warning and went ahead, a hand on the saddlebag in which he kept his pistol. She followed unhesitatingly.

"Hallo! Is somebody there? Can ye hear me?" Now there was an edge of desperation to the voice. She saw Burke dismount and run toward something, and then she saw the disabled farm cart and the man lying underneath it. "Thank ye, God! Thank God somebody's cum at last!" He was obviously a farmer, middle-aged and dressed in sturdy homespun. He lay in a ditch under his cart, a wheel lying beside him. A horse was peacefully grazing on ferns by the side of the road some distance away. The man's face was pain-wracked and tear-stained, but he grinned with relief at the sight of Burke bending over him.

"Are you badly hurt?" Burke asked, surveying the scene quickly.

"Aye, I've broke me legs," he gasped, "through me own stupidity, which don't make the pain any easier."

Katherine sprang from the mare, slithered down the muddy bank, and knelt beside Burke and the farmer. A look of wonder crossed the injured man's red, sweating face as she wiped his forehead with her handkerchief. "Is the pain terrible?" she asked softly, touching his cheek.

Burke snorted and stood up. "No, farmer, you aren't dead and in heaven. Now, pay heed. If I can lift this cart up a foot or so, do you think you can get out?"

The man shook his head ruefully. "Nay, son, ye'll never heft it, big, strong lad though ye be. 'Tis a job fer two men at least."

"You may be right, but it bears trying all the same. Stand aside, Kate." He was stripping off his jacket and rolling up the sleeves of his shirt.

"Can't I help?" asked Katherine. "If you can lift it, I can be helping to pull him out."

Burke thought a moment and agreed. "Only be careful not to slip in the mud," he cautioned; "we've no need for two of you to be stuck under there."

"Aye," the man on the ground told them, "that's just how it happened to me. Me wheel cum halfway off and I thought I could put it back on meself. But I skittered in the wet earth and slid underneath, and the bloody thing cum down atop me. Beg pardon, ma'am.''

Facing away from the farm cart, Burke grasped the sides of the wheel-less axle in his hands. He was straddling the prostrate farmer's upper body. "If I lift it, haul him out between my legs, Kate." She nodded and knelt down at the man's head, ready to seize him under the arms. "Ready—now!" Burke flexed his powerful legs and strained upward with all his might. He turned his blood-darkened face skyward, teeth bared, the muscles in his neck and shoulders bulging with effort. The cart moved— but only a fraction of an inch. Interminable seconds passed, but the heavy cart rose no higher. With a groan of frustration, he lowered it back down, gently, and stepped away. "I'm sorry," he said simply, flexing his fingers and breathing deeply.

"Nay, ye did yer best," the farmer reassured him. Sweat had broken out on his face again and his lips were gray. "I've three sons at home, lad. If you or the lady could fetch 'em—"

"Of course," Burke agreed immediately. Then he frowned, perceiving his dilemma. If he went, what was to prevent Katherine from running away? Then again, if she went, how could he be sure she'd return? The solution was for them both to go, but he shrank from that, unwilling to leave the farmer alone again in his pain.

"I'll go," Katherine said quietly. "Where shall I find them?" she asked the injured man, still kneeling by his head.

'' 'Tis only a mile and a half from here. Ye go back the way ye've cum until ye see a turn-off to yer left. There's a tumbledown sheepfold there, ye can't miss it. That trail will lead ye straight down across the dale to my little farm and no other. Me boys will be either in the house or in the barn behind it. Tell 'em to cum on the other horse and bring blankets. And some rum!'' he added, his pain-glazed eyes twinkling for a moment.

"Yes.'' Katherine stood up and faced Burke. "I *will* fetch them,'' she told him defiantly. She knew exactly what he was thinking.

"If you don't, you'll be sorry for it,'' he growled. He did not like anything about the situation, but he could see no way out.

"May I take the stallion?'' she asked, ignoring his threat. '' 'Twould be much faster.''

"Nay, Kate,'' he retorted grimly, "I may be a fool but I'm not a moron. Take the mare and be quick.''

She made a face, then knelt by the farmer's side once again. "Dinna worry,'' she said very softly, "I'll no' be long.'' She touched his grizzled head lightly, and his face relaxed. His eyes cleared and he even smiled at her.

Burke scrambled up the wet bank and stretched out a hand. She took it and he pulled her up beside him on the road. They walked to where the mare was standing; he seized Katherine around the waist and lifted her into the saddle. Then he stared up at her, his lips set and his eyes their coldest blue.

"I'm warning you, Kate—''

"Oh, have done, Major,'' she snapped, exasperated. "I've said I will fetch them.''

"Yes. But will you come back with them?''

"Ah, well. You'll just have to wait and see, won't you?'' Her smile was deliberately teasing. Burke made a grab for the bridle, but she'd already turned the mare and begun to trot away from him.

"You gave your word!'' he shouted after her.

"Aye! And I keep my word as well as you keep yours!''

It was a taunt, undeniably a taunt, and afterward he heard a trill of laughter before the bend in the road took her out of his sight and hearing. He almost jumped on his horse and went after her, but he did not. He stood in the road indecisively, clenching and unclenching his fists, until the time to catch her had passed, and then he scrambled down the enbankment and rejoined the farmer.

"Tell me again about yer lady." The injured man gulped down another mouthful of brandy and closed his eyes.

"She's not my lady," Burke said automatically. He suspected the farmer was a little drunk. He took a small sip from the bottle himself and glanced up again at the sky. It was still only mid-afternoon, but it seemed to him Katherine had been gone for much longer than an hour.

"Aye, so ye said before. I'll warrant ye're thinkin' that's a pity," the farmer smiled; his eyes were still closed so he missed the slight curling of Burke's lip. "I know I ain't exactly a man o' the world, but I been to four furrin countries in my life, not countin' Ireland, and I never recollect seein' a woman as fine-lookin' as that one. Lord, the way she smiled, the way she looked down at me—" He broke off, seemingly overcome by the memory. " 'Tis a pity about her husband bein' killed by Bonnie Prince Charlie's soliders and all, but lucky you was there to help her out and take her home to Lancaster," he continued in a moment. Burke grunted, smiling. "Funny, though, she don't talk like a Lancashire woman. More like a Highland Scot, I'd almost say, but more refined, like. Where do she come from, exactly?"

"Farmer, hadn't you better save your breath to keep up your strength?" Burke knelt down and held the bottle to his lips once again, noting his sweaty pallor. Where were the man's sons? They should have arrived by now. And where the bloody hell was Kate?

"Mayhap I should, but jawin' takes me mind off the pain," the farmer said feebly. Suddenly his eyes opened wide. "There! I hear 'em! Oh, thank the Lord."

Burke heard them a second later. He sprang to his feet

and was up the muddy bank in one leap. What he saw rounding the bend in the road in the next moment brought a truly vile oath to his lips. A horse, a wagon, and three men—and that was all.

The farmer's sons scrambled down from the wagon hurriedly, barely glancing at Burke.

"The woman! Where is she?" He had to pull one of them by the arm to get his attention. "Where did she go? The woman, damn it!"

"She went the other way," the youngest one told him hastily, trying to pull away.

"What do you mean? Where?" His grip was unrelenting.

The boy looked at him for the first time. "She told us where you was. She come with us as far as the main road, then she rode off west fer Thirlmere." He shook his arm free and plunged down the bank to join his brothers.

Burke ran to the stallion. With a foot in one stirrup, he stopped. He strode back to the top of the embankment and called down. "I have to go unless you need me! Can the three of you manage with the cart?"

"Aye, we can heft it," one of the sons told him. They were already positioning themselves to lift the heavy wagon.

"Farewell, then, farmer! And good luck to you."

"God bless ye, son," the farmer called to him gratefully. "And give me thanks to yer lady!"

"I shall give her much more than that!" Burke promised. In three strides he was atop the stallion, and then he was away.

He saw her across a field of bracken, skirting the northern shore of a lake. She was still nearly a quarter of a mile away, but he knew it was she because of the way the afternoon sun lit up her flaming hair like a signal beacon. He spurred his horse to a faster gallop and bent low over the mane, every sense intently tuned to the fleeing figure in the distance. Within minutes, he'd halved the space between them. She heard him and threw a panicked glance over her shoulder, and he had the deep satisfaction of seeing a look of profound dread darken her beautiful face. Suddenly her horse veered to the right, away from the lake and into a thicket of trees. Burke grinned approvingly: his horse's superior speed wouldn't be an advantage here in the woods. He could hear her mount thrashing through the undergrowth ahead, not more than thirty yards away now. Then they were out of the thicket and in the open again. He saw a waist-high stone wall bounding the northern edge of the field they were traversing, and Katherine riding straight for it. It was an easy jump; beyond it was another broad, empty field. He smiled. He would catch her there.

All at once his heart stopped as the mare halted, suddenly and inexplicably, three feet shy of the wall, and Katherine seemed to fly straight up in the air. He heard her land on the other side with a sickening, bone-crushing thud; but an instant later, miraculously, she was on her feet and running crookedly away from him.

His horse cleared the wall easily and trotted after her. When she veered and ran to the right, he followed; when she turned and fled the other way, he pursued, always keeping a short, teasing distance away. There was nothing for her to hide behind, no obstacle to put between them in the wide, level meadow. He heard her breath coming in high, panicked gasps, and saw that her legs were no longer obeying her. At last she stopped, winded and shaken, and turned slowly to face him. He halted the stallion ten feet away. For interminable seconds they watched each other, lost in fear and enmity and a thirst for punishment.

Very deliberately, he reached around for the coil of rope behind his saddle. Katherine blanched. She held up one hand and took a shaky step backward. He dismounted leisurely, smiling a slight, victorious smile. She backed up

another step. Now all the color had left her face; even her
lips were a chalky white. He walked toward her slowly,
playing with the rope in his hands, almost caressing it,
while an evil glint lit his ice-blue eyes and the little smile
deepened maliciously.

"Oh, Burke," he thought she murmured. "Oh,
please," he heard her say clearly.

He hesitated.

In that second she turned and darted away, panic
breathing new life into her exhausted limbs. He sprang
after, exhilarated by the chase, thinking of a red fox just
before the kill. When she was an arm's length away he
lunged, seizing her around the hips in both arms and
bringing her down with a crash, himself on top. He
thought he'd knocked the breath out of her, she lay so
still. He rolled her over, and suddenly it was like trying to
hold on to a windmill in a hurricane. Arms, legs, hands,
feet, elbows and knees, teeth and nails—every physical
weapon she possessed was unleashed on him in a violent
attack born of the sheerest terror. He cursed repeatedly,
shielding his face, his groin, his throat from her frenzied
assault. Once she managed to squirm from under him and
get a knee on the ground. She was on the point of
springing away when he tackled her again from behind,
this time coming down on top with his full weight and
hearing her gasp for air. He held her down savagely, his
thighs pinning her thrashing legs. When he reached for
her wrists, she screamed and crossed her arms in front,
lying on top of them. It took him long, exhausting
minutes to wrestle her hands back out from under her, and
his own wrist was red from the mark of her teeth. He
picked up the rope. She bucked wildly and he had to brace
his booted feet on either side to stay on top of her. He
brought one of her hands down and put his knee on her
open palm, pinning it to her side. Knotting a loop in the
rope, he wound it around her other wrist and pulled tight.

Katherine was making a gurgling sound in her throat, as though she were choking. Without a pause, he joined her wrists together and coiled the remaining rope around them, leaving no slack. He tied three knots in succession, pulling viciously after each one, and then he rolled off her and lay on his back, panting for breath and feeling the sweat roll down the sides of his face.

It was the silence that finally stirred him. He sat up, rubbing his sore wrist, and looked down at the rumpled figure beside him. Though he stared intently, he could detect no breathing. In one swift motion he put his hands under her arms and hauled her to her feet. He had to steady her when she wobbled backward and nearly fell against him. He turned her around and studied her face, fighting back a wave of alarm. It was bloodless and drawn, pupils dilated, white lips clamped shut. She stood as rigid as a board, every muscle tensed as if to protect herself from some imminent and unspeakable onslaught. "Kate," he said, clutching her shoulders. She shuddered. "Kate!" She was looking directly at him, but he had the eerie sensation she wasn't seeing him. He shook her lightly, and for a fleeting second she seemed to focus on him, but then the veil dropped back and the uncanny glazed look returned.

He shook his head, as if to rid himself of second thoughts. He wiped the dirt from her face and picked the bits of dry grass from her hair, brushed the dust from her gown. All the while she stood stock still, as though his touch were a torture she had to bear stoically, and yet she still seemed somehow not to be aware of him at all.

He assured himself she could stand unaided and went to fetch her horse. He pondered whether to seat her side-saddle or astride and decided on the latter, for with her hands tied behind her back she would need to use both knees to stay aboard. He put her up with difficulty; she was docile enough but she remained stiff. He arranged her skirts so her bare legs were covered. Then he mounted the stallion and, taking up the mare's reins, led horse and rider by a circuitous route back to the main road.

Two hours of daylight left, he estimated from the position of the sun. He knew of no inn in the vicinity, so they would probably have to sleep outside. But that was just as well; he had no intention of untying his prisoner until they reached Lancaster, and her appearance would be bound to raise awkward questions in a public hostelry.

He glanced at her uneasily. She was motionless except for the restless, unceasing twisting of her hands behind her. After that he stared straight ahead, though the countryside may as well have been populated with unicorns for all the notice he took of it.

To avoid examining the possibility that he had behaved cruelly, he went over in his mind the lengthy catalogue of abuses she'd heaped upon him in the brief time he'd known her. She'd shot him in the head. She'd pulled his own knife on him and would have used it had he not been quicker. She'd lied to him since the day they'd met. She had cold-bloodedly seduced him. She was probably a spy; she was certainly a whore. "I am a Scotswoman—my word is my bond!" she'd vowed to him only that morning. Her voice had rung with passion and he'd believed her. And then she'd tricked him again. Oh no, he had not been too harsh; if anything he'd treated her too gently, and she was only getting now what she richly deserved.

He looked again at the horizon. The sun didn't appear to have moved at all; the afternoon was crawling by with agonizing slowness. He spoke sharply, telling Katherine to hold tight to the back of her saddle. They were on a rough, wet path and he was fearful her horse might slip. He saw her forehead was beaded with sweat, though the late afternoon was chilly. She seemed intent on some awful inner vision, a private hell into which he could not enter. He felt a prickle of fear and called to her loudly, but it was like talking to a mannequin. He focused again on his anger and wondered when this hellish, interminable afternoon would end.

Finally they left the winding, slippery path and entered a gentler landscape, where a quiet tarn was nestled among wild rhododendrons and graceful, overarching alders. The windward end was sheltered by the bulk of an enormous boulder, and a little sandy beach stretched down to the shore. There was still another hour before the sun would settle over the scree cliffs behind them. But when Burke glanced at Katherine this time, he saw she was shivering uncontrollably. Her eyes were wide and staring but her shoulders were hunched and her chin had sunk to her chest. Without another thought, he led her horse down the grassy incline to the lake.

Her legs gave way and she fell against him as he pulled her from the mare. He picked her up and carried her to the softest spot on the small beach, then went back to his horse and got his heavy cloak from the saddlebag. When he returned, she'd fallen to her side, knees drawn up in fetal position, and was shuddering convulsively. His voice had a grim edge to it as he called her name, and he knew that whatever terrifying thing she associated with being bound had her at the limits of her endurance. With unsteady hands, he fumbled for the knife in his pocket.

Katherine felt the sudden release of pressure on her wrists, followed immediately by the onset of a hot, searing pain as the blood rushed into her hands. She heard a cry, but was not clear-headed enough to recognize it as her own. Vaguely she knew Burke was with her; she could hear him cursing about something. She looked down and saw through a haze that her wrists were raw and bloody, and then she drifted away again. Not to the black, whirling pit she'd been in before, but as if floating in and out of the

mouth of it, now fearfully close, now blessedly far away.
Time had no reality. Burke was there and then he was not
there. It was warm, and in a moment of clarity she knew
he'd made a fire. Later she felt her wrists being gently
washed and wrapped in something soft. Now he was
holding her and she felt soothed, then frightened, then
soothed again. She'd almost stopped shaking when she
felt his breath on her cheek, so light and warm. She sighed
deeply. His lips touched hers with feathery softness, the
merest whisper of a kiss, and at first she recoiled as a
terrible image rose in her mind and then receded. But he
held her so softly, caressed her so gently, she lay her head
on his shoulder and let it go. She floated along in a
neutral, pleasant cloud of unreality, thoughtless and
detached. After a long time or a short time, she didn't
know which, she felt his fingers carefully unbuttoning all
the buttons down the front of her dress. She lay still in his
arms, transfixed. The fire was warm on her bare breasts,
and she could hear Burke breathing in a slow, heavy
rhythm. His hands were so big, they covered her completely. His palms were rasping across her nipples in a way
that made her put her head back and take a deep gulp of
air.

Then, shatteringly, the awful vision returned and it was
someone else who was touching her, hurting her, making
her want to die of shame. She cried out in anguish and
began to flail blindly, sobbing in great hiccuping gulps.
She was being sucked back into the vortex and battered
with a mindless violence when, by some miraculous
redemption, the reality of Burke's voice, tender and
healing, penetrated her consciousness and led her back
from the brink. Gradually the touch of his hands brought
peace instead of revulsion, calming her like a man
soothing a frightened bird. She lay looking up at the stars,
and she knew where she was and whose arms were around
her, whose body lay warm and firm along the length of

hers. "I'm sorry, Kate," she heard him murmur twice, three times into her ear. She nodded and closed her eyes, and her sleep was deep and dreamless.

CHAPTER 12

Katherine awoke with the early sun slanting across her face, amid an intimate entwining of arms and legs with Burke under his warm cloak. She lay still, pondering this interesting circumstance. After a minute or two, Burke's breathing changed and she knew he was awake, too. She turned her face toward him. He smiled sleepily; without thinking, she smiled back. How strange we are, she thought. Yesterday they'd been bitterest enemies; she'd deceived him and he had brutalized her. Today it somehow seemed natural to wake up in each other's arms, smiling.

He disentangled himself reluctantly and stood up, saying something about wood for a fire. Katherine stayed where she was, unwilling to face the morning chill yet. She felt unaccountably rested and at peace, as though something inside her had healed overnight. And that was stranger still, considering what had happened yesterday. She held her wrists up to examine the bandages Burke had put on them. He'd used one of his silk shirts, she saw; somehow that moved her. Her wrists stung a little, and that was all. How odd, she thought again.

"What, still abed?" Burke dumped an armful of dry sticks on the sand nearby and stood over her, rubbing his hands. "Up, woman, or I'll kindle this fire beneath your rump."

Katherine smiled in spite of herself and prepared to rise, but he squatted down beside her, his face sobering.

"How are you? How do you feel? Let me see your arms." He reached for her hands and examined the bandages around her wrists. Satisfied, he asked again, "How do you feel?"

"I feel—" Perversely, she didn't want to tell him she felt perfectly well; he didn't deserve to know that. "I feel a little tired, but otherwise—" She shrugged bravely.

He watched her a moment in silence. "Why do you fear it so, Kate? What happened to you?"

The directness of the question took her by surprise. For an instant she thought of telling him the truth, actually telling him the whole awful story. She pulled herself together. "I can't talk about it," she stated with finality. Yet in the next breath she heard herself say, "Some—men hurt me once, a long time ago. Please don't ask me again, Burke. I can't, I just can't talk about it."

"All right, Kate," he said quietly, although she'd told him nothing more than what he'd already guessed. He touched her cheek fleetingly. "I'm sorry you were hurt."

She thought she was going to cry. With a shock she realized how badly she wanted his comfort, his sympathy. He was still holding her upturned hands; she thought he wanted to say more, but a minute went by and he didn't speak. She needed to tell him something. "Burke, I'm sorry I broke my word. I wouldn't blame you for not believing me, but in truth, it's not my way." In a corner of her mind, she wondered why it was so important that he believe her.

He cleared his throat. "What happened afterward, Kate—" He stopped; finally he raised his gaze from their clasped hands to her face. "It's not my way, either," he finished abruptly. Then he stood and walked away to kindle the fire.

They rode together that day in an atmosphere of peace.

Burke treated her with uncommon gentleness, and their conversation was easy and spirited. They spoke of comfortable, everyday things almost like old friends, and if she had not been on her way to a military prison, Katherine would have felt something strangely close to happiness. But there was a heaviness on her heart that grew more burdensome as the day wore on, a wistful melancholy she didn't care to examine closely because she knew it was not caused solely by their imminent arrival in Lancaster. They stopped for the night in Windermere and shared a quiet supper in their room; afterward they slept without touching on a narrow feather bed. If she had looked more closely and been able to penetrate Burke's calm facade, she might have noticed that his spirits were as sunken as hers, despite the light-hearted chatter he kept up to cheer her. The next day he slowed the pace of their horses with every passing mile, but her thoughts were turned inward and she never realized it.

They arrived at Kendal in the afternoon, where a fair was in progress. Dozens of tents and booths had been set up in a field east of town, bordering the main road to Lancaster. Traffic on the road was thick with carts, wagons, horses, and pedestrians, and Burke finally gave up trying to pick a way through the mob. He led the horses off the road and down a rough path to a cottage, where he paid a man half a crown to let them gaze in his tiny pasture while he and Katherine had their dinner.

They ate meat pies standing up, watching the crowd milling past. Afterward, instead of leaving, he surprised her by suggesting they go for a stroll around the fairgrounds. He took her hand and they began to walk about unhurriedly, watching a troupe of acrobats, a conjuror, a puppeteer. They saw a play called "The Creation of the World, with the Addition of Noah's Flood," and stood around a rope-sided ring while two women fought a boxing match. The sun slid lower, but Burke showed no interest in leaving. They were only hours from Lancaster now, and his disinclination to depart confused and upset her. She had no wish to reach their destination; for all she cared, Lancaster could disappear from the earth in a puff of smoke. But this was torture. So was the way Burke was touching her. She knew they looked like lovers, and the thought only deepened her unhappiness. But she hadn't the will to extricate herself from the arm he put around her waist or her shoulders, the hand he slipped in hers. She leaned back against him to gaze up at a tightrope walker, and went blind to everything when he folded her in his arms and rested his chin on top of her head. She was vibrantly conscious of the hard feel of his forearms under her breasts, his breath on her cheek when he bent his head to speak to her. If only this day, this moment, could last forever! But when she looked at the sky, she saw it was getting dark.

Burke bought supper from a woman selling fried fish and potatoes, and they ate sitting under a tree a little distance away from the jostling crowd and watched the moon come up. Torches began to dot the fairground; in the distance someone lit a bonfire. Presently music began to play and couples drifted off to dance around the fire. The night air was cooler but still unusually mild. Katherine leaned her head against the tree and finally spoke aloud what was on her mind.

"I've enjoyed myself so much today, Burke, but I don't understand why we stopped. Shouldn't we have ridden on to Lancaster this afternoon?"

"Mmm," he hummed noncommittally. He was staring up at the moon. "Probably."

"But aren't they expecting us?" she persisted. "And won't Colonel Denholm wonder why you've not returned?"

He yawned. "I doubt Denholm is even at Dumfries anymore. He's probably chasing your Bonnie Prince somewhere around Manchester, and he's more than welcome to do that without me. As for the authorities in Lancaster, they won't be wondering what's become of us because they don't know we're coming."

She absorbed this information in silence.

"Of course, that's not the real reason we stopped," he went on after a moment.

She waited. "What is the real reason?" she asked finally. He was lying on his side next to her, leaning on one elbow, and his face looked so handsome in the moonlight she couldn't stop looking at him. Her eyes were drawn in fascination to the tiny scar that marred his beautiful mouth's perfect symmetry.

He drew her folded hand from her lap and caressed it, playing with her fingers. She waited motionlessly. "The real reason"—his lips brushed her knuckles with the softness of a whisper—"the real reason is that I couldn't let you go out of my life without . . . dancing with you."

She expelled her breath in a long, soft sigh. He kissed her open palm and her eyes closed involuntarily. "Where will we spend the night?" she murmured after a time.

"Ah, I hadn't thought of that." His lips, then his tongue, lightly touched her wrist. "Would you sleep outside again, Kate?" His eyes caught and held hers; his hot breath on her palm made her shiver. "There'll be no rooms in the town because of the fair."

She was thinking she would sleep on a bed of nails if he would only . . . She cleared her throat and sat up straighter. "I expect we shall have to," she said, striving for a more formal demeanor. The effect was not all it might have been, since she let him keep her hand. "Perhaps the man we left the horses with will let us stay in his barn."

"Mmm." He'd put her ring finger in his mouth and was doing something unbelievably erotic with his teeth and his tongue. Her breath caught between a sigh and a moan. She reached out with her free hand to touch his face, but her fingers stopped in midair. She strove to recover herself. "Didn't you—say you wanted to dance? Oh, Burke, let's dance."

He smiled a slow, bewitching smile. He dropped her hand and sat up. "If that's what you really want, Kate," he said casually, but a muscle jumped in his jaw. He rose to his feet and reached down for her. She stood and they walked toward the music and the fire, not touching.

It was a beautiful night, star-filled and moonlit, and the sparks from the bonfire ascended like millions of fireflies rising up from captivity. A dozen couples were dancing in the ruddy glow while Katherine and Burke watched from the shadows a little distance away. It was a simple, exuberant country dance, and yet she was completely unfamiliar with the steps. She was more accustomed to the slow, stately minuet and other sophisticated court dances, and she imagined Burke was, too. But, as Katie Lennox, she knew she was supposed to know how to perform this rustic dance.

"Actually, I'm—not much of a dancer," she hedged, hanging back.

"I find that impossible to believe," he said softly. He had stopped watching the dancers and was gazing down at her, his hands clasped behind his back. "Actually, it wasn't dancing I wanted to do with you, anyway."

"No?" She was suddenly breathless again.

"No."

"What was it—actually?"

He touched the side of her face with his long, strong fingers while she stared fixedly at the buttons on his shirt. He tilted her chin up until she had to look at him, her lashes slowly unveiling the indigo depths of her eyes in the flickering firelight. His voice came in a whisper. "This—"

"Whoa, hullo, 'scuse me an' all, but what might be the chances o' me havin' this dance?" A tall, well-built young man with dark brown hair and matching eyes was standing beside them. He was dressed as a farmer or a laborer, and he was grinning a cheerful, impertinent grin.

"Very slender," Burke murmured, hardly glancing at him.

"Oh, but say, it's the Bolingbroke Reel," he insisted loudly, not moving.

Finally Burke dropped Katherine's arm and turned to stare at the intruder in incredulous silence.

"You know, you have to dance with someone you've never danced with before. And I told my mates I'd dance with this lady 'cause she's the prettiest girl here."

"Tell them you lied," Burke intoned boredly.

"Well, I couldn't do that, could I?" The man had never stopped smiling. "I could tell 'em she turned me down, o' course."

"Yes, you could do that," Burke agreed. Both men turned to Katherine expectantly.

She was looking from one to the other with wide, staring eyes. If it had been brighter where they were standing, they would have noticed she had gone very pale. Her voice when she finally spoke was soft and strained.

"I would like very much to dance with this gentleman."

"There, then!" The brown-eyed man seized her arm in a hearty grip.

Burke stood stock-still, his face unreadable. Katherine did not try to read it, though; she didn't look at him at all. She turned her back on him and went off to dance with Ewan MacNab.

CHAPTER 13

"Well, Kath, I see you've quite hurled yourself into your new role. Did you forget you were only supposed to seduce Maule?"

If he hadn't been holding both her hands, she'd have slapped his leering face. As it was, she could only hiss through clenched teeth, "Why did it take you so long to find me?"

"Did you really want to be found?" He laughed at her expression. "My dear, I not unnaturally assumed you were still with Denholm's troops, so I've been following them around for the past week. It took a sizable bribe to discover you were heading south in the company of one solitary English major. I must say, he's a lot better looking than Maule, and probably much pleasanter between the blankets, eh?" She tried to pull away, but his hurtful grip on her wrists prevented it. "Easy, your soldier's watching," he warned. His smile never wavered, but there was a cruel glint in the dark eyes.

She gave up and tried to smile back, but her lips were stiff with anger and mortification. "What is your plan, Ewan? How are you going to get us out of here?"

"There, that's better." He put an arm around her waist intimately and swung her around in time to the music. "Wade's troops are at Hexham," he resumed after a few moments, still smiling but speaking quickly. "Charles's army is very near, moving toward Manchester, and there are English scouts everywhere. We couldn't get through to the north alone; we'd be stopped and questioned. We'll have to take your friend with us. He'll tell any English soldiers we meet that we're his prisoners and he's taking us to the general himself at Newcastle.''

''You mean Burke—Major Burke? But why would he do that?''

Ewan MacNab stared down into her astonished face to see if she was joking. She was not. ''Because he'll have a gun at his back, my dear Katherine,'' he enunciated slowly.

Comprehension dawned. ''Oh,'' she breathed. ''You mean we'll *force* him to get us past the English soldiers. Yes, of course. But we can't leave until it's light, Ewan; what will we do with Major Burke tonight?''

''I won't do anything with him; what *you* do with him is your business.''

''But—''

''I'm already occupied for the evening.'' He nodded in the direction of a pretty young woman standing apart from the dancers, hands on hips, with a terrific, falconlike scowl of jealousy trained on the two of them.

Katherine was furious. ''You are an idiot!'' she cried, trying with little success to keep her expression pleasant. ''I've no doubt you were with someone like her the night I went to your room with Maule's papers. None of this would have happened if you'd—''

''If you'd come the next night as you were told!'' His anger matched hers. ''What happened, Kath? Was Maule too much of a man for you? Not enough like your beloved Michael, the late lamented saint, hero, and milksop? Tell me, is it true my cousin never even bedded you before he died?''

She wanted to scream at him, rake her nails across his evil, grinning face, but he kept her pinned close in an unbreakable hold as he swept her along to the music.

"Dance, Katherine," he said into her ear; "you're stomping about like a wounded cow. What must the major be thinking?"

She was afraid to look and find out, though some inner antenna told her exactly where Burke was among the circle of onlookers. With difficulty she subdued her passion, even resumed the smiling countenance she'd lost in the heat of her anger. "Very well, Ewan. Come tomorrow morning." Quickly she told him where they would be spending the night.

"A barn, Kath? How romantic," he sneered.

She ignored him. "And remember, you're still Ewan Ramsey, the gin-selling gambler from Edinburgh, rescuing your—mistress."

"What?" His surprise was genuine. "But why? What difference does it make now?"

"Don't be a fool! Major Burke is escorting a suspected spy to Lancaster. If she's rescued by her lover—not her partner and cohort in treason—there'll be a much smaller chance of serious pursuit after we let him go."

"After we—!" He stopped, recollecting himself. "Ah, yes, you're right," he said smoothly. "I hadn't thought of that."

The music stopped.

"Come early in the morning," Katherine urged, pulling away when he would have continued to hold her.

"I'll come when I can," he retorted. "If I'm late, I'm sure you'll think of something to keep him there." He drew her close and gave her a quick, hard kiss on the mouth. She was too stunned to speak. Grinning again, he led her away from the dancers. "Smile, Kate, your lover's watching. Christ, he looks like a baited bull."

She tried to compose her features, but she hardly knew what she was doing. A feeling of dread stole over her as they neared the unsmiling figure at the edge of the circle.

"Well, Katie—Miss Lennox, I mean—thanks fer the lovely dance. Here, I'll turn 'er over to you, friend, and it's a lucky sod you are. Goodbye, Katie, until we meet again." He touched an imaginary hat, grinning his cocky grin, and diappeared into the shadows.

She stared after him, putting off the moment when she must turn and face Burke. The silence between them lenghtened until at last she had no choice and was about to speak, say something flighty and inane, when another man accosted her and asked for a dance. He was short and stocky, with a cowlick and an eager manner. She opened her mouth to decline politely when Burke laughed a harsh, brittle laugh and reached for her shoulder.

"Go on, Kate, dance with him. Perhaps he's got friends and you can dance with all of them. If they've got enough money, you could pleasure them all afterward in the field. Eh? Have you got money, young fellow? It won't take much, she's not an expensive piece. Go on, Kate, what's the matter?"

She jerked from his grasp and stumbled into the darkness, blind to everything but the need to get away from him. "Not tonight, love?" he called after her. "Sorry, friend, she's not herself." She heard him following and hastened her steps, but almost immediately he caught up to her and put a hand behind her neck, twining his fingers in her hair and forcing her to stop.

"Are you ill, love? That must be it; nothing else would make you turn down such an easy profit."

"Let go, you're hurting me."

But he wasn't through. With his free hand he opened the front of her dress, so quickly she didn't begin to fight until it was too late, and then he fondled her insultingly with expert fingers. She tried to knock his hand away, appalled that she was suddenly exposed this way when people were all around them. He held the back of her neck more firmly and thrust his thigh between her legs, keeping her off balance. "What's wrong, Kate, don't you like it? Isn't this what you're used to?"

"Stop it!"

"Is it the money, love? Should I pay you first?"

She took a breath to scream, but his mouth came down, muffling her. His kiss was passionless and mean, more punishment than caress, and his fingers on her breast were not delicate. She pounded on his chest and shoulders to no effect, feeling as though she were suffocating. After a moment he lifted his head and took a deep, ragged breath. Something in his eyes kept her motionless. Then, before she could react, he drew her bottom lip into his mouth and nibbled it, at the same time lightening his hold on her neck and slipping his other hand into her shift so he could touch her bare skin. Now was the moment to escape, when he was holding her almost tenderly. But her limbs felt suddenly heavy, weighted down. Confounded, she let the moment slip away. Her body softened; her mouth opened to him.

"Do you like this?" he breathed between her lips, pinching her nipple with excruciating gentleness and sending sparks of fire into her vitals.

"Yes, yes," she managed to answer, incapable of lying.

He kept it up until she was trembling all over. A weak and quickly gone flash of reason told her this was madness. Seconds before, his hands and mouth had chilled her; now, incredibly, they were heating her blood and bones, making her cling to him as though he were a rock and she a drowning woman. Oh God, he was the devil! With all her heart she wanted to slide down to the ground with him, right here, right now, and let him take her in the dirt. Her fingers wound through his straight black hair; her tongue met his and shyly explored his mouth, his lips. She heard his breathing slow and grow heavy, and knew with an unaccustomed thrill of power that she had moved him.

His hand moved from her breast to her buttocks,

stroking her intimately. "And this?"

She could only murmur incoherently. If she had any doubts of his arousal, the hard, lustful swelling against her belly dispelled them. She knew they could not go on like this for much longer, but she was unprepared when he suddenly let her go and stepped back, leaving her stranded, arching toward him as if drawn by a magnet.

"Cover yourself, Kate. For once you look like the slut you are."

It took her a moment to believe her ears. She couldn't see his expression in the dimness, but his voice was as cold as death. She felt swamped, as though a tidal wave of frigid water had knocked her to the ground. She brought her hands up slowly and spoke in an aghast whisper. "You whoreson bastard, James Burke. *I hate you.*"

She turned around and tried to button her dress; it took a long time because of the unsteadiness of her fingers. Her knees felt wobbly and her breath was coming in painful gasps. She had to work very hard to keep from crying. She finished buttoning her gown and looked up at the sky. The bright, impersonal stars were strangely soothing. She saw that in all likelihood no one had observed them because the blazing glare of the bonfire blinded the eyes to everything in shadow. But it didn't matter much to her anymore.

She turned around. Burke hadn't moved. She patted her hair and smoothed her skirt. "Well, Major, what did you expect? 'Tis only what I've been telling you for more than a week. The mystery is why you couldn't believe it before."

"Why, indeed," he agreed tightly, tonelessly.

They stood for another minute, neither one speaking. Finally Katherine said evenly, "Should we not be going, then? I expect you'll want to be setting out early tomorrow for Lancaster."

There was an infinitesimal pause before he answered. "I expect so."

He took her arm in a stiff, impersonal grasp and steered her through the dwindling crowd. The moon was waning and it was difficult to see. Once she slipped and would have fallen backwards if he hadn't caught her around the waist and held her upright. In spite of everything, the touch of his hands made her want him to hold her again, and she felt a helpless wave of anger at her own flesh. He stepped away immediately, seeming anxious to end the contact as quickly as possible. Anguish welled up in her, but she shrank from considering what, beyond hurt feelings and wounded pride, might be the source.

They arrived at the end of the short lane leading to the farmer's cottage where they'd left the horses. She waited while he went inside to make arrangements for the night. She felt unbearably cold, even though the air was still mild. Soon he returned, carrying a lantern and an armful of blankets. She stepped into the small circle of light the lantern cast, and together they made their way across the hard-packed yard to the barn.

Burke examined the horses briefly to make sure they'd been treated properly, then spread the blankets across a bed of clean straw. He began to undress as though Katherine weren't there.

"Take off your clothes," he ordered shortly when she didn't move.

She shook her head. "I'm cold."

"Suit yourself."

She sat down on one of the blankets and removed her shoes. She was suddenly very tired. Everything went black when Burke put out the lamp, and afterward she could hear him fumbling a bit in the dark and then stretching out beside her. Katherine lay still, listening to him breathe.

After a long time she whispered into the dark, "Good-bye, Burke."

He must not have heard; he didn't reply.

*   *   *

"Wake up. It's time to go."

She opened her eyes. He was standing over her, frowning, hands in his pockets, nudging her with the toe of his boot. She had the distinct impression he'd been standing there for some time. She sat up. "What time is it?"

"Time to go."

"Is it dawn yet?" Very little light was coming through the chinks in the windowless walls of the barn. If it were very early, Ewan wouldn't arrive before they left. She felt a flutter of fear.

Burke walked over to the horses and began to saddle his stallion.

"What time is it?" she repeated, trying to keep the strain from her voice.

"What difference does it make? Get up. There's a privy behind the house."

Without a word, she put on her shoes and went outside. She searched the sky anxiously; it was still dark except for a faint pearling of light in the east. Her heart sank.

She used the privy, then returned to the barn. Burke had finished saddling both horses and was leading them out to the yard.

"Ready?"

"Wait." She went back inside, pretending she'd left something. She wrung her hands and stared about wildly, searching for something, anything, that could delay their departure. There was nothing. With a nervous jolt, she remembered what Ewan had so offensively suggested she could do if he were late—though in truth she'd never really forgotten.

"Come on, Kate." Burke's voice was impatient; he was standing in the doorway, hands on his hips.

"I—I thought I left my shawl."

"Your shawl? It's in my saddlebag."

"Oh." She didn't move. "Burke, can't we have

breakfast before we go?''

"We'll eat on the way. Now, come." He turned half-way around, then stopped when he saw she wasn't following. "Are you coming?"

"Why are you so anxious to be rid of me?" she blurted out breathlessly.

He turned back slowly. He leaned one arm on the side of the door and regarded her through narrowed lids. "What?"

"We won't see each other ever again after today," she said quickly, the words tumbling out without pre-meditation.

"I know."

"Don't you care?"

He didn't answer.

She flushed hotly but didn't look away. "Last night you wanted me, Burke, but you were angry." Swallowing hard, she wondered how she would get the words out. "Have me now."

For an instant his eyes registered total shock, then his brows came down in a hard, suspicious scowl. He stared at her for a full minute. She quailed when he strode toward her purposefully. "Why?"

"Because I want you to," she whispered. Wonderingly, she realized it was the simple truth. She wanted him to make love to her now in spite of his cruelty last night, and she knew regardless of what he said or how hatefully he treated her, he wanted it, too.

She thought he would touch her then, but he didn't. He continued to stare into her face while she resisted an impulse to put her arms around his neck. Finally when she thought she couldn't bear the silence another minute, he answered.

"No." His tone was firm, but he didn't move away.

The word echoed between them.

"No?"

He shook his head.

"Must I beg you?" she murmured, scarcely able to breathe.

His mouth twitched with the ghost of a smile. "Yes."

She moistened her lips with her tongue and spoke without thinking, never taking her wide-eyed gaze from his face. "Then I do. You know what happens to me when you touch me. I try to hide it but I can't. I'll die if you never touch me again. Please. At least kiss me one last time. Please, Burke, please kiss me."

She would have gone on pleading, her pride a useless, forgotten luxury, but it wasn't necessary. He reached for her and held her face in his hands like a fragile treasure, then kissed her with fierce, overwrought passion. Katherine's heart felt swollen with emotion, and for the first time she held nothing back. They dropped to their knees together on the straw-colored floor, and she was shocked by the words coming from her mouth, half-coherent entreaties that he end this longing, this sweet, urgent misery. Too impatient to undress, they strained in single-minded frustration against the hateful restriction of their clothing. It was if they were on fire and in a frenzy to extinguish the flames. "God, Kate! Oh, love," Burke rasped into the tangle of red hair at her neck, kneeing her legs apart and pressing himself against her. She helped him when he reached down to pull her skirts up, her fingers clumsy with eagerness.

Suddenly she froze. He searched her face as he drew the heavy material over her thighs. She was staring over his shoulder, eyes wide with something other than desire. Then he heard the click of the hammer of a pistol in his ear.

He made an instinctive move to shield her more completely with his body, but a booted foot slammed against his shoulder and rolled him off of her. He grunted with pain and looked up to see who had kicked him. The man pointing the barrel of a gun at his head was the one who had danced with Kate last night at the fair.

Abruptly the pieces fell into place. With sickening certainty he knew who it was. Ewan Ramsey, Kate's gambler lover.

"Katie, girl, you put too damn much enthusiasm into yer work. Get up, now, or I'll make you sorry. Fix yer dress, you bleedin' tart. You, soldier, stand up and step away from 'er."

Katherine rose to her knees, staring wildly between the two men. Burke's face was a study, and she was too distraught to decipher it. Behind Ewan's look of triumph she saw an unmistakable gleam of lust, and she hastily pulled at the top of her gown to cover herself. She wanted to speak, to say something that would change this horrible situation and make it bearable, but she was too beside herself to utter a sound.

"Stand up, I said!"

Burke got to his feet slowly and stepped back from Katherine, flexing his fingers. "There's no need to shoot me, Ramsey," he said coolly, though his lips were stiff with shock and anger. "She was used goods to begin with. I only helped myself to a little of what she was giving away." Katherine drew in her breath and looked away. "It wasn't that remarkable, believe me; just the usual cheap fare you can buy at any brothel."

She rose unsteadily and went to stand beside MacNab, her face ashen.

"Don't talk about 'er like that," Ewan said, half-smiling in appreciation. "She may be a whore, but she's my whore." He chuckled at Katherine's gasp. "What's he got fer weapons, girl?"

"A knife in his pocket. A pistol in his saddle." Her voice came out high and unnatural.

"Get 'em."

She couldn't move. Every instinct rebelled against going closer to Burke.

"Get his knife, damn it," MacNab barked, shoving her.

She made herself take one step and then another until she was in front of him. Haltingly, she slipped her hand inside his coat. The heat from his body was like a brand on her quaking fingers. Her eyes flew to his face involuntarily. She saw contempt, disgust, and malice, focused on her in a look so cold it froze her blood. She would have recoiled but her hand closed on the knife then and she jerked it out of his pocket. She stumbled blindly backward until Ewan was beside her again.

"Now get the gun. If you see anybody, holler."

She ran outside, thankful to be alone even briefly. The air was cool on her flaming cheeks. She went to Burke's horse and searched in his saddlebag until she found the heavy pistol, and the familiar feel of it in her hand brought back the memory of the night she'd shot him. She leaned her head against the stallion's flank and closed her eyes. Something was warring within her, an insight, a realization struggling to be recognized. Fear and dread and pride fought against it and won. For now.

It was barely dawn yet; no one stirred and no trail of smoke came from the farmer's cottage. She could hear voices raised inside the barn. When she lifted her head, Burke was emerging from the dark doorway, his hands in the air, a trickle of blood coming from the side of his mouth.

She went toward him without thinking but stopped after only a step or two, recollecting herself. "Why did you do that?" she cried, turning stormy eyes on Ewan. "What did he do?"

"What did he do?" His outrage sounded genuine, but she thought she saw a glimmer of calculated amusement in his dark eyes. "He put his filthy hands on my woman, that's what. And unless you want a taste o' the same right here and now, you'll shut yer trap. As it is, Katie, I'm gonna deal with you later.''

She opened her mouth, then closed it. She tried to look chastened, as Katie Lennox might, but succeeded only in looking mutinous. She would deal with *him* later, she promised herself furiously, when Burke couldn't overhear them.

''Here, hand over that pistol before you blow yer foot off.'' She relinquished it gladly. She almost gave him the knife as well, which she'd unwittingly put in her pocket, but even as she reached for it she had second thoughts. She wasn't sure why, but it seemed a good idea to keep it.

She stole an unwilling glance at Burke. At Ewan's command he'd put his hands behind his back; he was standing a little distance apart, his face impassive. He had just been surprised in a supremely unguarded moment, he was unarmed and covered with a pistol by a man nearly as big as he was, and yet there was nothing remotely submissive about him. With his legs spread and his knees slightly flexed, his chin jutting aggressively, he looked capable of almost any violence. Despite his rigid control, he couldn't hide a murderous gleam in his eyes. Staring into those eyes, Katherine understood perfectly that if it were unleashed, his violence would be directed at her first, Ewan later.

MacNab grabbed her abruptly and pulled her close, still pointing the gun at Burke. ''Used goods or not, she's still mine,'' he gloated. The hand he'd put around her waist slipped up until he was touching her breast. ''And Katie, you'd best not be forgettin' it again or I swear I'll take my belt to you.''

Damn the son of a bitch! She understood his game now, the cowardly bastard. This was what he'd been wanting from her for four years, and she had stupidly handed him on a platter the means to get it. What a fool she'd been for not realizing before that he would be sure to exploit the situation.

"You're a pig! Let go of me." She elbowed him in the ribs with all her strength; he released her rather than give Burke a chance to spring at him. "Your woman, puh! Don't make me sick. I suppose I was your woman the night you used me for a stake in your bleeding card game. Don't ever touch me again, Ewan Ramsey, or I'll gouge your eyes right out of your head."

She could see he was angry, too, but he had the wit to keep playing the game. "Now, there's gratitude for you! I spend days huntin' all over this horrible country fer you so you won't have to get hung fer a spy, and this is my thanks. All right, Katie, since ye're doin' so well on yer own, you can stay with yer pretty Englishman and let 'em string you up from the tallest tree in Britain for all I care. Is that what you want?"

He had her and he knew it, and yet for the longest second she actually considered not allowing him to rescue her. But reason soon resurfaced and she shook her head reluctantly. "Nay, of course not. Only don't think saving me gives you any special rights, that's all."

"Only the rights I've always had, sweetheart," he retorted maddeningly.

"We'll talk about it later," she snapped, nearing the end of her ability to act out the charade.

"Oh, aye, we'll talk about it." He grinned, then turned his attention back to Burke. "Now, look here, Englishman, here's how it'll be. I ain't tyin' you up because we don't want to attract attention to our little party. Katie rides in front, ye're in the middle, and I'm behind with my pistol pointin' between yer ears. If you so much as resemble a man with escapin' on his mind, I'll cut you in half. Anytime we see English soldiers and they ask us our business, you tell 'em ye're a major and ye're escortin' the two of us to Newcastle on orders from General Wade.

You'll be carryin' yer pistol like you was guardin' us, only it'll be empty. Mine won't be, though, and if you try any tricks I'll shoot you as sure as I'm standin' here. Now get up on that stallion. After we get a ways away from here, we'll stop so's you can change saddles and ride Katie's nice, slow mare.''

Katherine wondered what sort of accent Ewan thought he was using. It wasn't a brogue, it wasn't even particularly Scottish. If anything, it sounded English. It reminded her of the speech of a loutish stablehand her father had once employed. But it was rough, uneducated, and mean; she supposed it would serve.

They mounted and filed out of the farmer's barnyard in the order Ewan had decreed. Dawn was breaking, but already gunmetal clouds blown on a chill wind were obscuring the sun. They headed due north. The mild weather of yesterday was over, and Katherine shivered as a blast of cold air blew into her face.

They rode all morning at a bone-rattling pace. They passed several travelers and even a small company of English infantrymen marching south to Manchester, but no one challenged them or even paid particular attention to them. She began to wonder if forcing Burke to go with them had been necessary after all. In a way it made things worse. Now he knew for certain they were going to Edinburgh; if they let him go as soon as they reached the Cheviot Hills, he only had to make his way to Hexham and alert the soldiers under Wade that they'd escaped. Maybe they should take him all the way to Edinburgh and set him free in the city. As far as she knew, Charles's troops still controlled everything but the castle. Ewan could continue north and find safety with his family in Inverness; she could disappear into her mother's elegant townhouse in Belmont Crescent, the last place anyone would think of looking for Katie Lennox.

No, she could see that wasn't a good idea. Besides, the

sooner they were rid of Major Burke, the better. If it were up to her, she'd stop right here, tie him to a tree by the side of the road, take his horse and weapons, and gallop northward for home as fast as she could. Then she wouldn't have to feel his eyes boring into the back of her skull, wouldn't have to endure the sharp stab of his enmity like a knife between her shoulder blades. She didn't have to try hard to imagine what he was feeling; she knew she'd humiliated him and that he would hate her forever. However unintentionally, she'd wounded him in his most vulnerable area, his pride. She didn't ask herself why this mattered so much, or how it had come to be that she would rather hurt herself than hurt Byrke, because to entertain even for a moment the possibility that she cared for him would be unthinkable. Impossible, intolerable. It would make a mockery of everything she'd thought, felt, believed, and dreamed for the last four years. It would betray Michael and dishonor her family. And Burke would laugh at her. She had much courage, but not enough for that.

She had plenty of time to think about Ewan MacNab. She'd known him all her life and had never liked him. He came from a good family of sober, pious Episcopalians, the fourth son of seven children. All the others were credits to their straitlaced parents, but Ewan was a rebel, with a streak of meanness in him. As a little girl, she'd once bitten him on the knee when she saw him beating his horse. Neither had ever really forgiven the other for that, though since Michael's death Ewan had made a point of pursuing her in a nasty, offensive way. Women fell in love with him easily, and he despised them for it. Katherine believed he only kept after her because he knew how much she disliked him and her hostility intrigued him. She would never have had anything to do with him at all, Michael's cousin or not, except that he'd proven a useful source of information about the clans, the political climate among the Lowland lairds, the status of the revolution in general. She knew he had friends in the thick of things, that he himself went on secret missions for the Jacobites. When her father died and she'd made a decision to become personally involved in the revolt, she'd reluctantly gone to Ewan for advice, and it was he who had introduced her to Owen Cathcart.

Owen Cathcart. The mastermind of the plan that had gotten her into this predicament. As soon as they stopped and were out of Burke's hearing, she would ask Ewan where Cathcart was and if he'd spoken to him. She hoped he hadn't been arrested. He was a calculating and rather cold man, but she believed he was fundamentally decent. And his devotion to the Stuart succession was genuine, whereas she suspected Ewan's was merely an excuse for recklessness and knavery.

On and on they rode into the raw afternoon. She thought they would stop at Penrith, but they didn't even slow down. She was drooping with fatigue, hardly able to see the ruts in the road anymore in the dusk, when at last MacNab called out to her to stop. At his direction she turned into a dirt lane between high, leafless hedges, and after a short ride they arrived at a cottage in a clearing with a scattering of outbuildings behind it. There was a light in one window and smoke coming from the chimney.

Ewan told Burke to dismount, then handed his pistol to Katherine. He was tying Burke's hands behind him when the door to the cottage opened and a man stood in the threshold. He called out quickly, "Hullo, it's Ewan! Don't come out, I'll come to you!" He finished with the rope and shoved Burke back against his horse. "Don't move," he said shortly. "Katie, shoot him if he moves." Then he strode off toward the house.

Warily, Katherine jumped from her horse, holding the gun in her fist and hoping that in the dusk Burke couldn't see she didn't have her finger on the trigger. She pointed it at him and tried to look purposeful. "Don't try anything," she warned, though what he could do with his hands tied, standing six feet away beside his horse, she couldn't imagine.

"The farthest thing from my mind," he said tiredly, hunching his shoulders to ease the ache in his back, "is to try anything."

"Then you believe I would shoot you?"

"With the greatest of pleasure. And doubtless with better aim this time."

She swallowed. "Doubtless."

"Then again, perhaps you'll hand that privilege over to your gallant cavalier, Kate, in a spirit of sacrifice."

"Perhaps." She tried to shrug offhandedly.

"Yes, I think you will. Though I'm sure you'll at least want to watch while he does it; your magnanimity doesn't extend to missing out on the pleasure of watching me die."

"Burke, for God's sake—" She stopped, not knowing what she wanted to say. She wanted to put things right between them, but that was impossible. "Can't we at least be civil to each other?" she implored, running a distracted hand through her hair. " 'Tis only for one more day, and then we need never see each other again."

"Civil?" His mouth curled in a snarl. "I'm on the wrong end of the gun for civility, love. You want us to be friends, eh? Why, to ease your conscience?"

"No—"

"I'm not interested. I keep my friends separate from my enemies. That way when a snake crawls up my leg, I don't invite it to sit on my lap."

She drew in her breath. "I don't deserve this cruelty. You and I—"

"You call that cruelty, Kate?" Anger flared in his eyes and across his carefully controlled features. "Untie my hands and learn what cruelty is. I dare you. What a pleasure it would be to put my fingers around your throat and throttle the life out of you.''

Her head jerked back as if he'd struck her. He couldn't read the look in her eyes because of the dimness, but pain was etched plainly in the set of her lips. It should have made him feel triumphant. Instead he felt slightly sick. It astounded him to realize he still wanted to touch her, not to hurt her but to erase the stricken look from her face.

He watched her fighting for composure, striving to steady the gun that was making her thin wrist quiver. He spoke gruffly, surprising himself. ''Very well, we'll be civil to each other. As you say, it's not for long. I suppose I can stand anything for one day.''

Katherine blinked rapidly and shifted her gaze from beyond his shoulder to meet his eyes. ''Do you mean it?'' she asked with a wary hopefulness that almost unmanned him.

''Aye, I mean it. But in return, you must do something for me.'' He looked past her to see MacNab coming toward them from the house.

''What?''

He smiled slightly at her distrustful frown. ''Make the son of a bitch give me a drink of water.''

Her face cleared. Ewan joined them at that moment and stood for a second looking suspiciously between them. He plucked the gun from her hand and told her to go inside the cottage.

''Why? What are you going to do?''

''Do what I tell you,'' he snapped, irritated. She didn't move. ''Damn it, woman, I'm escortin' yer soldier friend to his quarters. He's spendin' another night in a barn, only this time he won't have yer lovely rump to keep him warm. Now go along like I said, or I'll turn you over right here and leather yer bare backside in front of him.''

She turned a deep shade of purple. She couldn't bring herself to look at Burke. Oh, she would deal with Ewan

MacNab! She could hardly wait for them to be alone so she could tell him what a bastard he was. Meanwhile a hundred horrible curses died on her tongue. With a last, shriveling look, she turned and stalked rigidly away.

CHAPTER 14

Caught up in a rehearsal of the vile but eloquent speech she meant to give MacNab when next she saw him, she neglected to knock and marched straight into the cottage as though she owned it. She stopped in the doorway, halted by the startled looks of a man seated at a table and a woman straightening up from tending the hearth at the back of a rather large, comfortable room.

"I beg your pardon. How do you do? I'm Ka—" She cut herself off in mid-word. Who were these people? it occurred to her to wonder for the first time. Friends of Ewan, of course, since he'd called out his name to the man on their arrival; *political* friends, she assumed, since he must have told them why he was locking an English soldier in their barn. Surely it was all right, then, to tell them her real name.

"I'm Katherine McGregor. I believe my friend Ewan means for us to stay with you tonight. I thank you for your hospitality."

The man stood up and bowed, murmuring "Lady Katherine." So Ewan had told them who she was; she didn't know what to think of that. The woman came forward and curtsied respectfully, though there was a look of intense curiosity on her face, and something else as well. Hostility? They introduced themselves as Donald and Flora Ross and invited her to sit on the bench in the chimney corner. Mrs. Ross, a pretty woman with light

brown hair worn on top of her head in a bun, brought her
a steaming cup of tea, which she sipped gratefully while
warming herself by the fire. Donald Ross, who was considerably older than his wife and evidently a man of few
words, sat down at the table and went back to work
cleaning his rifle. At first Katherine tried to make small
talk; her efforts were greeted with courtesy but no warmth.
Presently she realized they were watching her when they
thought she wasn't looking, and once she caught them
exchanging a glance that seemed full of meaning, though
what the meaning was she had no idea. After that she sat
quietly and stared into the fire.

Ewan soon joined them. Mrs. Ross asked Katherine if
she'd like to freshen up before supper, and she followed
her hostess into the bedroom.

"Here's water for bathing, Lady Katherine." She
indicated a pitcher and basin on a washstand by the bed in
the small, simply furnished room.

"Please, Mrs. Ross, I wish you would call me
Katherine."

Mrs. Ross merely pursed her lips, and pointedly did not
ask Katherine to call her Flora.

She sighed inwardly and prepared to bathe, unbuttoning the sleeves of her green velvet gown. She looked down
with dismay at the stained and wrinkled skirt, brushing
ineffectively at the dirt and dust.

"Your dress is a sight," Mrs. Ross commented
suddenly.

Katherine though it was the first sincere thing the
woman had said. She smiled slightly and nodded in sad
acknowledgement.

"You must have one of mine."

"Nay, I couldn't possibly."

"It's not anything so fine as what you're used to, I'm
sure, but at least it's clean and decent." She was pulling a
gown out of the bottom of a trunk at the foot of the bed.

She shook it out and Katherine saw it was a simple dress of woolen homespun, blue-gray and trimmed sparingly with light green ribbon.

"It's extremely kind of you, Mrs. Ross, but really I couldn't."

"Why not? We're much the same size. I suppose it's because it's not grand enough."

"Gracious, no! 'Tis a perfectly nice dress, I like it very much, it's only that you don't know me at all and I've nothing to give you in return, no money or—"

"Money!" She sniffed and raised her chin.

"Oh, dear, I've offended you. Please forgive me." The woman made her nervous. She had an idea. "I'll make a bargain with you. I'll accept the gown and thank you very kindly for your generosity, but only on condition that in return you'll take mine." Mrs. Ross cast a dubious eye over the stains and wrinkles, and Katherine couldn't help laughing. "Truly, it was quite a nice dress when it was new, and it could be again with only a little care." She held the skirts out persuasively and turned around once. "Well? Do you accept?"

For the first time Mrs. Ross smiled. It was a small, tentative smile, but a smile nonetheless.

She went away to make supper soon afterward, and Katherine was left alone to wonder exactly what Ewan had told the Rosses about her. Everything? That would certainly explain their coolness. She could imagine what they must think of her—a woman of birth and title who would sleep with English soldiers for a political cause. At that moment it seemed preposterous to her, too. She couldn't continue to delude herself that patriotism had played much of a part in her decision to become involved in this mad adventure. Closer to the mark were recklessness and a desire for self-destruction. And, of course, a thirst for vengeance. For the first time she considered that her motives might be ugly, not noble; for the first time she allowed herself to feel ashamed.

Supper was a simple but well-prepared meal at the table in the main room. The conversation was principally between Ewan and Donald Ross, and exclusively about the uprising. Ross was exultant because at Manchester Prince Charles and his small army of rebels had finally met a fine welcome. Several men of good family had joined the cause there, as well as farmers, tradesmen, and over a hundred common men. Now they were moving south to Derby, and Ross was confident a successful siege of London was only a matter of time. Momentum was in Charles's favor, if troop strength decidedly was not. With the exception of the castles at Edinburgh, Stirling, and Dumbarton and a few forts in the north, the whole of Scotland was under his control.

Ross's enthusiasm was contagious. Katherine felt the old familiar spark, and comforted herself in the knowledge that she really did care; it wasn't after all *only* her personal war with the English that had brought her to where she was. She had grown up waiting and hoping for the revolution, even if her understanding of its consequences had been naive and childish. She thought of what Burke had said once, that sides in a war were never good or bad but only men killing each other on foreign soil for obscure reasons. Was that only cynicism, she wondered, or the next step in political wisdom?

"Cumberland's a butcher," Ewan was saying, interrupting her thoughts with his vehemence. "He's at Lichfield now, you know." Donald Ross nodded. "Wade's a fool and Cope is hardly any better, but the Duke of Cumberland is a man to fear."

"I agree," said Ross. "Besides being the king's son, he's the most skillful general England's had in a long time. He's a harsh man, but his policies are working."

"He's a butcher," Ewan repeated. After a moment he pushed his plate away and leaned back in his chair. "Well,

Kath,'' he said with a barely concealed sneer, ''aren't you curious to know how things went at Carlisle?''

''Aye, of course.'' She could hardly look at him, she disliked him so much; she forced herself to be courteous out of consideration for her hosts.

''It fell as easily as Edinburgh. They surrendered completely, even the castle, without a fight. The Highlanders lost only two men.''

''Thank God.''

''As I mentioned to you, Donald, Lady Katherine had a small but important role to play in the victory. Didn't you, Kath?''

''No, I did not.'' She felt herself beginning to flush. She could not believe he was saying this.

''Now, don't be modest. It's true, you weren't able to carry out your assignment to the letter; but knowing you, I'm sure you quite threw yourself into the *spirit*.'' There was total silence around the table. Katherine's ears rang with anger and embarrassment. ''You may not know it, Donald, but the Lady Braemoray has a very special gift, a unique talent, you might say, and it's the Stuart family's good fortune that she's so very willing to enlist it in their cause. I fear not many women would make the ultimate sacrifice for what's usually considered a man's bailiwick anyway—the overthrow of governments.'' He smiled, but there was a vicious glint in his eye. ''It's a pity there aren't any medals or awards for your *particular* kind of valor, Kath; I'm afraid you'll have to settle for our silent admiration.''

She stared sightlessly down at her folded hands, aware that her face was flaming and the silence at the table was lengthening. What she longed to say to Ewan MacNab was not appropriate for polite company. But what really tied her tongue was the profoundly uncomfortable thought that his insults were deserved and that he was only expressing in unspeakably offensive terms precisely what she'd chided herself for less than an hour ago. It was time to take a candid look at what she had done, to examine her motives and actions in the bright light of honest self-evaluation. She didn't shrink from the task, but she considered she had the right to postpone it. Above all, she didn't want to cry in front of Ewan MacNab.

She drew a shaky breath and raised her head. She was about to speak when Mrs. Ross laid a light hand on her arm.

"Aye, it does seem to be a man's province, though I've never understood why. The kind of government we live under affects us all, doesn't it, man or woman? And although nobody asked, I'll say straight out I don't think the men have done such a wonderful job at governing up to now." She paused, then continued mildly. "A woman may care deeply about who has power over her and her family and her countrymen, but what can she do? She can't take up arms and fight, she can't make speeches in Parliament, she can't even vote for the men who do. That doesn't leave a woman with many weapons, does it? But she's still got one. And if she chooses to use it, maybe you can explain to me, Mr. MacNab, how that's worse than picking up a musket and blowing someone's brains out."

Now Katherine knew she was going to cry; she could feel tears stinging behind her eyelids.

Mrs. Ross stood up. "Will you help me with the dishes, Katherine? I'm sure the men would like to smoke their pipes and discuss all kinds of difficult things that would only confuse you and me."

Ewan's laugh sounded nervous and insincere. Mr. Ross was looking at his wife with a small, unsurprised smile, his eyes warm with affection. Katherine swallowed the lump in her throat and pushed back her chair. She and Mrs. Ross cleared the dishes from the table while the men went to sit in front of the fire.

They worked in silence until the older woman handed

her a plate to dry and Katherine took the opportunity to squeeze her hand. "Mrs. Ross—"

"Flora."

"Flora." She smiled and blinked back another unexpected tear. "Thank you for what you said."

"There's no need to speak of it."

"Nevertheless, I'm grateful. I only wish I were as strong and noble as the woman you described; I think you are much more like her than I."

"Ach! What nonsense. We only do what we must, all of us." And she turned away and would not hear any more on the subject.

Mrs. Ross was a plain but generous cook, and there was a good deal of food left over after the meal. Tentatively, Katherine broached the subject that had been on her mind all evening.

"Flora, the man in the barn, he's—a sort of hostage for us until we get past Hexham or wherever Ewan thinks the English soldiers may stop us. If you can spare it, I'd like to take him something to eat. It's been a long day, and he's done nothing wrong, he's—"

"Well, of course you must take him something! I thought Mr. MacNab had seen to it."

"No, he—didn't think of it."

"For heaven's sake." She clucked her tongue and began to tie up a bundle of food in a cloth; at Katherine's request, she filled a flask with water from the pitcher on the table.

"It's turned so cold, do you think—"

"Oh, aye, he'll need a blanket. We've an extra one here in the chest. One should be enough; it's warm in the barn."

"Thank you, Flora."

"And you'll want a candle. Now, will you be all right? Shouldn't Mr. MacNab go? Or we could send Donald."

"I think it would be better if I went," she said carefully.

"I'll be quite safe. Actually, Ewan and the Englishman don't—get along very well, you see, so I thought—" She broke off, reluctant to explain more fully.

"Yes, I see. Go along, then, and be careful of the ruts. Here's your shawl."

It was cold and clear outside, with a platinum half-moon rising above the bare branches of a sycamore. The largest of the outbuildings must be the barn, Katherine deduced, setting out across the stony yard with her bundle in her arms. She heard a noise behind her and looked back to see the cottage door closing and Ewan striding purposefully toward her. She turned to face him, mentally bracing herself. She knew exactly what he was going to say.

"Where do you think you're going?"

She sighed. "To the barn, Ewan, to give Major Burke his supper," she answered quietly and, she hoped, unprovocatively. She didn't want to fight with him now.

"Give it to me; you're going nowhere."

She stood still, staring at him across his outstretched hand. "The man hasn't eaten since last night. He's a prisoner of war, if you like, and should be treated with decency. I'm taking him this food and a blanket, Ewan. Good night."

She turned to walk away. MacNab grabbed her shoulder and spun her around. He grasped one end of the blanket and yanked it out of her arms, knocking the bundle to the ground. He seized her upper arms painfully and shook her. "But I've tied him up, Katherine, did you forget? So there's no point in going to him; he can't put his hands all over you—like this!" One hand moved down and he tried to touch her intimately, but she twisted free and pushed him back. Her face was livid with outrage. "You like it when *he* does it!" he snarled. "I saw you with him, don't forget, moaning under him like a bitch in heat. An *Englishman*, Kath! My cousin is turning in his grave."

"Aye, an Englishman! And a better man than you'll

ever be, Ewan MacNab. You're a bully and a brute, and I would rather be debauched by the devil himself than have you lay one finger on me!''

His arm shot out and he struck her across the face, sending her stumbling backward. Tears momentarily blinded her. The next thing she knew he was holding her around the waist with one arm and pulling her head back by the hair so he could kiss her. The taste of his mouth disgusted her. She struggled and tried to twist her head aside, but his grip on her hair was agonizing. She remembered the knife in her pocket and went limp.

"Oh, Kath," he breathed, taking her sudden stillness for acquiescence. Her hand fumbled softly in her skirts. Her forced his tongue between her lips, but she would not open her mouth to him. "I want to lay you down in front of him, Kath. Strip you bare and take you while he watches."

Her fingers closed around cold steel. She brought her arm up slowly, as though to embrace him, then held the knife under his chin. "And I want to thrust this blade into your throat. Take your hands off me and step back."

He jumped away with an oath, eyes wide with disbelief. They stared at each other, both poised for violence, until finally Ewan lowered his hands to his sides.

He bared his teeth in a nasty, humorless grin. "You win for now, love. But we've a long journey ahead of us. I'll have you before it's over, I promise you. And I'll make you sorry for this." He jerked his head toward the knife. She still held it in a stiff, steady grip, pointed at his throat. "Go ahead, take the major his meal. Enjoy yourself. But remember, Kath, it isn't free; in the end you're going to pay."

He smiled again, and she felt the hairs rise on the back of her neck. Then he turned and walked away. She watched him until the cottage door closed behind him, and only then did she lower her arm. Her fingers were so stiff, she had to pry them away from the handle with her other hand. As she did so, she saw her hands begin to shake, and in the next second her whole body was trembling. She bent to pick up the bundle she'd dropped and clutched it to herself until the shaking stopped. Stars blinked coldly overhead and a thin wind blew dead leaves across her feet. She raised her chin and went resolutely toward the darkened barn.

It was quiet except for the occasional stamping of the ancient cow in the stall across the straw-strewn floor. In the pitch black, Burke lifted his bound arms behind him a fraction of an inch to try to ease the ache in his shoulders, but it was useless; there was almost no feeling anymore in his forearms, and the ropes around his wrists made his hands feel like swollen claws. For the hundredth time he cursed his situation and all the separate events that had led up to it. How could he, a well-trained, battle-tried officer and sometime-intelligence operator, a man familiar with every kind of deceit and trickery on the part of the enemy—how could he have fallen for what must surely be the oldest, most time-tested ruse in the thick book of female tricks? His mind would not stop replaying, with lurid and obsessive accuracy, the moment that had brought about his downfall: Kate squirming under him, her face taut with longing, and then the sound of the gun cocking and the vicious kick on the shoulder that had sent him sprawling. He ground his teeth in humiliation, but the scene wouldn't go away. The only good thing about it was that he'd still had on his breeches. Thank you, God, for that, he thought with impious sarcasm.

But the worst thing, the stupidest part of the whole wretched affair, was that he still wanted to see her. Incredible! Even though his present situation was the ignominious proof of it, still he could not quite believe her passion had been completely feigned. And it wasn't only wounded pride that made it so hard to accept, though his had certainly been wounded. He knew perfectly well that simulated desire was an accomplished whore's stock in trade, but Kate—Kate was different. She had the most enticing innocence, as though everything she did with him were for the first time. He thought of how she'd taken her clothes off for him in the inn at Helvellyn, with that mesmerizing combination of shyness and sensuality. And then the way she kissed him, with such tentative sweetness, as though she didn't quite know how to do it but was eager to learn. . . .

He was infatuated with her. There, it was better to admit it. Still, the thought brought him no pleasure; it festered in his gut like a cancer. Awful, horrible, unbearable situation. It explained why he hadn't tried to escape yet. There had been a number of times today when he could have made a run for it on Kate's mare, bolted suddenly and taken a chance on Ramsey's shot missing him, but he'd been too full of apprehension that a stray bullet might hit her instead. He brought his head forward and butted it back painfully against the post he was tied to. It hurt and it took his mind off his aching arms momentarily, but otherwise it was not a satisfying punishment. He was still tied up in a barn, facing nothing but a long night in which to contemplate his own folly.

He opened his eyes and peered blindly into the darkness. Was he imagining it or had he heard a sound outside? Now he could hear a soft scrabbling at the door. His muscles tensed involuntarily and he took a deep breath to calm the pounding of his heart, but the truth was he did not relish the idea of a beating from Ramsey while his hands were tied behind his back.

The door opened noiselessly. A beam of moonlight lit up a head of coppery hair like a candle on rich mahogany, and he released his breath in a long sigh.

He watched her quietly as she gazed into the barn, her

body poised cautiously in the doorway. "Major Burke?" she called lightly, musically, and he felt his blood begin to stir.

"Aye!" he grunted. "I'm here, tied to this goddamn post to your right."

She closed the heavy door and he heard it latch. He sensed rather than heard her moving toward him in the darkness, and the unmistakable scent of her came to his nostrils. Now she was next to him; he could just make out her black outline against the lighter blackness.

"I've brought a light," she said, whispering for some reason, and feeling around in a sort of bundle she had with her. After a prolonged interval the darkness was lit by the glow of a candle which she carefully placed on a railing over her head. Then she turned, and he was startled by the change in her. She looked pale and agitated, and at first she scarcely even seemed to see him. He watched her in silence while she appeared to calm herself with deep breaths, and then she stared down at him with her hands on her hips. An infuriating smile of satisfaction slowly lifted the corners of her delectable mouth.

"What the hell are you grinning at?" he asked irritably, as if he didn't know. God, how this must please her. He wished she weren't so beautiful in the candlelight or that her impish expression weren't so damned adorable.

She crouched down to see him better and clasped her forearms around her knees. "This is a rare treat," she began. He leaned his head back against the post and cocked a resigned eyebrow. " 'Tis not every day a poor girl like myself gets to see a great major of the mighty English army trussed up like a wild turkey." She laughed delightedly and even clapped her hands. He returned a baleful stare. Her voice lowered. "At last, Major Burke, the tables have turned, and I admit to you it's sweet, very sweet. It warms the cockles of my heart."

"You have no heart," he growled.

She laughed again. "Ach! How can you say such a cruel thing? And after I've gone to all this trouble to bring you your supper."

"Are you going to untie me so I can eat?"

She made a sound of disgust. "Really, Major, I know you have but little respect for my girlish intelligence, but you ought at least to give me credit for being sane." He snorted. "Nay, indeed, I shall not untie you. I shall *feed* you." She rummaged around in what looked to him like a bundled up blanket and produced a green water bottle. "Are you thirsty?"

"Aye." It was an understatement.

She leaned closer and held the bottle to his lips. He drank from it in great greedy gulps. "More," he said sharply when she started to pull it away, and she sobered. After that she fed him his meal in contrite silence.

"I take it your friend disapproves of this," he said between bites, nodding toward the food. She shrugged noncommittally. "It would be much better if I starved to death. That would save him the trouble of killing me."

"What nonsense," she scoffed, pushing the last bit of bread into his mouth. " 'Tis Englishmen who murder their prisoners, not Scotsmen," she said grimly.

"Are you really that naive?"

" 'Tis not naive, 'tis a fact!"

Burke shook his head wearily. "Ah, Kate, Kate, your pigheadedness is going to get me shot. I didn't realize you hated me so much."

She considered this while tidying up from his supper. "I don't hate you," she said judiciously. "We're enemies, that's all. We can't trust each other. 'Tis not personal; we both do what we must."

"Even if it means one of us murdering the other?"

"Murdering! Why do you keep saying that? No one is going to be murdered."

He spoke slowly, as if to a retarded child. "Tomorrow.

After we're past any English troops near Hexham. Ramsey is going to kill me.''

"That is not true," she retorted, looking him in the eye. "Ewan is not that kind of man." Burke shook his head in disgust. "After you've gotten us safely past Wade's men, you'll be set free. Perhaps he'll tie you so we'll have a head start, but to think he would shoot you is ridiculous. Why would he do it?"

"Because you've kidnapped a British soldier, a crime against the crown punishable by hanging, and because I know who you are. Don't be so damned simpleminded."

She drew herself up with dignity. "There's something you don't understand, Major Burke, something you never will understand. We're Highlanders. We do not murder in cold blood to save our skins. We take our chances openly and honestly. To kill a man because he would tell the authorities about us is unthinkable. 'Twould be craven and cowardly and against everything we stand for. We—"

He let her go on, sinking back against the rough post with heartfelt fatigue. When she saw he wasn't going to argue anymore, she stopped. She felt dissatisfied. She stood up and brushed crumbs from her skirt, then took a few turns around the dirt floor. She felt a strange unwillingness to go.

"Will you be cold? I've brought a blanket."

He said nothing, only stared up at her wearily, his long legs stretched out in front of him. His arms had begun to throb again and he felt a heavy sense of dread. She was about to leave and tomorrow he might die. At that moment both eventualities struck him as nearly equally bleak.

"You have new clothes," he observed after a time.

She stopped her pacing and looked down at the dress Flora had given her. "Aye." She felt self-conscious, knowing he was appraising her.

"It must feel good to be clean."

She spoke with assurance. "This time tomorrow, you'll be in an inn somewhere in Northumberland, lying in a big tub full of soap suds, drinking wine and eating fresh fruit. And flirting with the maid who brings you more hot water." She laughed a trifle uneasily.

"And you, Kate? Where will you be?"

"I? Oh—" She looked away, taken off guard. For a few seconds she allowed herself to think what she would do, after tomorrow. Why, she would go home, of course, or at any rate to Edinburgh, to the big house in Belmont Crescent that had been her family's city home for a dozen years. Darragh was gone, and she would never see its high stone towers again. She'd never see another sunset through the leaded-glass windows of her father's library, never quake in delicious terror at another thunderstorm from the stone parapet. Her mother was in Edinburgh, though, and Katherine knew with a melancholy resignation that it was time for her to go home. Home. Her lip curled with bitterness. Would her own mother know her, or had she slipped even further into madness by now? And what else awaited her in Edinburgh? Would the revolution fail, and she be forced to watch while the English king took from her every possession, every tradition, every last shred of her family's pride? She took a deep breath to stifle what came dangerously close to a sob.

"Kate?" Burke's voice, sharp with surprise, brought her back to the present.

"I shall take a position," she said quietly, staring beyond him into a dark corner of the barn.

He stirred sullenly. He didn't want to ask what kind of position, but he did anyway.

His tone of voice annoyed her. "What kind do you think?" she snapped. Hostility floated between them like a sudden fog. "What kind do you think?" she repeated, daring him to answer.

"Is there no skill, no—"

"What? A governess? I can't read. A companion? Who would employ me? I'm unschooled and unskilled, and fit for only one thing. Do you not approve, Major?"

He shrugged. "It's nothing to me what you do."

"Ah, good. I thought I detected disapproval." She looked away, then back at him; perversely, she couldn't let the subject drop. "And yet I think you've been taunting me with the reality of what I am since the day we met. Can you deny it?"

Burke studied the toe of his boot. "If I've made you feel . . . unworthy in any way—"

"Puh!" she exhaled disgustedly. She unfurled the blanket and knelt in front of him. "You will be cold." She tucked it around his shoulders, keeping her hands impersonal, and yet a spark of feeling went through her like a jolt of lightning at this simple touch.

"You're kind," he said stiffly, watching her face.

She stopped, her fingers resting lightly on his chest, and looked him straight in the eye. "I would do it for a sick animal." Their gazes held until she drew her hands away, slowly. She stood. "Good night. I'll leave you the candle." She went to the door and opened it.

"Kate!" he called unwillingly. He could hardly see her in the gloom.

"Yes?"

"He means to kill me, Kate."

Silence. Then, "You're wrong, Major Burke."

She closed the door and left him in the shadowy darkness.

Katherine fluffed up the goose-feather pillow and gave a final tug to the quilt, smoothing the top. On her side, Mrs. Ross did the same. They'd shared the bed last night; the men had slept on the floor in the other room by the hearth.

The older woman picked up a small bundle from the

bureau and held it out to her. "Here, Katherine, I want you to have this."

"What is it?"

"Nothing at all, an old nightgown of mine."

"Oh, Flora."

"No telling how long you'll be on the road, and you ought to have something to sleep in besides your shift."

The two women embraced with genuine affection. Katherine had sorely missed the companionship of a woman and felt truly sorry to be leaving.

As they stepped outside, all three men were emerging from the barn—Ross leading the horses, Ewan behind Burke with his gun in his hand. Burke was rubbing his wrists and flexing his shoulders painfully; he looked pale and tired. Katherine said good morning with great formality, and a tiny, sardonic smile flitted briefly across his face. "Good morning," he returned, with an exaggerated bow. She colored slightly and didn't look at him again.

As before, she mounted his stallion and he her mare, and the three of them set off down the lane away from the cottage. Katherine turned around to wave to Flora, who waved back from the doorway and, unexpectedly, blew her a kiss.

It was another cold, gray day. Burke rode hunched over his saddle, watching Katherine and thinking about what Ewan Ramsey had just said to him: "If you try anything today, Major Burke, I'll shoot her first and then you."

"Good," he'd retorted after an instant's startled pause; "that'll give me the edge I need to get away."

Ramsey had only smiled.

The words kept coming back to him as they pushed farther north, nearing the time when they would be likely to meet soldiers. Of course, he was probably bluffing. He was a mean, ruthless bastard, but to think he could shoot Kate . . . It didn't bear thinking about. All the same,

throughout the long, exhausting day, he made no move to
escape.

At last, in mid-afternoon, they reached Brampton,
where there was a small encampment of British soldiers
much like the one near Dumfries at which Katherine had
been held. If they were going to be challenged, it would
be here. They all knew it, and the tension among them
was at its height.

"Drop back and ride beside me, Major," Ewan ordered.
"Katie, stay in front of us."

The only road north skirted the encampment on its
western edge; they passed small groups of soldiers on foot
and on horseback, but no one spoke to them. Burke was
getting used to the way men looked at Kate when she
passed and the effect she had on them afterward, as
though they'd witnessed a miracle. Today it was a useful
distraction—passersby wondered who *she* was, not who
they were; but the phenomenon still had a peculiar way of
irritating him.

And then the encampment was behind them and the
danger was past. After analyzing it, Burke realized that the
feeling uppermost in his mind was relief. And why is that?
he asked himself, already knowing the answer. It blared
back at him like a child's taunt: because you don't want
Kate to get caught.

"Stop!" MacNab called out after another hour of hard
riding. "We'll stop here."

Where? Katherine wondered, then noticed that beyond
the woods edging the right side of the road was a clearing,
a small field, bare but for a large, leafless elm tree in the
center. She turned around, following Burke, and her heart
lurched in her chest. She had been expecting this moment
all day, but she wasn't prepared for it. This was the place
where they were going to leave him. She commanded herself not to look ahead, to live only in this moment, get
through this space of time; after it was over, tonight or

tomorrow, she could think about what it had meant.

They came to the middle of the clearing. She jumped from her horse impulsively: she had decided she would shake hands with him in farewell.

MacNab ordered Burke to dismount. He was pointing the pistol at his head, and there was an excited light in his eyes that puzzled her. Burke got down from the mare slowly, watchfully. His face was grim. She wondered what he was thinking, if he cared at all that they were about to part forever. "There's rope in here," she said, groping in the stallion's saddlebag. "And he must have his horse back, Ewan." She anticipated a fight with him over this, and prepared to be firm.

"Don't bother with the rope."

"Aren't you going to tie him?" They'd need a head start. She continued to fumble in the saddlebag.

"No, I'm going to shoot him."

CHAPTER 15

Katherine whirled around, her mouth wide with shock. The two men were standing twelve feet apart. MacNab held the gun with both hands, pointing it straight at Burke's heart. Burke was measuring the distance between them, his body poised, knees flexed, ready to jump.

"No! Ewan, don't, don't!" Her voice was shrill with panic. "For God's sake!"

"Shut up." He cocked the hammer. "Watch this, Kath, watch him die."

"Stop!" She stumbled closer, trying to make him look at her. "You can't! No, *don't!*"

She knew in the brilliant flash of an instant that he was going to do it, she could never dissuade him, and Burke wouldn't have time to dodge out of the way. In a reaction as natural as breathing, she threw her body in front of the gun, just as it fired. She felt the bullet slam into her right breast, spinning her around in a circle. Her legs buckled and she dropped to the ground on her knees.

She looked up in astonishment. MacNab was holding the smoking gun and staring back at her with a face full of horror. The pain assaulted her suddenly, hot and sharp like a twisting sword, and she slumped and had to shut her eyes. Still kneeling, she pulled her hand away from the front of her coat and saw that it was covered with bright red blood. Warm and wet, it ran down her wrist and into her sleeve. She moaned as black dots shimmered in front of her eyes.

Time might have passed; around her she could hear terrible, frightening sounds of violence and dimly saw struggling figures. "Be careful, he has a knife," she warned, but Burke couldn't have heard because she could only whisper. She wanted to stay on her knees, it was important not to lie down, but the ground was steadily rising up even as she pressed down hard with her palms to keep it away. Now her face was in the grass and she could smell the damp earth. I am dying, she thought, with deep sorrow.

But not if she didn't lie down, she reasoned, and began to pull herself by painful inches toward the elm tree. She reached it after a long, long time, though it was not far away, and pressed her cheek against the rough trunk. It seemed now she would die if she closed her eyes, so she studied the bark of the tree and, lifting her hand, the way her flesh formed tight, intricate whorls on the tips of her fingers. There was a sound in her ears as of rushing water. The pain was so intense she was afraid to move. Where was Burke? How could he leave her now when her life's blood was slowly draining away into the hard earth? Her heart broke and a tear of perfect sadness slid down her cheek.

"Oh, Burke! You're here," she breathed a second later. He was kneeling beside her, clutching at her hands. Now she could close her eyes, perhaps even lie down. She turned her head slightly to see his face. It was white and haggard; she'd never seen him so distraught. "Are you hurt?" she asked, even though he didn't look wounded.

She blinked when he began to mouth a string of awful curses. Why was he so angry? He was peering into her pinched and frightened face, demanding to know, "Why, Kate? *Why?*"

"Why?" Why what? The question made no sense. She would not regard it, even though he seemed to want to know the answer so badly. She had something more important to ask him. "Burke, am I dying?"

"No!"

Immediately she felt better; the pain didn't seem nearly as bad. Her eyelids closed and she sighed.

"Lie down," he said sharply. He wanted to hold on to his anger, but it was fast dissipating and turning into a cold, shaking fear. Holding her shoulders and the back of her head, he lowered her to the ground. She lay still while he unbuttoned her coat; but when he tried to probe the wound through the torn material of her dress, she flinched violently and they both went a shade paler. He examined the small, ugly hole with his eyes, not wanting to hurt her again. The bullet had entered an inch below and to the right of the nipple. Blood oozed steadily, but mercifully not in pulsing gushes. "Can you take a deep breath? Slowly, now."

She drew in her breath shakily, afraid of the pain, until there was a sharp catch in her chest.

"Did that hurt you?"

"Only a little." Perspiration beaded her upper lip.

"For God's sake, don't be brave!" he almost yelled at her, furious again. "Did it hurt?"

"Yes!"

He pushed the hair back from his forehead distractedly. Certainly a rib was broken, maybe two, but he didn't think her lung was punctured. But, God, there was too much blood! He took out his handkerchief and put it into her hand. "Hold this to the wound and press on it as hard as you can," he told her, trying to keep his voice calm. "Can you do that, Kate?" She nodded and held the cloth gingerly to her breast, wincing. "Good girl. I'll be right back; I'm going to get my cape."

She closed her eyes, and it seemed he was beside her again an instant later, carefully tucking the warm wool around her. For the first time she remembered MacNab.

"Where is he?" she asked, fearful of the answer. "I mean Ewan."

"Dead. I killed him. Kate, I'm so sorry," he whispered bleakly, seeing the anguish on her face as her eyes overflowed with tears. "You did love him." He felt as though a strong-fingered hand was squeezing his heart.

She shook her head in futile denial. How could she explain that she wept because of guilt, not grief? "All my fault," she uttered brokenly, full of terrible remorse. "Stupid. Stupid."

"Be quiet; don't talk anymore. We have to leave here and find a place where you can be warm." She heard him go away again, then return leading the big stallion. "I'll have to lift you, love. Can you put your arms around my neck?" She could put her left arm around him, but moving her right was too painful. He slid his hands under her shoulders and knees and slowly stood up, watching her. Her head dropped against his shoulder and she tried to take short, even breaths. The roaring in her ears returned, diminished slowly, and Katherine passed out.

Pain roused her, induced by the gentle but excruciating jarring of the horse's footsteps, and pain soon brought oblivion again. When next she could see and hear with a clear head, Burke was shouldering open a door, with her in his arms, and standing in the only room of what had once been a cottage but was now little more than a hovel. "Good lord," he breathed, glancing around. Dirt and dust were everywhere, competing for space with cobwebs and spiders. A tilting table, a chair, and a filthy pallet on the floor were the only furniture. There were light-filled gaps in the thatched ceiling, and the window was a piece of cloth nailed over a hole in the wall. But the brick fireplace still stood, and on a shelf over it were broken kitchen utensils and a dusty box of candles. It would have to do.

He laid her, still swathed in his cloak, on the pallet; then he took off his coat, folded it, and put it under her head for a pillow. "I'll be right back, love."

"Don't go." She turned her face away, hating this weakness, this fear.

"Kate, I must. The knife and some brandy are in the saddlebag, and we're going to need them both." He bent over and lightly touched the side of her face. "I'll be back in two seconds."

She closed her eyes and waited, thinking about nothing, until she heard a disembodied voice and realized he was kneeling on the floor beside her. "Sip this slowly so you don't cough. Good. Now a little more." She made a face as the fiery liquid burned her throat and made her eyes water, but she took another swallow obediently. She knew as well as he that she was going to need it. "Now let me look at you." Very gently he pulled her hands away from the blood-soaked coat. She made a small, frightened sound of protest. "I won't hurt you, I promise. Let me take a wee look, love." Because of his voice or the softness of his hands or the lessening of the pain a little, she let him unbutton her dress, then the shift, and separate the folds of cloth with infinite care. Her breast lay bare, and she closed her eyes in senseless shame. He touched her, his fingertips barely grazing the mutilated, exquisitely sensitive tissue. The brandy took hold then and she had trouble focusing on his face.

"It's bad, isn't it? Tell me the truth, Burke. Am I dying?" He ignored her and continued to probe gently with his fingers. Unconsciously she covered her other breast with her hand. "Please, I want you to tell me."

Finally he sat back on his haunches and looked at her "Nay, Kate, you'll not die," he said gruffly, "not if I can get that bastard's ball out of you in time. Now, lie still and don't move." She obeyed, falling almost immediately into an uneasy half-sleep.

Burke stood up. If he was going to play surgeon, he would need a fire and more light. God, she was so pale. The bleeding had slowed considerably, but he knew from grim experience that she might already have lost too much blood to survive. He peered about for something to use with his knife to remove the bullet. He needed something like pincers, two pieces of wire or metal, or . . . He spied an old fire shovel hanging from a nail on the wall by the hearth; into its handle was welded a thin but strong V-shaped wire. If he could pry it out of the handle, it would serve as a crude forceps. Filthy, of course, like everything else in the room, but he could boil it along with his knife. He'd seen many wounds during his career, watched many hastily performed operations in the field, and he'd learned an important lesson from observing who died and who didn't: the cleaner you could keep everything that touched the patient, the better chance he had.

When Katherine woke again, he was kneeling before the dirty hearth, blowing on dry tinder and kindling until the flames caught. Orange light glowed on his long-fingered hands, and she unconsciously relaxed at the sight of their strength and sensitivity. "Blessed Mother, help us both," she prayed, and when she saw him look up sharply she realized she'd spoken aloud.

"Why, Kate," he said, smiling, as he rose and came to stand over her, "do you really think we'll need the intercession of Our Lady? I think it won't come to that. After all, everyone knows a Scottish ball couldn't hurt a baby in nappies, much less a mean-spirited, saber-tounged Highland lass such as yourself."

"You're a damned English parasite," she retorted reflexively. "If I die it'll be through your clumsiness, you pudding-fingered—" Then all thought fled when he sat beside her on the edge of the pallet, causing a sudden movement of her body that sent a scalding arrow of agony through her bosom. She gritted her teeth, and her breathing stopped while the pain rocketed around her in circles. When she opened her eyes, her face was bathed with perspiration and her vision was clouded. She tried to speak, but it was as if her lips had suddenly grown thick and immovable. Her fingers sought his hand and held on weakly.

"God, Kate," he breathed; he was sweating, too. He reached for the brandy and made her drink again..

It went down more easily this time. After a while the warmth reached her veins and her grip on his hand loosened. She felt light-headed. "Aye, may the Blessed Virgin, the Holy Spirit, and all the heavenly angels smile down on us now"—she giggled blasphemously—"for never did a poor girl put her trust—nay, her *life*—in the hands of a less experienced physician."

He couldn't help smiling at that, though it came very close to the truth. He pulled his bloody handkerchief out of her hand and began to tear it into strips. Her smile faded as she watched him warily, suspiciously, through a haze of pain and brandy. When he reached for her right wrist, she drew back with a hiss and might have scratched his face if he hadn't jerked away.

"You'll not," she whispered, aghast. "Get away, I'd rather die. Nay! Get away, you bastard!"

"Kate, shut up, for God's sake—" He seized her arms in a steel grip and held them down by her sides. Her body continued to writhe beneath him, and when he looked, blood had begun to gush again from the wound. "Be still, woman, do you want to kill yourself?" he cried desperately, throwing a leg over her thrashing hips. He held her wrists down with his knees and grabbed her shoulders. "Hush, Kate! Hold still, love, you must. Listen to me."

She subsided for a moment, out of weakness, but the panic on her face remained. "Don't, Burke, please don't. Don't tie me, I'm begging you."

He had to turn away from the entreaty in her eyes. Her

voice was low and urgent; she was striving mightily for self-control. It hurt him to hear her beg him for anything; whatever happened, he vowed he would never remind her of this moment. "Listen to me, Kate. If I could, I would take this pain from you and make it mine. But I can't. I'm going to have to hurt you to get the bullet out, and you won't be able to hold still."

"I will!"

"You won't. And if you move while I've got the knife inside you, I'll hurt you more than you've already been hurt."

"Try! Oh, Burke, try, I'm strong, you don't know me, try it, and if I move you can tie me then, I swear I won't even say anything—" She ran out of breath; she was almost babbling from panic.

He bowed his head for a long moment, considering his choice. Finally he looked up and nodded. "All right, love," he said quietly. "We'll make a try." He watched as a little color returned to her cheeks. "But will you remember your promise?"

"I swear I will!" She closed her eyes as he let go of her shoulders and gently extricated himself. Her heart felt unburdened, as though she'd narrowly avoided a terrible catastrophe; what was about to happen couldn't possibly be worse than what she'd escaped. She could hear him doing something by the fire again, and then she heard the high-pitched, grating sound of metal on metal. Unexpectedly, a sickening stab of fear jolted through her, causing her to doubt if she really did have the courage to endure what was coming. A memory of Rory came to her suddenly, and of Michael. For years she'd lived with the pain and confusion of knowing that, for no reason in the world, they had died and she had lived. She would be strong for them, she resolved. And for her kind and gentle father, who had suffered a cruel death in the service of the same cause that had brought her to this moment. "For you, Papa,'' she promised fervently, and opened her eyes.

Burke was standing over her. His face was so troubled, she sent him a tremulous smile for encouragement. He shook his head in wonder and sat down carefully beside her. He put his knife and something else, some ugly metal instrument, on a cloth by her shoulder, and she suppressed a shudder. "Let's get some of these clothes off you," he said, gently pushing her coat, dress, and shift over her shoulders and helping her to pull her arms out of the sleeves. She lay back weakly, naked to the waist until he covered her with his cloak. "Are you cold?" She shook her head; he'd made a huge fire in the hearth and it was warm, almost hot, in the small room. He held her head and made her take one more swallow of brandy. And then it seemed there was nothing else to do but begin. He reached out and touched her cheek, stroking her jaw with his thumb. "Are you ready?"

Her hand found his and squeezed it softly. "Aye, I'm as ready as I'll ever be." Her smile flickered again briefly; then she dropped her gaze before he could see the dread in her eyes. She felt him pull the wool cape away from her breast and heard a metallic clatter. She clenched her teeth. The first piercing touch shocked her so that she involuntarily jumped. She threw him an anguished look, terrified he wouldn't give her a second chance, but he only clamped his lips together grimly and wiped his damp brow on his shirtsleeve. He dropped to the floor on one knee to have better access to the wound, and Katherine gathered handfuls of his cloak in each fist for something to hold on to. Now that she knew what to expect, the second stab of pain was almost bearable; still, she couldn't stop herself from pressing back with her whole body into the pallet, as if that could lessen the torment.

"Breathe," Burke commanded; but she was afraid if she took a breath she would start sobbing. Surely he was killing her, for it felt as if he were drilling a white-hot spike into her bosom. Tears slipped past her tightly closed eyelids and she despaired; she'd been so determined not to cry. "Breathe!" he repeated. She was frightened by the note of alarm in his voice as she sucked in a gulp of air. Now the pain was excruciating and unrelenting, and she realized with a desolate whimper that she was not going to be able to bear it. All of a sudden she felt a keen, harrowing thrust deep inside, and despite her resolve she opened her mouth and screamed. She had a quick vision of her heart being pulled from her body, and then a warm, compassionate blackness swallowed her up.

She was floating up through a thick black fog to the mouth of a vertical tunnel. She could see a rim of darkness above her, beyond it the clear sky, and then her head and shoulders burst through the black and into the light. She blinked, dazzled by the brightness and completely disoriented. She saw a dark-clad figure sitting by her side but facing away from her, and her eyes widened until she recognized Burke. Elbows on his knees, he was resting his forehead in his hands; she thought he might be asleep. She lay still so as not to wake him, remembering everything. There was a slight piercing stab in her chest at the top of each breath, but otherwise she was free of pain. She felt as if she'd awakened from the deepest sleep of her life.

She raised her hand to her breast and explored the area of the wound with tentative fingers. There was nothing to feel but a bandage. But it was dry, so she knew the bleeding had stopped. She was wearing Flora's white nightgown, open down the front. The room looked almost tidy in the dim candlelight. It was black outside the window directly across from the bed, but she had no idea what time it was or even what day it was. She realized that the mere act of moving her arm had wearied her to the point that now she could only lie motionless. Still, she must have made some sound or movement because Burke turned just then to look at her.

His face was strained and pale; he looked exhausted. There was a deep line between his eyebrows and she wanted to smooth it away with her thumb, but she couldn't lift her arm. He looked into her eyes with a hopeful intensity that was new and slightly unnerving, and asked the question she'd been about to ask him.

"How are you?"

"Very well," she murmured after a second's thought. "Everything considered."

He smiled, and his whole face changed. She'd never seen it look so open and unguarded; she couldn't stop staring at him.

"Burke, did I move? I can't remember."

He took her hand and brought it to his lips. "No, sweet, you didn't move. You stayed as still as a rock at Stonehenge."

She sent up a swift prayer of thanks. "I fainted, though, didn't I?" Her brow creased in a disapproving frown.

He nodded, moving his mouth softly back and forth across her knuckles. "Yes, thank God. The bullet is out and I've sewn you up with a needle and thread. Quite a nice job, too, if I say so myself."

"You sewed—me up?" she repeated, dumbfounded.

"Indeed I did. The scar shouldn't be too bad, either. In time you may come to think of it as a beauty mark. Not that you need anything there to make you more beautiful."

She blinked; she was getting so tired, she could hardly follow his words. "And the room?" she asked drowsily. "Did you hire a maid while I was sleeping?" He smiled again and she watched his lips in fascination as he kissed her fingers one last time and then carefully returned her hand to her side. She remembered what she'd wanted to tell him before. "Burke, you were right—I was so stupid. I had no idea he was planning to kill you, I swear it. You believe me, don't you?''

"Yes, of course.'' His eyebrows rose in surprise.

She smiled sheepishly. Yes, of course. Otherwise she wouldn't be lying here, would she?

"Go to sleep, Kate.''

She obeyed instantly.

"What do you think you're doing?''

"I'm taking your bishop with my knight, that's what.''

"That's not a knight, it's a rook.''

"Burke, if you're going to cheat again—''

"Cheat! You're the one who cheats. I've told you three times that knights are stones and rooks are twigs.''

"Except when you want it to be the other way around.''

"Now, that's a childish lie, completely unworthy of you.''

"Why don't you write it down, then?''

"There's nothing to write with. Just *remember*, Kate: pawns are pebbles, bishops are bark—''

"I know all that. *You* remember.''

Burke sighed and leaned back on his elbow, cradling his head in his hand. They were sharing the pallet, the makeshift chess board he'd fashioned resting between them, holding its odd array of sticks and stones and leaves. Katherine smiled faintly, enjoying his exasperation. He couldn't help smiling back. "How do you feel?'' he asked, for the dozenth time that day.

"Much better.'' It was her standard answer. But sometimes she was in pain, and when it was very bad he would lie beside her and hold her, talk to her and tell her stories until the pain lessened or she fell asleep. Whatever happened later, she knew she would always be grateful to him for that.

"Make your move, then, tortoise.''

"I made it.''

"Make a *legitimate* move.''

She clucked her tongue, but shrugged and moved a different piece, muttering, "Some men just can't stand to lose to a woman."

She won that game but fell asleep in the middle of the next, waiting for him to take his turn. Burke lay quietly beside her, watching her, thinking his thoughts, and after a time he fell asleep too.

He dreamed they were kissing, lying on the ground, he on top of her. A gun cocked in his ear. Someone fired a shot and he felt a bullet trace a hot path through the center of his body, then through Kate's. But there was no pain, and instead of dying they were fused together, heart to heart.

"I'm starving."

He opened his eyes. Her turquoise ones were blinking sleepily at him, her head turned toward him on the pillow.

"Feed me."

He had an all but overwhelming urge to kiss her. Instead he said, "You know, Kate, your illness has given you an unattractive bossy quality." She only smiled a slow, drowsy smile. He got to his feet and stretched, groaning and rubbing his face. "Would you like rabbit and onions this evening, my love? Or onions and rabbit?"

"Mm, you decide. Both sound equally . . . equal."

He set about heating the bland stew they'd been dining on for two days. Katherine lay back against the wad of clothing they were using for a pillow and watched him, content to be silent, utterly at ease. They hadn't exchanged a cross word in three days, she realized with a feeling of awe. It couldn't last, of course, especially now that they knew she wasn't going to die—indeed, she'd begun to get a little stronger, though her right arm was still useless. But for now the harmony between them was lovely, and she meant to enjoy it while she could. What would happen when she was well enough to travel was a subject they were leaving alone, for now, by unspoken agreement.

When the stew was ready, he helped her to sit up a little and then fed it to her with his fingers—there were no forks or spoons in the cottage. He could never quite get over the element of sexuality involved in feeding her this way, nor could he tell from her expression whether she shared his perspective. Sometimes she would put out her tongue to lick a drop of broth from his fingers, and he would go rigid with a hard, aching lust. Tonight she actually sucked his thumb for a second, and he had to struggle to maintain his facial composure.

"Are you doing that on purpose?"

She finished chewing the last bit of rabbit and swallowed. "Doing what?"

He scrutinized her expression of baffled innocence for a long minute. "Nothing," he growled. He set the bowl aside, got up to stir the fire, then resumed his place beside her on the pallet. His body was turned toward her, one shoulder propped against the wall behind them.

"What?" she said, puzzled by the lengthening silence and his air of hesitancy.

"Kate . . ." Oh hell, he'd just ask her. "Why did you do it?"

"Do what?"

His lips pulled sideways with impatience and she looked away. He took one of her clasped hands out of her lap and held it tightly. "Tell me why."

It was absurd to pretend she didn't know what he meant. But the truth was, Katherine didn't know the answer. She hadn't given the subject any thought, before or since. And she didn't want to start now. "Because I didn't want him to shoot you." She colored, knowing how inadequate that sounded. His hand on her jaw made her look at him directly. "Well, that *is* why." The blue intensity of his gaze held her; she was mesmerized by the firelight on his skin, the beauty of his mouth when he spoke.

"That's not good enough." He leaned nearer, his voice only a murmur. She looked so beautiful to him in the shadowy light of the fire and the single candle beside them. Learning the answer to his question began to seem less important than holding her. "You threw your arms over your head," he whispered, "trying to make as big a target of your body as possible. It was deliberate, not an impulse. Why?"

He was stroking her throat, his lips a breath away. Her eyes closed. "What do you want me to say?" she managed, one hand pressing against the flat of his chest to hold him away, or to touch him.

He didn't really know. There were things he couldn't say to her either; but now that his hands were sliding over her warm skin, he thought he knew a way to show her. "Why do you always smell so good?" he asked, distracted, nuzzling the hair behind her ear.

She couldn't answer that either. She had some idea that if she kept her eyes closed, she could pretend this wasn't really happening. Oh, but it was. "Burke, what are you doing?" Her fingers tightened on his shirtfront when his mouth came down. She'd wanted him to kiss her all day, but she shuddered when he nudged her lips apart and sleeked his warm, wet tongue inside. She made a weak mewl of protest that turned into something else as he began to caress her softly, with a sweetness she'd never known with him before. "Burke, don't," she finally got out when he left her mouth and started kissing her eyelids, her cheekbones; but her fingers threading his hair sent another message.

"I want to." He was skillfully undoing the buttons down the front of her nightgown and she wasn't doing anything to stop him. "And you want me to." Watching her eyes, he slipped his hand inside and cupped her left breast in his palm, stroking it with slow, lazy passes until she had to hide her face from him. "Do you like it?" Her answer was incoherent. He kissed her hard little nipple while he listened to the quick, helpless moans she couldn't smother.

"Why are you doing this?" Her toes were clenching, her breath coming in rapid pants. For answer, he jerked the covers back and threw them to the foot of the bed. "Oh God, no, we *can't*—" But he already had his hand under her gown, and now he was coaxing her legs apart while he kissed her. "This—this isn't good for me," she gasped into his mouth, knowing in secret that that couldn't be true. "You told me not to move, you said—"

"Hush. Lie still, I'll do everything." He couldn't have stopped now if she'd begged him. He'd wanted to give her this pleasure for days, driven half-crazy by the nearness and the sweet intimacy of her body, and even more by this rare and extraordinary gentleness between them. "Let me, Kate. Yes." He found her secret place, heard her breath catch. She was struggling for control, but his patience was endless. "Let go," he murmured against her throat, "I'll catch you." Katherine made a last, desperate try at self-restraint, and failed. Her response was stark and unmistakable as he kept up the lovely, merciless assault, until all at once her mouth opened on a soundless cry. Her head went back against the pillow and he saw the cords in her slender neck stretch taut, felt her stiffen against him. He kissed her over and over, crooning her name, and then he held her while the long, shuddering tremors subsided.

There were tears on her cheeks. "Did I hurt you?" he whispered. "Are you all right?" She didn't answer. "Why are you crying, Kate? Are you embarrassed?" She turned her face away. He wanted to soothe her; he felt as satisfied as if the pleasure had been his. Her skin was moist and sweet. He touched his tongue to the hollow behind her ear, blew on it with his warm breath. He tried to kiss her on the mouth again, but she wouldn't let him.

She wanted to push him away, but she couldn't move yet. When she finally spoke, it was in a quavery falsetto that made him smile. "You shouldn't have done that. I didn't want you to."

This was manifestly untrue, but he maintained a gallant silence while he stroked her ribs and breathed in the scent of her hair.

"You took advantage of me," she insisted. "At my weakest, most vulnerable moment. You behaved like a cad."

He nodded meekly.

"It was *despicable*." She was warming to it now. "What sort of man would do such a thing to a helpless invalid? Certainly not a gentleman!"

This was too much. He sat up. Her eyes, still damp from weeping, were glittering with righteous indignation and there was hectic color in her cheeks. "Excuse me, but you—"

"I couldn't fight for fear of hurting myself! And you knew it, and took the meanest, most contemptible advantage of my condition. Damn you, James Burke—"

"Now, hold on a minute, Kate. You were not that unwilling and you know it."

"You scurvy son of a—Stop *leering* at me, damn it! Out! Get *out*!"

"Out? It's the middle of the night!"

"I don't care."

She was pushing at him with all her feeble strength, and he was afraid she really might hurt herself. He gave her a quick kiss, which she immediately wiped off, and said, "All right, all right, I'll go." Maybe he would chop wood for a while; it might take his mind off his body's needs, which were beginning to reassert themselves. She turned her back on him and he stood up. "There's no reason for you to feel ashamed, love," he said to the top of her head. She only went more rigid. "And don't expect me to apologize, because I'm not sorry." He lowered his voice intimately. "And neither are you." She made a furious, inarticulate sound. He crossed to the door, but paused with his hand on the knob. "Oh, and Kate. You were spectacular."

"Go!"

He chuckled. "I'm going." And out he went.

Katherine sank back on the pillow and covered her face with her hands. The tears came immediately, streaming down her cheeks and into her ears, tickling and making her shiver. When she grew tired of crying, she wiped her eyes and commenced to curse, calling James Burke every horrible name she could think of, out loud. She only subsided when she'd depleted her storehouse of vile expressions. After that, there was nothing to do but think.

That coward, that bully! He'd *tricked* her, that's what. And then he'd had the nerve to tell *her* not to feel ashamed. What had *she* to be ashamed of? He was the one who had manipulated her, callously *used* her in a weak moment, and she had only . . . she'd only . . .

She covered her face again and went back to crying. She had only wanted every slow, scorching caress the way a starving woman wants food. Oh God! How *could* she have let him touch her that way? And then to—to let him see her while she . . . She cringed and hid her face in the covers. Oh, she would never live this down. But it was his fault! He was no better than an animal, and he deserved a vicious thrashing for what he'd done.

She had a vague sense that she was overreacting. It had happened, that was all, and now it was over. Besides, she was no slave to her own passions, she was a reasonable, intelligent woman. This was a fluke, an aberration. He'd caught her when her defenses were down, that was all. *Any* man could have done it.

But her nerves still tingled from the feelings he'd aroused, and dangerous memories flooded back. How right it had seemed, how sweet, how—inevitable. And he'd been so gentle these last few days, her island of safety in a harsh sea of pain and fear. They'd treated each other like friends, almost, or even lovers . . .

Lovers! Ha! What an idiot she was. Her fingers twisted in the covers, would have torn them if she'd had the strength. Lovers! He'd only been kind so he could lull her into trusting him and then *humiliate* her. But she would pay him back. Someday, somehow. She didn't know what she would do yet, but one day he would writhe with mortification the way she did, and she would laugh at him and be glad.

She wiped her eyes again and buttoned her nightgown. She felt better. Stifling a groan, she sat up, leaning her weight on her arms behind her. She dragged her legs across the low pallet and dropped them over the side.

That was a mistake. A nauseating wave of dizziness engulfed her and before she knew it she had fallen over backwards. She stared up at the ceiling, trying to breathe normally and hoping she hadn't hurt herself. There was a dull throbbing in her breast, but it wasn't too bad. After a minute she grabbed hold of the sides of the pallet with both hands and hauled herself upright again, panting with effort. She sat still, recovering her breath, then pushed herself closer to the edge. There was no post to help her to rise; she would have to stand up on her own power. The floor was cold on her bare feet. In the back of her mind she knew she wasn't ready for this, but the need to get strong, to throw off this degrading vulnerability and stop being Burke's victim, was a powerful goad to foolish and precipitous behavior. She stood up.

Immediately the room began to spin and she broke out in a cold sweat. She stood, swaying, teeth clenched, knowing that if she fell she would do herself serious harm. After a while the room was only swimming, not spinning, and she took a tentative step forward. Then another. She was wobbly but determined; she made it to the far side of the small room in less than two minutes. She clung to the wall, breathing in great gulps and beginning to tremble. The trembling turned into a palsied shaking, and tears of helplessness splashed down her cheeks when she realized she wasn't going to be able to make it back to the bed. And if she obeyed her quaking knees and slid down the wall to the floor, she would never get up again. The thought of crawling to the bed was somehow appalling; what if Burke walked in and saw her? She let out a pitiful, hopeless wail and banged her head against the wall. Burke came through the door at that moment.

He saw her at once—she was standing only a little to his left; he sucked in his breath and dropped the pile of wood he was carrying. "What the hell do you think you're doing?" he cried, anger battling with worry on his proud face.

"Don't talk to me like that!" she shouted back, dashing telltale tears from her cheeks. "And don't touch me! Ever again, you cowardly whoreson bastard! I'm walking, that's what, and I don't need you to—to—" To what? "To tell me I can or I can't!" she finished lamely. "Now, get away, I'm busy." She took a confident step sideways, away from him, and the floor rose up with amazing speed. He caught her around the middle just before she would have hit the ground. She lost consciousness briefly; when she came to, they were both on the floor, she in his arms, he rubbing her wrists and looking intently into her face. "I did not faint," she insisted, her voice a quaver. "I did *not*."

"No indeed."

"Don't humor me."

He smiled, and she felt her anger begin to drift away meekly, like a cloud after a storm. She tried to call it back but it was too far off now, floating softly out of sight. I'll still pay you back, James Burke, she promised. But it was only a solemn statement of fact now, devoid of rancor. What she really wanted was to close her eyes and let her head fall against his chest. The beating of his heart was strong and steady and the sound of it pleased her enormously. She felt his lips on her forehead, where it seemed to her they ought to be. A dreamy half-smile touched the corners of her mouth and she drifted off into a lovely, warm sleep.

It wasn't quite dawn yet when Katherine heard Burke get up, pull on his clothes, and go outside. He certainly wasn't sleeping well lately, she reflected, moving her feet over to the warm place he'd vacated. She, on the contrary, was sleeping almost twenty hours a day, and beginning to recover a little of her strength. After he'd caught her trying to walk the day before yesterday, he'd made her promise not to get out of bed again unless he was there to help her. Yesterday she'd gotten up two times and walked around the room on his arm. The first time she'd done remarkably well, staying on her feet for at least ten minutes; the second, she'd tired out soon and had to lean on him heavily as he steered her back to bed. She expected to do better today, but she was impatient with her progress. She wanted to be well *now*, immediately.

She shifted restlessly, watching the sky lighten through the window. She was hungry, but a steady diet of rabbit and onions was beginning to wear on her. Shivering, she pulled Burke's cloak more tightly around her shoulders; the room was drafty and almost always cold, regardless of how big a fire he built. They were fortunate it hadn't rained yet, but she knew their luck couldn't last much longer. It would not be pleasant to lie on this pallet while water streamed through the sizable hole in the roof directly overhead. Burke, she knew, was as anxious to leave as she, probably more so; it was only the agonizingly slow progress of her healing that kept them here.

She'd promised not to get out of bed unless he was with her, but that had been when she was much weaker, much more prone to dizziness and falling. Surely the promise didn't apply today, she told herself, shoving back the covers and slowly pulling herself to her feet.

There. She felt fine, hardly dizzy at all. She would go stir the fire, make herself useful for a change.

She had to bend down to pick up the stick Burke used for a poker. That was not, she swiftly realized, a wise move. She leaned her forehead against the mantel-less brick front of the fireplace and breathed evenly, waiting for the spell to pass. A log snapped, a spark flew. She looked down. Her nightgown was on fire.

She uttered a frightened sound and began to beat at the gown against her knees with her palms. More sparks flew, and in a trice the shirt Burke had hung to dry over the hearth was spitting short, angry flames into her face. She shrieked and jumped away, still slapping at the hot sparks that leapt and danced at the hem of her nightgown. The wooden pole Burke's shirt had hung upon went up in a whoosh of smoke and sparks, and Katherine began to cough violently. Water, she needed water—she spied the cup beside the bed, seized it, and dashed the contents at the nearest flames. The only effect was a hissing sound as, with mind-numbing quickness, fire began to creep over the dry floorboards and flick past the narrow column of brick toward the walls. The noise and heat doubled, tripled while she watched. The cloth that half-covered the window ignited and disappeared in a fierce shower of sparks. Coughing and in pain, transfixed and unable to think or move, at last Katherine remembered Burke's cloak. She pulled it from the bed with panicked, jerky movements and tried to suffocate the flames engulfing the hearth under its heavy woolen weight. If she'd thought of it even a minute sooner, it might have helped; now it was too late. She knew it, and stepped back. Tears were streaming down her cheeks and she couldn't get her breath; the heat was so intense, she felt as if her flesh were melting.

She had to get out or she would perish. But then the cottage would burn to the ground—where would they go? Her brain wouldn't take her further into the future than this moment. If only she could lift the pallet from the floor and somehow hurl it on top of the flames—but even if she'd had the strength it was much too late for that, she perceived in the next instant: the fire was spreading to the ceiling, sending down flaming chunks of thatch and igniting the desiccated straw mat that had once been a rug. Smoke was thick, inky, suffocating. Her choices had narrowed to one. Staggering, she scooped up her shoes from the floor by the bed, her coat from a nail by the door, and stumbled out into the cold, clean air.

She collapsed on the ground a little distance away, leaned her shoulder against the trunk of a tree, and watched as the cottage fell in on itself with a deafening roar. Her head throbbed and the burnt stench that clung to her nostrils was nauseating. Her breath wheezed in her throat, every inhalation an agony to her scalded lungs. She began to shudder convulsively as if she were freezing, though her skin was still hot to the touch. Without thought, her lips formed Burke's name, and out of nowhere he appeared.

But he hadn't seen her, he was running toward the heap of still-blazing rubble, and now he was kicking aside piles of snapping, sizzling straw. She thought he was calling her, but it was impossible to hear over the spitting sound of the flames.

''Burke! I'm—'' She barely got the words out before her throat closed and she began to cough again. He was wading in deeper, oblivious to the thigh-high wreckage burning around him. Somehow she got to her feet. She must finally have forced out an audible sound; before she was halfway to him, he turned and saw her.

He reached her at the moment her knees gave away; he lifted her in his arms and ran, cursing violently, until they were a safe distance away.

Fear and unspeakable relief rendered him furious. "You bloody idiot! How did you manage it, Kate? What the hell are we going to do now, you stupid, bungling—" All the while he reviled her his hands roved over her body, searching out the myriad places she'd hurt herself. His rage faded when he realized she was in deeper distress than he, not mortally wounded but frightened and in pain. He pulled her into his arms and crooned her name, gentlehanded, sighing comfort into her hair, and held her close against his body until she stopped shaking.

"How did it happen?" he asked at last, speaking in a quiet, reasonable tone.

"I—" She gestured helplessly. "It's a long story." Her voice came out a raw croak.

"I'm sure." He blew ashes out of her hair and gathered her close again, listening to the labored sound of her breathing. "Can you ride? We can't stay here any longer."

"Where will we go?" she managed in a husky whisper, wincing with effort. "I don't think I can ride all the way to Lancaster."

He gave her a tiny, impatient shake. "We're not going to Lancaster, Kate. We're going home."

"Home," she echoed weakly. "Yes, Burke, let's go home."

PART III

CHAPTER 16

"You don't *live* here." Katherine's voice was a croak from disuse. She rested her head against Burke's chest and stared up at the three-story mass of columns, turrets, balconies, and salmon-colored brick that was Wedding-stone. It was so immense, it was hard to imagine one man and his rather small family living here. On first sight, she'd thought it must be a government building of some sort, or perhaps one of the royal residences; at the very least, a grand hotel.

"Home, sweet home," Burke assured her. His tone held a mixture of pride and deprecation. He slowed the horse's pace as they trod a long, stately avenue of lime trees.

Late afternoon sun was warming the rose brick walls, making the house seem slightly more human, less monumental. Katherine blinked sleepily and tried to imagine Burke as a small boy, growing up in this enormous place. It wasn't hard to do, she realized; in fact, it explained quite a lot.

"Good God, what's that?" She looked up to see what he was scowling at: three floors of scaffolding surrounding a good deal of the east wing. "Another of my stepmother's projects," he guessed sourly. "Now, pay attention, Kate. Are you awake?"

"Yes, I'm awake." She'd slept much of the way,

slumped sideways against him.

"Your name is Katherine Pell; you're a widow. There was a fire in our hotel in Bewcastle this morning and you were injured. I'm bringing you to my home to recover. Have you got that?"

She nodded mutely. There was something significant in the fact that Burke was shielding her identity from his own family, but she was too ill and exhausted to understand what it was. She would think about it later. Meanwhile, she was staggered by the audacity of the new role she had to play: a lady pretending to be a whore pretending to be a lady.

"How do you feel, love?"

"I'm glad we're here," she whispered. She was too tired to tell him she would have keeled over and died if they'd gone another mile.

An elegant carriage drawn by four fine matched bays was waiting at the bottom of a three-way marble staircase, while a coachman and two footmen in crisp livery stood by. Burke reined in the stallion a little distance away just as the massive front door opened. A butler stood aside and three fashionably dressed ladies swept past, heading for the carriage. Seeing the new arrivals, they stopped in unison on the top step. The youngest, a tall, willowy girl of about sixteen with black hair and gray eyes, let out an unladylike screech and bolted, with a slight but noticeable limp, down the stairs. Katherine smiled at the new and unwonted sound of Burke's laughter, spontaneous and full of pleasure, as he jumped from the horse's back. Almost before he could turn around the girl was upon him, wrapping her arms around his neck and hugging him with all her strength. He lifted her from the ground and spun her around twice while she shrieked with delight. Ill as she was, it was impossible for Katherine not to laugh with them, so evident was their joy at seeing each other.

"James."

The girl stepped out of his embrace at last as the second of the ladies to reach them, a striking-looking woman with hair so blonde as to be almost white, said his name with a more subdued kind of excitement. She glided into his arms and kissed him full on the mouth. Katherine looked away, and saw the black-haired girl staring up at her with undisguised curiosity.

"Olivia," Burke said with a faint smile, gently disengaging the long, slim arms from around his neck. "How lovely to see you. And you, Renata." He bowed over the hand of the third, a middle-aged matron with a huge ostrich feather curled around her carefully coiffed gray hair.

"Well, James, you've come home. Your father will be overjoyed to see you." Lady Renata was trying to smile graciously, but it was difficult for her to take her eyes from the strange and astonishingly disheveled young woman still seated above them on Burke's horse.

Burke raised his arms to Katherine. She put her left hand on his shoulder; her right arm wasn't working very well and hung limply at her side. She almost collapsed against him as he lifted her from the saddle, and the ground under her feet felt wobbly and dangerous. She put a hand on the stallion's flank to steady herself, then gazed back at the three staring women with as much poise as she could summon. The scorched hem of her nightgown was plainly visible beneath her coat, and her bare ankles looked white and vulnerable above her brown leather shoes. Her hair was dirty and tangled, her face smudged with soot. She was beginning to shiver again, and the smile she was laboring to sustain was faltering. She heard Burke's voice as if through a tunnel, introducing her as Mrs. Pell and saying something about a fire. The older woman was his stepmother, the beautiful blonde his stepsister. The girl was Lady Diana, his sister. Katherine knew if she curtsied her knees would give way and she would fall down, so she bowed her head instead. Then Burke was moving her forward, his hand pressing lightly at the small of her back, and she was gazing up at a monstrous pile of dazzling white marble steps that suddenly seemed higher and steeper than any of the Pyramids. She took a step up, then another. Another. On the fourth or fifth step the yellow stars in front of her eyes multiplied a hundredfold. Vaguely alarmed, she felt herself falling over backwards. Someone screamed. Burke grabbed her arm at the last second, wrenching her shoulder painfully. Then everything went black.

When she opened her eyes, she saw a veritable constellation of faces bobbing above her, peering down with differing degrees of curiosity and concern. She sought Burke's face among them, like the North Star on a cloudy night, and realized he was the one holding her hand. She started to speak.

"I know," he said, forestalling her; "you didn't faint." She smiled, and the intimate look that passed between them went unnoticed by no one. "Put your arm around my neck." She did, and he lifted her up from the cold marble as easily as if she weighed nothing at all.

"Mrs. Pell is ill," he explained unnecessarily. "Is there a room made up?"

"Of course," Lady Renata spoke up. "The Blue Room in the West Wing will do, I should think." Her voice had a way of capitalizing the rooms and wings at Weddingstone.

Diana frowned in puzzlement. "Oh, but surely—"

"The blue room will be perfect," Burke interrupted. Her Ladyship doubtless had her own reasons for wanting the invalid far away and out of sight; so did he.

The tall, stately butler appeared at his side. "Shall someone fetch the doctor, my lord?"

"Not yet, Knole. I'll let you know if it's necessary."

"Very good, my lord."

Katherine rested her cheek against the lapel of Burke's coat and blinked wearily at Olivia, whose head was on a level with hers. She was undeniably beautiful, with a pale complexion made paler by the liberal application of rice powder. Her lavender velvet coat and saucy pink hat were the pinnacle of *haute couture*, and her maid must have labored for hours to perfect the complicated coiffure for her strange, silvery-blonde hair. There was no friendliness in the cool blue eyes that were examining her face and person with openly rude interest. Katherine had seen the look many times—that of a woman taking the measure of a potential rival. The very thought of doing battle with Olivia over anyone or anything sapped what little energy she had left. She closed her eyes in temporary surrender, and was glad when Burke turned around and started up the steps.

The entrance hall was two-storied, and as magnificent as the outside of the house promised. The walls were of pastel stucco, delicately carved; the ceiling was a painted fresco high overhead. Busts of illustrious ancestors stared down from niches inset below a massive cornice. The spectacular curving staircase was oak inlaid with walnut, with a filigreed wrought-iron bannister.

It looked as if all three ladies meant to follow them upstairs, as well as the butler and two of the housemaids. Burke turned around and confronted them.

"Renata, would you tell my father I'm here and will be down to speak to him presently? Knole, I won't be needing you. I look forward to seeing you at supper, Olivia. Diana, come along and help me, will you?"

A look, carefully controlled but nevertheless communicating perfectly a sense of mounting alarm, passed between Olivia and her mother. Burke missed it but Katherine did not.

After that it seemed to her they climbed hundreds of steps and moved down dozens of high-ceilinged hallways,

all richly adorned and fabulously appointed. Servants
bowed or curtsied and stood aside, respectfully lowering
astonished eyes only to gape after them in wonder. Diana
looked ready to burst with questions, but good breeding
prevented her from asking them in front of Katherine. At
last they arrived at a closed door at the end of a long,
somewhat gloomy hallway. Diana opened it and Katherine
had a quick impression of a large, comfortable bed
chamber with blue damask wall hangings and a polished
wood floor. The wide four-poster bed was of massive
mahogany and could have accommodated three or four
people.

"Pull back the covers, would you, Di?" said Burke. He
laid Katherine down on the white silk sheet and sat beside
her. "Close the door." Diana did, then stood by the bed a
bit uncertainly, her hands clasped in front of her.

Katherine, who was not in pain but was nearly numb
with fatigue, gazed dreamily up at the two of them,
fascinated by the resemblance. Diana had Burke's black,
shiny hair and pale but healthy complexion, and they
shared as well the same long, straight nose and regal
bearing. But Diana's eyes were a soft gray and her sweet,
feminine mouth lacked the hard, sensual beauty of her
brother's. She had a calm and dignified beauty even at
sixteen, despite the limp she tried unsuccessfully to hide.
She was looking expectantly at Burke, and her eyes
widened to saucers when she saw him unbutton
Katherine's coat and then her nightgown.

"I'll g-get the maid," she stammered, turning away.

"No, Di, don't. Come and sit down." He indicated the
other side of the bed. She hesitated, then did as she was
bid. "I see you're all grown up, pet," he smiled, his eyes
alight with affection.

"I'll be seventeen in two m-months."

"Yes, I know. You've turned into a lovely young
woman since I saw you last."

She colored and looked down, her expression indicating she did not believe him.

"I'm obliged to ask you a favor, pet. I wish I didn't have to, but I have no choice."

"Anything, Jamie. You know that."

"It'll involve keeping a secret." He smiled at her swiftly concealed eagerness. "A secret from everyone, even Father."

Diana looked at Katherine. "It's about M-Mrs. Pell, isn't it?"

"Yes. Whom you may call Katherine." The two ladies nodded formally, to Burke's amusement. "Now, listen, before Renata sends the maid up. It's important, for reasons I can't explain, that the exact nature of Mrs. Pell's illness not become known. Therefore she'll need someone to help her with things like bathing and changing clothes. The maid can wait on her most of the time; but for the intimate chores, we need someone we can trust."

Diana was wide-eyed. "What *is* the n-nature of Mrs. Pell's illness?" she inquired softly, shyly.

"A bullet wound in the breast."

Katherine blushed deeply and put a hand over her eyes. She felt called upon to say something, but nothing came readily to mind.

"Oh. W-*well*." Diana was experiencing the same difficulty.

"The details aren't important, but you should know Mrs. Pell was hurt while trying to save my life." He reached out and gently pulled Katherine's hand away from her face, looking into her eyes as if the answer to a question might be read there. She stared back guardedly, giving nothing away. After a long moment she transferred her gaze to Diana, whose mouth had formed a perfect O.

"I would be grateful for your help," she said in a hoarse whisper. "I'm sorry it means keeping a secret from your family, and I understand perfectly if you feel you would rather not.''

Diana looked from one to the other in growing wonder and finally found her voice. "Of course I'll help!"

"Good." Burke stood. "The first thing you can do is head off the maid; tell her to come back in half an hour. Then find some clean cloth to use for a bandage, and make sure no one catches you at it. Then come back and I'll show you how to change the dressing. Go along now, and hurry."

"Yes!" She squeezed Katherine's hand on an impulse and stood up. "Don't worry," she whispered conspiratorially, "I'll be right back."

Katherine laughed softly and watched her go. She and Burke exchanged fond glances, almost like parents over a beloved child. Then he sat beside her again and began to elaborate on the story he was making up to explain her presence. He hadn't gotten far when he realized she was fast asleep.

Neville Burke, the eleventh Earl of Rothbury, was young-looking at sixty, with snow-white hair and his son's silver-blue eyes, which had not softened at all with age. Tall and slender, with prominent cheekbones and a strong beak of a nose, he was an older, slightly effete version of his virile son, and practically a caricature of the wealthy, titled aristocrat. One could almost see the blue blood coursing through his veins.

He rose from his uncluttered desk when he saw Burke in the doorway to his study and held out a hand. The two men greeted each other affectionately but with no more outward emotion than was seemly. Burke waited for his father to resume his seat, then sank tiredly into the armchair in front of the desk. He looked around at the familiar hunting prints on the paneled walls, the globe in its stand by the mullioned windows; he sniffed the familiar odor of ink and old books. He thought how very little had changed since he'd been here last. The reflection was at once soothing and depressing.

"Well, Father," he began, clasping his hands around one updrawn knee.

"James. Naturally I'm delighted to see you at home, but puzzled over what brings you."

"Nothing, really. I'm between assignments, and it's nearly Christmas. I wanted to see my family." It sounded reasonable. His father's pleased expression gave him the heart to go on. "Last night I was stopping at a hotel in Bewcastle. At supper I met a lady, a widow from Edinburgh returning from a visit with her late husband's family. Later, around four o'clock in the morning, there was a fire. The lady, a Mrs. Pell, roused several of the sleeping guests, myself included. She was subsequently overcome by the smoke and flames and very nearly didn't survive. Out of gratitude, and because there was no suitable place nearby, I brought her here to recover. She saved my life, and I was certain you'd be eager to receive her."

"Indeed, indeed! Why, how extraordinary. Renata told me there was a—a person with you, but I had no idea. How extraordinary!"

"Isn't it. So tell me, Father, how have you been?" He thought it politic to get on to another subject quickly.

"Eh, fairly well, fairly well. My family is spending me into the poorhouse; otherwise I'm tolerable. You've seen the east wing?" Burke nodded. "Renata wants to do it over in marble, ever since we returned from Italy. Marble! Makes me cold to think of it. And the lawn! You won't believe this, my boy. She wants to pull up all the flowers and shrubs in the gardens and plant a 'landscape,' whatever the bloody hell that is. The newest thing, in case you didn't know, is making nature look more natural." He curled his lip in disgust. "Meadows, lakes with swans, and I don't know what else. Why, someone told me Lord

Finchley put a dead tree in his park so it would look more 'natural.' Hah!''

Burke chuckled and slid lower in his chair, crossing his legs.

''And Olivia is worse, if anything. By God, I never knew one woman could spend so much money on clothes. Now she wants imported paper from China for the walls in her bedroom. Bought a fighting cock for three hundred pounds, wagers on it against the birds of her idiotic friends. Wants me to buy her a *monkey*. So it can ruin the new carpet from Persia she's ordered for the sitting room, I suppose.''

''Poor Father. I used to wonder why you never adopted her; now I understand.''

''Ha! Renata wanted it, too, but I wouldn't even discuss it. Ah, how dearly Olivia would love to be a 'Lady' instead of a mere 'Miss,' '' he gloated with unconcealed relish.

''And Julian? How is he?''

Neville's smile faded, replaced by an angry scowl. ''My stepson is an embarrassment to me, James. My only hope is that he'll get into so much trouble one day, he'll be deported. Or hanged; that would be even better.''

''I heard some unsavory stories,'' Burke acknowledged.

''All true, I assure you. I don't even want to discuss him.''

''Why do you put up with all of it? The house, Olivia—''

''Why? I suppose because it's easier to do what Renata wants than listen to her nagging.''

Burke cupped his chin in his hand and asked something he'd never thought of asking before. ''Do you love her, Father? Or did you when you married her?''

''Love?'' Lord Rothbury repeated the word as if it were in a foreign language. He seemed genuinely puzzled. ''Renata is capable, reasonably intelligent, and still attractive. More to the point, she was a dowager baroness.

Her husband had been a respectable fellow with a sizable fortune, who hadn't acquired his wealth from trade. She and I may not have been a brilliant match, but there was certainly nothing to be said against it.''

Burke wondered why he'd asked. For some reason he thought of the time Kate had asked him if he were a snob. He hadn't answered her, hadn't thought the subject merited his attention. Perhaps he would think about it someday.

''Did you love Mother?'' The question was as much a surprise to him as it evidently was to his father.

His Lordship looked embarrassed. He opened a drawer in his desk and made a show of looking for something. ''Of course, of course,'' he muttered.

Burke looked away, equally embarrassed. He longed to ask, Yes, but did you *really* love her? Did she love you? Were you happy together? Why were you always so cold to me?

He stood up.

''James, before you go.'' Burke waited politely. ''Just between us, of course.''

''Of course.''

''Renata's taken it into her head that you must marry Olivia. The two of them buzz about it all the time when they think I can't hear. I hope I needn't tell you such a match is unthinkable.''

If Burke hadn't been so tired, he'd have laughed out loud. ''No, Father,'' he said solemnly, ''you needn't tell me.''

''Good,'' said Neville with relief. ''Don't relax your guard, my boy. The two of them together can exert a strange and mysterious power.'' He chuckled, seeing Burke's look. ''I'm serious. It's positively uncanny.''

''Let me put your apprehensions at rest, Father. We are in no danger whatever from that quarter.''

''Mmm.'' Lord Rothbury sobered. ''I want you to make

a good marriage, James.''

"And I shall. Someday.''

"Lord Westley's girl, now, she's almost of age—''

"Good God! That hyena-faced nincompoop? Put it out of your mind forever.''

"Very well, very well.'' His lips twitched. "But don't tell me you mean to marry for love, my boy; it's simply not practical.''

"No, but I won't marry an ugly woman. The sight of a man's wife in the morning ought not to make him wish he were dead.''

"Indeed not. No indeed.'' Smiling, His Lordship stood up and came around the desk. "Had enough of soldiering yet, James?'' he asked, resting a casual hand on his son's shoulder.

Burke was not misled by the seeming idleness of the question. What surprised him was the answer. He'd left home after Oxford and bought a commission in the military in order to escape the life of a leisured, professionless lord and to see something of the world. He'd seen enough now, and it astonished him that the idea of entering politics or involving himself in his father's business affairs did not fill him with loathing, as it had when he was twenty-one.

"I believe I may have, Father. But let's speak of it later; I'm dead on my feet.''

"Fine, fine. Go have a nap.'' Neville clapped him on the back, trying unsuccessfully to mask his delight. "See you at supper, my boy.''

"Breakfast, more like.'' Yawning hugely, Burke left the study and went to his room.

"Weddingstone
Northumberland
December 15, 1745

"Dear Colonel Denholm:

"My apologies for not writing sooner, but I have been ill

with fever for better than a week and am only now sufficiently recovered to hold a pen.

"I regret to inform you there will now be no need for anyone to decide whether the prisoner, Miss Lennox, was a spy or not, as she is unfortunately deceased. She died when she unwisely got in the line of fire between me and Ewan Ramsey, whom you will remember as the man who gambled her away in a card game. Ramsey made a foolish and unsuccessful attempt to rescue his mistress near Newcastleton, and died in the effort.

"What in bloody hell were we doing near Newcastleton, you are undoubtedly asking. The circumstances were complicated and, to be frank, somewhat embarrassing to me professionally. Suffice it to say for now that Miss Lennox's desire and ability to escape punishment for her sundry misdeeds were stronger than I expected. I will brief you on the sordid details when I see you.

"It was soon after this inglorious incident that I fell seriously ill, and was brought home in a coach, not expected to survive. I have outwitted the best efforts of my physicians, however, and hope to be able to return for duty in two to three weeks. I have heard that the Bonnie Prince is in retreat and means to spend a quiet winter in Scotland, so it seems there is no pressing need for my services now anyway.

"I understood from Miss Lennox that her only living relative was a mother residing in Edinburgh. I will undertake the duty of attempting to inform this lady by post of her daughter's death.

"Hoping this letter finds you well—indeed, that it finds you at all—I remain your obedient servant,

"Major Lord James Burke, Viscount Holystone"

Burke tapped his pen against his teeth and stared thoughtfully out at the pinkening dawn through his window. It wasn't a particularly believable story, but on the other hand, Denholm had no reason to disbelieve it. It

worried him that if even half the lies in his letter were
discovered, he would doubtless end up in prison. Still,
what choice did he have? One couldn't repay a girl for
saving his life by turning her over to the hangman, could
one? He didn't know if Kate was a spy or not, and he
didn't care. As soon as she was well enough, she was free to
go.

He got up from his writing desk and walked to the
window. The lovely old formal gardens, soon to be a
"meadow," looked coldly dignified in their winter browns
and grays. Somewhere a thrush chirped a lonely, tuneless
song, and Burke shivered with a sudden chill. The source
of the hollow feeling inside him was the thought of Kate
leaving. He knew it, but it was a subject he was unable to
explore any deeper. He'd never known anyone like her and
he believed he never would again, and yet he could think
of no other ending to their story. None.

Burke knocked softly on Katherine's door and pushed it
open. Diana, reading by a dim lamp near the bed, put a
finger to her lips and rose, gesturing for him to join her in
the window seat on the other side of the room. He trod
silently across the polished floor, catching only a glimpse
of the sleeping Katherine as he passed.

They sat beside each other on the velvet-upholstered
pillows, knees touching, practically in darkness. "How's
the patient?" he asked, keeping his voice low.

"Oh, Jamie, she's so much b-better. She's had no fever
all day and she's hardly in any pain. She won't take the
laudanum anymore."

"Did she eat supper?"

"M-most of it. She says tomorrow she wants a real bath.
I told her I'd ask you."

"I suppose it's all right. Make sure the room is quite
warm before you start. Are you tired, pet? You've been
sitting here all evening."

"I don't mind a bit. I like her so much, Jamie, don't you? She's been so kind to me."

Burke raised his brows. "Who wouldn't be kind to you?" he wanted to know.

"We talk a lot. Or—" she blushed—"I suppose *I* talk a lot. Mostly she just listens."

He felt a warm rush of affection. He touched her cheek, sensing her loneliness. "I wish I could be with you more often, Di. I've missed you very much."

"I've m-missed you, too," she said in a small voice, surprised by his unexpected openness.

"Olivia's not much of a sister to you, is she?"

"Not much," she admitted.

They sat in silence for a few minutes. Then Diana stood and said she'd better go as it was getting late. "Are you coming?"

"In a minute."

She nodded in understanding. "Sometimes when she's asleep, I just sit and stare at her. She's so *beautiful*."

Burke was silent.

"Good night, Jamie."

"Night, pet. Oh, I forgot to tell you. Edwin Balfour is coming to visit tomorrow. He sent a note by his servant."

Immediately Diana's face lit up and became a radiant vision of happiness. She hugged herself and closed her eyes tightly for a second. "Oh, Jamie," she whispered joyfully, "now I have everything!" Then she was gone.

Burke shook his head in wonder and concern. Was there ever a truer, more ingenuous soul? How could anyone so artless ever hope to survive in the wicked world? With all his heart he prayed God would protect her.

He walked over to the bed slowly, hands in his pockets, feeling an odd reluctance. He understood exactly what Diana meant: he'd already done a good deal of staring at Katherine while she slept. Knowing she would soon be gone made him almost not want to see her now. Almost.

He pulled a chair close to the bedside and sat down.

Illness hadn't diminished her loveliness, only changed it; her coloring was less vivid but more subtle, her features softer and, if possible, even more fragile. The thick, dusky lashes couldn't conceal the delicate blue hollows under her eyes. She looked frail and worn out; but Burke's desire for her, he realized after a moment, was neither. He picked up her pale, long-fingered hand, at once feminine and strong, and she moved her head, sighing softly. God, she was beautiful. He remembered with a lurch in his chest how easy it had been to arouse her that day in the cottage, how passionately she'd responded to caresses she swore were unwelcome. Afterward he'd felt a little ashamed: for gallantry or gentlemanly conduct, perhaps it hadn't been his finest hour. Still, what an intense pleasure it had been to touch her, excite her with deliberate skill, and then watch her while she achieved her release. He felt an almost unbearable tightening in his groin and knew he wanted to touch her like that again, now. What sort of a man was he? He dropped her hand, and Katherine's eyelids fluttered open.

He tried to look away, embarrassed by his lustful thoughts, but her clear turquoise gaze, frank and unguarded for once, drew him like a magnet. She held out her hand and he took it back without hesitation. She smiled up at him trustingly. He told himself she was anything but innocent, yet it was hard to hold on to that conviction when all he could see was sweet, guileless loveliness.

He cleared his throat with difficulty. "My sister says you're better."

"I am better." The whispery hoarseness was gone; now there was only a slight huskiness. "I think I could get up tomorrow for a few minutes. And, Burke, I'm dying for a bath—"

"I know, Diana told me. But I'm confused. Is this the

same girl who once professed to hate baths?''

She shrugged, hiding a smile. "I know, but you made me take so many, I've grown quite fond of them."

"I see. I suppose it's all right, if you think you can manage with only Diana to help you."

"I'm sure I can."

"If not, you know I'd be more than happy to lend a hand."

"Thank you, that won't be necessary."

"It wouldn't be the least little bit of trouble."

"I assure you, your assistance won't be required."

"Well, if you're sure."

"Quite sure." They both smiled, enjoying the rare friendliness of the moment. "I like your sister, Burke. She's been so kind to me." He sent her a bemused look, nodding. "Your stepsister came to see me this morning."

"Olivia?" This was a surprise. "What did she want?"

"To—welcome me, I suppose. In a way. She said she hoped I'd recover soon so I could be with my own family for Christmas."

"Did she indeed?" He was smiling and frowning at the same time. "I think you may disappoint her there, Kate; you won't be able to travel by Christmas."

"No, probably not, but I didn't like to tell her. She seemed so set on it." She looked away and then back. "Burke?"

"Yes, love?"

She blushed; he used the word so freely, it upset her for some reason. "What's going to happen?" He looked blank. "I mean after I'm better. What are you going to do with me?" He watched her for a long time without speaking. When he pushed back his chair and stood up, her worst fears were confirmed. "You're taking me back to Lancaster, aren't you?" she accused him bitterly. "I *knew* it." He shook his head, but she wouldn't look at him. "Would you please go away now? I'm very tired."

"Don't worry about this, Kate. Worry about getting well."

"Why? So you can be rid of me sooner? Please, just leave."

He frowned down at her, hands behind his back, wondering why he didn't tell her the truth. If he admitted he was going to let her go, risking his name and his career in the process, she might think, might reasonably conclude, he was doing it because he had feelings for her. She wouldn't see he was acting solely out of gratitude—duty, really—and merely seizing the opportunity to pay her back for the sacrifice she'd made for him.

He sighed, resigned to her enmity. "Good night, then. Sleep well." She put a hand over her eyes and turned her head away. "Try not to worry, Kate." She'd find out what his intentions were soon enough anyway, he told himself.

"Get out," she said through her teeth.

"I'll send the maid to you." He went quietly from the room.

The days passed quickly and, in spite of Katherine's apprehension about what would happen to her when she was well, not unpleasantly. She could feel herself slowly growing stronger, requiring assistance less frequently for every tiny chore as time went by. Each afternoon she walked on Diana's arm around the room in a slow, stately procession, an activity they both found agreeable. The progress of their friendship was quick, their attachment nonetheless strong. Katherine had no wish to lie to her friend and make up a complicated history of herself, as she once had for Burke, so she was obliged to be either vague or silent about her past. Diana attributed this to natural reticence, a quality she possessed in some degree herself, and never pressed for details. Under Katherine's gentle encouragement and unfeigned interest, the younger

woman abandoned her usual shyness and opened her heart
as though to the long-wanted sister she'd never had. She
was sweet-tempered, with a keen intelligence that saw
through people's vanities and weaknesses, and a kindly
disposition that allowed her to forgive them. Her only flaw
was a complete inability to recognize her own worth. She
had suffered a small limp from birth, owing to one leg
being very slightly shorter than the other; when nervous or
excited, she was apt to speak with a mild stutter. These
handicaps caused her profound embarrassment and con-
tributed to her deep and abiding conviction that she was
an unattractive misfit—an opinion her stepmother and
stepsister never challenged. She was sure she would
forever, and rightfully, be in the shadow of the beautiful,
glamorous, and worldly Olivia. It was a tribute to the
kindness of her heart that this certainty never caused her a
moment's envy.

Katherine heard a great deal about Edwin Balfour and
developed a strong curiosity about him. He was a near
neighbor, younger than Burke but older than Diana, who
had known him all her life. He was a baron; when his
father died he would be an earl. Listening to Diana speak
of him, watching her face grow animated at the very
mention of his name, she concluded the man must either
be a god or a sorcerer. He had the handsomest face, the
manliest physique, the most delightful manners; he knew
more than anyone about almost everything; he rode as well
as Burke and he never lost at cards. All that seemed to be
wrong with him was that he wasn't often enough at home.
But even that shortcoming was lately not in evidence as the
poor health of his father made him tarry this Christmas at
Blyth Park and kept him longer away from London, where
he was thought to be a bit of a rake.

Diana had loved him all her life. He'd never made fun
of her limp or her stammer, and with Burke away in the
army he'd become as close as a real brother. Later, when

Edwin himself was hardly ever at home, she'd listened to stories of his escapades with a sweet pang of sadness. Every day she expected to hear of his engagement to someone beautiful and perfect, knowing that after that they could never be friends again as they were. Everyone in the family knew of her devoted heart, but no one thought much of it. They took it for granted. So, apparently, did Edwin Balfour.

Olivia never visited again. Burke appeared infrequently and hardly spoke; Katherine wondered why he came at all. Once he informed her that Prince Charles's ragtag army had gotten as far south as Derby and then retreated. She pretended complete ignorance and disinterest, as though she couldn't imagine why he would be telling her such a thing. But afterward she was despondent and depressed, longing for more news and wondering if this meant the revolution was finished.

One afternoon she had a new visitor, and the manner of their meeting gave her something to worry about for several days afterward. She was lying on the blue and gold satin day bed, where she'd fallen asleep watching birds circling the wintry sky through the window, when something awakened her. She sat up jerkily, clutching the top of her robe, which had fallen open during her nap. Under it she wore a plain silk nightgown, sheer but buttoned to the throat. She had the irrational but powerful impression that someone had touched her, intimately; but of course that was impossible, she was alone in the—

"Good afternoon. I'm sorry I woke you."

She almost screamed from shock. A man came out of the shadows behind her and bowed deeply.

"And I see I've startled you as well. Can you forgive me?"

"Who are you?" She put a hand over her heart to still its racing.

"Julian Lowndes." He reached for her other hand and

bent low over it; his lips felt cold and somehow unpleasant. He had a slurring, disdainful kind of voice, as if
the effort to speak were almost too much for him. "The
stepson," he added cynically, seeing no recognition on her
face at the mention of his name.

"Oh, Olivia's—"

"Brother. Precisely. And you are the heroic Mrs. Pell,
the beautiful and mysterious widow of whom we hear so
much, and yet really so little. My curiosity overcame me; I
had to make your acquaintance. What Diana said of your
loveliness was a hideous understatement. How long have
you been a widow?"

"I beg your pardon?" Her mind wasn't functioning
well; she could hardly follow him. And still she had the
vague, intrusive idea that he'd put his hands on her,
although that now seemed impossible, insane. He was
obviously a gentleman; he dressed almost foppishly. He
was Burke's stepbrother, he couldn't possibly—

"I say, how long has Mr. Pell been away from us? Your
late husband, you know."

"I—Would you mind lighting the candle? I can hardly
see you."

"*Mais oui*, madame."

She studied him while he lit a taper at the hearth and
touched it to the branch of candles on the table beside her.
He was of medium height, thin, with yellow hair and odd,
honey-colored eyes. His face was bony and debauched; it
didn't seem to fit with his soft, womanly lips. He took a
pinch of snuff from a tortoiseshell box and touched a little
to each nostril, then sneezed delicately into a scented
handkerchief.

"My husband's death was recent. I would prefer not to
talk about it." She had recovered her equilibrium and was
beginning to conceive a dislike for Julian Lowndes.

"Ah, yes, of course. He was English, I believe; but
you're Scottish, if I interpret that delightful bit of brogue

correctly.'' Katherine nodded acknowledgment. ''Where was your husband from?''

She cast about in her mind hurriedly. ''Surrey. Forgive me, Mr. Lowndes, I'm not well. Would you mind—''

''A thousand pardons, madam! I've tired you with my stupid questions. Allow me to help you to your bed and then I'll take my leave.''

''Thank you, that's not necessary. I'll ring for the maid.''

''But I insist. It's the least I can do after being so thoughtless.''

''Really, I couldn't ask you.''

''Please, madam, allow me. Material proof that you forgive me, what?''

It seemed ridiculous to keep arguing with him. She let him take her arm and help her up from the sofa. To her dismay, he passed his hand around her waist and rested it on her hip in a most intimate manner. She turned toward him to protest. There was a light tap at the door, it opened, and Burke came in.

No one spoke for several seconds. What astonished Katherine was that Julian Lowndes did not immediately remove his hand, but instead smiled across at his stepbrother, who had not moved from the doorway, almost with an air of proprietorship.

''Ah, James,'' he said at last. ''I thought you might follow me up. I was just leaving.''

''Were you?'' Burke's voice was neutral, controlled; his eyes moved watchfully between them.

Katherine stepped out of the circle of Julian's arm and walked to the bed unassisted, where she pulled hard on the bellrope for the maid. She turned back to the two men, her arms held stiffly at her sides. ''Good afternoon, Mr. Lowndes,'' she said tightly. ''Major Burke, I'm a bit weary of visitors. Do you mind?'' She knew what he was thinking and it infuriated her.

"Not in the least," he said, smiling thinly.

"Good, you can walk down with me," said Julian. "There was something I wanted to ask you anyway. Mrs. Pell, I fear the pleasure of meeting has been all mine. Pray forgive me if I tired you. I look forward to seeing you again soon."

Katherine inclined her head fractionally.

Burke held the door. He turned to look at her before closing it, his face a careful blank. She saw his lips curl and whirled away from him before he could say something to hurt her. After a second she heard the door click shut.

Julian was waiting for his stepbrother on the landing to the second floor. His first words set Burke's teeth on edge.

"You've bedded her, of course. What was she like? A hot one, eh? Come, tell me, you really must." His strange yellowish eyes, normally lifeless from boredom or inertia, were bright with excitement.

"Don't be an ass, Julian, I haven't touched her. She's a grieving widow, for God's sake."

"Oh, Christ, James, why be coy? I *know* you've had her; I can tell by the way she looks at you. I mean to have her myself, by God. What a beauty! If you hadn't come in when you did, I swear she'd have let me toss her then and there."

Burke laughed harshly. "You're lying." He sensed that the younger man was testing him for some reason and kept a tight rein on his anger. "Leave it alone, Julian. She's not your type." But wasn't she? Wasn't someone like Julian exactly who she would want? They were speaking, after all, of the woman who had bedded Lieutenant-Colonel Maule and been the mistress of Ewan Ramsey. The longer he knew her, the more inconceivable that became; and yet it was incontrovertibly true. As far as Kate's bed partners went, the unsavory fact was that it behooved him always to believe the worst.

"How long has Mr. Pell been dead?" Julian was asking

offhandedly.

"I've no idea."

"Where was he from? English, wasn't he?"

"English, yes. Lincolnshire. What was it you wanted to ask me about? A loan, of course. Anything else?"

Julian laughed self-consciously. "Only a couple of hundred pounds, as a matter of fact. You can spare it. I owe my tailor, and he's getting a trifle noisy. Snuff?" He held out his little box.

"No."

"And it's only till the first of the year, when your father graciously gives me my allowance."

"You don't look well, Julian." In the stark, unforgiving light of late afternoon coming through the window on the landing, Julian looked almost ill. His skin was sallow, his now-dead eyes sunken into dark hollows. His breath was bad from a rotten tooth, and the lilac scent he doused himself with couldn't disguise his need for a bath. "I heard you've begun to smoke opium. You look it."

"Nonsense. Only rumor, I assure you."

"Was it rumor that a young girl died at one of your swinish friends' 'entertainments' last summer?" Burke asked heatedly.

"Ah, you heard about that, did you? That saddened me, James, truly it did. The poor child wasn't up to the exertion, as it turned out. Bad heart. Naturally I was cleared of any wrongdoing in the unfortunate incident."

"I've no doubt you bribed the magistrate." Julian didn't deny it, and he turned to go.

"Wait, James, there was one other thing."

Burke turned back impatiently.

"I was wondering if you might put in a good word for me at your club."

He almost laughed. "My club! Are you serious?"

"It's the sort of social entree I need at this time in my

life. I'd meet all the right sort, of course. I should think you'd be glad of that; certainly your father would.''

Burke shook his head in awe. "You amaze me, Julian, you really do. The answer is no. The men at my club don't belong simultaneously to a club where the principal amusement is tying up girls and whipping them." Julian had the grace to blush. "But you're beyond that now, aren't you? The last I heard, it was young boys you liked to tie up."

"You've been listening to slanderous gossip. Don't believe half of it."

"If I believed half of it, I'd try to have you locked up." He started down the steps; if he stayed another minute with Julian, he was afraid he would throw him over the bannister.

"You won't do it, then?"

"Of course not."

"You always were a bastard, James. I won't forget this!"

"And forget about the loan, Julian," he called over his shoulder.

"You son of a bitch! You'll be sorry!" He was red-faced with fury, but he kept his voice low. It wouldn't do to alienate his stepfather by fighting with his son on the stairs, after all.

Burke kept going without a backward look.

CHAPTER 17

Christmas Day dawned sunny and unusually mild at Weddingstone. Wisps of cloud rode slowly across the bright blue sky and hopeful birds sang as if spring were almost here, not three months away. Katherine sat in the window seat in her room, feeling the warm sun on her face and gazing absently at a bowl of fresh hothouse flowers on the sill. Diana had brought them for a present this morning before leaving for church with her family. The house was quiet with everyone out, and she had plenty of leisure, if not much inclination, to recollect all the Christmases of her past. This was the first one she'd ever spent away from Darragh, away from her family. But now, of course, there was no family, and no home; only a mother who couldn't recognize her own daughter.

She straightened her shoulders. How easy it would be, she chided herself, to sink into a comfortable mire of self-pity and never climb out. Things could be much worse, after all. She could be in prison already, or facing a hangman's noose tomorrow instead of sometime in the future. She sighed and rested her forehead on the cool glass. She picked a white chrysanthemum from the bowl and began to shred it in her fingers.

Footsteps sounded in the hallway. Oh God, she thought, don't let it be Julian. He had come almost every day since they'd met. Usually she contrived to have Diana or the maid in the room, but sometimes he outwitted her and caught her alone. He never again tried to take any sort of liberty, and she'd almost abandoned the disturbing idea that he could have touched her while she slept that first afternoon—it was simply too absurd, too fantastic to be true. And yet she never enjoyed his visits and found his presence unsettling. He asked too many questions, for one thing, and it was exhausting to make up plausible answers. But mostly it was the way he looked at her—watchful, patient, predatory. Dangerous. His yellow-brown eyes reminded her of a wolf, and sometimes she felt as if he were waiting for a chance to devour her. Ridiculous, of course. She was sure he was a gentleman; his conversation was conventional in the extreme, his manner of address politeness itself. And yet she couldn't feel comfortable with him. There was something almost corpselike about him, something rotten, corrupt . . . She shivered, and the door opened.

"We're back!" It was Diana. She was a vision of youthful freshness in a pale green gown figured with tiny blue and white flowers. She came straight to the window seat, kissed Katherine affectionately, and plumped herself down beside her on the pillow. "How are you?"

"I'm very well."

"Good! Edwin came home with us and means to stay for dinner. I want you to c-come down and meet him, Katherine. He's dying to make your acquaintance after all I've told him about you."

"And I, his," she smiled. "But perhaps another time."

"Oh, but you said you were feeling well! You look wonderful. You needn't dress, you know—you could wear the new dressing gown Father gave me for Christmas."

"I don't think so, Diana," she said gently. "Much as I'd like to meet this paragon, I'm not quite up to it today."

"Oh, poo." She sighed with disappointment. "Look, there are Jamie and Olivia," she said a second later, looking past Katherine's shoulder through the window. "She's showing him the new garden house." Katherine followed her gaze across the park to a small hexagonal structure of painted stone, complete with circular dome and Doric columns. "Isn't it too, too? Notice it has a 'vista.'" Diana pursed her lips, mimicking Olivia's voice perfectly, and pointed to an artificial fish pond some distance away, surrounded by an assortment of bronze garden sculptures.

Katherine scarcely heard her; she was watching the elegant couple walking arm-in-arm toward the garden house.

"She wants to marry him," Diana said softly. "She wants to be a countess more than anything in life." Katherine said nothing. "She loves to go to cock f-fights." Still she didn't speak. Diana fired her last volley. "She beats her maid."

Katherine turned around. They looked at each other for a long time, their faces solemn, eyes serious. Katherine plucked another flower from the bowl and brought it to her nose. "You know," she said casually, "perhaps after all I will go downstairs today."

She leaned lightly on Knole's arm as she made her slow and careful way down the final staircase to the front hall. Diana was behind them, smiling proudly and offering frequent cautionary advice, a mother duck managing her offspring's first outing. Katherine had refused to borrow her new dressing gown, but after much cajoling had at last consented to wear her old one, a soft, comfortable robe of apricot velvet. Diana had also insisted she do something with her hair, which hung a bit wildly about her shoulders, and together they'd devised a simple but becoming style with a few pins and a bit of ribbon. Studying herself in the full-length mirror before they set out, Katherine had decided she looked as nice as she could, considering she was not in perfect health.

"I think we might rest a moment," Diana suggested in the middle of the stairway, and the butler stopped obediently. His normally stoical face was almost animated; if one didn't know better, one might have said Knole was enjoying himself.

The front door swung open, and a richly garbed Olivia swept into the hall on a rush of fresh air. There was already a peevish, dissatisfied look on her pallid countenance; when she saw the trio on the stairs, it settled into unqualified annoyance.

Burke was behind her. He closed the door, he saw Katherine, and he stopped in his tracks.

He hadn't seen her in days, though she'd rarely been out of his thoughts. She looked so exquisitely lovely now in his sister's old dressing gown and slippers, it was as if he were seeing her for the first time. He stood unmoving, vaguely conscious that Olivia was speaking to him, hanging on his arm in her leechlike way. What had she done to her hair? It looked like a heavenly cloud, and she was like an angel come to earth. She was smiling her sweet, dazzling smile as if at him alone, and her eyes sparkled with all the wit and intelligence he'd been missing. For the first time in days he felt truly alive.

Olivia's voice, shrill with poorly concealed displeasure, finally reclaimed his attention. "You don't look at all well, Mrs. Pell; are you sure you ought to be up?"

No one even troubled to respond to this fatuity.

"I think Edwin is in the drawing room," said Diana, with the air of one who has accomplished her mission and is content now to let events take their course. "Shall we?"

Burke felt Olivia's grip tighten as the party on the stairs descended the rest of the way and came toward them. He bowed for Katherine and Knole to precede him, to Olivia's intense irritation, and then took his sister's arm on his other side. The five moved in a slow, stately procession down the hall to the drawing room.

Edwin Balfour was idly casting dice at a table, right hand against left. When he saw the company in the doorway, he jumped to his feet, a welcoming grin lighting up his handsome, cheerful face. Diana performed the introductions and Katherine curtsied to him, calling him "my lord." He took her hand and bowed over it. "Diana's told me so much about you, I feel I've known you all my life. You must call me Edwin or I'll think you're addressing my father."

She smiled, pleased by his open manner and amazed that Diana hadn't after all been exaggerating his good looks or his amiability. "Then I hope you'll call me Katherine, for I too feel as if we're already friends."

"Shall we have a 'nuncheon'?" Olivia suggested rhetorically after everyone was seated. Her accent was too consciously refined to sound natural. "Knole, have the maid bring a tray of cold meats and fruit. And some cheese cakes, I think."

Diana caught Katherine's eye and mouthed the words in mock perplexity, "a *nuncheon*?" and Katherine had to look away, stifling a hysterical urge to laugh.

Olivia had taken particular pains with her hair and dress today, but her stiff brocade gown of wide yellow and white stripes did not become her. She held up her wrist to show off a bracelet, gold with purple stones. "I *adore* my new bracelet, James. How terribly sweet of you to remember that amethysts are my favorite gem. I think it's quite *comme il faut*, don't you? In fact, quite *à la mode*." She seemed to be addressing Katherine.

"Yes, and right in fashion, too." She kept her face straight but her eyes were dancing. She heard Burke give a strangled cough. True, they weren't speaking to each other these days, but she couldn't resist a chance to make him laugh.

Olivia was eyeing her in amazement and distrust.

"What do you think of this uprising, Mrs. Pell?" she asked abruptly. "Are you in sympathy with the rebels?"

The directness of the question startled her. She gave her stock answer: "Oh, I've no head for politics."

"No, of course not," Olivia agreed, as though no decent woman had. "But I'm sure you share our happiness over the news that their little army is in retreat."

She swallowed, not knowing how to respond. She glanced toward Burke, but he only looked back at her in interested silence.

"Edwin," Olivia went on, fiddling with the bracelet on her wrist ostentatiously, "tell Mrs. Pell what you were saying earlier about the behavior of the so-called 'Bonnie Prince' at Thornhill."

"Oh, well," Edwin demurred, embarrassed. "A bit of mischief, perhaps."

"Mischief! Shall I tell you what his troops did at Drumlanrig Castle?"

"I feel certain you're going to," Katherine murmured.

"They put *straw* in all the rooms for beds, except the prince's chamber. They killed forty of the duke's sheep *inside the house*. They got into the cellars and drank or spilt most of the wine; they broke the furniture and melted down the pewter. And when they left they tried to make off with the linen and blankets, but the Duke of Perth stopped them."

Katherine could not think what to say to this.

"Yes, but they behaved quite gallantly at Glasgow, you know," Edwin put in. "Some thought they'd sack the city, but they didn't."

"How *handsome* of them," said Olivia sarcastically. She turned back to Katherine. "Tell me, Mrs. Pell, something I've always wanted to know. Why *do* the men wear those funny little skirts? 'Kilts,' do you call them? Don't they get terribly cold? And is it true that even women in the so-called 'upper classes' never wear shoes, not even in winter?''

Katherine went rigid with annoyance, but she was saved from the necessity of a reply by the entrance of Renata on the arm of her son. Her Ladyship was splendid in puce satin and gauze, but her eyes narrowed in an expression of dismay identical to her daughter's at the sight of the invalid on the sofa. ''Ah, Mrs. Pell. Feeling better, I see. How nice.''

Edwin had risen on her arrival. When she was seated, he turned back to his spot on the couch beside Katherine to find it taken by Julian. Frowning, he went to stand beside Burke at the fireplace.

Katherine was no more pleased with the substitution than he. Pale and trembling, Julian looked as if he'd just awakened from a very bad night. He was wearing a coat of pale green taffeta with a pink sheen, and the color did little for his sallow, lifeless complexion. His stagnant eyes brightened minimally as he proceeded to monopolize her with his dull chatter. She found it curious that he gave the impression of paying no more attention to what he said than she did, but instead seemed to be watching her closely and thinking his own strange, unwholesome thoughts while his tongue rattled away. Out of one ear she could hear Burke, Edwin, and Diana discussing a new book by Mr. Fielding, and she longed to join them. Out of the other she heard Olivia and her mother talking excitedly about a ball they were giving next week at Weddingstone: ''She's a very *vulgar* person, and a dead bore; quite odious, in fact. But, my dear, she has a hundred thousand pounds a year; we could *not* but invite her.''

Presently Diana went to the spinet and began to pick out a quiet, rather sorrowful tune. Edwin followed her, and she immediately went on to something more cheerful. ''Join us, Katherine,'' she urged. Without a second's hesitation, she got up from the couch and went to them, happy for the excuse to leave Julian.

Diana played a popular melody while Edwin sang along in a robust tenor. Katherine joined in at their urging in her clear, slightly off-key soprano. "Do you play?" asked Olivia, wandering over. Katherine shook her head, lying; Mrs. Pell might, but Katie Lennox definitely did not play the spinet. "Sing something in Scottish," Olivia pressed, as though it were a foreign language like Greek or Sanskrit. "I think it's so quaint the way you Scots speak the king's English."

"You mean the king's *German*," Katherine corrected, eyes downcast. She heard Burke behind her, clearing his throat in warning. She couldn't resist. She began to sing, *a cappella*, a song whose chorus went, "Wha' the deil hae we got for a king, but a wee wee German lairdie!" interspersed with several abusive verses. Burke took her arm in mid-chorus and led her away to the tea table, his face a study, while Olivia clucked her tongue in shocked disbelief.

Edwin joined them in a few minutes, and Katherine was glad for the chance to speak to him. Her favorable first impression held up; she was relieved that Diana's regard was for a man who might be worthy of her. He was tall and athletic-looking, with a ruddy complexion that bespoke a love of the outdoors. He wore his own curling, reddish-blond hair rather long. His features were strong and regular, his brown eyes bright and amused. He flirted just enough to be agreeable but not offensive. She asked him somewhat frankly about his life, and he readily told her of his father's illness and how it had necessitated his staying home more often to manage the estate. He loved all sports—riding, shooting, gaming, hell-raising—but of late a more contemplative side of his nature had surfaced as he watched his father draw closer to death. He admitted to a certain restlessness. He struck Katherine as a man on the brink of deciding to settle down.

"Mrs. Pell, I wonder if I might have a word with you in private."

Katherine recognized the disdainful, droning tone and turned toward it without enthusiasm. There was almost nothing she less wished to do than have a word with Julian in private. "Certainly," she said, and followed him into a windowless alcove across the room.

"Forgive me for tearing you away from the others. I'm going away soon and this may be my last chance to speak with you until I return." Her spirits lightened at this news, but she tried to look suitably grave. "As you must know, I find you very attractive," he continued, and her heart sank. He was going to make a declaration.

"Mr. Lowndes—"

"Please, allow me to finish. I'm not a rich man but I am comfortably off; my father was a baron and my stepfather is an earl."

"Really—"

"Mrs. Pell, hear me out." She wanted to step back, away from his sour breath, but there was no place to go. "I can provide for you rather handsomely, I believe." He laughed deprecatingly. "Certainly as well as the late Mr. Pell."

Katherine felt rather affronted by this on behalf of her nonexistent husband. It seemed to her, though, that Julian was being deliberately obnoxious despite his polite manner. She cut him off almost impatiently. "I'm honored, Mr. Lowndes, and extremely grateful for your kindness and condescension, but I must decline. I shall never marry again."

To her surprise, Julian laughed, cutting off what she was going to say next. "You misunderstand me, madam," he told her with a falsely rueful smile. "I wasn't asking you to be my wife."

Katherine blinked in confusion. "Then—"

"I was asking you be my mistress."

She was utterly speechless.

"Do I take it from your silence that you decline?" he asked after a pause, not seeming the least bit disconcerted.

"You—yes!"

"Ah, too bad. I confess I'm not surprised, however. It hasn't escaped my notice that you feel a certain coldness toward me. It's my misfortune that your attitude hasn't extinguished my ardor; *au contraire*, it's fanned it, you might say."

The absurdity and offensiveness of the conversation were beginning to overwhelm her. Without another word, she moved to shoulder her way past him, but he planted his feet and wouldn't budge.

"One more thing, Mrs. Pell. As I say, I'm going away for a little while. When I return, I think I'll have something to tell you that will make you change your mind."

"Mr. Lowndes, the likelihood of that is small beyond measure. Please get out of my way."

He laughed again. "I *will* have you, you know."

She was too amazed to respond; his effrontery took her breath away. She pushed against him forcibly and this time he stepped back, allowing her to pass.

Slumped in a chair by the fire, Burke watched her as she steered a somewhat blind path back to the piano. She was pretending to listen to the music, but he could see she was agitated. What had the swinish Julian said to her? Her nostrils were flared, a sure sign she was angry. He studied her profile, the graceful way she carried herself, the way she smiled. He couldn't help wondering what he would have done if he'd met her at a party at his stepmother's or a ball at Blyth Park. He'd have been captivated, of course. She put every woman he'd ever met to shame. He would have set out to win her and not stopped until she was his.

But he hadn't met her at a party, he'd met her in gaol. She looked like a lady, but she wasn't. A lady didn't let herself be used as a stake in a card game, nor become the mistress of villains and brutes because they had money.

His thoughts were eating away at him, making him feel reckless and mean. He was tired of watching Katherine

with other people; he wanted her for himself. Olivia was
baiting her again; he couldn't hear the words, but he saw
her recoil in hurt and bewilderment and knew her temper
was about to explode. He rose and went to her swiftly.

"You're looking tired, Mrs. Pell. Allow me to escort
you back to your room."

"Surely the butler can do that, James," Olivia said
sharply.

He ignored her and tucked Katherine's hand in his arm.
Edwin bowed and said he was enchanted to have met her.
Diana grinned and said she would see her soon. Renata
and Olivia nodded frostily; Julian was nowhere to be seen.

"Christ, Kate, you look as mad as a hornet," Burke
observed in the hallway, his good humor suddenly
restored. He had to pull her by the arm to get her to slow
down.

"Did you hear what she said?"

"No, what did she say?"

She was fuming, sputtering, hardly able to get the
words out. "She called us b-barbarians!"

He chuckled. "Called who barbarians?"

"Scotsmen! All of us! That pudding-faced, stuck-up,
white-haired—"

He laughed gleefully and put his arm around her.
"Compose yourself, love. I want you to meet my father."

Before she could react, he rapped at the door they were
standing opposite and there was a brusque "Come in!"
He swung the door open and stood aside for Katherine to
enter.

His Lordship stood up, taken aback by the sight of a
beautiful red-haired woman in a dressing gown standing at
the door to his study.

"Father, let me present Mrs. Pell to you. Katherine, this
is my father, Lord Rothbury."

Katherine curtsied as deeply as she could. His Lordship
inclined his head but did not trouble to come out from

behind his desk. "Ah, yes, Mrs. Pell. Let me express on behalf of my son and my family our heartfelt thanks for your very brave actions. You're certainly a courageous young woman." Katherine murmured something suitable but inaudible; she'd forgotten all about saving Burke's life in a fire. "Pell, Pell," His Lordship was repeating. "Would that be any relation to the Winston Pells of Bath?" he inquired, staring down his long beak of a nose.

"I don't believe so, my lord."

"Mm." He seemed to lose interest. "Let's see, I had something here; where is it? Ah." He found a slip of paper on his desk and picked it up. "Here, a draft for you. For saving James and all that, you know." He came toward her, arm outstretched.

Katherine stepped back, staring at his hand as if it held an insect. "Thank you," she said stiffly; "I could not possibly accept it." Her tone told him further discussion would be pointless.

"Ah! Well, then. In that case I won't detain you. A pleasure to have met you, madam." This time he did bow, his brow creased in some perplexity. Katherine walked out into the hall. "James?" he called before Burke could close the door. "A very short word with you, if I may?"

Burke sent Katherine a look of apology and went back into the study.

"I noticed a certain—atmosphere," his father said in a low tone. "I hope I didn't offend her; I thought a reward suitable for a woman of her class. She is quite a *common* person, isn't she? At least this is what Renata has told me."

Burke's face was set in hard lines. There was a cold little pause before he answered shortly, "Yes, Father, quite common." He turned on his heel and left His Lordship standing in the middle of the floor.

He caught up to Katherine halfway to the stairs and put a hand on her arm to detain her. "My father meant no offense, Kate; I'm sorry if his offer insulted you.''

She was already regretting her haste. On reflection, she realized Katie Lennox would have snapped up Lord Rothbury's bank draft before he could blink. "Oh, I wasn't offended in the least," she told him airily; "I only thought *Mrs. Pell* might be."

He stepped back. "How stupid of me," he said with an ugly smile. "It's a mistake I won't make again."

How she hated that cynical quirk of his lips, the sudden arctic coldness in his eyes! She shivered, chilled to the bone, and began to walk away from him.

When she reached the stairs, he caught her and took hold of her arm in a stiff, unkind way, as if touching her were distasteful to him. A dark pall settled over her spirit and grew heavier with every step as she contemplated the rest of this day, and tomorrow, and the next. He would never come to see her now because he despised her and there was nothing she could do about it. And she had to continue playing a role that *guaranteed* he would despise her, forever. Today she'd had flickering moments of happiness, moments when he'd looked at her not with disdain but admiration, or smiled at something she'd said, and at those times her heart had been light as a bird. But that was over now. It was time for the return of Katie Lennox. And time as well for Katherine to confront something much worse: the awful possibility that she was in love with Burke.

There, the horrible thought was out at last. She couldn't keep ignoring it; like a noxious weed it always returned, stronger for the pulling. And it did no good to try to camouflage it by calling it gratitude or mere sexual attraction. This was something much stronger, much more upsetting. What a cruel joke! She, Katherine Ross Lennox Brodie McGregor, in love with an Englishman. How could it have happened? When had it started? When she thought she'd killed him, on her frantic ride from Helvellyn? Or before that, when they'd made love in the inn? Perhaps even before that, when he'd told Mrs. Parkington she couldn't read without her glasses. Or the night he'd saved her from the lecherous landlord, and held her in his arms afterward until she fell asleep.

Oh, what did it matter? It was so hopeless, she wanted to laugh. She imagined his reaction if she told him who she was, and then she wanted to cry. He wouldn't believe a word she said. She'd been too clever, made the deception too perfect. And he would have to deny the evidence of his own senses to believe he was her first and only lover. There had been no blood, no cry of pain that first time.

They were at the top of the staircase in the upper hall, pausing for her to catch her breath. She felt as if a heavy stone lay on top of her heart. She couldn't, she simply could not bear it that they were almost to her room, that he would leave her there, and that she wouldn't see him again for God knew how long. In a low tone, without looking at him, she said, "I'm really not tired, Burke. Would you show me a little of the house?"

He glanced at her coolly but shrugged his shoulders with indifference. At the next corridor he steered her to the left instead of going straight on to the third-floor staircase. They passed door after paneled door, some open to reveal stately bedrooms luxuriously furnished in the richest, most fashionable style, many being readied by maids for the forthcoming ball. Katherine asked how many rooms there were at Weddingstone.

"I don't really know," he answered, with the insouciance of the very, very wealthy. "Forty-seven bedrooms, I think. Renata gives lots of parties, so it's not quite as useless as it sounds."

They walked through an archway and the hall opened into an enormous gallery, with floor-to-ceiling windows on both sides for light and between them a seemingly endless collection of family portraits. They began with the original

Rothbury earl, ennobled in 1488 by Henry VII, the first
Tudor king, and ended with Neville, the current and
eleventh earl. The more recent paintings were at the far
end of the gallery, and it was these Katherine most wished
to see.

"Is that *you*?" she exclaimed, standing in front of a
full-length picture of a very handsome and richly dressed
young lord, posed against a background that was meant to
be either the countryside or heaven.

Burke laughed. "No, not quite my style. That's my
father."

She took note of the silky, blue-black hair, the proud
cheekbones and haughty, ice-blue eyes, and shook her
head in wonder at the resemblance. But no, now that she
looked more closely, Burke's mouth was kinder, and certainly more sensuous; and his eyes had more humor and
intelligence than this young man's.

There were pictures of Diana at various ages, sometimes
solemn, sometimes laughing, always sweet. When they
came to portraits of Burke as a child, a young boy, a man,
she wanted to stop at each one and study it, but he kept
pressing her to move along. A portrait of a tall, black-
haired woman with striking gray eyes was so compelling,
she halted in her tracks and would not be moved.

"My mother," he said quietly to her unspoken
question. "Her name was Anne."

"She was very beautiful," she said inadequately. For
some reason the painting affected her profoundly. "When
did she die?"

"Sixteen years ago. I was fourteen, Diana was an
infant." He was silent for a moment. "She was killed by a
band of Scottish cattle thieves on a raid over the border."

Katherine felt as if a thunderclap had gone off in her
ears. She went dead white and her whole body tingled.
She had to lean back against the wall to keep her knees
from sagging. "My God, my God." Her mouth was dry;

she could hardly get the words out. She turned anguished eyes to him. "Don't you hate us?"

"No, Kate, of course not," he said softly. "That would be stupid, to hate a whole race of people because of what four men did." When she didn't speak, he said lightly, "I've hated *you* at times, but never because of your country."

"I've hated you, too—" She couldn't finish the thought. It was both too early and too late for confessions. Would it have made any difference if Innes had shot Wells, too? Was knowing he was alive somewhere in the world part of what made her so full of hatred and bitterness? No, she didn't think so. If he were executed tomorrow, she doubted it would bring her any peace. Revenge was a hollow, craven motive: she would renounce it. But it was her oldest companion—what would take its place? What in the world would animate and sustain her in the long days to come?

Burke took her cold hand and held it in both of his, wondering at the gentleness of his feelings now when he'd been angry with her ten minutes ago. "Do you hate me now?" he asked, bringing her fingers to his lips. She didn't look at him. He brushed a stray lock of hair back from her face and touched her cheek with his fingertips. "Look at me, Kate."

She did, and his heart gave a wild lurch. Her lashes dropped before he could believe what he'd seen in her eyes, and then she stood on tiptoe and kissed him on the mouth.

Their arms went around each other in a warm, spontaneous embrace. To Katherine it seemed like the first time she'd kissed him of her own free will, uncoerced by circumstances or the role she had to play. His lips were gentle and urgent at the same time; they made her want to tell him with hers what she could never say in words. Her lonely heart opened and took him in, and she knew with a mixture of joy and grief that she would love him until she died.

He held her as tightly as he dared, not wanting to hurt her but wanting to feel every inch of her against his hard, yearning body. It was always like this with Kate, he thought feverishly; his desire for her was so hard to control, he was like an adolescent boy with his first woman. But this time there was a difference, a new warmth in her, some message of unbearable sweetness she was communicating to him with her mouth, her soft fingertips. He raised his head to look into her eyes, and there in the blue depths was the shining, unequivocal truth he'd caught only a glimpse of before. "Kate, Kate," he murmured unbelievingly, kissing her again. His heart was racing; he knew of only one way to make sense of his feelings.

He took her hand and pulled her with barely controlled eagerness through the opposite archway and into a new hall containing countless smaller rooms. He threw open the first door they came to and drew her in, almost slamming it behind them.

Katherine looked around in dismay. She'd had time to regain her reason, if Burke had not, and her surroundings brought her the rest of the way down to earth with a rude plop. They were in a tiny room, almost a closet, used for storing extra furniture. It was cramped and dusty, permeated with the smell of mildew and beeswax. She said his name, but he muffled the rest of her words with a passionate kiss. She could feel him trembling and she let him hold her for a little while, but then the inevitability of where this would lead sobered her and she pushed him gently away. He hardly noticed the interruption; he reached for her again and held her head while he entered her mouth with his tongue. With his other hand he caressed her breast, softly but urgently, now tugging on the sash that knotted the front of her robe. A hard, wrenching ache of desire shuddered through her. She knew in another second they would be of the same mind unless she ended it now. She pulled her mouth away and said as calmly as she could, "Don't, Burke, please let me go." He shook his head as if to shoo away an annoying fly and bent to kiss her again. "*No*." She turned her face sideways and pushed hard against his chest. "Let me *go*."

He released her, blinking in disbelief. "Don't do this to me again, Kate."

His warning tone brought a quick flash of anger. "What would you do, lay me down on that sofa, or bend me over the chair? I won't be treated like a servant, Burke!"

"You won't—" Still shaking with desire, he fought down an impulse to throttle her. "Where, then?" he almost shouted. "Tell me where!"

"I'm sorry," she uttered in near-despair, turning away from his anger. The hopelessness of it all assailed her in force. "What are you offering me?" she asked, more to herself than him.

"What do you mean?"

"Nothing. Nothing." What *could* he offer her? Nothing respectable. Even as Lady Braemoray, her station was lower than his, and she knew that such things mattered to him. A lady as respectable as the Widow Pell had been beneath his proud father's notice, and Burke was cut from the same mold. Well, he might be ten times richer than she, but his blood was no bluer, and she would not let him take her like some chambermaid in a closet. She reached for the door handle.

Burke had misunderstood her question. "Wait!" His hand closed around her wrist. "Is it *money* you want?" he demanded incredulously. "My God, how *stupid* of me not to have thought of that!"

Enraged, she wrenched her arm free and jerked open the door. She was halfway down the hall before she realized she didn't know where she was going. She could hear him behind her and hastened her steps.

"Why didn't you take my father's money, then?" he hurled after her furiously. "Because you're accustomed to giving your hide in return and he didn't mention that in the bargain?"

She stopped. When he was level with her, she pulled back her hand and slapped him across the face with every bit of her strength. She saw the shock in his eyes and walked on. Blinded by tears, she called out to a servant ahead of her and told him in a choking voice to take her to her room.

CHAPTER 18

Katherine slumped against the headboard of the bed, her knees drawn up, and stared listlessly at the opposite wall. She was weary of staying in bed, weary of wearing nightgowns, weary of being sick. She hadn't been out of her room in two days, pleading illness after her first, eventfilled excursion downstairs, but in truth she'd exiled herself in order to avoid meeting Burke in the house. Her anger had dissipated somewhat—after all, he only believed of her what she'd taken such pains all these weeks to make him believe—but she doubted whether *his* had and she wasn't strong enough yet to confront him.

At least she hadn't had to deal with Julian; he hadn't returned from wherever he'd gone, and for that she was profoundly grateful. His offer to make her his mistress still astounded her, but now it seemed dreamlike and unreal. It was the fight with Burke her mind constantly replayed, not the scene with Julian.

There was a light tap at the door and Diana entered. Katherine looked forward to her visits because she always managed to cheer her up, at least until she went away. But today, judging by the despondent look in the younger girl's level gray eyes, it was going to be the other way around. That was surprising; if Katherine recollected correctly, this was the day Edwin Balfour was coming to visit.

"Is anything the matter?" she asked diffidently, watching Diana sink down into a chair.

"No." She folded her hands and gazed off into space.

"Have you seen Edwin?"

"Yes."

Silence. "How is he?" she prodded at last.

"Fine." Diana sighed as if her life were ending. "He's leaving. The day after the b-ball. His father's a little better and he says he feels restless. He's going to London."

Katherine didn't know what to say, how to comfort her. Diana had never told her she loved Edwin, not in words, and Katherine felt obliged to return her reticence. "You'll miss him terribly," she offered tentatively, looking for an opening.

"Yes." Diana closed her lips and turned her head away, inconsolable.

There was silence.

"What will you wear to the ball?" she asked finally, thinking to distract her.

Diana looked up in surprise. "Why, nothing; I'm not going. I n-never dance."

Katherine sat silent, thinking. After a long time, with grave misgivings and as much delicacy as she could bring to the subject—they had, after all, never spoken of Diana's limp, not even indirectly—she mentioned that she'd heard there were special shoes for people with her difficulty. To her immense relief, Diana blushed slightly but was not at all angry with her for broaching the topic.

"I know," she explained patiently, "but Renata won't allow me to have them."

"Why ever not?"

"She says it's vain to want something God has chosen not to give you."

Katherine's eyes widened. The two women exchanged one of their silent, loaded glances. "Diana," Katherine said carefully, fully aware that this was none of her affair but unable to stop her tongue, "*that's nonsense.*" Diana stared back, wanting to believe her but not ready to take the plunge. Katherine made a decision to go further. "Ask yourself why your stepmother wants you to stay in Olivia's shadow. You are more beautiful than she by half, and Renata knows she couldn't stand the competition!"

Diana laughed, truly amused, and marshaled her thoughts to begin denying all this, but Katherine cut her off impatiently.

"How can anyone as intelligent as you be so willfully blind?" she asked in exasperation. "Diana, you're a lovely woman! God's seen fit to give you the tiniest little infirmity, and in your mind you've made it into a terrible affliction!"

"I s-stutter, too," she said miserably.

Katherine clucked her tongue and looked heavenward for patience. Then she saw the tears on her friend's face and came off the bed. She sat on the edge of the chair and enfolded her in her arms, blinking back tears of her own. What Diana needed was a mother, she thought, years ago, someone who could have put her foolish self-doubts to rest and her fears into perspective. She took her handkerchief out of the pocket of her robe and dabbed at the girl's cheeks, then briskly blew her own nose.

"Now." She stood up, all business. "First of all, you *are* going to the ball. And you're going to dance."

"I can't—"

Katherine interrupted with an impatient gesture. "There's no time to have these special shoes made; we'll have to improvise. You must go to the village tomorrow and buy two pairs of shoes."

"Two—"

"Two *identical* pairs of shoes, only one pair must be larger than the other." Diana frowned in puzzlement. "Which leg is shorter?" Katherine asked, tired of mincing words.

"This one." She colored but indicated her left without hesitation.

"Then we must raise it. With extra stockings or—no, that would show when you picked up your skirts to dance. With cotton, then, or some sort of material laid thickly on the sole so your left foot is raised. It's only a wee little *bit* shorter, Diana, so not much needs to be done. But don't you see, if we stuff the larger shoe with something, your foot will be higher and the tiny little limp will disappear!"

Her confidence was contagious. Diana clapped her hands and almost squealed with excitement before the old doubt and worry descended again. "What if it doesn't work?" she asked, and Katherine's heart ached with pity.

"If it doesn't work, you needn't go to the ball if you don't want to. And then we'll just think of something else."

Diana rose slowly and went to look out the window. Katherine waited in suspense, hoping she hadn't meddled too far in her friend's business, and praying that if Diana agreed to the unorthodox suggestion it would work. Finally Diana turned around. "Yes. I'll do it, I'll go to the village tomorrow. And I'll buy a g-gown, too, Katherine, a ball gown! I've never had one before, you know." Her eyes were shining with hope; she looked radiantly beautiful. "Oh, Katherine, think! In three nights I might be dancing with Edwin!"

The chair appeared to be Louis XIV; she couldn't break that. The picture over the bed was probably some illustrious forebear; in good conscience she couldn't hurl it through the window. The pitcher? Delicate china, probably worth a fortune. Katherine threw back her head and screamed very softly, then resumed her frustrated pacing.

That odious man! How dare he insult her again? And to think she'd been glad to see him when he came upon her

and Edwin Balfour walking outside—actually glad! Oh,
she should have stayed locked away in her room until it
was time for him to take her back to Lancaster, and not
risked exposing herself to his unbearable hostility until she
had to! But she'd finally ventured out today, overcome
with boredom and the need for fresh air, and had met
Edwin in the garden. They'd been chatting companion-
ably, enjoying the mild afternoon and each other's
company, when Burke had suddenly descended on them
like some avenging god. He'd sent a confused Edwin away
with a rude remark and then turned to her with eyes
sparkling with anger.

"Did it ever occur to you that flirting with him causes
my sister pain?" he demanded, bending over her in a
threatening way.

When she got over her astonishment, her fury easily
matched his. "You are a fool!" she told him pointedly.
"First of all, I wasn't flirting. I don't care if you believe me
or not!" she flared, incensed by his disbelieving snort.
"And second, if you think she's in love with him, why
don't you speak to him about it? He's your friend, too,
after all. And you're her brother—'tis your duty to take
care of her!"

"I'm so grateful to you for pointing these relationships
out to me," he gushed sarcastically, causing her to grind
her teeth. "But you must forgive me if I find your advice
ridiculous. It would do no good to speak to Edwin; it
would only hurt and embarrass Diana and put an end to
their easy friendship."

"But—"

"Edwin's a man of the world. He's not interested in a
sixteen-year-old child barely out of her ladies' academy,
who's never been to court, never even been out of the
country for more than a week at a time."

"But she's *not* a child!"

"Leave it," he said with finality. "And leave Edwin

alone, Kate. I swear to you, if you hurt my sister, you'll be sorry."

And he'd turned on his heel and walked away, leaving her seething with indignation.

"Katherine!" The door opened and Diana burst in, interrupting her ill-tempered and profitless thoughts. She threw the two bulky boxes she was carrying onto the bed and walked over to the window seat to push back the curtains. "Why are you in the dark? Look how pretty it is outside!"

"I've been out."

"Have you?" Diana wasn't really listening; she seemed distracted, excited. She walked to the bed and fluffed the pillow unnecessarily, then turned to Katherine with wide, staring eyes. "What's that you're reading?" She walked to the sofa and picked up a book about Italian paintings.

"Nothing, just pictures." Katherine started suddenly. Her eyes widened, too. "Diana!" she cried, and the younger girl flew into her arms, laughing with joy.

"It works! Oh, Katherine, it works! Look at me." She walked slowly to the door, turned, and walked back. The limp, slight to begin with, was completely gone. The two women embraced again, and afterward they both had to dab at their eyes. "Oh, my dearest friend, how can I ever thank you?"

"But you already have. Seeing you so happy is more thanks than I could ever deserve." She sniffed, smiling, and changed the subject in embarrassment. "What are these, gowns?" She indicated the boxes on the bed. Diana nodded. "Shall we choose one, then? Open them and let me see!"

Diana smiled broadly. "I've already chosen the gown I'm wearing. The other one is for you."

Katherine glanced at her to see if she'd misheard. "For me? What do you mean?"

Diana laughed gaily. "You're coming to the ball!" She

ignored her friend's sadly smiling shake of the head and opened one of the boxes. "Look! Oh, Katherine, it's *perfect*. I like it better than mine," she laughed, "only Renata would never let me wear one with so much bosom showing. Isn't it exquisite? Try it on." She held up a lush-looking gown of burgundy velvet, simply but stunningly trimmed in cream-colored silk lace.

"Diana—"

"No, now, I don't want to hear this. I know everything you're going to say, and all your arguments don't amount to a pinch of salt. You're going."

"Diana—"

"Because if you don't go, I'm not going either."

Katherine stood still in helpless consternation. The look in Diana's eyes told her she was speaking the simple truth. "That's blackmail," she said, trying to sound angry.

"Blackmail is an ugly word," Diana retorted, pressing down a smile. "I mean it, Katherine, I won't go without you." She paused for a second. "By the way," she said offhandedly, "I think Olivia means to announce at the ball that she and Jamie are engaged."

Katherine felt a small explosion in her chest and reached for the bedpost to steady herself. "Really?" was all she could say.

"Unfortunately, she hasn't told Jamie a thing about it."

"Oh." Color came back to her white face and her breathing returned to normal. She decided to call Diana's bluff. "Well, I think it's a great deal too bad. Edwin would have enjoyed dancing with you in your new dress. He's leaving the next day, isn't he? 'Twould've been your last chance to see him." She clucked her tongue in disappointment. "Ah, well, so it goes. What will we do, do you think? Play cards in my room or yours?"

"Oh, yours, I expect. It'll be much quieter, farther from all the guests and the music." Diana put the top back on the box containing the burgundy gown, picked up both boxes, and carried them to the door. In one swift, nonchalant movement, she opened the door and hurled the boxes out into the hall, where they landed with a muffled crash. Then she went back to the bed and sat down, gray eyes downcast, and began humming a careless tune.

Katherine whirled around, but her shaking shoulders gave her away. She heard an explosion of laughter behind her and turned back. She went to the bed and half fell, half sat beside Diana. They couldn't stop laughing; they collapsed against each other in helpless hilarity.

Finally Diana recovered. "Come, Katherine, we have to hurry," she hooted softly, wiping her eyes. "We've only one more day for you to teach me how to dance!"

CHAPTER 19

"To the king!" came the toast. "To the king!" Lord Rothbury's Whig friends responded in cheerful obedience. Burke quaffed his wine automatically, looking without enthusiasm over the rim of his glass at the assembly of notables around him. It was the usual crowd of earls and countesses, a duke or two, some lesser nobles, and a great number of the rich and untitled with whom his stepmother found it easier, if not as socially gratifying, to consort. His practiced eye had picked out the two or three attractive women he hadn't met before, but so far they hadn't conquered his inertia sufficiently to lure him away from the corner of the ballroom nearest the punchbowl where he'd spent the last thirty minutes. Olivia would haul him off to dance soon enough anyway, he was sure. He'd told his bland story of being between assignments to anyone who'd bothered to ask, but most people took his presence at home at Christmastime as unremarkable and not requiring an explanation. He picked up another glass of wine from the table and moved away before Lord Clifton, one of his father's transfixingly boring friends, could capture him, and went to stand beside a pillar near the orchestra. A moving target is harder to hit, he reasoned, thinking again of Olivia.

His wandering eye flickered over a familiar black head, and he stood up straight. Diana. His face softened as he watched her. By God, she was *dancing*. And she was beautiful. Who was her partner? He waited until the lines of gentlemen and ladies assumed their original formations. Edwin, eh? Good. Nothing would come of it, but it would make her happy for a night.

Burke considered his choices. He could have another drink and begin the work of getting seriously pissed, or else he could find Olivia and dance with her, speak civilly to his father's cronies, and meet new women with the object of seducing them. He headed unswervingly to the punchbowl.

Midway there, he halted. Ahead of him, gliding through a high, gilded archway into the ballroom as if she made spectacular entrances every day, looking as regal as any duchess and incomparably more beautiful than any other woman in the room, was Kate. Burke set his glass down with nerveless fingers and stared.

Thank God she'd seen him first, Katherine thought, searching frantically for Diana among the crowd of dancers and trying not to look as nervous as she felt. This was a mistake, she should never have come down, it didn't matter that she'd given Diana her promise. Maybe she could go back, no one but Burke had really seen her yet—

She thought of a profane barnyard expletive that always reminded her of Rory when a burly but foppishly dressed young man accosted her. "I say, are you really *alone*?" His monocle dropped out of his eye as the magnitude of his good fortune began to dawn on him.

"Hullo, how do you do?" said a wafer-thin, effete-looking fellow in a turquoise waistcoat. Behind him, puffing audibly, came a corpulent older gentleman wearing a black wig. There were others approaching; Katherine could see them on the periphery of her vision. The dance had ended; if only Diana would see her!

"Mrs. Pell. I've been waiting for you."

She looked behind her and there was Burke, taking her

by the hand. She didn't know whether to be glad or sorry. He led her away from her whining, disgruntled admirers without a word, and sudden, uncomplicated gladness filled her almost to bursting.

He took her to a currently unpopulated portion of the room and dropped her arm. Scowling, he tried to think of something cross to say. It was difficult; she was unbearably lovely and she was looking at him with soft and, one would swear, genuine gratitude. "What are you doing here?" he finally ventured, keeping his tone level since he couldn't make it stern.

"Diana asked me to come. 'Twasn't my idea, I promise you." She looked around as if the hall were crawling with cockroaches instead of lords of the realm.

"You look beautiful." He had to say it; only a blind man could keep from saying it. She stared fixedly at his shirtfront and blushed. His defenses crumbled a little more. "But you shouldn't have come."

"No."

"It's possible there are men here who know Colonel Denholm or have heard of my assignment. It's even possible someone might recognize you."

Her delectable mouth opened in alarm. "I never thought of that!" Then she frowned in thought, and immediately he realized his mistake. "But, Burke, what difference would it make? What have you told them?"

He scowled again, becoming annoyed because his mind was a blank and he couldn't think what to tell her, when Diana and Edwin arrived and saved him from the necessity of trying.

The two women kissed as if they hadn't seen each other in days, and admired each other's gowns as though they hadn't gotten dressed together. They were a striking pair, one fair and one dark, their lovely faces animated with suppressed excitement, communicating in some wordless, sisterly fashion that excluded Burke and Edwin but nevertheless drew them like moths to radiant candles.

Diana surprised her brother by asking him to lead her in the next dance, and Edwin was quick to claim Katherine for his partner. She accepted with grace, though a little wave of disappointment washed over her heart; she would have given much to dance with Burke at that moment. He sent her a narrow look of warning as she went off on Edwin's arm, but she turned her face away to avoid it. She would not let him spoil her tenuous happiness already; it would be over soon enough, she knew, without his hastening it along.

The music was fine and the dance was lively; it was a pleasure to whirl about among the colorfully dressed lords and ladies, feeling almost as if she belonged there. But she tired quickly and had to ask Edwin to take her away before the dance was half over.

"Are you ill?" he asked anxiously, searching her face as he led her into an alcove on the edge of the marble dance floor.

"Nay," she assured him, " 'tis only that I'm not used to dancing. Do you think we might have a glass of punch?"

When he went away to get refreshments, she made a decision. Edwin was leaving for London tomorrow. She knew she risked a great deal by speaking, yet it seemed the consequences of remaining silent were bleaker still.

He handed her a glass of punch and offered to share a plate of tidbits from the buffet. She watched him eat hungrily, admiring his handsomeness and the way he radiated masculine good health. She mentioned she'd heard he was going away.

"Aye, for a time. Father's better, you know." He didn't sound particularly enthusiastic about leaving.

"Yes, I was glad to hear that. Diana will miss you."

"God, I'll miss her, too," he said heartily. "She's the best part of coming home."

Katherine set her glass down on a little table and clasped her hands. "Edwin," she began nervously, "we hardly know one another, and yet already I've a—a very high regard for your character and integrity."

"Thank you," he returned in some surprise. "And I for yours."

"I believe you're kind and decent, and probably no more backward in affairs of the heart than most men." He returned her smile in polite puzzlement. "I hope you'll forgive me for speaking so frankly, but we're both going away soon and there's simply no time for propriety or discretion or the—slow and orderly progress of events." A certain look on his face made her laugh suddenly and hasten to assure him she was not about to declare herself in love with him; he had the good manners not to look relieved.

"Madam, I'm deeply disappointed."

"I must also apologize for speaking on a subject that is so patently none of my business, 'tis hard for me to believe I'm really doing it! And I assure you, if another would only speak instead of me—" She drew a breath. Edwin looked patient but bewildered. There was nothing for it but to plunge in. "Diana's been so kind to me during my convalescence, and I've gotten to know her quite well considering the brevity of our acquaintance. She's a bright, warm-hearted, loving young woman. She's remarkably intelligent and her judgment is sound beyond her years. She hasn't a shred of vanity, although she is of course very beautiful." She paused again. Oh, heavens, what if she were only making everything worse?

"I'm in complete agreement with you on every particular," Edwin acknowledged readily. "Diana's a wonderful girl."

She leaned nearer to him in her earnestness. "But she's not a girl. She's a woman. And in her woman's heart she holds a secret she believes no one knows but herself. But she's too good, too transparent to be able to hide the most important thing in her life. Edwin—'' she touched his sleeve, praying she was right to say it—''Diana is deeply and passionately in love with you.''

It took a moment for her words to sink in, and then his face registered complete shock. It was as she'd expected: he'd had absolutely no idea. How could such a bright man be so stupid? she thought wonderingly, but kept her lips closed.

He continued to stare at her unseeingly. ''You mean—as a brother, a—''

''No, in the way a woman loves a man.''

''But she's only a child!'' He looked across the way and saw Diana speaking with two men. She neither looked like nor did they hover over her as if she were a child. ''Good God.''

Katherine sagged a bit against the wall. She'd done her best and could do no more; she only hoped she hadn't done too much. But Edwin was a gentleman; if he could not love Diana, she was confident he would never deliberately hurt her, and certainly he would never reveal by word or implication that they'd had this conversation.

He was still standing there mutely, looking as if he'd been thrown from his horse, when she caught sight of Burke advancing on them menacingly. She hurriedly excused herself, leaving Edwin barely aware of her departure, and tried to melt into the milling crowd on the edge of the dance floor. Hopeless, of course. He caught her before she'd gone a dozen paces. She felt an icy foreboding as his hand clamped down on her shoulder. She faced him with false calm, but the sight of his face made her heart pound.

''Burke, don't. I wasn't—''

''Shut up. I told you not to hurt my sister or you'd regret it.''

''But I didn't—''

"If you're well enough to dance, you're well enough to travel. I'll make the arrangements for you to be gone from here in two days. If you go near Edwin Balfour in the meantime, I'll break your arm." The punishing grip he had on her elbow made her believe him. He gave her a small but vicious shove and walked away.

Almost immediately someone claimed her for a dance and she went off with him, his face a blur to her, his voice a meaningless hum. Burke snatched a glass of wine from a moving tray and drank it down in one swallow. Olivia found him a little later leaning against the wall near the spirits table, staring sullenly out at the dancers. It was either courage or stupidity that caused her to take his arm and try to lead him out on the floor. He looked at her as if he couldn't quite place her; then his head cleared and he shook her off impatiently.

"Methinks you're a trifle foxed," she said playfully but nervously. She looked as if she wanted to tell him something. "I'll come back when you're more yourself."

Two of her friends came up behind her; Burke vaguely remembered the man's name was Worthy and the girl was Lady Annabelle something.

"If it isn't the happy couple!" sang out Worthy in ringing tones. "Congratulations, James, you fortunate sod, you. When's the lucky day?"

"What lucky day might that be?" Burke asked softly, looking at Olivia. She'd gone beet red under the rice powder; her mouth opened and closed soundlessly while she held up a hand to try to silence Worthy.

"Oh, I know it's a secret," the latter continued smilingly, "but Olivia couldn't help dropping a hint of the engagement to me and Annabelle, seeing as we're such old friends."

"James," Olivia trilled in a too-loud voice, "do let's dance!" She pulled at his arm in a subdued kind of frenzy, to no avail.

"The engagement?" Burke repeated with interest. Under any other circumstances he'd have done the chivalrous thing—accepted her friends' congratulations in silence and chastised her later when they were alone. But Olivia's timing was execrable: she'd gotten caught in a mammoth lie at a moment when Burke was verging on drunkenness and in a mood that made a poisonous snake seem lamblike in comparison. "I must be old-fashioned," he said brittlely. "I thought it was customary for the bride-groom to be consulted in these matters."

"Really, James." Olivia's laugh was embarrassingly false; she let go of his arm and began to back away. The other two were listening attentively.

"I'm sorry I won't be able to oblige you, my dear. But I wish you luck in finding someone who'll like you better than you like yourself."

It was fortunate Olivia wasn't holding a glass; otherwise Burke would have received the contents in his face. As it was, she drew herself up with all the dignity remaining to her and told him he could go straight to hell. Worthy and Lady Annabelle melted away, and Burke toasted Olivia's retreating back with cynical satisfaction. Good riddance, he thought sullenly.

Sick of wine punch, he told a passing waiter to bring him a bottle of brandy. He drank steadily while he watched Katherine dance with every man who asked her. She began to look pale and ill but she kept it up, endlessly. After a while he noticed he wasn't the only one watching her. There was detestable Julian, evidently just arrived because he was still in his riding clothes, absently thumping his booted calf with his crop while he stared at her. The music stopped and he went to her like an arrow shot from a bow. Her face was turned away, but Burke saw her shake her head twice at something he was saying. He leaned close and spoke for a moment in her ear. She seemed to go rigid. Then she let him take her hand and lead her off the floor.

Burke found himself following them without volition, hardly knowing what he did. They left the ballroom and went down the main hall to a seldom-used and dimly lit corridor. He walked softly and kept his distance, watching as Julian opened a door and stood back for Katherine to enter. Then he was alone in the silent hallway, listening to the beat of his own heart and wondering if the rising nausea in his belly meant he was going to vomit. He imagined all the violent, unspeakable things he wanted to do to them. Then he turned slowly around and walked back to the ball. He wouldn't interfere; after all, they were made for each other. Above anything, he wanted a drink.

"My dear, you were right to wear no jewelry. Your dress falls in such lovely sculptural folds, no other decoration is required."

"Tell me what you meant, Julian."

"But then your hair is so vivid and your coloring so delicate, jewels would always be a mere distraction."

"Stop it! What did you mean?" Come with him or see Burke imprisoned as a traitor, he'd whispered to her in the ballroom. It was absurd, of course; absurd! Yet she felt queerly apprehensive.

"Don't you want to know where I've been?" he asked. They were in a book-lined study of sorts, furnished with a desk, a large table, easy chairs, a sofa. Julian went to the window and pulled the heavy draperies closed with a flourish; his deliberately dramatic gesture gave her a chill, but she only stared back at him levelly. She watched him pour a glass of sherry from a decanter on the desk. "Well? Don't you?"

"Not particularly. What I want is for you to tell me what nonsense you've got on your mind. Tell me now, Julian, or I'm leaving."

He laughed delightedly. "This is so enjoyable, you know, hearing you tell me what to do. Because very soon it will stop, and you'll begin to do exactly what I tell *you* to do.'' He moved toward her until he was standing quite close. She resisted the urge to step back; he frightened her, but it wouldn't do to let him know. "You're so lovely," he whispered, touching her hair. She lifted her hand to swat his away, but he grabbed her wrist. His strength surprised her. "It's no wonder," he went on in a different tone, "James couldn't bring himself to turn you over to the Lancaster authorities."

She paled, but frowned as if in confusion. "What?"

He laughed again. "Good, very good. Just the right note of bewilderment. I think I'm going to like you, Katie Lennox."

"I don't know what you're talking about," she said softly.

"No?" He let go of her wrist and moved back, sipping from his glass. "I've just returned from Dumfries. Does that tell you anything? No? There's an army encampment near there. Dragoons, you know; waiting out the winter, hoping Charlie will come back south and have another go. A Colonel Denholm's in charge of this particular regiment. One of James' superiors, I believe. Anything ? I had a long, interesting chat with a charming corporal named Blaine; Freddie, I believe his first name was. He had a good deal to say about the girl James left with for Lancaster over a month ago."

He knew. All right, then. It was too bad, but there was no cause for panic. It would mean some unpleasantness for Burke with his family, that was all. "Are you finished?"

Julian's strange yellow eyes narrowed. "*Mais non*, my sweet, I'm just coming to the best part." He tossed down the rest of his sherry, put the glass on the desk, and came toward her again. "The best part," he murmured, lowering his voice to an oily, insinuating sneer, "is what you're going to do to keep me from telling Colonel Denholm where you are." She frowned, and his thin-lipped smile widened. "You're going to be my mistress."

Katherine laughed. Detecting no hint of fear in the sound, Julian's eyes glinted dangerously. "You must be mad," she told him, sounding almost relieved. "I've met Denholm; he's a reasonable man. I don't know what Burke's told him to explain the delay, but certainly none of it was *his* fault. Even if Denholm's angry, he'll be mollified when we finally arrive in Lancaster next week. We're leaving in two days, Julian." She looked at him almost pityingly and turned to go.

His grip on her shoulder was cruel as he spun her back around. "You may be leaving in two days, but not for Lancaster," he snarled fiercely. "Denholm will be interested to know you're here because James has told him you're dead!"

"What?"

"Dead!"

He pushed her backward so hard her shoulder struck the door frame painfully. She held one trembling hand to her throat and leaned weakly against the wall. Dead, he'd told them she was dead. What did it mean? Her brain felt sluggish. It meant he wasn't taking her back to prison—it meant—oh God, he was letting her go! Sudden hot tears cascaded down her cheeks; she bit down on her knuckles to keep from sobbing out loud. She heard Julian coming toward her again and saw the rage in his eyes. He pulled her hands away from her face and slapped her twice, three times, infuriated by her tears.

"Stop it, stop it!" he yelled. Finally it sank in that she couldn't stop crying if he kept hitting her. He took her by the shoulders and shook her. "*I* make you cry," he raged, "no one else!" He drew out his handkerchief and rubbed it roughly against her red, smarting cheeks. "Fix yourself!" He turned his back on her in disgust.

He was mad, he had to be. She blew her nose and took deep breaths, trying to gather her wits. She knew he was blackmailing her, but she hadn't yet made out what the terms were. She was quaking with fear, but at the same time a tiny voice inside sang joyfully, He was letting me go!

"Tell me what you want, Julian," she said quietly when she felt she had herself under control.

He turned around slowly, smiling again. He'd put his riding crop down on a chair; he picked it up now and came closer. "As of now," he said softly, "you stop telling me what to do. Is that clear?"

She swallowed and nodded. "I'm sorry."

He shook his head impatiently. "No, no, too much contrition, much too soon. Besides, I know you're lying. All that will come later." He raised the crop and rested it on her shoulder. "Listen to me, Katie. You and I are leaving for London in the morning. You'll stay at my townhouse for as long as I like and do anything I tell you to do. Corporal Blaine says you're a whore, though I find that difficult to believe. But so much the better if you are, for then you'll catch on faster to my little games. Even if you're very experienced, some of them may surprise you."

Katherine shuddered. "And what will you do in return?" she asked in a barely recognizable voice.

"I won't have James court-martialed. It's quite as simple as that."

The blood drained from her face. If only she could think! "If you try to do that, his father will disinherit you. He'll throw you out of the house."

"Not if he doesn't know it was I. You shouldn't have come down, my dear. A hundred people have seen you, and yours isn't a face they'll forget. Any of them might tell Denholm of the lovely redhead spending Christmas at Weddingstone."

That's what Burke had meant when he'd told her she shouldn't have come! Now she understood, now that it was too late.

"Well?" Julian brought the crop up under her chin and

rubbed her throat with it in a grotesque caress. "Do you agree?"

"No."

He drew in his breath. "What do you mean? Do you think I won't do it? Let me assure you—"

"I'm certain you will do it. I don't agree to your terms. I will go with you tomorrow and be your mistress or your slave or whatever you like. But not for as long as you want, Julian. Only for one month."

"You're telling me what to do again," he said warningly, prodding her with the crop. "That will be the last time." The childish anger died out of his eyes quickly, replaced by a feverish excitement. "A month, eh? Yes, very good. I fancy I'll tire of you sooner than that anyway. Come, let's drink to our bargain. Don't shake your head, Katie; you'll drink if I say you'll drink. Here, take it."

The thick, sweet sherry almost made her gag, but she got it down. Julian took her arm and led her away from the door. "You're not terrified yet, are you?" he said with his feminine smile. "You're thinking somehow you'll trick me, somehow you'll get away. But you won't, you know. Even if the opportunity arises, you won't take it because you know what I'll do."

"How did you know I loved him?" she asked unexpectedly. "I didn't know it myself."

"We won't ever speak of him again," he said patiently, like a schoolmaster. "Or if you were thinking to distract me, you must give it up. Our unique relationship begins this minute." He threw the riding crop down on the sofa. "I'm so pleased your gown opens in front; I like to see a woman's face when I undress her. Especially if it's against her will." She didn't move when he put his hands on her; that made him smile. He undid one button. "No, I've changed my mind, I want you to do it. That would be better the first time—a symbol of your submission. Yes, Katie, unfasten your dress so I can look at you."

She was shaking and her breath was coming in shallow little gulps. She reached up and unbuttoned her gown, seeing Julian's face through a mist.

He stopped her before she got to the last button. "There—just there. The nipples not quite showing yet. It's more wanton somehow than completely naked. Now let me tell you something I particularly like to do."

When he finished, she said, "It sounds ludicrous; I shall try not to laugh."

Fury flashed across his face. He bent swiftly and picked up the crop. "Oh, you won't laugh. I promise you won't laugh." He dragged the leather up and down between her breasts and she had to will herself not to scream. His hand slid inside her dress. "I did this before, did you know? Touched you while you were sleeping. I've wanted you ever since. Lie down on the couch on your stomach."

In spite of all her resolve, she started to cry. At that moment, while his hand still cupped her bosom, there was a deafening crash as the door burst open and smashed against the wall. Katherine's scream of fright broke off when she realized it was Burke swaying on the threshold, a bottle dangling from his fingers and murder in his eyes.

It was the look of ready violence that stopped her from going to him. She stepped away from Julian, covering herself with her hands, wondering who in the world would speak first. A feeling that this had all happened before flitted through her mind—but no, that was Ewan, interrupting her and Burke on the floor of a barn. The thing that was the same then and now was that Burke had everything backwards. Which was going to hurt her more, she mused with a peculiar fatalism, captivity with Julian or salvation with Burke?

Over and over Burke had imagined what they were doing here, but he hadn't really believed it until this moment. He could hardly stand to look at her, wide-eyed, half-naked, waiting for him to do something. Oh, he would do something. He threw the bottle of brandy against the wall behind her, enjoying the way she jumped and tried not to scream again. He liked the way she looked now, scared to death, trying to tell him something with her big blue eyes that would make him stop. He liked the way Julian looked, too, like a rat in a trap. Squirm, you bastard, he thought with satisfaction, moving toward him. Then he stopped, blinking in surprise. Why, the little prick had pulled a gun out of his pocket and was pointing it at him. A little silver woman's gun. Kate had both hands over her mouth and was making soft, scared sounds. He remembered what she'd done the last time somebody held a gun on him, and suddenly his head cleared.

"Don't come any closer, James, or I'll have to shoot." Julian's yellow, dissipated face was taut with nervous excitement. "There's no need for all this *turmoil*, dear boy; you can even have her when I'm finished. Say, in about a month. It's not as though she's going with me against her will, after all. Are you, Mrs. Pell?" He glanced malignantly at Katherine but kept the gun pointed at Burke. She neither spoke nor moved.

Burke said one word. "Why?"

She lowered her hands from her face. She tried to speak, but her lips were trembling too much. Finally she got it out. "Money."

Everything went still. The sound of her voice seemed to echo in the small room while nobody moved or even breathed. At last Burke clasped his hands behind his head and looked up at the ceiling. Julian relaxed and smiled at Katherine in triumph. That was the moment Burke kicked the gun from his hand and lunged.

The struggle was short and bloody. "You'll kill him!" Katherine cried when it seemed Julian's head would split open if Burke slammed it against the wall one more time. He released him with deep reluctance; instead of slumping to the floor, Julian made a lopsided dash for the door, and

Burke caught him in the hall. She covered her ears to muffle the awful sounds of violence, and in a minute it was over. Burke staggered into the room and moved toward her. She shrank back, certain she was next, but he was heading for the bottle of sherry on the desk. He upended it and poured the contents down his throat and onto his shirtfront, wiping his mouth with the back of his bloody hand. He hurled the empty decanter at the same wall he'd broken the brandy bottle against and came after her.

She held up her hands protectively. He was so drunk. Talk was probably useless, but she had to try. "Burke—" That was all she got out before he caught her wrists and flung them apart so he could grab hold of what was left of the front of her dress and rip it open to her navel. She screamed as loud as she could. He only laughed and let her go long enough to slam the door shut with his foot. She looked around for a weapon. "Don't, don't, don't," she mumbled through fear-stiffened lips, backing up, one arm across her bosom and the other straight out to hold him off. He threw something at her. She heard a clatter and looked down at a gold coin on the floor. He tore off his coat and came at her again.

She had nothing to fight him with but the truth. "Julian was f-forcing me." Her tongue was thick; her voice wouldn't rise above a whisper. "H-he said if I didn't go with him—No!" She put her hands up to ward off a blow, but instead he spun her around and jerked the gown over her shoulders and down her arms. Fear and a new fury gave her the strength to fight for a few more seconds, but then she felt him shove the dress over her hips and knees to the floor and panic engulfed her.

He wrestled her to the couch with childish ease, intrigued by the way her whole body was shaking. Her fear was making her weak; he laid her on her back and opened her legs, and all she did was twist her head back and forth and stare up at him with her huge eyes. If she would lie still he'd make her enjoy it, he thought suddenly, stroking the smooth skin of her thighs.

"If you do this, you'll be no better than Julian," she said in a whisper he could barely hear.

"Shut up." He unbuttoned his breeches.

"Burke, I love you!"

A red mist rose up in front of his eyes. Snarling like an animal, he covered her with his body and drove slowly into her. Her short, choked-off scream almost made him stop. She held her face away and bit down hard on her knuckles. In spite of everything, he still wanted to arouse her. "Kate," he said, holding still inside her, trying to kiss her. She made a sound of fear and revulsion that turned his blood to ice water. He finished in a few short, violent thrusts and stood up.

He found his coat and went to the door. He couldn't move fast enough. With his hand on the knob, he turned back to look at her. She was curled in a ball on her side, her hair covering her face. He said her name again, he didn't know why, and she put her hand over her ear. He started shaking. He opened the door and went out.

Diana gazed out at the snow through the window, watching the diving, swirling flakes with a dreamy half-smile. The ball had lasted till dawn, and she was the first one in the dining room at this early hour. But she'd been too excited to sleep late, too excited to have breakfast in her room; she had to *tell* somebody.

Her face lit up when she saw her brother come in, then it sank in dismay. He went straight to the sideboard and began to drink glass after glass of water from a silver pitcher.

"I thought you were ill, but now I see you're only drunk." She stood at his elbow, staring at him in surprise and wrinkling her nose at the smell of him. He still wore

his evening clothes, though they were torn and stained
beyond recognition. His hair, normally tied back neatly in
a ribbon, fell all about his face in disarray, and there was a
crusty scab over one eye from an untended cut. His skin
looked pasty and gray; the hollow-eyed stare he turned on
her was dull and seemingly unconnected to any functioning intelligence. "You *are* ill," she amended in concern.

He shook his head. "Hangover." Uttering the word
seemed to require all his strength.

Then she noticed the matted hair and bulging, blood-
encrusted lump over his ear. "Jamie, your head!"

"It's nothing."

"Oh lord, it looks awful, let me—"

He shrank away from her raised hand, not looking at
her. "It's nothing! Let me be, Diana."

"Are you sure?"

He nodded, wincing.

Diana sighed, watching him try to pour a cup of coffee
with hands that shook so badly he spilled most of it on the
table. He picked up the cup and raised it to his lips with
both hands like an old man, swallowing the entire scalding
contents in a few loud gulps.

"Jamie, can I please, please talk to you? I want to tell
you something so badly, I think I'm g-going to explode!"

"Tell me," he said with difficulty, pouring more
coffee.

She looked around. "Not here, someone might come
in. It's *private*."

He closed his eyes in pain. "Hall."

She almost skipped out of the room. He followed much
more slowly, holding himself as if his body were made of
glass.

"What?" he said when they were in the center of the
entrance hall and standing under the massive chandelier,
the candles melted away to nothing now. Diana opened
her mouth and then stopped. She closed her eyes and put

her fingers on her lips, savoring it. Even in his diminished condition he could see that whatever it was, it was very good. He said his question again laboriously.

"Edwin asked me to marry him."

His mouth went slack. "Edwin?" he repeated stupidly.

Diana nodded in solemn happiness. She began telling him about it while he backed up to the bottom step of the staircase and sat down. When she finished, his upper body sagged against the bannister limply. "Jamie, you *are* sick."

"Katherine told him you loved him." His dry lips moved slowly and carefully over the words as if he were trying to make sense of meaningless syllables.

"Yes, but you mustn't tell her I've told you because Edwin says she told him in confidence and he really shouldn't even have told me!" She giggled at her own giddiness. "I can't wait to tell her the news! But I had to tell you first. Don't tell Father—Edwin's coming this afternoon to ask for my hand. Oh, kiss me, Jamie, I'm so happy!"

He did, as best he could, then heard her start to run up the stairs. "She's not there."

Diana stopped. "She's not?" She came back down slowly. "Where is she?"

He shook his head. "I thought she was with you." Suddenly he put his head between his knees, feeling sweat pop out all over his body. He gulped convulsively while his mouth seemed to manufacture water faster than he could swallow. With deep, even breathing he finally controlled the nausea; when he lifted his face it was as white as the marble floor under his feet.

"Excuse me, my lord." It was the butler, come from nowhere to stand by his shoulder.

"Yes, Knole, what is it?" said Diana.

"I thought his lordship would want to know right away. The stableman says your horse is missing, sir; the gray stallion.''

Burke stood up slowly. If he looked ill before, now he looked dead. Knole instinctively reached for his arm. "What do you mean? It can't be."

"I'm afraid so, sir. And a saddle and bridle as well."

"Jesus. Oh God, no." His voice trailed off as he hauled himself up the stairs using the railing. At the top he shouted down, "Have another horse saddled, a fast one!" Diana and the butler were staring up at him in silent confusion. "Do it *now!*" Knole rushed off.

He ran down one hall and then another, soon out of breath and again overcome with nausea. In the middle of the third-floor staircase he paused long enough to vomit what seemed like gallons of water and bile, then staggered up the rest of the steps and down the hall to Katherine's room. He threw open the door and looked around hastily. The bed was made, everything was tidy. He went to the wardrobe and opened it. There it was in a torn heap on the floor: her burgundy gown. He heard a sound behind him.

"What's happened? Is it Katherine? What is it?"

"What's missing?" he demanded, taking Diana by the arm and pulling her to the wardrobe. She looked at him blankly. "What's missing?" he yelled.

She looked. There was the apricot dressing gown, another robe, her nightgown. "Where's the dress I lent her to wear downstairs?" she wondered aloud. "I gave it to her a few days ago. And her coat—"

Burke slammed the door shut in a fury and Diana jumped. "She's gone!"

"Gone? She can't be. You think she took your horse? Jamie, that's impossible. It's snowing out, she's not well enough to ride—Why would she go?" He looked at her with a face she'd never seen; she shrank back in apprehension. "What did you do?" she whispered.

He put his fist on the wall and leaned his sweating forehead against it. "I hurt her."

"You—" She felt afraid; she didn't want to know more. "Find her," she said quickly. "Go now, Jamie. Find her, don't let her be hurt."

He raised his tortured face and saw the tears on his sister's cheeks. He tried to smile. "It's all right, baby, I won't let her be hurt."

But there was a shaky, haunted feeling in his chest that wouldn't go away even as he busied himself with preparations to leave. Within an hour he had bathed, dressed, eaten a little, and packed enough clothes and supplies for a journey of unknown length. In the stable, he was mounting his horse—a fast black gelding—when he saw Julian come toward him, snow flying in the doorway behind him. He found it minimally warming to see someone who looked worse than he did. Julian's face was a mass of blue and yellow contusions; he held one arm at his side and walked with a limp. The honey-colored eye that wasn't swollen shut was bright with hatred.

"You'll never find her. It's a blizzard. She's gone and you'll never—" Burke rode his horse into him; he stumbled backward to avoid being trampled. "If you go after her, I'll tell Denholm she was here! You'll be court-martialed!" Burke stopped. "Katie Lennox. That's her name."

"How do you know?"

"She told me! We laughed about it. She—"

"Liar." He took his boot from the stirrup and kicked Julian hard in the chest. He lurched backward and fell onto the straw-covered floor.

"I'll write Denholm today!" Julian shouted after him, leaning against the stable door. "You'll never find her! She'll be dead!"

The demented scream died out quickly in the heavy, muffling snow and the whistling wind, but it echoed in Burke's ears for miles and miles.

PART IV

CHAPTER 20
Edinburgh
February 1746

Belmont Crescent was a quiet, eminently respectable enclave in the southern portion of the great city, situated on a slight rise so that on almost any day Edinburgh Castle could be clearly seen in the west. Today a cold, biting wind rustled dead leaves across the avenue and whipped at the ribbons of a black funeral wreath on the door to No. 6, the third townhouse on the eastern side. The door opened and a man with a small bag descended the steps to a waiting carriage. He wore a grim, dissatisfied look, and it was mirrored in the countenance of a tall, stoop-shouldered man who stood in the doorway, oblivious to the bitter cold, and watched him go.

The carriage rattled away and the tall man went back inside. With a heavy tread, as if his boots were weighted with lead, he crossed the tiled entrance hall and climbed the stairs, hanging onto the bannister in the manner of a much older person. At the top he stood quietly, staring at the closed door at the end of the hall; the lines in his weathered face were deep and etched with worry, and he passed a hand through his long, graying hair in a gesture of hopelessness. A middle-aged woman came through the door quietly and hastened forward when she saw him in the dim corridor.

"Mr. Innes," she said in a subdued but anxious voice, "wha' did he say?"

Innes leaned against the cheerfully papered wall in fatigue and dejection. "The news is no' guid, Mary. He says she'll follow 'er mother before spring if she keeps on in this way."

"Lord help us!" exclaimed the woman. "Bu' I'm no' surprised, no' a'tall. Only look at the tray she sent back; hardly a bite did she eat from it, and 'tis been tha' way fer nigh three weeks."

"Doctor says her wound's healed and there's naught bu' her ane misery keepin' her from bein' weel. If she weren't such a pitiful bundle o' bones lyin' in tha' grea' bed, I'd take her by her skinny shoulders and shake her, it makes me tha' mad t' see wha' she's doin'!"

"Go in and talk to her, Mr. Innes. Mayhap she'll listen t' you. I've aboot flapped my lips off tryin' t' make her see reason."

"Do ye think I've no' done the same?" he asked indignantly. "Nay, bu' ye're right, Mary, I'll try again. 'Tis all we can do for her now, it seems."

The room was gloomy with the draperies closed; the only light came from the fire in the grate and one candle beside the bed. Though spotlessly clean, there was a musty sickroom smell, as of unaired linen and long-dead flowers. Innes went to the hearth and added a log to the fire, kicking it with his boot in a deliberate attempt to make a loud, unexpected noise and dispel the atmosphere of funereal quiet. The figure on the bed opened her eyes and watched him, but otherwise made no move. He walked to the window and pulled back the curtains, letting in a little wintry light.

"Please not," came a low, uninflected voice from the bed, and he closed the draperies on a long sigh.

He went to the bed and stared down, hands on his hips.

He tried to look stern and unsympathetic, but there was a sudden lump in his throat. Her face, pale as the pillow, was all cheekbones and eyes; the only spot of color was her hair, still an irrepressible flaming copper, plaited in a thick braid and resting on her shoulder. Her eyes had lost their turquoise brightness and now seemed dark and cloudy with pain. One bony hand grasped the coverlet; it was still and waxen, like a corpse's hand, and the sight of it made Innes look away and shiver.

He pulled the chair closer to the bedside and sat down. "Miss Kate," he began, almost angrily, "the doctor says ye're behavin' like a parfect fool. He washes his hands o' ye and says no' t' call him again till ye're dead, he's tha' tired o' lookin' at yer peaked face. Mary has aboot decided the same thing, bein' fed up wi' preparin' mouth-waterin' meals and havin' 'em sent back ice-cold and undented." The enormous eyes, which looked even larger because of the dark, bruised-looking circles under them, swiveled away from his face to stare blindly at the wall. "It seems ye've decided on a course t' kill yerself, which I wouldna ha' believed had I no' seen it wi' me ane eyes. I've known ye all yer life bu' I hadna suspected ye were tha' stupid and tha' selfish. I'm ashamed o' ye, I am, and sae would yer Pa be if he could see ye today. And yer Ma hardly cauld in 'er grave yet—I vow she'd rise up and hector ye hollow if she knew ye were plannin' t' join her as quick as ye can. I thought ye were brave! I thought ye had yer Pa's courage and could bear the bad times tha' cum to us all. But nay, now I ken yer naught bu'—Here, now, what's this? Lord, Miss Kate, dinna cry, I meant no' a ward, 'twas all drivel, I swear—" He couldn't bear the sight of the tears pouring down her pallid cheeks like raindrops on a window, while her shoulders shook and her still face collapsed in helpless grieving. He moved to the bed and lifted her from the pillow, holding her in his arms and blinking back his own tears.

"Oh, lass, lass. Ye're breakin' my heart as sure as if ye'd set a sword to it. If ye'd only speak o' wha' happened to ye whilst ye were awa', and how it cum aboot tha' ye retarned to us half dead in a coach, wi' a wound in yer breast and all yer will t' live gone. Or if ye canna bring yerself t' tell me, then tell Mary; she loves ye like a daughter and her woman's heart would understand. Bu' if ye will no' speak of it, 'twill fester in yer soul and lay ye low, as it's begun t' do. Can ye no' talk t' me?"

Katherine strove to check her weak, unwanted weeping, but it seemed she had no control over it anymore. She reached for the handkerchief that was never far from her hand and wiped her eyes. After a minute she was a little better; she pressed herself gently away from Innes and sank back against the pillow. "You're right, I am an awful coward," she said brokenly, waving away his protest. "I'll try to do what you and Mary want me to do—eat more, get out of bed sometimes. But more than that I beg you will not ask me again, Innes, for I will never, ever speak of it. Never. I cannot!"

More tears splashed down her cheeks and he patted her shoulder soothingly, afraid he was making her worse. "There, then. Never mind, lass, I gi' ye my ward I'll no' mention it again if that's wha' ye want. Rest now and try t' get strong. Mary'll bring ye some hot broth in aboot an hour. Dinna cry anymore."

He got up and went from the room, closing the door quietly behind him. Katherine lay as he'd left her, exhausted in body and spirit. She felt as weak as she had after the shooting, and yet the doctor said her wound was healed and there was nothing physically wrong with her. Innes' words had stirred her enough to give her a sense of guilt but no real interest in getting strong. One had to want to get strong *for* something, she thought tiredly. In her case, that wasn't possible.

A few days later she had a visitor. "I won't see anyone,"

she told Mary with a pathetic attempt at firmness, but the housekeeper held her ground.

"He says he *must* see you, Miss Kate. Here, he sent up his card."

Katherine stared at the name engraved on the square of stiff paper for a long time. Finally her hand dropped to the coverlet and she raised her eyes. "Very well, I'll see him. But I won't get up, he'll have to come here. Help me to sit up a little, Mary."

In a few minutes she was as ready for company as she could be. The gentleman Mary ushered in was middle-aged and balding, with exceedingly thick spectacles and a small, neat beard. He stopped short when he got near enough to see clearly the slender figure propped against the pillows, and the cheerful greeting he was planning died on his lips. "My dear child," he said feelingly, and took her hand.

"I'm glad to see you, Owen."

"They told me downstairs you were ill, but I had no idea—! Perhaps I should come back another time."

"Nay, it's all right; I wanted you to come up."

"I shan't stay long. Katherine, I was so very sorry to learn about your mother." She inclined her head and murmured thanks. "Were you able to see her before she passed away?"

"No. She died a week before I came home." She looked away. It was another failure she must live with, for if she hadn't undertaken a mission in the service of a cause that meant less to her than her own need for vengeance, her mother would not have died alone. And if she hadn't encouraged her father to set out on a course that was against his nature, he would not have been killed. If she hadn't given her love to a man who despised her . . . She put her hand over her eyes and shuddered.

Owen Cathcart made a sad, sympathetic sound. "So. You're all alone now."

"Aye, all alone."

He watched her for a second, then looked away from the pale, bleak face. "Have you heard that the prince's army is in retreat?" he asked presently, taking a seat in the chair at the bedside.

"Aye, I heard. But Innes says they won the battle at Falkirk, so I don't understand why they're marching north."

Cathcart grimaced. "It's a mystery to others besides yourself, I assure you. The prince himself is against it, but most of the clan leaders are in favor. There've been so many desertions, it's thought the rest of the winter would be better spent in taking Inverness and Fort Augustus. By spring, it's hoped the French will join us and a new army can be raised."

"What do you think?"

He looked at her candidly. "I think it's the beginning of the end of our cause."

"Surely not!"

"I hope I'm wrong. Meanwhile, the work goes on."

"It must be difficult for you now that the English occupy Edinburgh."

"I have to be more careful, that's all."

"Ewan's dead," she said quietly, after a pause.

"Is he?" He didn't seem surprised. "How did that come about?"

In a few lean sentences, she told him what had happened, including the fact but not the manner of her own wounding. He listened carefully, paying close attention when she spoke of having stayed for several weeks at Weddingstone.

"I sincerely regret I couldn't have been of more help to you, Katherine," he said when she was finished. "I sent McNab to try to help you, but it was absolutely necessary that I myself return to Edinburgh."

"It doesn't matter," she said tiredly.

Cathcart cleared his throat. "This Major Burke," he began, then stopped. Katherine stared fixedly at the coverlet. "You stayed at his home?" She nodded. "May I ask the nature of the relationship you had with him?"

She raised her disturbing eyes to his. "Why?"

" 'Tis not idle curiosity, I assure you. And it is important."

"I was in love with him," she said quietly, not looking away. "I am not anymore."

"Ah. You—had a disagreement?"

She gave a little strangled laugh, then nodded.

"You were lovers? Forgive this rude probing, my dear; I have a good reason for needing to know."

Now a little color began to suffuse her cheeks. "We—were intimate. We were not lovers."

Cathcart frowned but thought better of pressing further. "He's here. In Edinburgh."

She came off the pillows and sat straight up, holding one arm out toward him in an odd, beseeching gesture. Her face was alive with the first evidence of animation he'd seen. "Burke? In Edinburgh?"

"Looking for you. Or for Katie Lennox, I should say."

She sank back in a weak collapse. He thought she'd fainted until he noticed the twin spots of pink on her cheeks. "How do you know? Are you sure?" She looked away into the middle distance and bit her knuckle in an old gesture of distraction he remembered.

"He's been here for at least two weeks, according to my people." He waited a few seconds, then asked, "Why would he be looking for you, Katherine?"

She shook her head and didn't answer.

"My dear, I want you to see him."

"Why?" The word was almost inaudible.

"I want you to give him some information to take back to his superiors. It will be false information. Will you do it?"

There was no sound except the hissing of the fire in the grate and the ticking of the clock on the mantel. She stared at the palms of her hands in perfect stillness, thinking of all the things she had lost. Honor, pride, innocence. Respectability. A chance at happiness. She'd thought there was nothing left but self-hate, but she was wrong. She also hated James Burke.

"What will happen to him?" she asked after a long moment.

"Nothing dire. He's a viscount, he's extremely wealthy. A slap on the wrist. If you hope to cause him a lot of trouble, you'll be disappointed."

She shook her head. "You misunderstand," she murmured, but did not explain. After a few more seconds she sat up straight. "Aye, Owen, I will do it," she said positively. There was light in her eyes, and her voice had a new resonance. "Hand me my dressing gown, will you?" She pointed to the robe at her feet; he brought it to her and helped her into it. She threw back the covers and got out of bed, sliding her feet into slippers. "Would you like some tea?"

"No, thank you," he said wonderingly.

"If you don't mind, I would." She pulled the bellrope, and a maid entered almost immediately. She took the order in happy surprise and ran off.

Katherine paced slowly between the bed and the window in subdued excitement. "When shall we do it? How shall we arrange it? No more card games, Owen, you must promise me!" She laughed almost gaily.

"No indeed." He couldn't stop staring at her. "Tell me, Katherine, what does Major Burke think of you? Today, now."

The pacing stopped. She looked at the floor, then into his eyes fearlessly. "He thinks I'm a whore." Her attempt at audacity couldn't completely hide her bitterness.

Cathcart stroked his beard. "You're serious? Do you

mean literally? A prostitute?''

"That's exactly what I mean.''

"Good God, the man must be an idiot. Very well, we'll use that; leave the details to me. Prince Charles wants to winter in Inverness, Katherine, but the town is occupied by government troops. We must find a way to lure them out so Charles and what's left of his army can slip in. Once there, it'll be impossible to dislodge them. I shall be thinking of something for you to tell Major Burke that will help us toward that end. May I come and see you again tomorrow?''

"Yes, certainly.''

"One more thing. Time is precious. It would be disastrous if the major left Edinburgh before we could make use of him. On the other hand, you've been ill, you're still not well—''

"Owen, don't distress yourself on that account. My own doctor says I am not ill. Regardless of that, nothing in the world could prevent me from doing this. I would get up from my deathbed for a chance to make a fool of James Burke!''

Cathcart felt a small shiver from the icy glitter in her eyes and the hard, implacable note in her voice. "Very well, my dear,'' he said quietly, "I'll arrange everything as quickly as possible.''

"Good. I will be ready.''

The Unicorn looked, from its unprepossessing two stories of stucco surmounted by a shingled, many-chimneyed roof, like any other alehouse-cum-hostelry in this middle-class, nondescript section of the city. In fact, it was the finest brothel in Edinburgh. This was immediately apparent to any fortunate gentleman allowed past its stout front door and daunting welcoming party, for once he was past these the exotic beauty of the place was revealed. If one had a fondness for ancient Greek and Roman antiqui-

ties, one was doubly enchanted, for all the rooms—all
except a few special ones in back—were decorated in that
style, and all the women wore togas or robes or anything
else that passed in Edinburgh in 1746 for Greco-Roman
garb.

Burke knew no password, no name of an influential
patron who might have sent him; he did, however, have
plenty of money, and thus the door was thrown open to
him in gracious welcome. He was escorted by a footman
dressed as a Roman page to an anteroom where his hat and
greatcoat were taken, and then into a large lounge made to
look like a kind of underground grotto. The walls and
floor were of rough stone, as were the benches and small
tables scattered casually about. Marble statues of naked
gods and goddesses stood in every corner, some bearing
flaming torches, and the walls bore richly woven tapestries
depicting countless lewd sexual conquests. In the center of
the room was a sunken pool surrounded by rocks, real
moss, and more torches; two nearly nude women reclined
in the water and spoke desultorily to a fully clothed
gentleman nearby, who was amusing himself by tossing
grapes at them. In a corner, a young girl dressed as a dryad
played the harp softly. Over everything was a warmly
flattering pinkish light, created by the judicious placement
of oil lamps covered in gauze netting. Burke hoped the
place wouldn't catch fire until he could finish his business
and be gone.

He walked over to a stone platform that looked like an
altar but was really the bar, and a man wearing a toga
handed him a glass of champagne before he could say a
word. "I prefer whiskey," he began, but the barman
shrugged.

"Sorry, mate, we only serve bubbly," he told him in an
accent incompatible with his costume.

A florid Scotsman with copious sidewhiskers came
through an archway hung in diaphanous silver draperies
and joined him at the bar. "One more, Tommy," he told

the barman, then turned jovially to Burke. "Quite a place, eh? Don't think I've seen you here before." He straightened his cravat and ran his fingers through his whiskers in a hasty toilette.

Burke mentioned it was his first visit.

"Ha! Not your last, I'll wager. They've got everything here a man could dream of." He drank his champagne down in one gulp and belched. "Lord, I hate to go, but my wife's got one of her idiotic supper parties." He made a comical face of disgust, and Burke smiled. "Well, I'm off. Oh, but I say, if you haven't been here before, you won't have heard about Lenore."

"Lenore?"

"Aye. I've just come from her." His face took on a singular look of pride mingled with awe. "She's new, but she's the best girl in the house, by God. Ask for her," he advised, punching a large index finger into Burke's lapel, "and you won't go wrong." He turned to go, and Burke looked down at his drink, missing the quick wink that passed between the Scotsman and the bartender.

He leaned back against the bar and idly watched the two women in the pool, thinking how ludicrous the place was. This was the strongest lead he'd had in the weeks he'd been searching for Katherine in Edinburgh, yet he knew he wouldn't find her here. She was a mystery to him in many ways, but of one thing he was certain: she didn't work in a brothel. He had a swift vision of himself tossing a coin at her feet, and his brain cringed. The truth, which should have been obvious to anyone but an imbecile, was finally clear even to him: she had been telling the truth when she said Julian had forced her. He understood as well what Julian had used to coerce her—the threat of exposing Burke to his superiors for hiding a suspected spy in his home. And for her pains, for her willingness to submit to Julian's degrading whims in order to save him, he had brutalized her.

It was an abomination. He still reacted with physical

revulsion whenever he thought of it, and he thought of it almost constantly. It was a sin for which he would rightly burn in hell—except that he was in hell already.

At least she was here, in a city, where presumably someone was taking care of her. When he'd thought she was sick and alone somewhere in the frozen Scottish countryside, he'd almost lost his mind. He thought of all the doors he'd knocked on, all the blank stares his frantic questions had elicited. He remembered the last door, in a tiny village near Kelso, and the kind-eyed woman who'd resolutely shaken her head to everything he asked her. He'd led his horse back to the lane and was about to mount when a little boy, no higher than his knee, called to him from the hedge, "Are ye lookin' fer the beautiful lady?"

Burke's sudden fierceness almost frightened the boy away. He reassured him somehow, then listened in torment while the lad told him of finding a half-conscious woman there in the lane one morning more than a week before. He'd run to Crawfords'—pointing to the cottage Burke had just come from—and gotten Mrs. Crawford to come out; together they'd lifted the lady and taken her into the house.

"She's there? Now?"

"Nay, she's gone."

"Gone! Where? When?"

The boy fell back in fear. "All I know, Mr. Crawford took 'er in his wagon to Kelso two days ago for t' meet the coach goin' to Edinburgh."

"Edinburgh!" Burke closed his eyes and repeated the word like a prayer. He gave the astonished boy a sovereign.

"Is she goin' t' get weel?" he called as Burke began to ride away. "She had the saddest eyes. Is she goin' t' get weel?"

He didn't know the answer. But at least now he was sure she was here, somewhere, even though it seemed as if the city had swallowed her up. He marveled at how little he actually knew about her. That was what was hampering his search, the fact that he didn't know where to begin. She could be anywhere.

Anywhere but here, he amended, looking around with distaste. He was wasting time, but the thought of returning to his empty hotel room was not inspiring. When the barman handed him another glass of champagne, he took it.

"Good evening."

He turned his head. There was a woman beside him. She had jet-black hair, white skin, and red lips, and she wore the requisite flowing robe. "Are you enjoying yourself or is there something I could do to increase your pleasure?" she asked softly. She had a breathy, childlike voice and she used it to good effect.

"I'm looking for a girl," he told her.

"Yes,' she agreed, returning his smile.

"A particular girl," he corrected. The woman pouted prettily. She was very beautiful; he wondered why he had no interest in her whatever. "Her name is Katie Lennox. Or Kate, or Katherine."

"I'm afraid we have no Katies, Kates, or Katherines. What a shame." She slid her arm through his.

"It may not be her real name. She's tall and slender, with bright red hair and turquoise eyes. She's very lovely. Her skin—"

The woman removed her hand from his waistcoat with a little frown of irritation. "That's Lenore," she said tiredly, as though this had happened before.

"No, I don't think so," Burke smiled; "you must be mistaken."

She shrugged. "Perhaps, but the woman you describe is Lenore. But she's always busy; I doubt if you could see her tonight anyway. You could try, though—there she is."

He looked across the room and saw a girl coming through the archway with a man on either arm. He couldn't see her face at first, just her soft, slender throat as she turned her mouth up to accept one man's kiss, then the other's. The two men moved away, and the girl looked straight at him.

It was Kate.

His glass slipped from his fingers and shattered in a hundred pieces on the stone floor.

CHAPTER 21

The crash of the glass shattered what was left of Katherine's nerves. Through sheer power of will she returned his utterly shocked, disbelieving gaze without flinching. How could she have thought she would relish this moment? She wanted to bolt for the door, or better, to fall through a hole in the floor and die. Instead she took a step toward him, then another, excruciatingly conscious that the ridiculous gown they'd made her wear was all but transparent and under it she was stark naked.

When they were near enough to speak but not near enough that he could touch her, she stopped. "What are you doing here?" she asked, trying for the right note of angry surprise.

It should have made her feel smug that he still couldn't speak, could only shake his head in mute denial, but it didn't. She repeated her question, and finally he found his tongue. "You don't work here." He looked around and laughed with mirthless wonder and said it again. "You don't work here."

"I don't? I wonder why I'm so tired in the mornings. What is it you want, Burke? A girl? There are plenty here; I'll go and find you one." He seized her bare arm when she turned as if to leave and pulled her close, growling. She didn't know what he intended, and there wasn't time to be afraid before a very tall, very broad individual dressed as a Roman soldier loomed up between them and put a ham of a hand on Burke's shoulder.

"This cove botherin' you, Miss Lenore?"

"Yes!"

"Take your hand off me or I'll kill you," Burke said to the Roman soldier in utter seriousness. Katherine put a shaky hand to her throat; things were not going the way they were supposed to.

"Thank you, Bob, you may go, I think," came a low, husky voice to her right. She turned to see Cara, the still-beautiful owner of the Unicorn, the "madam," as it were, standing by her shoulder and smiling pleasantly at Burke. "Now, sir, how may I help you? I see you've met Lenore. I regret to say she's occupied for the evening, but there are countless lovely ladies here who would be honored to serve you."

The burly soldier lumbered off, and Burke's grip on Katherine's arm loosened. "I daresay you're right," he said smoothly, suddenly all reasonableness and calm, "but you see, I've got my heart set on . . . Lenore."

Cara laughed lightly. "In that you aren't alone, sir, but I'm afraid it's impossible."

"Why?"

"She's engaged."

"Ah." He reached into his inside coat pocket and pulled from it a heavy, bulging purse. "Perhaps she's free now."

The proprietress took it from him in seeming surprise, weighed it in her hand with professional quickness, and smiled. "Yes, I believe after all she is."

Katherine watched the transaction in sick fascination. When Cara smiled, she closed her eyes for a second and thought, Never, never can it get any worse than this; this is the bottom. The thought was cheering in a horrible kind of way.

"I won't go with him," she protested, suddenly remembering her role.

"Nonsense, Lenore. No more of that, now." Cara smiled coolly.

"I mean it. You can't make me go with him—I hate him!"

Cara took her wrist in a wiry grip and led her through the curtains in the archway. "Brace yourself, dear," she whispered in the dimness, then brought her hand up against Katherine's cheek in a loud slap. She yelped in pain and astonishment. Burke came through the draperies at the moment when Cara took her by the shoulders and began to shake her.

"Stop it," he said menacingly.

"Are you finished with this foolishness, girl?" the older woman asked sternly, and Katherine nodded, blinking back genuine tears. "Good." She patted her on the shoulder briskly and turned to Burke. "You may spend the night if you like; a late supper will be sent up, and naturally there's champagne. But I believe you wanted whiskey?" He bowed, impressed. "One more thing. Violence of any kind is not permitted in the rooms. If you fancy it we have another place for that, closely supervised, and you must pay extra. Understood?"

Burke's face became even harder. "I'll let you know if it becomes necessary."

"Fine." She threw a last sharp glance at "Lenore" and was gone.

They stood in the small vestibule staring at each other for a few tense seconds before Katherine's nerve failed and she headed for the stairs, Burke close behind. The lighting was dim and determinedly romantic; the walls had been roughly plastered to resemble stone. On the wide landing they passed a girl dressed as a wood nymph, sitting on a rock in an artificially sylvan setting, playing the flute. Under other circumstances the sight would have made them both laugh; tonight it didn't stir a smile.

At the top of the stairs the hall branched off in three

directions; Katherine kept going straight, past innumerable closed doors, her ears resolutely closed to the
low sounds coming from most of them. She was acutely
aware of the way she looked from the back in this flesh-
colored silk dress, and of how in certain lights it seemed
she was wearing nothing at all. By the time she reached
"her" room, through the last door facing them at the end
of the hall, she was in such a state she hardly knew what
she was doing.

Not surprisingly, the main feature in the rather spacious
room was the bed, high and wide and swathed in rich
velvet draperies, and adorned with a canopy on which was
painted a scene depicting a mythical orgy. The mantel was
supported by two marble goddesses, naked; a fire burned
warmly in the grate. There was a miniature torch burning
in a sconce by the door, providing the only illumination
except for the fire and a branch of candles on a table beside
the bed. The other furnishings were sparse but func-
tional—a small table laid with service for two near the
fireplace, one comfortable-looking upholstered chair, a
long, low sofa, an ottoman.

Burke took it all in at a glance. He wanted to pinch
himself and wake up from this dream. None of it seemed
real, least of all the wide-eyed girl standing in front of him
in a goddamn toga. But it was Kate, his Kate. The woman
he'd sought for weeks so he could tell her he was sorry he'd
raped her. And she made her living under that lurid
canopy every night with men she didn't know. She was a
whore. He repeated the word to himself carefully, trying to
believe it. He couldn't. He shook his head, staring at her.

"You don't work here," he said for the third time. It
sounded ridiculous even to him, but he couldn't seem to
get past it.

"Not that again." Her laugh was brittle, patently false.

She looked like a whore in that dress, God knew. The
only thing holding it together was a sort of rope under her

breasts; it was cunningly knotted so that one little tug would untie it and open the whole front of the gown. Not that he couldn't see almost everything through it anyway—the shape of her breasts, her nipples, her navel, the triangle of hair between her thighs. The longer he looked at her, the less important it became that he understand what she was doing here.

He saw he could still make her blush. Her face was crimson from his scrutiny. What sort of whore blushed when a man looked at her?

He sat down on one of the chairs at the table and began to pull off his boots. The sight rocked her. Her imagination had never taken her beyond this point. He would come, she would give him Cathcart's information, he would leave. If he really thought she was a prostitute, he wouldn't want her. How could he? He was Lord High and Mighty James Burke, the Viscount Bloody Holystone! But now he was taking off his cravat and throwing his coat and waistcoat on the floor.

"What do you think you're doing?"

"I think I'm taking my shirt off," he said mockingly; and indeed, he'd started unbuttoning it. "Hadn't you better do the same? But with a dress like that, I imagine you can be naked in seconds. That must be convenient. Let's see you do it." He stood with his hands on his hips, bare-chested, legs apart, watching her appraisingly. His look was insulting. "Take it off, Kate. I want to have a look at what I've paid for."

Anger leapt into her chest like a flame. "And I want you out of this room in five seconds, you arrogant son of a bitch!"

His bark of genuine laughter was disconcerting. "Not bloody likely," he snarled, coming toward her. On second thought, he wanted to undress her himself. His fingers were itching to pull on the little rope.

She stepped back quickly, and soon there was no more

room; he had her against the wall between the fireplace and the bed. She tried to bring her knee up into his groin but he was pressed against her too closely, there wasn't enough space. He was frowning with concentration, discovering that the gown was more complicated than he'd thought.

"Why did you come here?" she cried. "What do you want with me? I thought I was *rid* of you, damn you!" She felt the rope give way and moaned in despair. His eyes were shining with hellfire, his hands covering her bare breasts. "No!" she gasped when he used his thumbs to stroke her nipples. "Damn you, damn you." Her head rocked back and forth while she pulled on his wrists with all her strength. He kissed her behind her right ear and she jerked backward as if he had leprosy, striking her head against the wall. "I'll kill you if you do this!" she flung at him hysterically.

His face made her quail. "And I'll kill you if you don't." She could swear he meant it. "I paid a fortune for this night and I want my money's worth. Stop fighting me, Kate, or I'll take you to that special room where they 'carefully supervise' the violence. Do you think I won't?"

"Oh, I know you too well—I think you would do it with pleasure!"

Her answer made him even angrier. He gripped her shoulders so hard they ached and brought his face level with hers. "Am I really that repulsive? How many men do you open your legs for in one night? Are they all that much better than me?"

She brought her hand back to hit him, but he caught her wrist in mid-swing. He laughed, his teeth flashing whitely in the firelight. With the other hand he pushed her dress back over her shoulders. Sickened, Katherine felt it fall to the floor and land in a heap around her ankles. She gave a desolate cry and tried to turn away, but he wouldn't let her. He made her face him while his burning gaze swept over the soft upswell of bosom, the flat stomach and too-prominent rib cage, the flare of her hips and her smooth thighs. She felt weak and uncoordinated, and he jostled her over to the bed with ease. Still, she wouldn't make it easy for him. While he took off his breeches, she rolled away and almost reached the far side of the bed before he grabbed her around the middle and pulled her back so she was pinned under him. He seized her wrists and pulled them over her head, and now she was helpless. She felt his knees roughly opening her legs, felt his hardness against her thigh. Tears she'd sworn not to shed welled in her eyes and streamed down her cheeks. She heard herself say in a voice choking with grief, "Burke, for the love of God, don't."

A shudder went through him as sweat fell from his face onto her breasts. He saw her tears, heard the anguish in her voice, and made himself stop. I can't do this, he thought; of course I can't. It's pleasure I want to give her, not pain. Frustration made his skin tingle.

Without releasing her hands, he shifted himself so most of his weight was on his left side but his right thigh was over her body, still holding her down. He transferred her wrists to his left hand, freeing his right to pull her chin gently around until she faced him. The look in her eyes was bruised and battered; it made him feel ashamed. He lowered his head and kissed her. She pulled away and his lips trailed along her jaw softly to her ear. He kissed the curls at her hairline, the trails of tears on her cheeks.

"Don't," she said brokenly. "Stop." But he wouldn't stop, and when she tried to move her arms he held them still. This can't be happening, she thought. Why is he—why can't I? . . . Her thoughts flew off in tattered confusion. He kissed her eyes and her nose, then returned to her lips. Over and over he kissed her with hot, searing kisses until he heard a moan deep in her throat. Her mouth opened and he entered her with his tongue, caressing, tasting. His free hand moved softly to her breast. "No, *don't*—" But he would never stop now and they both knew it. When he let go of her wrists she hardly realized it. She made one last attempt to push him away but her heart wasn't in it. But when he put his lips on the scar under her nipple, she stiffened. "Don't, Burke. It's ugly."

"Shh. Everything about you is beautiful."

She sighed and felt something like joy well up in her. Now he was doing something to her nipple with his tongue that sent sparks of delicious pleasure shooting through her. He kissed her with loud, shocking sounds that thrilled and embarrassed her. She felt him move lower, sliding his warm lips down her belly and moving inexorably on to the place between her legs. "Burke?" She stopped breathing. He couldn't be doing this; this was—this—Oh God, he was, he was opening her will-less legs with his hands and kissing her *there*, with a sweetness she'd never known existed. Conscious thought floated into thin air and she was aware of nothing but hot rings of pleasure that spread out and grew wider and wider as her mind tapered off to nothing. There was no question of holding back or waiting for him, the rings were taking her too far too fast, beyond rationality or control. And then she felt the fierce explosion inside, beginning where his mouth was but radiating through her belly and thighs, her toes, her whole body, so intense she thought she was dying. Was she crying out his name? Her hips were jerking spasmodically, but more slowly now as the rings receded, grew fainter, disappeared. She was being set ever so gently back on solid ground. Ah, sweet, sweet. Her muscles felt like jelly. She would never move again. She drew a shuddering breath and looked down at Burke. He was resting his cheek on her thigh and smiling, his eyes closed. She had never known such peace.

It was short-lived. Before the sweat could dry on their

bodies, Burke sat up and moved away from her, saying in a voice that was like a glass of cold water in her face, ''There, Kate, we're even.''

He'd been lying there in such selfless contentment, thinking how wonderful she was, how he would swear no man had ever done that to her before, when reality hit him like a blow to the sternum. He had a vision of the hearty Scotsman combing his whiskers, of the two faceless men kissing her upturned mouth, and his fantasy shattered into fragments. Not once did he consider that it might all have been staged. Kate's gift, he clearly saw, was an ability to make every man who had her feel like the first.

Katherine was chilled to the bone. Such a precious moment, and he'd trampled on it. But what had she expected? She sat up quickly, ashamed of her wanton posture, and grabbed for the thin robe at the foot of the bed.

She went to the window. The black square sent back a clear reflection of herself, pale, trembling, distressed. The bitter, bitter truth assaulted her without mercy: she still loved him. Even rape couldn't destroy her love, nor callousness, nor cruelty. What kind of a woman was she? She began to cry.

Anger finally stopped the tears, at Burke and at herself. She despised her weakness; she would rot in hell before she'd let him see it. She needed to be alone. The thing to do was tell Burke what Cathcart wanted her to tell him, and then he would go away and she could be by herself.

She turned toward him. He was still sitting on the edge of the bed, staring moodily into the fire. Before she could speak there was a discreet knock at the door.

''Come in,'' said Katherine.

It was the maid, bearing a tray. She didn't bat an eye at the sight of the naked man, and Burke was equally unmoved. Katherine, however, was discomforted sufficiently to go to the wardrobe, take out the conveniently placed man's dressing gown of soft blue wool, and toss it to him. The

maid set out fruit, bread, and a bit of meat on the table, as
well as Burke's whiskey and a carafe of wine for Katherine.
After tending to the fire, she murmured, "Anything else,
Miss Lenore?"

"No, Sally; thank you." She watched her go, then
stood uncertainly in the center of the room, casting about
in her mind for a way to begin. "Why did you come
here?" she asked suddenly. It wasn't what she'd meant to
say at all.

He got up and walked past her to the fireplace, where he
stood gazing down sightlessly as though he hadn't heard
her. Finally he straightened. "To apologize." She stood
still; a traitorous little bird in her heart began to sing.
"And to make sure you were all right." He looked around
the room with undisguised contempt. "You seem to have
landed on your feet."

The song died as she watched his lips twist cynically. But
his words provided the opening she'd been looking for.
She poured a glass of wine and carried it to the opposite
side of the mantel from him. "I know you told Colonel
Denholm I was dead. I'm grateful to you for that."

"Julian told you?"

"Yes." She waited for him to say more; when he
didn't, she continued. "Following me here to Edinburgh
must have further jeopardized your standing with the
colonel."

"Don't distress yourself on my account," he said coolly.

"Yes, but I should think you're in a bit of trouble,
Burke."

"What difference does it make to you?"

She drew herself up. "You misjudge me if you think it
gives me any satisfaction to know I've caused trouble for
you or your family. That was never my intent." She stared
thoughtfully into her glass, then looked up as if something
had occurred to her. She opened her mouth, closed it,
started again hesitatingly. "Burke, I know something that

might help you." He folded his arms and watched her dubiously. "Two nights ago I was—with a man. Here, in this room. I won't tell you his name or his rank, but I'll warrant to you he was in a position to know what he was talking about. We were speaking of the uprising, as you can imagine happens often these days—"

"Oh, I'm sure a lot of *talking* goes on in here," he interrupted sarcastically.

"Do you want to hear this or not?" she snapped. He bowed in exaggerated apology. "Anyway," she went on stiffly, "this man told me something he probably shouldn't have, something that's going to happen." She hesitated again, seeming to weigh her words, then took a deep breath as if she'd made a decision. "In about five days from today, three ships are to land at Kessock. French ships, carrying a total of six hundred men."

"Kessock?" he repeated, frowning.

"Across the Moray Firth from Inverness."

He turned away and Katherine held her breath. He looked back at her. "French ships?" She nodded. "It's too few, too late," he said, more to himself than her. "Charlie's finished."

She shrugged. "Still," she offered tentatively, as if thinking it out for the first time, "if the landing is successful, I suppose more could follow." She took a sip of wine.

There was a pause while Burke seemed to be thinking. "Why would you tell me this?" he demanded all of a sudden.

"I told you why. It might help—"

"I don't believe you. You support the prince, even though you try to hide it."

She smiled almost pityingly at his naivete and shook her head. "You said it yourself—the Jacobite cause is finished. English troops occupy the city now. I'm in a somewhat delicate position here, as I'm sure you can appreciate. Let's say it . . . behooves me to cast my lot with the winning side.''

She looked back into his repelled face for as long as she could stand it, then casually transferred her gaze to the fire. She didn't try to lift her glass again; her shaking hand would have given her away.

"What a bitch you are," he said quietly.

Her heart contracted as if he'd plunged a knife into it. "I try to help you and you insult me," she said weakly; she couldn't seem to rally the strength to defend herself. "I don't care if you use this information or not; 'tis nothing to me. For God's sake, why don't you leave now?"

"Leave?" He smiled in amusement. He went to the table, sat down, and poured a small amount of whiskey into a glass. "Come over here, Kate."

She didn't move. Her heart was in her throat. He was going to touch her again and it seemed wrong, it seemed like a sacrilege. He despised her, with good reason. How could he possibly want to make love to her?

"I said come here."

"Why?"

He didn't answer, only waited patiently for her to come. At last she did, telling herself it wasn't because she wanted to but because she had no choice. She stood beside his chair, trembling already at the mere thought of his hands on her body. How much more was she going to have to endure? At that moment she didn't give a damn about Owen Cathcart or the Jacobite cause. Even the deaths of her father or Rory or Michael couldn't justify this sacrifice. She wanted Burke. She wanted him to know who she was and how much she loved him, wanted him to touch her with—*affection*, not this compulsive lust that drove them both to hurt each other, shred each other's hearts until there was nothing left between them but distrust and contempt.

He reached for her then, his patience gone, and pulled

her onto his lap, where she perched as stiffly as if she were sitting on an anthill. For a few moments he was content just to hold her, inhaling the sweet scent of her. It occurred to him she didn't smell or taste like a prostitute, like a woman who slept with many men every night. Tonight she was as fresh as spring, as she always was, as honey-sweet as a young virgin. He opened the front of her robe and kissed the place between her breasts, breathing deeply. Her hand pushing against his shoulder was halfhearted.

"Kiss me," he ordered.

"Only because you're making me," she said primly, lowering her lashes to conceal the desire she knew was shining in her eyes.

"Oh, that goes without saying."

She touched her lips to his demurely and drew away.

"More," he growled softly.

It was what she wanted, too, but she held back. "Burke—"

"Quiet. No talking."

"Why do you still want me when you hate me so much?"

He looked at her with an odd expression. "I don't hate you," he murmured, taking them both by surprise. A nearly primitive fear surfaced in his mind, blocking out whatever he might have said next. He desperately wanted this conversation to end. He put a hand behind her head and kissed her hungrily, devouring her with pent-up, inarticulate passion. He pushed aside her robe and stroked her silky thighs, her buttocks. Her unrestrained moan of pleasure was music to him as she pressed closer, flattening her breasts against his hard chest. He could feel her arms trembling as she held him tightly, back arched, her mouth clinging to his.

He stood up and carried her to the fire. He would take her there on the rug—the low couch and the ottoman struck him as obscene. He didn't want Kate in a posture of submission; he wanted her like a lover, like his Kate, passionate and giving, hot, responsive, wanting him as much as he wanted her.

He lay on top of her and her legs parted eagerly, enfolding him. She didn't hide her face away when he came into her, but looked boldly into his eyes and let him see whatever he cared to see—the excitement, her nearly unbearable pleasure, all the love in her heart. It was too much for him. He buried his head in her wild hair and took her with strong, shuddering strokes.

"Oh, Burke, my God. Burke, Burke," Katherine cried when it was over. She couldn't stop saying his name; her heart was bursting. "Kiss me. Oh, Christ, kiss me."

He shook with fear and excitement. He wanted her again, but that was impossible. Above all, he didn't want to speak: his tongue was a traitor and might say anything. So he kissed her over and over, until finally their hearts slowed and their bodies ceased straining toward each other.

"Kate," Burke said after a long time, watching the way the flickering firelight made her hair look like burnished gold flecked with rubies.

"Yes, love?" The word slipped out so naturally. She wanted to snatch it back, but he didn't seem to have noticed.

"How long were you by yourself after you left Weddingstone?"

She drew back. "Let's not talk about it."

"But I want to. Tell me."

"I can't remember. A few days, then someone helped me. I don't want to talk about it."

"What was it like?"

"I don't remember."

He sighed. "I'll tell you, then." He pulled her closer and held her in a tight embrace while he spoke. "It was

hell. The snow was blinding, and the wind almost blew
you off your horse. You were freezing cold and sick at
heart. You could hardly see the road; you never knew
exactly where you were. You were in pain, and frightened
because you knew you were ill and needed help, but you
were also numb inside. Something so awful had happened
to you, you couldn't think about it." He felt her tears on
his cheek and held her even closer, smoothing her hair
back and kissing her softly. "And what had you done to
deserve such treatment?" he went on in a husky whisper.
"Sacrificed yourself to a monster on my account. It's true,
isn't it?" She wouldn't look at him. "Lord, Kate, you'd
have gone with him, wouldn't you? You knew what he
was like and still you would have gone." He recoiled in
horror at the thought.

"Only for a month," she said in a small voice. "I made
him agree to that."

"My God, my God." He held her so tightly she could
scarcely breathe. "I was drunk, Kate. That doesn't excuse
it, but it helps explain it. When I saw you together, he was
touching you like this. Something happened, an explosion
in my head. I wanted to kill him. And you—you I just
wanted to punish. But also to be inside you, to claim you.
To take you away from Julian and make you mine." He
loosened his paralyzing grip on her and looked into her
eyes. "I don't deserve your forgiveness and I won't ask for
it. But I want you to know I've suffered too, and that I'll
never stop remembering what I did or being sorry for it."

Her face was grave, her cheeks still wet from her tears.
"Burke, I know you only believed what you saw, and I
wish I could tell you I forgive you with all my heart. But I
cannot. Not yet." He bowed his head. "But I thought you
wouldn't care about what happened, and so I'm moved by
what you say."

"Lord, Kate, how could you think that?"

"I thought you would say it's impossible to rape a

whore.''

His expression was unreadable. He lay on his back and stared up at the ceiling, the back of one hand resting on his forehead. "Why do you work here?"

She died a little inside, acknowledging his shift from denial to acceptance. She realized how much she had treasured his disbelief. "That I will not talk about."

"Tell me."

"It's none of your business."

"For money, of course." She said nothing. "That's the reason you gave for going with Julian, though, and that was a lie." He sat up and stared at her fixedly. An inner trembling started in her chest and spread quickly to her limbs. Guess! her heart begged him. Guess the truth about me, Burke! But instead he reached for her and kissed her savagely, muttering against her lips, "It doesn't matter. Tonight you're mine, only mine." His hands were rough, his kisses violent and demanding. She responded with her own urgency, and their lovemaking was tinged with unmistakable desperation. She lost track of how many times they made love, sometimes frantically, even painfully, sometimes with excruciating tenderness. Once, deep inside her, he demanded to know how many men she'd slept with. "How many, Kate?" he panted above her. "How many in one night?"

"Hundreds! Thousands!" she flung back. "No one, Burke, only you. You're the only man I've ever loved!"

"Shut up, shut up. I've given away all my money, I can't pay for your lies. This is all I want from you."

But her words echoed in his ears and sent him careening over the edge, for once without her. Oddly, she felt no despair at his cruelty, for a tiny seed of hope had taken root in her mind and was sending out little green tendrils into all the dark corners of her heart. It was possible—it was possible!—that her beloved was an even bigger liar than she was.

Toward dawn, when desire was finally eclipsed by

exhaustion, she told him of her mother's death. His sympathy was so compelling, he held her with such tenderhearted affection, that for the first time the pain and grief inside her began to be comforted. He let her cry for a long time, then told her freely and without reserve how it had felt when his own mother died. She was immeasurably soothed. Then he told her that Diana was to marry Edwin, and the last of her sadness disappeared. "I am so happy," she said simply.

"How many ways have I been a fool?" Burke wondered on a tired sigh, kissing her shoulder and laying his head on her breast.

She ran her fingers through his hair, loving the cool, silky feel of it under her hand. More ways than you may ever know, my love, she thought silently. Then she fell into an exhausted sleep.

An hour later Burke was up and in his clothes, gazing down on her sleeping form. He went to the fire and put on the last log so she wouldn't be cold when she woke. He moved quietly, but it wasn't really necessary; she was sleeping the sleep of the dead. Or of the well and truly loved, he smiled to himself. How literally true that was he hadn't been able to face earlier, not when she was straining in his arms with sweet passion and he was so close to admitting everything. But she was asleep now; she couldn't hear him when he knelt beside her and whispered into the air, "I love you, Kate! God help me."

He lifted a long copper strand of hair and brought it to his lips in farewell. Desire flared in him again, but was soon quelled by a rush of despair. His plan had failed utterly. Not only had he not gotten her out of his system, but the long night of lovemaking had taught him the bittersweet lesson that he would never have enough of her. The joke was truly on him. The Viscount Holystone was in love with a whore.

CHAPTER 22
March 1746

"I'm sorry, m'lady, he says he canna talk now, he's tha' busy, and fer you t' gang along hame and wait fer him t' call upon you."

Oh, he does, does he? Katherine's brows lowered ominously and the little maid moved back a step. "Go to him again. Tell him I'm not leaving until he sees me," she ordered, removing her gloves and beginning to unbutton her cape as if she had every intention of staying.

"Yes, m'lady."

The maid made the mistake of leaving the door open while she went to speak to her master; Katherine slipped through and closed it as soon as her footsteps died away. The sound of voices at the end of the modest hallway drew her forward. She stopped when a movement overhead caught her eye. A child of about eight was staring down at her through the wooden bannister rails. "Hello," Katherine said, smiling. The little girl smiled back but was too shy to speak. "I've come to see your papa," she called up softly, feeling some explanation was due under the circumstances, and kept walking.

Owen Cathcart was in his study, remonstrating with his maid, when Katherine walked in and abruptly cut off their conversation. "I'm sorry, Owen, but you *must* see me."

He stood up, obviously irritated, and sent the maid

away. "You shouldn't have come here, Katherine. It's more dangerous now than ever for you to be seen with me."

"I don't care about that. Besides, I was careful. Why haven't you answered my notes? I have to know what's happening, I can't wait at home any longer."

"I have answered your notes—"

"With evasions and vagueness!"

"I told you all I knew. The plan worked, the prince is safely quartered in Inverness. Grant surrendered the castle peacefully, and the Highlanders are using the city as a base from which to hold the coast and take the western forts."

She listened impatiently. "I know all that."

"What you did has been an immense help, and we're very grateful to you. With Inverness at his back, Charles has done an extraordinary job over a vast amount of country in the dead of winter, with fewer than eight thousand men."

"I'm glad of that, certainly, but—"

"Still, I won't try to tell you things are going well." He seemed to want to keep talking to avoid having to deal with her. "The army is out of money, the men are being paid in oatmeal. Many have deserted. It's certain now the French will send no help." For the first time she noticed a grimness about his mouth and eyes. "I'm making plans to move my family to France."

"What?" she cried, shocked. "Surely the end can't come this soon!"

"I'm afraid it can, and will." He looked stricken, and much older than when she'd seen him last.

"I'm so sorry, Owen," she said earnestly. It was a tragedy, but something else was on her mind, and to her it trivialized the cause for which they'd all sacrificed so much. "What is the news of Major Burke?" Her voice shook because she was afraid of his answer; she'd lived with an awful mounting dread for more than a month, and part of her was relieved when Owen hadn't responded to her letters and inquiries. But she had to know the truth.

Cathcart looked uneasy. "There is some news," he said, and Katherine put her hand on the back of the chair. "He's in prison. He was arrested in February, soon after he left here and went north with the information about the French ships." He blinked uncomfortably behind his thick spectacles, disturbed by her deathlike stillness, but went on. "He was charged with harboring a suspected spy, deserting his regiment in wartime, and aiding the enemy. He was convicted of treason and sabotage, and awaits sentencing at Dunkeld. My dear—!"

He caught her before she could slide to the floor; with an arm around her waist he half-lifted her into the chair. "I'll call Sara," he muttered, frightened by her pale, perspiring face.

She shook her head and hung onto his hand, taking in short gulps of air until the room stopped spinning. Her brain was pounding with the hellish echo of his words. She felt leveled, cut down. Rather than sink into uncontrollable sobbing, she took refuge in anger. She snatched her hand away and tried to stand. "Damn you, Owen! A slap on the wrist, you said, and I believed you! You lied, damn you to hell—"

"My dear, listen to me, I sincerely thought it was true!"

"You've known for weeks, haven't you? You knew, and yet you didn't tell me. Oh God! If I'd known, I could have gone there and told them the truth!" She was unconsciously tearing her handkerchief to shreds.

"That's precisely why I didn't tell you! You'd have been arrested yourself and hanged, don't you see? And nothing you said could have helped his situation one whit in any case."

She stood up shakily and walked away from him, unwilling to face the truth of this. "What are we going to do?" she asked in a desperate voice.

"Wait. I still think he's too eminent and too rich to

receive a prison sentence. A heavy fine and dismissal from the military is much more likely. At most, they'll strip him of his title.''

''My God.'' She put her head in her hands.

''Above all, you must not go to Dunkeld, Katherine. Do you understand me? You would endanger not only yourself but a whole network of operators. If you were caught, they would force you to tell all you know.''

''Never!''

He came closer. ''Listen to me. You're not an innocent any longer, and this is not a game. You would be tortured and you would admit anything. Believe me, I know what I'm talking about.'' She looked unconvinced. ''If you won't think of yourself, then think of the men and women who've sacrificed so much for the Stuart cause. Would you betray them for the sake of one Englishman, whom you couldn't save anyway?''

''Yes!'' But she thought of Flora and Donald Ross, and all the others unknown to her, and of the little girl upstairs who'd smiled at her through the railing. ''No,'' she said miserably. ''Very well, I will not go. But, by God, Owen, you must swear you'll tell me any news as soon as you hear it!''

''I swear.''

She went to the window and stared out at the small, neat garden. ''When is he to be sentenced?''

''There's no prescribed time. It could be tomorrow, it could take weeks.''

She closed her eyes to absorb this. ''Is he being treated well? Does his family visit him?'' She tried to imagine the Earl of Rothbury in a prison cell, or Olivia or Renata. Surely Diana would go, and Edwin. She couldn't hold back her tears any longer.

''I'm sure he's being treated well; his money can at least buy him that. Don't distress yourself on that score, you'll only make yourself ill again.'' He watched her for a minute in pained silence. "Katherine, why didn't you tell me you were in love with this man? I never thought this would happen to him; all the same, I'd have chosen someone else for the pawn in the game if I'd known what he meant to you."

"It's my fault, all my fault," she said in despair. "I'm sorry I blamed you; this was not your doing." She turned her stricken face to him and confessed. "I wanted to punish him for a wrong he had done to me. Owen, revenge is a base and cowardly motivation, and it's been mine for the whole of this godless adventure. I renounce it!"

Cathcart didn't know what to say. He went to her and patted her shoulder helplessly.

"I must go." Already she felt restless, keyed up. How could she possibly wait at home for news and do nothing?

"How did you get here?"

"I hired a carriage in the High Street. I made certain no one noticed me."

"Don't come here again, Katherine; wait to hear from me. And please, my dear, try not to worry."

Four weeks later, Katherine mounted the short flight of steps to her front door and pushed it open wearily.

"Lord, Miss Kate, ye look half dead."

"Thank you, Mary. I can always count on you to buck me up when I'm a bit down." A tired smile took the sting out of her sarcasm. She handed her hat and coat to the housekeeper and smoothed her soft muslin skirts. "Nearly six o'clock, and see how light out it still is," she commented absently.

"Oh, aye, I expect tha' means ye'll just wark *longer* hours at yer dearly beloved orphanage now," said Mary, with a hint of her own sarcasm.

Katherine loved to hear Mary say "orphanage"; it sounded something like "arphneege." "Aye, Mary, I expect I will," she agreed mildly. Briefly she considered how impure her motives were for her numberless works of charity: she worked herself to exhaustion nearly every day in order to keep from thinking about Burke at least as much as she did it to help lonely children or sick people or paupers. "Are there any letters?"

"Aye, there on the table. And callin' cards from a fair host o' admirers, as usual. A Mr. Fairchild, said as how he met ye at Miss Wilkins's card party or some such; and another one named Smith or Smythe, a handsome devil who said he recollected ye from the same affair. Oh, and Lady Susan Drake stopped in, said as how she'd call again tomorrow."

Katherine wasn't listening. She was staring at a small white envelope on the table, addressed in Owen Cathcart's neat, clerkish hand. So it had come at last.

Mary was saying something about supper. "Yes, yes, anything," she muttered, picking up the square of paper with trembling fingers.

"But yer tea farst in the drawin' room, Miss Kate. Ye look tha' peaked, I'll have the gel bring it right awa'. Go along, now, and have a sit-down, do ye hear?"

Katherine was so used to Mary ordering her around, she went without a word. She carried the letter to the window seat and sat down, holding it in both hands as if it might fall to dust. She closed her eyes and said a hasty, urgent prayer. Then she broke open the wax seal, took out the single sheet of paper, and read.

"20 April, 1746

"My dear Katherine,

"By now you have heard the dreadful news. The High-land clans were defeated four days ago at Culloden in a savage and cruelly decisive battle. A thousand men died on the field; hundreds of wounded were slaughtered where they lay, their bodies stripped and plundered. The

Duke of Cumberland gave the order to allow no quarter, and even now the captured are being hanged or allowed to starve to death in dungeons. The prince is in hiding, with a £30,000 price on his head. Government troops are marching into rebel clan strongholds to burn the houses, destroy the corn, and drive off the cattle. Anyone wearing the kilt, plaid, or any tartan garment is to be killed.

"Our cause is finished, Katherine, and a reign of merciless brutality is beginning. The prince came too close to toppling the throne; London was badly frightened and now means to wreak a fearful punishment. You are probably safe; no one has ever made the connection between you and K.L. Your father's property has already been forfeited and nothing more can be taken from you. For me, things are more difficult. My family has already left the country; I am to follow in a matter of days.

"As for the person you are most concerned about, I have nothing but more evil tidings. In keeping with the vicious tenor of the times, he is to be executed. His sentence will be carried out on the morning of 2 May. It is said he might have been spared if he had spoken a word in his own defense, but throughout the proceedings he remained silent.

"I am deeply sorry, and accept full responsibility for this tragedy. My error was in underestimating the Duke of Cumberland's savagery.

"Goodbye, my dear, and may God be with you.

                                        "Your dutiful servant,
                    "O."

Katherine crumpled the letter in her hands and shot to her feet. "Mary!" she cried in a voice like the crack of doom.

The housekeeper came on a run. "Miss Kate?" She stared at her mistress's white face and rigid posture, struck dumb by the holy fire in her eyes.

"Tell Innes to have the carriage brought round. Bring my coat. Quickly!"

"Aye, m'lady!"

Her Ladyship took long, strong strides between the window and the door while she waited for her carriage. Her hand was still clenched around the wrinkled missive; on her fourth trip to the window she threw it into the cold, empty hearth as if it were burning her fingers. "Oh, no, my friend," she said aloud in clear, wrathful tones, "you'll not be leaving Edinburgh just yet. Not until you've seen to a bit of unfinished business at Dunkeld!"

CHAPTER 23

The military prison at Dunkeld was a dismal place, a hulking pile of stone and brick and iron from which escape was a rare and dangerous achievement. Evil smells and the sounds of hopelessness filled the dank spaces between its thick walls; something in its reeking, oozing atmosphere called forth men's basest instincts and made it a diabolical pit of cruelty for prisoner and keeper alike. It was a small gaol, but adequate if the deserters, thieves, drunkards, and brawlers chained to the walls in the wretched common area were confined close enough to one another. The resultant violence and perversion were considered a natural and not undeserved consequence; indeed, a fitting part of the punishment.

No one in this room was to be executed, and thus the mood was sullen and miserable but not altogether desperate. Only one prisoner was presently awaiting death, and he was housed alone in a tiny cell next to the warden's room. For him, the comparative comforts of solitude were offset by his physical condition and, of course, the grimly temporary nature of his stay. Until this morning he'd been kept chained to the wall with manacles to his wrist and ankle; but the latest beating from the guards had rendered him so laughably incapable of escape, his bonds were thought pointless. So he was free. Or as free as he could be in a cell that measured four feet wide and six feet long,

and considering he could barely move. Yesterday they'd
performed a mock hanging, to give him a taste of the real
thing to come three days hence. Now his neck was raw and
bleeding and he couldn't speak. He reckoned he had three
or four broken ribs, and something inside felt wrong; perhaps it was his spleen. The only part of him they'd left
alone was his face, so he would exhibit no signs of the
violence done to him when hanging day came.

At least it was to be hanging, not drawing and quarter-
ing followed by disemboweling, as it might have been. He
had his position to thank for that, if nothing else. Or,
more precisely, his former position: James Burke was no
longer the Viscount anything.

He turned painfully in his louse-infected cot, half-
listening to the myriad prison sounds he knew so well—
dripping water, the furtive scurrying of rats, the seemingly
constant drone of muffled weeping. He wasn't tortured by
hunger any longer, but he was always cold. His clothes
were in tatters and they'd taken his boots, and the ragged
blanket he huddled under did little to keep out the unhealthy dampness of the place. Before the sentencing he'd
had a fairly clean cell, decent food, even a few amenities,
but all that changed when he was condemned to die. He
was thankful he'd had time to say goodbye to his family
while still housed in those kinder quarters, for he would
not have wanted them to see him here. Diana had tried to
visit him again, but he hadn't allowed it. He'd made
Edwin take her home, not wait in Edinburgh for the
execution.

Ah, Diana! How her tear-streaked face haunted him; it
made him weep to remember their last moments together.
She'd tried so hard to be brave for him, but she was only
seventeen and her dearest friend was about to die. But she
had Edwin now, staunch and true-hearted, and he knew
she would be all right. His father would survive, too, in his
way. Nothing seemed to affect the earl very deeply,

though Burke had never been able to tell how much he was really capable of feeling. At their last parting he'd seemed more baffled than grieved, and not quite completely present, as if in his mind it were all happening to someone else.

He envied his father's numbness and wished he could achieve the same detached state; but alas, he could not. Everything maintained a dazzling, crystalline reality no matter how long his confinement went on or how brutally he was treated. He felt he ought to be letting go of earthly things and beginning to prepare for whatever came next. He wasn't afraid to die, or at least not more than most men. Only one thing still kept him chained painfully to the material world and wouldn't let him float free: Kate.

He was obsessed with thoughts of her. When he could sleep, he dreamed of her. Her image lit his dark cell; the sound of her voice echoed against the stone walls. Sometimes her delicate fragrance even penetrated the prison stench. Once in a while her memory brought him a moment's peace, but usually it tortured him. He knew full well she'd betrayed him and cold-bloodedly sent him off to die. Yet he'd kept silent throughout his trial to protect her, and he didn't know why.

He'd been afraid that if he admitted that Mrs. Pell was really Katie Lennox, they would trace her to Edinburgh as quickly as he had. For the same reason, he told them he'd heard of the French ships in a tavern from a man whose name he couldn't remember. Not surprisingly, they'd found this incredible. Meanwhile Julian had done his work well. True to his word, he'd informed Colonel Denholm that the spy whom Burke had been entrusted to deliver to Lancaster had been a guest in his home. When his step-father learned of this, he'd thrown him out; and with nothing left to lose, Julian had been eager to testify in court. Burke stood by his story that Katie Lennox was dead, but witnesses were called who had seen one woman or the other—Denholm, Maule, Corporal Blaine; Olivia, Edwin, even poor Diana—and it was soon clear they were all describing the same person.

The Duke of Cumberland, whom many regarded as a butcher and a monster, had written Burke a kind note expressing regret over his fate. The two men were not exactly friends, but had shared a mutual respect for each other's military professionalism. The powerful duke, the king's son, wrote that the matter was unfortunately out of his hands, that Burke was a victim of the times; that if he'd received a prison sentence instead of a death warrant, perhaps he could have helped him in a year or two after the national thirst for vengeance had been slaked. Thus Burke could add another irony—poor timing—to the seemingly endless catalogue of ironies that had put him where he was.

And so his silence had gained him nothing but the leisure to contemplate why he'd so steadfastly maintained it, and the answer to that remained as much a mystery to him as ever. He couldn't think of Kate rationally, only remember her in random, vivid pictures. He saw her lightly touching the injured farmer's face as he lay trapped under his wagon, or descending the staircase on Knole's arm like a fragile queen; sending him a shaky smile of encouragement as he bent over her with a knife in his hand, or moving away from him down a darkened hallway on Julian's arm. He remembered the way she held her head, the rare sound of her laughter, the way she would sometimes touch her fingertips to her lips when she was thinking. He saw her exchanging a secret, twinkling look with Diana, or kneeling beside him in a barn and gently holding a bottle of water to his lips. Most often his mind went back to their last night together, and then he would have to grapple again with the tormenting truth that what he'd taken for passion and tenderness were really cunning and treachery. "I know something that might help you," she'd said, and he could still hear the tentative, almost shy note in her voice as she stared into her wineglass. How skillfully she'd done it, and how easily he'd swallowed the bait.

Sometimes he played with the notion that she hadn't fully understood what would happen to him, but he knew that was folly. She had to know, she wasn't stupid. He'd underestimated her desire for revenge after he'd raped her. That was it; there was no other explanation. Once she'd jumped in front of a pistol to save him, but at Weddingstone everything had changed when he'd behaved like an animal. He'd denied her humanity and made her into an object of his anger and lust and jealousy. Could he blame her for the course she'd taken? Perhaps not, but he despised her duplicity. It would have been better if she'd stabbed him in the back while he slept.

So his thoughts went, round and round in circles. He found himself imagining in lurid detail all the humiliating things he wanted to do to her, most of which involved degrading sexual acts. But strangely, his erotic fantasies always ended with Kate crying out in pleasure, not pain. It was obscurely comforting that he had only three more days to live knowing he was the world's biggest fool.

He heard the rattle of a key in the lock, and his muscles tensed. He never knew if they were coming to feed him the verminous slop they called dinner or to bash him around for an afternoon's amusement.

"Get off yer arse, Lord Viscount," sneered the guard, kicking at him with his boot. He squinted, blinded by the dim candlelight, and tried to stand. "Up, I said!" He was seized by the collar, jerked to his feet, and shoved roughly through the door. He landed against the stone wall on the opposite side of the dank corridor and almost lost consciousness. He was sliding down the wall when the guard hauled him up by his coat and shook him. "I ain't carryin' you, you filthy pig! Walk!"

Not many days ago he'd have offered some kind of
resistance, at least a curse, regardless of the unequal
punishment such gestures always provoked. But lately it
hardly seemed worth it. So he walked, barefooted, down
the silent corridor toward a flight of stone steps leading to
a studded oak door. Not another beating, then? Those
were either in his cell or in the hall, and this was the door
to the warden's room. The guard rapped on the scarred
oak with his fist, and a metal grate at head height slid
back. Burke saw two eyes examine him dispassionately
before the grate closed and the door was unlocked from
the inside. He went in before the guard could push him,
shielding his eyes from the unaccustomed glare of
lanterns, and heard the door latch behind him.

He peered into a dim corner of the room and saw a tall,
stoop-shouldered man in the brown robes of a monk. He
recognized the habit as belonging to the priests from a
nearby monastery whose vocation was to minister to the
convicts and felons. So he'd come to pray over him, had
he? That was fine, Burke had no objection; he was sure his
soul could use it. He folded his arms around his middle
protectively and waited.

"Wha' the bloody hell have ye done to 'im?"
exclaimed the hooded monk in shocked tones, and Burke
blinked. It wasn't the usual idiom of a man of the cloth.

The warden, Lieutenant Wheeler, was a small, prim-
looking soldier with a deceptively mild manner. He was in
full uniform, buttons and boots polished to a high shine,
red jacket immaculately brushed. In his hand was a short
length of metal pipe; he was slapping it against his palm
with suppressed excitement. "Unfortunately," he said in
a clear tenor voice, pursing his lips, "the prisoner has tried
to escape on more than one occasion and the guards were
forced to subdue him."

"Subdue 'im? Ye call tryin' t' hang 'im ahead o' time
subduin' 'im? Look at his throat!"

Lieutenant Wheeler shook his head patiently. "The prisoner has been unusually disruptive, and it was thought this form of discipline would be instructive. And so, indeed, it's proved to be. As you see, he's so docile now we don't even chain him."

For answer, the monk spat on the floor, and Burke's eyes widened.

"It's after eight o'clock," observed the warden after a moment. "Why isn't the damned priest here?"

Burke blinked again and leaned against the wall weakly, awaiting events. He wanted to ask what the hell was going on, but he couldn't speak.

There was a sharp knock at the outer door.

"You, prisoner," the warden said quickly, "stand over there near the door. Move!"

Burke pushed himself off the wall and padded over to the place he was indicating. Nothing made sense; he saw no reason not to obey.

"Come in!"

The outer door opened and a soldier stuck his head in. "Brother William, sir," he announced, then stood aside as another robed and hooded monk came into the room. The soldier left, and the new arrival greeted the warden respectfully. Then he saw his double across the way and stared in confusion.

"I say, who are you?" he asked curiously, starting forward.

Burke would have liked to hear the answer to that, too. But at that moment the warden, who had come around behind the new monk and was standing beside Burke, lifted the metal pipe over his shoulder and brought it down with a short, chopping motion on top of Brother William's head. He collapsed on the floor in a billowing heap of brown homespun.

The first monk cried out in dismay and went to his fallen brother. "Ye weren't supposed t' brain 'im, damn yer hide! I think the bastard's dead!" The hand he brought away from the wounded man's head was covered with blood.

"He's not dead," Lieutenant Wheeler said derisively. "Give me credit for knowing how to render a man safely unconscious."

"Ye're a bloody, filthy swine," the other man muttered, laying the monk out flat.

"If you insult me, I'll only raise the price of this traitor's freedom. Speaking of that, I'll take the other half of the payment now."

The blasphemous monk rose and reached inside his habit. Lieutenant Wheeler took the large velvet pouch he held out and spilled its contents on his desk. Burke shuffled over in a kind of stupor, his eyes widening at the pile of gold glittering under the yellow light of the lantern. It was a fortune. Greed momentarily loosened the warden's pinched face before he pushed the coins back into the purse and straightened. "I'll secure this and return in a moment. See to the prisoner's clothes while I'm gone." He left through the inner door to the gaol, locking it behind him.

The monk glanced at Burke, then began to strip off the unconscious man's robes. "Are ye able t' ride, lad?" Burke nodded, but he was looking down and didn't see. "Eh?"

"Yes," he croaked, then clutched at his throat painfully, eyes watering.

"Jesus, Mary, and Joseph! Took yer boots, too, did they? Pigs is wha' they are. Put on the priest's shoes. Here, sit doon before ye fall. I'll help ye." Burke sat, staring dazedly down as the big, raw-boned man put the monk's shoes on his feet. Then he helped him settle the robe over his tattered shirt and breeches and raised the hood over his head. "Keep this on nae matter what," he admonished. "One look a' tha' wild beard o' yers and they'll commence shootin' fer a cartainty. Ye're sure ye can ride? Ye look as weak as a mouse.''

"Who are you?" Burke mouthed the words, touching the man's sleeve.

"My name's Innes. I'm a friend."

Burke nodded in agreement, looking down into the older man's face. His hood had fallen back, revealing his thick gray hair, lantern jaw, and honest brown eyes. They clasped hands briefly.

The inner door opened and Lieutenant Wheeler returned. He looked at the prisoner with distaste. "Can he walk?"

"Aye, he's fine," said Innes positively. "Now, we've only one wee detail left."

"I've been considering that. I don't think it's necessary that I too be found unconscious, like Brother William here. It will suffice if I'm only gagged and bound in my chair."

Innes shrugged indifferently. "Whatever ye say. Have ye a bit o' rope, then?" He took the proferred coil from the lieutenant and set to work tying him to the chair Burke had laboriously vacated.

"You may use my handkerchief for a gag; it's in my inner pocket."

"Ah, weel, mayhap we willna be needin' that after all." And he hauled back and punched the warden in the nose so hard his chair tipped over backwards.

Burke's jaw dropped. Silently he watched the big man rub his bruised knuckles and then haul the sagging, unconscious lieutenant upright, chair and all. "There, that's better, eh? More realistic, like. Bastard'll thank me later." He winked, and Burke had to hold in a laugh. "Now, lad, ye maun stand straight up, ye canna be holdin' yerself and hunchin' over when we walk past the guards. And needless t' say, I'll do the talkin'. Try t' look priestly, is all; I found it triflin' easy, myself. We've aboot a quarter of a mile t' walk to our horses. Then—'' he frowned and put a solicitous hand on Burke's shoulder—''we've a bit of a ride ahead of us. We're makin' fer the coast betwixt Perth and Dundee, where there's a vessel waitin'. 'Tis a distance o' mayhap twenty miles, and we maun make it before daybreak. Tell me the plain truth: can ye do it?''

Burke closed his eyes for a moment at the thought of what lay ahead of him. When he opened them they were full of fierce determination. He nodded and touched his clenched fist to his chest in solemn promise.

''Guid mon. I believe ye,'' said Innes quietly. ''Cum, then, let's be off.''

The hardest part was keeping himself upright as they trod the corridor to the main gate in full view of two guards, and then, after a bit of chitchat with the guards on the other side of the main portal—during which Innes exhibited an unexpected flair for pious, even long-winded rhetoric—keeping from breaking into a ragged run for freedom toward the darkened field beyond the prison lamps. He controlled that urge, swinging his legs gracefully under his skirts in the manner he associated with priests and monks, but the cost was tremendous. ''We've done it, lad, we've done it,'' Innes gloated in an excited whisper after a five-minute walk down a barren dirt lane and no alarm had sounded. ''We've beaten the bloody bastards, damn 'em all t' hell!'' By then Burke was dripping with sweat and every step was an agony. He began to be afraid his body wasn't going to obey him, that the bold deed of this brave stranger would be in vain. ''Steady, lad,'' said the Scotsman, as if reading his mind, but more likely catching a glimpse of his wet, drawn face in the light of the half-moon. ''The horses are just here.''

They rounded a bend in the lane, and there beyond a low hedge were indeed two horses, as well as a rider on a third. When they were close enough, he noted that the rider was also dressed as a monk, but otherwise he could make out nothing about him in the murk. Then he was too intent on mounting his horse without fainting to give the newcomer another thought. He had no idea who was rescuing him; if the pain in his ribs hadn't been so severe, he'd have thought he was dreaming. The whole of the last hour had a decidedly unreal quality, beginning with the unlikely monk's first words in the warden's office. The jolting canter of the horse, however, was altogether too real; and while he clutched at his middle to keep his bones together, he wondered again if his promise to the man named Innes had only been a foolish boast.

His name almost broke from Katherine's lips when she saw him. In her eyes there was an aura of light around him; she hardly saw Innes at all. She'd been numb with worry before, but not afraid; now a primitive, quaking fear seized her that they—that *he*—would be captured and taken back. She urged her horse to a walk almost before Burke could mount his, so impatient was she to get away. A cloud slid past the moon and she had a quick look at his face. Her breath caught. Was he ill? She didn't like the way he was holding himself. No, no, he must be all right; Innes would say or do something if he were not! They trotted out into the lane leading to the road for Perth and began to canter in single file—Innes ahead, Burke in the middle, Katherine in the rear. She remembered another tense and endless journey of three riders, only then it had been Burke, herself, and Ewan MacNab. She prayed this one would have a better ending.

She was so full of emotion, she could scarcely tend to the task of keeping her horse on the road. Incredibly, miraculously, the plan was working! Owen Cathcart had prepared the way, albeit unwillingly, with his saboteur's knowledge of who at Dunkeld was allowed access to condemned prisoners, who could and who could not be bribed. Everything was going exactly according to the scheme and no one was following them. In fact, things were going so smoothly, she was terrified. She imagined red-coated soldiers behind every tree and hedgerow, every turn in the road. She rode with muscles tensed, ears straining for the sound of pursuit. At the same time the wild, exciting thought danced joyously in the back of her mind that if things went on this way, Burke would be free! She thanked God again and again, tears of gratitude flowing incessantly, half-blinding her.

Innes slowed as they approached a clearing in the woods edging the lane. "We'll rest a bit," he called back softly. They were making good time but still had more than half the way to go. The horses formed a semicircle. "Do ye want t' get doon?" he asked Burke. He shook his head—slowly, Katherine thought, wondering again what condition he was in. She thought he peered at her, but he didn't speak. She'd deliberately positioned herself with the moon at her back so he couldn't see her face. Still, she had an uncanny feeling he must know her. How could he *not* when she was so intensely aware of him? But time passed and he said nothing. His silence reinforced her resolve to maintain hers, and no one spoke for ten minutes. "Weel, shall we be awa'?" asked Innes at last, and the bone-breaking canter began again.

They rode all night. She was thankful the weather was fine and mild for late April, not wet and muddy as it might have been. They passed the darkened cottages of farmers and laborers and roused many a sleeping dog, but not a living soul hailed them or challenged their right to the road. It seemed Innes was slowing the pace toward morning, and she felt a hot rush of impatience. Yet Burke was slumped over his horse's neck more than before, she saw in the pearl-gray, predawn gloom. Was he ill? she wondered for the hundredth time. She could smell the sea, and knew with a thrill of exhilaration they were almost there. Soon she would see him, and he would see her and know who had saved him, and he would . . . She made herself stop thinking such thoughts, shying away in superstitious fear from putting in words the thing her heart desired most. She concentrated on reaching the barren stretch of shore where a boat and tiny crew were waiting to take them to France.

They skirted a small village bordering the Firth of Tay and slowed to a walk. Katherine and Innes changed positions—she knew the way from here and he didn't—but Burke didn't even notice. He suspected he was losing consciousness at times without realizing it. At least they'd stopped cantering; he believed he could stay astride his well-behaved horse at a walk, though the muscles in his thighs were vibrating like harp strings. He tried to keep his eyes on the back of the rider in front, but a moment later he was jerking his head up and clutching his horse's mane for balance, and knew he'd passed out. He looked around, beginning to be able to make out shapes in the gray dawn. The trees had disappeared; they must be near the sea. There was a salty tang on the increasing wind, and their horses were treading sandy soil. A vessel, Innes had said. Bound for where? he wondered incuriously, his eyes drooping again.

Alertness returned when he realized they'd stopped. His companions were dismounting. With difficulty he worked his right foot out of the stirrup and swung it over the horse's rump; but when he tried to lower himself to the ground, his arms gave out. He would have gone sprawling over backward if Innes hadn't caught him around the waist and held him steady. He leaned his forehead against the horse's neck and waited for the strength to move again.

When he raised his head, the other monk was coming toward him. He had time to wonder if this one really was a monk, he moved so gracefully in his flowing robes. Then a quick breath of wind lifted the hood, and he saw her.

"You!" he uttered in a hoarse croak. Red hair cascaded down the sides of her pale face like a crimson waterfall, and the blueness of her wide, frightened eyes put the sea to shame. She was twisting her hands under her chin, almost smiling, exquisitely uncertain. A thousand half-thoughts rose and sank in his brain. He wanted to hurt her and he wanted to hold her to his breast. He took a step forward, arms stretched out.

"Here, now—" Innes said and moved in front of him, giving him a light, warning shove. In the ribs. Bright lights exploded in front of his eyes; he thought he heard her cry out as he pitched forward and slumped to the ground.

CHAPTER 24

The *Morning Glory* was a sturdy but not very glorious fishing vessel with two sails fore and aft and room in her hull for a galley and a cabin that could sleep four men in bunks. Two brothers named Dern owned it. They were dour, taciturn Lowlanders who asked no questions; it was sufficient for them that they would make more money in a week ferrying this strange couple to Calais than they would in a year of fishing for cod in the North Sea. It didn't matter to them that the gentleman looked half dead or the lady who was paying them tended to him all the time in the cabin; that only made them quieter passengers. Out of respect for the lady and because the weather was fine, they hung their hammocks on deck and slept under the stars.

Innes had wanted to sail with them when he'd seen how ill Burke was, but Katherine wouldn't allow it—Mary was expecting him home in two days and she'd be frantic with worry if he didn't return. So ran her argument, but her real reason was that it was too dangerous. Innes had already risked his life to save a stranger, for no reason except that she'd asked him. With luck, the search for them would begin in the Hebrides, where Lieutenant Wheeler was to say they were heading. But a man like that couldn't really be trusted, and if they were caught they would likely be hanged on the spot. Katherine was eager to take that risk for herself, but not for her friend. And so

she'd embraced Innes on the beach for the last time and
said goodbye. Both of them had wept, and Katherine had
felt a rush of fierce love for the bluff, honest Scotsman who
had been such a staunch friend all her life. He was her last
tie to home and family. All that comforted her was her
faith in their special kinship, which would never be
broken regardless of the distance between them.

On the second night out, Katherine held water to
Burke's lips, then sat down on the small stool near his
pillow and leaned her tired back against the wall. She
knew she ought to lie down in the opposite bunk and try
to sleep. But she needed to be near him, touching him.
Yesterday she'd bathed him and cleaned his wounds and
bound his ribs in bandages, horrified by the viciousness of
the abuse his body had taken. Fury at the brutes who had
done this to him was the only thing that kept her from
swooning at the sight of some of his most terrible wounds.
The recent, raw lacerations around his neck were the worst,
but there was a swelling on the right side of his abdomen
that frightened her. He was fretful and feverish, and
almost too weak to swallow the rich meat broth she
spooned into him at every opportunity.

Her hand strayed to his hair, dirty and unkempt, and
her fingers lightly massaged his scalp. She heard him sigh,
and her own eyelids closed. She was exhausted, and the
sound of the sea and the steady roll of the boat were
soothing, but in her mind she saw again the murderous
intensity of his eyes, his arms stretched toward her; his
choked ''You!'' was like an awful curse on her soul. How
different this voyage was from the one she'd allowed herself to fantasize in the last few weeks! She'd seen the two
of them standing arm-in-arm in the stern of some proud
vessel, watching its white wake while they laughed and
cried over all their past misunderstandings. How could she
have been so childish and self-deluding? Of *course* he
hated her; how could he not? Look what they'd done to

him, and all because of her! That night in the brothel
she'd imagined he felt something for her besides physical
desire, and her fantasy had grown over the long, difficult
months following until she'd nearly convinced herself they
were within a few explanatory sentences of being reconciled. Now she knew his enmity was a hundred times
stronger than it had been. The fact that she'd saved him
from hanging at great expense and risk to herself and her
best friend didn't seem to count for anything. At least not
in that instant when he'd recognized her. But perhaps, in
time, after he'd had a chance to think about things—

Ah, she didn't want to deceive herself again; the cure
was too painful. And she had her own pride, too. She
would bide her time and see what happened. What else
could she do? But if he could not forgive her, she would
never tell him who she was, even if it meant losing him.

It was a good resolve. She wondered how long she could
keep it.

By the third day, Burke's fever had diminished and he
was able to stay fully awake for longer periods. For
Katherine, it was a mixed blessing. She was glad, of
course, that he was getting better, but now his arctic-cold
eyes followed her everywhere and his silences seemed to
her sullen and dangerous. Even so, he was more restless
when she was gone from the room. But she could no
longer sit beside him as she had; there was an unmistakable anger radiating from him that frightened her,
making her want to keep a safe distance between them.
Once when she was changing the bandage around his
neck, he seized her wrist in a painful grip—even in his
debilitated condition he was stronger than she—and held
it away as if her touch repelled him. She met his malignant
gaze almost without flinching. "When are you going to
open your eyes?" she burst out. "Or are you set on living
your life like a blind man?" Rather than let him see her
cry, she pried his fingers away and went up on deck,

leaving him alone with his thoughts.

They were not sanguine. Who the bloody hell did she think she was? Blind man, was it? He tried to sit up against the pillow behind him, but the pain in his ribs was too severe and he fell back with an oath. What the hell did she want from him, gratitude? Whose fault was it he was lying on this cursed cot in the first place? He cleared his throat tentatively. It was better, definitely better; it wouldn't be long before he could tell her in detail exactly what he thought of her.

Damned witch. Gliding around him like a swan in her fancy new clothes, touching him all the time, pretending she gave a damn about him. But he'd been beguiled by Kate's well-acted innocence one time too many; this new role of compassionate nurse didn't fool him for a minute. How did he even know they were sailing to France? Maybe she'd decided hanging was too good for him and what she really wanted to do was drown him. Nothing would surprise him anymore! Besides, even if she had rescued him, he wouldn't have needed rescuing if she hadn't betrayed him in the first place.

So to hell with her. Wariness was the key. It would be a cold day in hell before he'd so much as turn his back on her.

They reached Calais on the afternoon of the fifth day. Katherine sent one of the Derns for a physician almost before the boat was anchored, although Burke's fever was gone and his wounds were healing quickly. Even the swelling in his stomach had disappeared, and he claimed he was free of pain. The doctor pronounced him weak but no longer gravely ill, and Katherine finally relaxed.

She decided they should remain on the *Morning Glory* in spite of its discomforts because it would be safer than renting a room if English agents were looking for Burke in France. The weather was fine and mild; in fact, it was one of the most beautiful springs anyone could remember. Burke was speaking now, but mostly in rude monosyllables and usually not above a whisper. He could get up, but he tired quickly and sometimes needed help getting back to his bed.

On the third afternoon in port, he made his slow and careful way up the companionway ladder to the deck, his first foray into fresh air since the trip began. Katherine hovered around him worriedly. The Derns were away and, as unlikely as it seemed, she didn't know what she would do if he should fall or faint and hurt himself again. But he achieved the deck without incident and lowered himself into a chair in the full sun, and she breathed a relieved sigh.

She'd brought her sewing scissors with her so she might give him a haircut. He grunted disinterested assent to her suggestion and she set to work. She'd only given Rory haircuts before, and Burke's straight black hair was different from her brother's tousled curls. Still, she imagined the principle was probably the same: you just kept cutting until it looked right. She loved the cool, sleek feel of his hair through her fingers, and found it a pleasure to shape it just so around his ears and the back of his neck. The sun was warm and lovely; an odor of blossoms stirred in the breeze. Katherine felt as light and buoyant as spring itself in a silk dress of palest pink, with a flower-sprigged bodice and lacy sleeves. How lovely to be out of heavy woolens and velvets, she sighed. And yet already she missed Scotland, and would have given up springtime in France forever, and much, much more, for the chance to go home again. But she was as much an exile as Burke now, and there would be no going back.

Burke stared across the bay sightlessly and gripped the arms of his chair, trying not to sink into a stupor of sensuality. Was she breathing into his ear on purpose? Did she know what it did to him when the warm wind blew her

hair across his cheek, his neck? The scent of flowers in the
air was indistinguishable to him from her own beguiling
fragrance. How did she do this to him? He was a grown
man, not an adolescent, but at that moment he felt as if he
were drowning in his own sexuality. He marveled at the
powerful effort of will that kept him from pulling her
down on the deck and ravishing her. He could do it, too;
he was getting stronger every day. Thank God for that—he
couldn't have taken much more of her mollycoddling.

What was she doing now? Snipping off a bit of ribbon
that held her own hair in place and tying his back with it.
Oh, good, he thought irritably; now they could be twins.
At least she was finished. She stepped back and inspected
him critically, nodded as if satisfied, and wandered over to
the rail to gaze out at the water. It was time to tell her what
was on his mind, although he would much rather have sat
there and silently filled his eyes with the dizzying sight of
her. That he hadn't spoken to her yet was a measure of the
enmity he still felt toward her, but he couldn't put it off
any longer.

He said her name and she turned around dreamily. The
sun on her hair was dazzling. "Come closer." It was still
hard to talk above a throaty rasp. She came a few steps
nearer. He wished there was another chair; she made him
nervous standing over him like that.

"What is it?" she asked when he remained silent, her
hands clasped in front of her. He was scowling ferociously;
she couldn't imagine what he had to say.

"This—" He waved his arm vaguely at the water and
the sky, then stopped. He rubbed his eyes, the back of his
neck; he drew a deep breath. At last he fixed his gaze on
her puzzled face and told her. "A little over a week ago I
couldn't have imagined myself being here, Kate. I'd said
goodbye to everyone I loved and, as much as I could,
reconciled myself to dying. I'd reduced the world to a
dark, stinking cell, and the people in it to a handful of

barbarians. That made the pain of leaving a little easier. Now, this—this is like a miracle. Sometimes I wonder if I'm deaming, or if I've died and this is heaven.'' He looked way from her shining eyes and finished. ''I know I haven't shown much gratitude these last days. I apologize for my conduct. I don't know how you managed it, but I thank you for risking your life to save me. I'm more grateful than I can say.''

That was an understatement. What a stiff, unsatisfying speech, not at all what he wanted to say to her. The trouble was, he didn't know what he wanted to say to her. Stifling a groan, he raised himself from the chair and walked away to stand at the rail and watch the seagulls soar over the bay. When he turned back, she was standing where he'd left her, staring blankly at his empty chair. ''Kate, would you do something for me?''

She looked up. For once he couldn't read her expression. ''Yes,'' she said levelly.

''Would you cut this damn bandage off me? It hurts worse than my ribs.''

She came without a word. He unbuttoned his shirt and she helped him push it down over his shoulders. With her sewing scissors she cut away the binding of cloth she'd wound around his torso, willing herself to keep her hands impersonal. It was unbearable to be this close to him and not be allowed to touch him. The sight of his wide, hard chest filled her with an unspeakable longing. There was a huge, purplish bruise under his breast. She watched her hand disobey her and stroke it gently. Burke stiffened and seemed to stop breathing. She knew she dare not look at him. When she reached up to pull his shirt back over his shoulders, there was a moment when she could have put her arms around his neck and held him. She did not, but the effort it took to control the impulse left her weak-kneed. She stepped away and leaned back against the rail beside him. After a few minutes, she decided it was time to return his little speech with one of her own.

"Burke, I want you to know I never intended any of this to happen. I knew you would get in trouble, but I thought they would only reprimand you. A—slap on the wrist. If I'd known what would happen, I would never have done it. I swear it."

She'd sworn lies to him before. She was saying what he longed to hear, but he would not be a fool again. "Why did you do it?" he asked sharply.

They were both staring straight ahead, not looking at each other. His voice made her shiver. "I did it to help the Jacobite cause." He turned incredulous eyes to her, and she gave a short, almost hysterical laugh. "No, of course that's a lie. I did it to get even for what you'd done to me. I did it for revenge."

The word vibrated between them. He bowed his head. He'd known that was why, but hearing her say it made a sharp pain slice through him.

She massaged the lump in her throat and tried to swallow. She desperately didn't want to cry in front of him, but a terrible sadness was bearing down on her heart. "Would you like me to write to your family?" she asked tightly when she could speak. "Tell them you're all right—"

"You mean give them a hint of my future plans?" he flared in sudden bitterness. "Tell them I'm a nameless, penniless fugitive without work, that I'll be hanged if I return to my own country, that I'll never see my home or Diana or my father again?" He watched her face turn ashen and looked away. "Anyway, I thought you couldn't write."

"You think many things about me that aren't true," she said in a choked whisper.

"Then tell me what they are so I can mend my ways!"

She shook her head slowly and steadily. "I think not."

The look in her eyes chilled him. Something final was

happening and he couldn't understand what it was. She made a move to leave and he grabbed her. "Don't go."

"Why?"

"I don't want you to." He ran his hands up and down her arms, hardly knowing what he was doing. "I don't know what happens next, Kate, but I want you to be with me. Will you be my mistress?" He'd put it a bit baldly, he supposed; he hadn't known he was going to say it until it was out of his mouth. Now that it was, it felt right.

"Your mistress?" When he nodded, she laughed. "Never! *Never!*"

He couldn't believe his ears. She'd laughed at him! His hands tightened on her elbows. "Why?" was all he could say.

"Why?"

He gritted his teeth. If she repeated his words to him once more, he was going to throw her over the side of the boat.

"Because if you want me, Burke, you'll have to marry me!"

It was his turn to laugh. Incredulously, wholeheartedly. Hanging onto the rail to stay upright. The look on her face only made him laugh harder. She whirled away and began walking toward the ladder to the cabin. "Kate, Kate," he gasped, coming after her. He really hadn't meant to insult her. He reached for her hand.

"Don't ever touch me again!" she cried. "You arrogant bastard, I detest you! You make me sick! Who do you think you are?"

"Nobody!" he shouted back hoarsely. "Nobody, and it's your fault!"

Her face crumpled and she flung away, not toward the ladder but to the bulwark closest to their mooring. There was no gangplank; to leave the *Morning Glory* you either had to climb down a rope ladder or jump for it. By the time he realized Katherine was opting for the latter, he only had time to call out her name before she threw her legs over the rail, paused a breathless second as if in midair, and then leapt the seven feet of deep, empty space to the dock. Her momentum tumbled her to her hands and knees on the splintered wood, but she was up and running almost instantly. He lurched to the rail and climbed over, considerably more slowly, muttering curses all the while. With one final oath, he flexed his knees and let go. A rush of air, and then a pain in his middle on impact that felt as if his legs were being rammed into his body. He fell to his side on the pier and lay there a moment in fetal agony, then got to his knees, and finally his feet. Katherine was a blur of pale pink up ahead. He started after her in a shuffling stagger.

His hoarse shout halted her in her tracks. She whirled around. God, *no*, don't let him be following! But there he was, holding his ribs, stumbling after her with bulldog determination. Outdistancing him would have been child's play; she stopped considering it when he tripped on a coiled rope on the dock and pitched to his knees. She stood still. A man spoke to her, made some crude suggestion in French; she barely heard. Burke was picking himself up and starting after her again. She gave up and went toward him.

"What are you doing, Burke, killing yourself? For God's sake—"

"Have you lost your mind, Kate? Do you realize what could happen to you out here alone? What the hell were you thinking—"

"—all the stupid things to do, on your first day out of bed—"

"—*trying* to attract attention to yourself? Surely there are easier—"

"—some kind of idiotic masculine need to *prove* yourself—"

And on and on as they made their way back to the boat,

he hauling her along, she supporting him. When they reached the *Morning Glory*, Katherine hailed a pair of sailors mending line on the ketch tied up across the dock from theirs. With the men's help, Burke ascended the rope ladder, insisting all the while it was *she* who needed help, but more in the head and thus beyond the scope of their assistance.

Once they were both safely on deck, the argument shifted to whether or not he ought to go below and lie down, with Burke maintaining he needed to stay above to drive off the vanguard of her newest admirers, and expressing surprise at Katherine's hitherto unsuspected taste for dockhands. Too riled to respond, she stalked to the prow, where she held onto the rail with murderous, curving fingers and stared at the blinding sunset.

She had to get away. His hostility was too strong; if she stayed any longer it would surely kill her. She'd lost the heart to tell him who she was. If she had to be Lady Braemoray to win him, she didn't want the prize.

She stared down sightlessly at the dark water. But how could she leave him? What would her life be without him? She could go to the American colonies, become some child's governess, begin some new kind of life. But it all seemed so grim, so outlandish, she couldn't even imagine it for more than a few seconds at a time. She *belonged* to Burke, but all he wanted her to be was his mistress. She closed her eyes against a hot rush of tears. When she opened them, he was beside her.

He'd recovered from his exertion; his face was no longer bathed with sweat and he wasn't clutching his ribs in pain. He stared without speaking at the merging bands of color in the western sky—orchid, silver, softest orange. The minutes lengthened, but still he said nothing.

"Kate," he finally managed.

Was he going to apologize? He looked uncomfortable enough for it. She stood still and waited.

"I'm sorry I laughed, before. It was insulting. But your . . . suggestion took me by surprise. I'd never—it just hadn't occurred to me before."

"Oh, I'm sure of that." She made a quick movement to leave, certain she didn't want to hear this, but his hand closed over hers on the rail and held her still.

Another lengthy pause. He took a calming breath. "But now I've had a little time to think about it, you see, and I don't find the idea quite so . . . extraordinary." Her body was turned completely away from him; he tightened his grip on her captured hand and swallowed hard. "Kate. Will you—" He stopped.

He simply couldn't get the words out. Marry Kate? Impossible. It was too absurd, it was preposterous. He was glad she wasn't looking at him; his mouth was opening and closing and he was sure he looked like a turtle.

"Will I what?" she asked, wondering how she could speak when there was no air in her lungs.

Somehow he got it out. "Marry me."

"I'm sorry, I didn't hear you."

He'd spoken softly, but they both knew that was a lie. Gritting his teeth, he repeated it, a little louder.

Here were the words she'd dreamt of hearing him say for so long. But Katherine didn't care for the tone of his voice. He'd said it the way a condemned man might say "For God's sake, hurry up!" to the executioner who had paused to sharpen the axe.

"Why would you want to marry me?" she asked, deliberately perverse, her voice unsteady despite her best effort. "You can't stand me. You tell me I've ruined you, and you think I'm a prostitute. So why would you?"

When she put it that way, he didn't know why himself. She was right about everything except him not being able to stand her. 'It's . . . it's not easy to explain, Kate, there's a lot of . . . Would you please turn around and look at me?''

"No." Out of the question. "Tell me why."

Oh, *now* he knew what she wanted him to say. He'd be damned if he would. "Why would you marry *me*?" he countered cagily.

"Who said I would?"

"I'm saying *if* you did. Why would you."

"Well, maybe I *wouldn't!*" She tugged out of his grasp and got half a step away before his hands on her waist hauled her back. He jostled her over to the wide mainmast and pressed her back against it, bracing his arms on either side of her head.

"But just pretend you would," he persisted, his face inches away. "Just for the sake of argument. Why would you? Mmm?" His fingers rubbed a gentle up-and-down pattern along the column of her throat. "Not for my money, we know that, and not my exalted position in the world." When she tried to speak he moved in, kissing her lightly, nudging her shocked lips apart with his. "There could only be one reason, Kate," he breathed against her mouth, while his restless hands stroked her sides. "You'd have to be in love with me."

She began to tremble. She was letting him touch her so she wouldn't risk injuring him by fighting, she told herself; she would let him do this until her coldness repelled him. By the time the weaknesses in this plan were clear to her, it was too late to institute another. She tried not to make a sound, but he was kissing her deeply, intimately, and she went limp. With a glad shudder, she heard her own helpless moan of defeat.

"You love me, don't you?" he whispered fiercely. "Say you do. Oh, say it, Kate, because I'm so in love with you, I couldn't stand it if you didn't."

"Oh God." She didn't really believe her ears. "You don't mean it. You couldn't mean it."

"I love you, I adore you. You're the best part of me, you're everything. How could I not love you?"

She clung to him desperately, eyes clenched shut, afraid to look at him. "But I betrayed you, Burke, all the things you said—"

"Over. Finished. Marry me, Kate. I love you."

She pressed backward and took a deep breath, her eyes brimming with unshed tears. "Of course I love you," she told him, as if nothing could be more obvious. "I've always loved you. But, Burke—" He pressed his lips to her hand in a fervent kiss and cried, "Oh, Kate!" with such unfeigned joy that a giddy laugh bubbled up in her throat. "Well, what did you think?" she wanted to know. "Why else would I keep risking my life to save you?"

He thought. "Guilt?" Her expression made him throw his head back and laugh. He pulled her close, smiling into her eyes. "Only one explanation. You must be crazy about me."

"I must be crazy!"

"No, you love me a simply unbelievable amount," he gloated. "Still, it's only half as much as I love you."

Her smile trembled and faded. "Impossible. Burke, you're my life. When I stopped being angry, I would have become your mistress," she confessed, unashamed. "I couldn't have let you go."

"I was an idiot to ask you, Kate. And I couldn't have let you go, either." He kissed her again and wrapped his arms around her securely. "This is the best argument we've ever had. Let's never stop fighting over who loves who more."

She sighed blissfully, agreeing, loving the long, hard feel of him against her. This was where she belonged. And how lovely to be holding each other instead of shouting, for once. Still—

"But, Burke?"

"No buts. I'm enjoying the peace. I think it's a first."

"Yes, but I was just wondering."

He gave a mock groan.

"How could you marry a woman who's had as many

lovers as I've had?''

If he'd looked into her eyes then, he'd have seen a mischievous twinkle. But he went very still, staring without seeing at the clear knife edge of the horizon, deep blue against ochre. "When we marry, Kate," he told her quietly, "we'll take vows of love and fidelity, and from that moment on we'll belong only to each other. What either of us did in the past won't matter. It won't exist."

The tears overflowed then and streamed down her cheeks. "Oh, Burke. My dearest, dearest love." She weighed nothing at all, she was buoyant with her perfect happiness. "But what about the Unicorn?" she pursued doggedly, sniffling, inexplicably determined to say the worst things she could think of. "How could you—"

"You never worked there," he said, realizing it as he said it.

She breathed a tremulous sigh, poised between laughing and crying. "No, I didn't. I certainly did not." She looked up. "Did you know I can read Greek?"

He shook his head, smiling with resigned wonder. "Now, that's a relief. I couldn't marry a woman who didn't read Greek."

"Latin too. My father was a great scholar, a great man. I want to tell you all about him."

"I want you to tell me. Ah, Kate, I want to give you so many things," he said suddenly, hugging her. "But I don't have anything at all. So you must think carefully about marrying me, because we won't—"

"Oh, I have plenty of money. I was going to give it all to you and go away. This is much better."

He looked down to see if she was joking. She didn't appear to be. "I believe we need to have a long talk," he said gravely.

"But not now, I hope. Don't you think we've been talking a very long time already?"

He nipped at the forefinger she was pressing against his

lips. "When are the Derns coming back?"

"Not for hours and hours. Oh, Burke, I'm so *happy*. Kiss me, I can't stand it another second."

He obliged. Exuberantly at first, then more tenderly as the last scales began to fall away from his heart, the old protective layers that had insulated him for so long from his deepest feelings. "I love you so much," he whispered, pressing her to him, stroking her back with gentle, hectic need. "Come below with me, sweet Kate. I want to lie with you in that narrow bed and show you how strong my love is."

She went weak in the knees. "But what about your poor body? I don't want to hurt you, Burke, and we—"

His tickled laugh cut her off. "Oh, Kate. What a quaint notion." He kissed her again. "Besides, a woman of your vast experience will surely think of a way to manage it so that I won't kill myself."

He was teasing, but she needed to be sure. "You know that's not true, don't you? That my experience is anything but vast?"

He sobered. "The answer is yes, though I remember taunting you once with having bedded half the English army. Now I wouldn't care if you had." Who was this woman in his arms? he marveled. He suspected he knew nothing at all about her, and the miracle was that he didn't care. He loved her and he would never let her go again. What else mattered?

"Somehow I doubt that," she told him, beaming, "though it's extremely nice of you to think it." They began to walk toward the companionway, their arms around each other. "What would you say if I told you you were my first and only lover?" she asked, leaning her head on his shoulder and smiling up at him.

To Burke she'd never looked so lovely; the sun seemed to set her hair on fire, and its slanting light warmed the pallor of her skin in a rose-tinted glow. "I'd say there must be a long, intriguing story behind such a remarkable phenomenon, and someday I'd like to hear it."

"Some *day*?"

"Mmm. I should think we might want to come up for air by, oh, Thursday or so." It was Sunday.

"Heavens." The very idea made her shiver deliciously.

The tiny, cramped cabin seemed beautiful to them. Soon they would need a lamp—or perhaps not—but now the soft afternoon light touched the room like a sweet benediction. They kissed for a breathless time, moved by their strange new tenderness, whispering guileless, extravagant words of love.

"Do you think once we're married," Burke murmured against her throat, "you'll call me by my Christian name? It's James, if you'd forgotten."

"Do you want me to? I suppose I could. But only on one condition."

"Kate you have the *sweetest* skin," he told her, distracted, "the most exquisite mouth." A little later he asked, "What condition?"

What? Oh . . . Now he was edging her dress down over one shoulder and kissing her bare skin with passionate, open-mouthed kisses. "The con . . . condition is that you must learn *my* name."

This was beyond him, but it didn't really matter. He tugged her gown lower, exposing one perfect, lace-covered breast. "I know your name," he said throatily, watching her face as he caressed her through the thin silk. "You're my beautiful Kate, my love and my life. And I'm dying for you."

Her turquoise eyes turned smoky-blue with desire. "Then you must have me. But only once more."

He growled low in his throat. "You're mad, woman, a hundred thousand times wouldn't be enough!" With urgent hands he pressed her to the bed and bore her head down to the pillow. "I'll never have enough of you,

Kate.'' His kiss was deep and hungry and achingly sweet.

"Nor I of you," she said when she could speak. "But you may only make love to Katie Lennox once more—and then you'll have me forever!"

DEBRA DIER
LORD SAVAGE
Author of *Scoundrel*

Lady Elizabeth Barrington is sent to Colorado to find the Marquess of Angelstone, the grandson of an English duke who disappeared during an attack by renegade Indians. But the only thing she discovers is Ash MacGregor, a bounty-hunting rogue who takes great pleasure residing in the back of a bawdy house. Convinced that his rugged good looks resemble those of the noble family, Elizabeth vows she will prove to him that aristocratic blood does pulse through his veins. And in six month's time, she will make him into a proper man. But the more she tries to show him which fork to use or how to help a lady into her carriage, the more she yearns to be caressed by this virile stranger, touched by this beautiful barbarian, embraced by Lord Savage.

_4119-7   **$4.99 US/$5.99 CAN**

Pure Temptation

Connie Mason

"Each new Connie Mason book is a prize!"
—Heather Graham

Spirits can be so bloody unpredictable, and the specter of Lady Amelia is the worst of all. Just when one of her ne'er-do-well descendents thought he could go astray in peace, the phantom lady always appears to change his wicked ways.

A rogue without peer, Jackson Graystoke wants to make gaming and carousing in London society his life's work. And the penniless baronet would gladly curse himself with wine and women—if Lady Amelia would give him a ghost of a chance.

Fresh off the boat from Ireland, Moira O'Toole isn't fool enough to believe in legends or naive enough to trust a rake. Yet after an accident lands her in Graystoke Manor, she finds herself haunted, harried, and hopelessly charmed by Black Jack Graystoke and his exquisite promise of pure temptation.

_4041-7 $5.99 US/$6.99 CAN

A Faerie Tale Romance

Prince of Kisses

COLLEEN SHANNON

Daughter of wealth and privilege, lovely Charlaine Kimball is known to Victorian society as the Ice Princess. But when a brash intruder dares to take a king's ransom in jewels from her private safe, indignation burns away her usual cool reserve. And when the handsome rogue presumes to steal a kiss from her untouched lips, forbidden longing sets her soul ablaze.

Illegitimate son of a penniless Frenchwoman, Devlin Rhodes is nothing but a lowly bounder to the British aristocrats who snub him. But his leapfrogging ambition engages him in a dangerous game. Now he will have to win Charlaine's hand in marriage–and have her begging for the kiss that will awaken his heart and transform him into the man he was always meant to be.

——52200-4 $5.99 US/$6.99 CAN

Dorchester Publishing Co., Inc.
P.O. Box 6640
Wayne, PA 19087-8640

The Gentle Beast

COLLEEN SHANNON

GIVE YOUR HEART TO THE GENTLE BEAST AND FOREVER SHARE LOVE'S SWEET FEAST

Raised amid a milieu of bountiful wealth and enlightened ideas, Callista Raleigh is more than a match for the radicals, rakes, and reprobates who rail against England's King George III. Then a sudden reversal of fortune brings into her life a veritable brute who craves revenge against her family almost as much as he hungers for her kiss. And even though her passionate foe conceals his face behind a hideous mask, Callista believes that he is merely a man, with a man's strengths and appetites. But when the love-starved stranger sweeps her away to his secret lair, Callista realizes that wits and reason aren't enough to conquer him—she'll need a desire both satisfying and true if beauty is to tame the beast.

_52143-1 $5.99 US/$6.99 CAN